the Righteous MEN

the Righteous MEN

SAM BOURNE

HarperCollins*Publishers*

HarperCollins books may be purchased for educational, business, or sales promotional use. For information, please write: Special Markets Department, HarperCollins Publishers, 10 East 53rd Street, New York, NY 10022.

FIRST EDITION

Designed by Joy O'Meara

Library of Congress Cataloging-in-Publication Data

Bourne, Sam.
The righteous men / Sam Bourne — 1st ed.
p. cm.
ISBN-13: 978-0-06-113829-4
ISBN-10: 0-06-113829-0
1. Journalists—New York (State)—New York—Fiction. I. Title.

PS3602.O8885R54 2006
813'6—dc22 2006043500

06 07 08 09 10 NMSG/RRD 10 9 8 7 6 5 4 3 2 1

For Sam,
born into a family of love.

the Righteous MEN

CHAPTER ONE

FRIDAY, 9:10 P.M., MANHATTAN

THE NIGHT OF THE FIRST KILLING was filled with song. St. Patrick's Cathedral in Manhattan trembled to the sound of Handel's *Messiah*, the grand choral masterpiece that never failed to rouse even the most slumbering audience. Its swell of voices surged at the roof of the cathedral. It was as if they wanted to break out, to reach the very heavens.

Inside, close to the front, sat a father and son, the older man's eyes closed, moved as always by this, his favorite piece of music. This may have been a preview, a warm-up for the Christmas season, but that did not lessen its power. The son's gaze alternated between the performers—the singers dressed in black, the conductor wildly waving his shock of gray hair—and the man at his side. He liked looking at him, gauging his reactions; he liked being this close.

Tonight was a celebration. A month earlier Will Monroe Jr. had landed the job he had dreamed of ever since he had come to America. Still only in his late twenties, he was now a reporter, on the fast track at the *New York Times.* Monroe Sr. inhabited a different realm. He was a lawyer, one of the most accomplished of his generation, now serving as a federal judge on the second circuit of the U.S. Court of Appeals. He liked to acknowledge achievement when he saw it, and this young man at his side, whose boyhood he had all but missed, had reached a milestone. He found his son's hand and gave it a squeeze.

It was at that moment, no more than a forty-minute subway ride across town but a world away, that Howard Macrae heard the first steps behind him. He was not scared. Outsiders may have steered clear of this Brooklyn neighborhood of Brownsville, notorious for its drug-riddled streets, but Macrae knew every street and alley.

He was part of the landscape. A pimp of some two decades' standing, he was wired into Brownsville. He had been a smart operator, too, ensuring that in the gang warfare that scarred the area, he always remained neutral. Factions would clash and shift, but Howard stayed put, constant. No one had challenged the patch where his whores plied their trade for years.

So he was not too worried by the sound behind him. Still, he found it odd that the footsteps did not stop. He could tell they were close. Why would anybody be tailing him? He turned his head to peer over his left shoulder and gasped, immediately tripping over his feet. It was a gun unlike any he had ever seen—and it was aimed at him.

Inside the cathedral, the chorus was now one being, their lungs opening and closing like the bellows of a single, mighty organ. The music was insistent:

> *And the glory of the Lord shall be revealed, and all flesh shall see it together: for the mouth of the Lord hath spoken it.*

Howard Macrae was now facing forward, attempting to break into an instinctive run. But he could feel a strange, piercing sensation in his right thigh. His leg seemed to be giving way, collapsing under his weight, refusing to obey his orders. I have to run! Yet his body would not respond. He seemed to be moving in slow motion, as if wading through water.

Now the mutiny had spread to his arms, which were first lethargic, then floppy. His brain raced with the urgency of the situation, but it too now seemed overwhelmed, as if submerged under a sudden burst of floodwater. He felt so tired.

He found himself lying on the ground clasping his right leg, aware that it and the rest of his limbs were surrendering to numbness. He looked up. He could see nothing but the steel glint of a blade.

In the cathedral, Will felt his pulse quicken. The *Messiah* was reaching its climax; the whole audience could sense it. A soprano voice hovered above them:

If God be for us, who can be against us?
Who shall lay anything to the charge of God's elect?
It is God that justifieth, who is he that condemneth?

Macrae could only watch as the knife hovered over his chest. He tried to see who was behind it, to make out a face, but he could not. The gleam of metal dazzled him; it seemed to have caught all the night's moonlight on its hard, polished surface. He knew he ought to be terrified: the voice inside his head told him he was. But it sounded oddly removed, like a commentator describing a faraway football game. Howard could see the knife coming closer toward him, but still it seemed to be happening to someone else.

Now the orchestra was in full force, Handel's music coursing through the church with enough force to waken the gods. The alto and tenor were as one, demanding to know:

O Death, where is thy sting?

Will was not a classical buff like his father, but the majesty and power of the music was making the hairs on the back of his neck stand up. Still staring straight ahead, he tried to imagine the expression his father would be wearing: he pictured him, rapt, and hoped that underneath that blissful exterior there might also lurk some pleasure at sharing this moment with his only son.

The blade descended, first across the chest. Macrae saw the red line it scored, as if the knife were little more than a scarlet marker pen. The skin seemed to bubble and blister: he did not understand why he felt no pain. Now the knife was moving down, slicing his stomach open like a bag of grain. The contents spilled out, a warm soft bulge of viscous innards. Howard was watching it all, until the moment the dagger was finally held aloft. Only then could he see the face of his murderer. His larynx managed to squeeze out a gasp of shock—and recognition. The blade found his heart, and all was dark.

The mission had begun.

CHAPTER TWO

Friday, 9:46 p.m., Manhattan

The chorus took their bows, the conductor bowing sweatily. But Will could only hear one noise: the sound of his father clapping. He marveled at the decibels those two big hands could produce, colliding in a smack that sounded like wood against wood. It stirred a memory Will had almost lost. It was a school speech day back in England, the only time his father had been there. Will was ten years old, and as he went up to collect the poetry prize he was sure that, even above the din of a thousand parents, he could hear the distinct handclap of his father. On that day he had been proud of this stranger's mighty oak hands, stronger than those of any man in the world, he was sure.

The noise had not diminished as his father, now in his early fifties, had entered middle age. He was as fit as ever, slim, his silver-white hair cropped short. He did not jog or work out: weekend sailing trips off Sag Harbor had kept him in shape. Will, still applauding, turned to look at him, but his father's gaze did not shift. When Will saw the slight redness around his dad's nose, he realized with shock that the older man's eyes were wet: the music had moved him, but he did not want his son to see his tears.

Will smiled to himself at that. A man with hands as strong as trees, welling up at the sound of an angels' choir. It was then he felt the vibrations. He reached down to his BlackBerry to see a message from the Metro desk: "Job for you. Brownsville, Brooklyn. Homicide."

Will's stomach gave a little leap, that aerobic maneuver that combines excitement and nerves. He was on the "night cops" beat on the *Times* Metro desk, the traditional training ground for fast-trackers like him. He might be destined to serve as a future Middle East correspondent or Beijing bureau chief, ran the paper's logic, but first he would have to learn the journalistic basics. That was *Times* thinking. "There'll be plenty of time to cover military coups. First you have to know how to cover a flower show," Glenn Harden, the Metro editor, would say. "You need to learn people, and you do that right here."

As the chorus basked in their ovation, Will turned to his father with a shrug of apology, gesturing to the BlackBerry. *It's work*, he mouthed, gathering up his coat. This little role reversal gave him a sneaky pleasure. After years living in the glow cast by his father's stellar career, now it was Will's turn to heed the summons of work.

"Take care," whispered the older man.

Outside Will hailed a cab. The driver was listening to the news on NPR. Will asked him to turn it up. Not that he was expecting any word on Brownsville. Will always did this—in cabs, even in shops or cafés. He was a news junkie; had been since he was a teenager.

He had missed the lead item, and they were already onto the foreign news. A story from Britain. Will always perked up when he heard word from the country he still thought of as home. He may have been born in America, but his formative years, between the ages of eight and twenty-one, had been spent in England. Now, though, as he heard that Gavin Curtis, the chancellor of the exchequer, was in trouble, Will paid extra attention. Determined to prove to the *Times* that his talents stretched beyond the Metro desk, and to ensure the brass knew he had studied economics at Oxford, Will had pitched a story to the Week in Review section on only his second day at the paper. He had even sketched out a headline: "Wanted: A Banker for the World." The International Monetary Fund was looking for a new head, and Curtis was said to be the frontrunner.

". . . the charges were first made by a British newspaper," the NPR voice was saying, "which claimed to have identified 'irregularities' in Treasury accounts. A spokesman for Mr. Curtis has today denied all suggestions of corruption." Will scribbled a note as a memory floated to the surface. He quickly pushed it back down.

There were more urgent matters at hand. Digging into his pocket, he found his phone. Quick message to Beth, who had picked up his British fondness for texting. With a thumb that had become preternaturally quick, he punched in the numbers that became letters.

My first murder! Will be home late. Love you.

Now he could see his destination. Red lights were turning noiselessly in the September dark. The lights were on the roofs of two NYPD cars whose noses almost touched in an arrowhead shape, as if to screen off part of the road. In front of them was a hastily installed cordon of yellow police tape. Will paid the fare, got out, and looked around. Rundown tenements.

He approached the first line of tape until a policewoman strolled over to stop him. She looked bored. "No access, sir."

Will fumbled in the breast pocket of his jacket. "Press?" he asked with what he hoped was a winning smile as he flashed his newly minted press card.

Looking away, she gave an economical gesture with her right hand. *Go through.*

Will ducked under the tape, into a knot of maybe half a dozen people. Other reporters. I'm late, he thought, irritated. One was his age, tall, with impossibly straight hair and an unnatural dusting of orange on his skin. Will was sure he recognized him but could not remember how. Then he saw the curly wire in his ear. Of course, Carl McGivering from NY1, New York's twenty-four-hour cable news station. The rest were older, the battered press tags around their necks revealing their affiliations: *Post*, *Daily News*, and a string of community papers.

"Bit late, junior," said the craggiest of the bunch, apparently the dean of the crime corps. "What kept you?" Ribbing from older hacks, Will had learned in his first job on the *Bergen Record* in New Jersey, was one of those things reporters like him just had to swallow.

"Anyway, I wouldn't sweat it," Old Father Time from the *Post* was saying. "Just your garden-variety gangland killing. Knives are all the rage these days, it seems."

" 'Blades: The New Guns.' Could be a fashion piece," quipped the *Daily News*, to much laughter from the Veteran Reporters' Club whose monthly meeting Will felt he had just interrupted. He suspected this was a dig at him, suggesting the *Times* was so snobbishly remote from the gritty reality of the streets, it failed to give the macho business of murder its due.

"Have you seen the corpse?" Will asked, sure there was a term of the trade he was conspicuously failing to use. "Stiff," perhaps.

"Yeah, right through there," said the dean, nodding toward the squad cars as he brought a Styrofoam cup of coffee to his lips.

Will headed for the space between the police cars, a kind of man-made clearing in this urban forest. There were a couple of unexcited cops milling around, one with a clipboard, but no police photographer. Will must have missed that.

And there on the ground, under a blanket, lay the body. He stepped forward to get a better look, but one of the cops moved to block his path. "Authorized personnel only from here on in, sir. All questions to the DCPI over there."

"DCPI?"

"Officer serving the Deputy Commissioner of Public Information." As if speaking to a dim-witted child who had forgotten his most rudimentary times tables.

Will kicked himself for asking. He should have bluffed it out.

The DCPI was on the other side of the corpse, talking to the TV guy. Will had to walk around until he was only a foot or two from the dead body of Howard Macrae. He stared hard into the blanket, hoping to guess at the face that lay beneath. Maybe the blanket would reveal an outline, like those clay masks used by sculptors. He kept looking, but the dull, dark shroud yielded nothing.

The DCPI was in mid-flow. ". . . our guess is that this was either score-settling by the SVS against the Wrecking Crew, or else an attempt by the Rockaway prostitution network to take over Macrae's patch."

Only then did she seem to notice Will, her expression instantly changing to denote a lack of familiarity. The shutters had come down. Will got the message: the casual banter was for Carl McGivering only.

"Could I just get the details?"

"One African-American male, aged forty-three, approximately a hundred and eighty pounds, identified as Howard Macrae, found dead on Saratoga and St. Marks Avenues at 9:15 this evening. Police were alerted by a resident of the neighbourhood who dialed 911 after finding the body while walking to the 7-Eleven." She nodded to indicate the store: *Over there*. "Cause of death appears to be severing of arteries, internal bleeding, and heart failure due to vicious and repeated stabbing. The New York Police Department is treating this crime as homicide and will spare no resources in bringing the perpetrator to justice."

The blah-blah tone told Will this was a set formulation, one all DCPIs were required to repeat. No doubt it had been scripted by a team of outside consultants, who probably wrote an NYPD mission statement to go with it. *Spare no resources.*

"Any questions?"

"Yes. What was all that about prostitution?"

"Are we on background now?"

Will nodded, agreeing that anything the DCPI said could be used, so long as Will did not attribute it to her.

"The guy was a pimp. Well known as such to us and to everyone who lives here. Ran a brothel, on Atlantic Avenue near Pleasant Place. Kind of like an old-fashioned whorehouse, girls, rooms—all under one roof."

"Right. What about the fact that he was found in the middle of the street? Isn't that a little strange, no attempt to hide the body?"

"Gangland killing, that's how they work. Like a drive-by shooting. It's right out there in the open, in your face. No attempt to hide the body 'cause that's part of the point. To send a message. You want everyone to know, 'We did this, we don't care who knows about it. And we'd do it to you.' "

Will scribbled as fast as he could, thanked the DCPI, and reached for his cell phone. He told Metro what he had: they told him to come in, there was still time to make the late edition. They would only need a few paragraphs. Will was not surprised. He had read the *Times* long enough to know this was not exactly hold-the-front-page material.

He did not let on to the desk, to the DCPI, or to any of the other reporters there that this was in fact the first murder he had ever covered. At the *Bergen Record*, homicides were rarer fare and not to be wasted on novices like him. It was a pity because there was one detail that had caught Will's eye but which he had put out of his mind almost immediately. The other hacks were too jaded to have noticed it at all, but Will saw it. The trouble was, he assumed it was routine.

He did not realize it at the time, but it was anything but.

CHAPTER THREE

SATURDAY, 12:30 A.M., MANHATTAN

AT THE OFFICE, Will hammered the Send key on the keyboard, pushed back his chair, and stretched. It was half past midnight. He looked around: most of the desks were empty. Only the night layout area was still fully staffed—cutting and slicing, rewriting and crafting the finished product that would spread itself open on Manhattan breakfast tables in just a few hours' time.

He strode around the office, pumped by a minor version of the post-filing high—that surge of adrenaline and relief once a story is done. He wandered, stealing a glance at the desks of his colleagues, bathed only in the flickering light of CNN, on mute.

The office was open plan, but a system of partitions organized the desks into pods, little clusters of four. As a newcomer, Will was in a far-off corner. His nearest window looked out onto a brick wall: the back of a Broadway theater bearing a now-faded poster for one of the city's longest-running musicals. Alongside him in the pod was Terry Walton, the former Delhi bureau chief who had returned to New York under some kind of cloud; Will had not yet discovered the exact nature of his misdemeanor. His desk consisted of a series of meticulous piles surrounding a single yellow legal pad. On it was handwriting so dense and tiny, it was unintelligible to all but the closest inspection: Will suspected this was a kind of security mechanism, devised by Walton to prevent any snoopers taking a peek at his work. He was yet to discover why a man whose demotion to Metro meant he was hardly working on stories sensitive to national security would take such a precaution.

Next was Dan Schwarz, whose desk seemed to be on the point of collapse. He was an investigative reporter; there was barely room for his chair, all floor space consumed by cardboard boxes. Papers were falling out of other papers; even the screen on Schwarz's computer was barely visible, bordered by a hundred Post-it notes stuck all around the edge.

Amy Grossman's desk was neither anally neat like Walton's nor a public health disaster like Schwarz's. It was messy, as befitted the quarters of a woman who worked under her very own set of deadlines—always rushing back to relieve a nanny, let in a babysitter, or pick up from nursery school. She had used the partition walls to pin up not yet more papers, like Schwarz, or elegant, if aged, postcards, like Walton, but pictures of her family. Her children had curly hair and wide, toothy smiles—and, as far as Will could see, were permanently covered in paint.

He went back to his own desk. He had not found the courage to personalize it yet; the pinboard partition still bore the corporate notices that had been there when he arrived. He saw the light on his phone blinking. A message.

Hi babe. I know it's late but I'm not sleepy yet. I've got a fun idea, so call me when you're done. It's nearly one. Call soon.

His spirits lifted instantly. He had banked on a tiptoe reentry into the apartment, followed by a pre-bed bowl of Cheerios. What did Beth have in mind?

He called. "How come you're still awake?"

"I dunno, my husband's first murder perhaps? Maybe it's just everything that's going on. Anyway, I can't sleep. Do you wanna meet for bagels?"

"What, now?"

"Yeah. At the Salonike."

"Now?"

"I'll get a cab."

He got there first, bagging a table behind a noisy group of thirty-something couples—all of them fitting the "new Brooklyn" demographic profile perfectly. He caught snatches of conversation, enough to work out that they were young parents buzzing with the thrill of a night out without the kids.

Then he saw her. Will paused for a split second before waving, just to take a good look. They had met in his very last weeks at Columbia, and he had fallen hard and fast. Her looks could still make his insides leap: the long dark hair framing pale skin and wide, green eyes. One look, and you could not tear yourself away.

He jumped up to meet her, instantly taking in her scent. It began in her hair, with an aroma of sunshine and dewberries that might once have come from a shampoo, but combined with her skin to produce a new perfume, one that was entirely her own. Its epicenter was the inch or two of skin just below her ear. He only had to nuzzle into that nook to be filled with her.

Now it was the mouth that drew him. Beth's lips were full and thick; he could feel their plumpness as he kissed them. Without warning, they parted, just enough to let her tongue brush against his lips, then meet his own. Quietly, so quietly no one but him could hear it, she let out a tiny moan, a sound of pleasure that roused him instantly. He hardened. She could feel it, prompting another moan, this time of surprise and approval.

"You *are* pleased to see me." Now she was sitting opposite him, shrugging off her coat with a suggestive wriggle. She saw him looking. "You checking me out?"

"You could say that."

She grinned. "What are we going to eat? I thought cheesecake and hot chocolate, although maybe tea would be good . . ."

Will was still staring at his wife, watching the way her top stretched across her breasts. He was wondering if they should abandon the diner and go straight back to their big warm bed.

"What?" she said, feigning indignation. "Concentrate!"

His pastrami sandwich, piled high and deluged with mustard, arrived just as he was telling her about the treatment he had gotten from the old-timers at the murder scene. "So Carl whatsisname—"

"The TV guy?"

"Yeah, he's giving the policewoman all this Raymond Chandler, veteran gumshoe stuff—"

"Give me a break here, you know I got a lawyer friend downtown." This between mouthfuls of cheesecake. Beth was not picking at it like most of the women Will would see in New York, but downing it in big, hearty chunks.

"Anyway, it was pretty obvious he was going to get the inside track, and I wasn't. So I was thinking. Maybe I should start developing some serious police contacts."

"What, drinking with Lieutenant O'Rourke until you fall under the table? Somehow I don't see it. Besides, you're not going to be on this beat long. When Carl whateverhisnameis is still doing traffic snarl-ups in Staten Island, you're going to be covering the, I don't know, the White House or Paris or something really important."

Will smiled. "Your faith in me is touching."

"I'm not kidding, Will. I know it looks like I am because I have a face full of cake. But I mean it. I believe in you." Will took her hand. "You know what song I heard today, at work? It's weird because you never hear songs like that on the radio, but it was so beautiful."

"What was it?"

"It's a John Lennon song, I can't remember the title. But he's going through all the things that people believe in, and he says, 'I don't believe in Jesus, I don't believe in Bible, I don't believe in Buddha,' and all these other things, you know, Hitler and Elvis and whatever, and then he says, 'I don't believe in Beatles. I just believe in me, Yoko and me.' And it made me stop, right in the waiting area at the hospital. Because—you're going to think this is so sappy—but I think it was because that's what I believe in."

"In Yoko Ono?"

"No, Will. Not Yoko Ono. I believe in us, in you and me. That's what I believe in."

Will's instinct was to deflate moments like this. He was too English for such overt statements of feeling. He had so little experience of expressed love, he hardly knew what to do with it when it was handed to him. But now, in this moment, he resisted the urge to crack a joke or change the subject.

"I love you quite a lot, you know."

"I know." They paused, listening to the sound of Beth scraping her cheesecake fork against the plate.

"Did something happen at work today to get you—"

"You know that kid I've been treating?"

"Child X?" Will was teasing. Beth stuck diligently to the rules on doctor-patient confidentiality and only rarely, and in the most coded terms, discussed her cases outside the hospital. He understood that, of course, respected it even. But it made it tricky to be as supportive of Beth as she was of him, to back her career with equal energy. When the office politics at the hospital had turned nasty, he had become familiar with all the key personalities, offering advice on which colleagues were to be cultivated as allies, which were to be avoided. In their first months together, he had imagined long evenings spent talking over tough cases, Beth seeking his advice on an enigmatic "client" who refused to open up or a dream that refused to be interpreted. He saw himself massaging his wife's shoulders, modestly coming up with the breakthrough idea that finally persuaded a silent child to speak.

But Beth was not quite like that. For one thing, she seemed to need it less than Will. For him, an event had not happened until he had talked about it with Beth. She appeared able to advance into the world all by herself, drawing on her own strength.

"Yes, OK. Child X. You know why I'm seeing him, don't you? He's accused of—actually, he's very definitely guilty of—a series of arson attacks. On his school. On his neighbor's house. He burned down one of those gyms for kids.

"I've been talking to him for months now, and I don't think he's shown a hint of remorse. Not even a flicker. I've had to go right down to basics, trying to get him to recognize even the very idea of right and wrong. Then you know what he does today?"

Beth was looking away now, toward a table where two waiters were having their own late-shift supper. "Remember Marie, the receptionist? She lost her husband last month; she's been distraught, we've all been talking about it. Somehow this kid—Child X—must have picked something up, because guess what he does today? He comes in with a flower and hands it to Marie. A gorgeous, long-stemmed pink rose. He can't have just pulled it off some bush; he must have bought it. Even if he did just take it, it doesn't matter. He hands Marie this rose and says, 'This is for you, to remember your husband.'

"Well, Marie is just overwhelmed. She takes the rose and croaks a thank-you and then has to just run to the bathroom, to cry her eyes out. And everyone who sees this thing, the nurses, the staff, they're all just tearing up. I come out and find the whole team kind of having this moment. And there in the middle of it is this little boy—and suddenly that's what he looks like, a little boy—who doesn't quite know what he's done. And that's what convinces me it's real. He doesn't look pleased with himself, like someone who calculated, Hey, this will be a way to get some extra credit. He just looks a little bewildered.

"Until that moment, I had seen this boy as a hoodlum. I know, I know—I of all people am meant to get past 'labels' and all that." She mimed the quote marks around "labels," leaving no doubt that she was parodying the kind of people who made that gesture. "But, if I'm honest, I had seen him as a nasty little punk. I didn't like him at all. And then he does this little thing that is just so good. You know what I mean? Just a simple, good act."

She fell quiet. Will did not want to say anything, just in case there was more. Eventually Beth broke the silence. "I don't know," she said, in an "anyway" voice, as if to signal that the episode was over.

They talked some more, their conversation noodling between his day and hers. He leaned over several times to kiss her, on each occasion hoping for a repeat of the open-mouthed treat he'd had before. She was denying him. As she stretched forward, he could see the bottom of her back and just a hint of her underwear, visible in the gap between her skin and her jeans. He loved seeing Beth naked, but the sight of her in her underwear always drove him wild.

"Check, please!" he said, eager to get her home. As they walked out, he slid his hand under her T-shirt, over the smooth skin of her back, and headed south into her trousers. She was not stopping him. He did not know that he would replay that sensation in his hands and in his head a thousand times before the week was out.

CHAPTER FOUR

Saturday, 8:00 a.m., Brooklyn

This is weekend edition. *The headlines this morning: There could be help for homeowners after the Fed's quarter-point rise in interest rates; the governor of Florida declares parts of the Panhandle a disaster area thanks to Tropical Storm Alfred; and scandal, British style. First, this news . . .*

It was eight a.m., and Will was barely conscious. They had not fallen asleep till well past three. Eyes still shut, he now stretched an arm to where his wife should be. As he expected, no Beth. She was already off: one Saturday in four she held a weekend clinic, and this was that Saturday. The woman's stamina astounded him. And, he knew, the children and their parents would have no idea the psychiatrist treating them was operating on a quarter cylinder. When she was with them, she was at full strength.

Will hauled himself out of bed and headed for the breakfast

table. He did not want to eat; he wanted to see the paper. Beth had left a note—*Well done, honey. Big day today, let's have a good night tonight*—and also the Metro section folded open at the right page. B3. *Could be worse*, thought Will. "Brownsville Slaying Linked to Prostitution," ran the headline over less than a dozen paragraphs. And in between was his byline. He had had to make a decision when he first got into journalism; in fact, he had made it back at Oxford, writing for *Cherwell*, the student paper. Should he be William Monroe Jr. or plain Will Monroe? Pride told him he should be his own man, and that meant having his own name: Will Monroe.

He glanced at the front page of the Metro section and then the main paper to see who among his new colleagues—and therefore rivals—was prospering. He noted the names and made for the shower.

An idea began to take shape in Will's head, one that grew and became more solid as he got dressed and headed out, past the young couples pushing three-wheeler strollers or taking their time over a café breakfast on Court Street. Cobble Hill was packed with people like him and Beth: twenty- and thirtysomething professionals, transforming what was once a down-at-the-heels Brooklyn neighborhood into a little patch of yuppie heaven. As Will made for the Bergen Street subway station, he felt conscious that he was walking faster than everyone else. This was a working weekend for him, too.

Once at the office, he wasted no time and went straight to Harden, who was turning the pages of the *New York Post* with a speed that conveyed derision.

"Glenn, how about 'Anatomy of a Killing: The Real Life of a Crime Statistic'?"

"I'm listening."

"You know, 'Howard Macrae might seem like just another brief on the inside pages, another New York murder victim. But what was he like? What had his life been about? Why was he killed?' "

Harden stopped flicking through the *Post* and looked up. "Will, I'm a suburban guy in South Orange whose biggest worry is getting my two daughters to school in the morning." This was not hypothetical; this was true. "Why do I care about some dead pimp in Brownsville?"

"You're right. He's just some name on a police list. But don't you think our readers want to know what really happens when someone gets murdered in this city?"

He could see Harden was undecided. He was short on reporters: it was the Jewish New Year, which meant the *Times* newsroom was badly depleted, even by weekend standards. The paper had a large Jewish staff, and now most of them were off work to mark the religious holiday. But neither did he want to admit that he had become so tired, even murder no longer interested him.

"Tell you what. Make a few calls, go down there. See what you get. If it makes something, we can talk about it."

Within minutes Will was wondering if it had been worth the trip. At the precinct he managed to speak to Officer Federico Penelas, who had been the first policeman on the scene. But he was a reluctant interviewee, offering only one-word answers.

"Was there a commotion when you got down there?"

"Nah-uh."

"Who was there?"

"Just one or two folks. The lady who made the call."

"Did you talk to her at all?"

"Just took down the details of what she'd seen, when she'd seen it. Thanked her for calling the New York Police Department." The consultants' script again.

"And is it your job to lay that blanket on the victim?"

For the first time, Penelas smiled. The expression was one of mockery rather than warmth. *You know nothing.* "That wasn't a police blanket. Police use zip-up body bags. That blanket was already on him when I got there."

"Who laid it out?"

"Dunno. Reckon it was whoever found the dead guy. Mark of respect or something. Same way they closed the victim's eyes. People do that: they've seen it in the movies."

Penelas refused to identify the woman who had discovered the corpse, but in a follow-up phone call the DCPI was more forthcoming—on background, of course. At last Will had a name: now he could get started.

He had to walk through the projects to find her. A six-foot-two Upper East Side guy in chinos and an English accent, he felt ridiculous and intensely white as he moved through this poor, black neighborhood. The buildings were not entirely derelict, but they were in bad shape—graffiti, stairwells that smelled of piss, and plenty of broken windows. He would have to buttonhole whoever was out of doors and hope they would talk.

He made an instant rule: stick to the women. He knew this was a cowardly impulse, but, he assured himself, that was nothing to be ashamed of. He had once read some garlanded foreign correspondent saying the best war reporters were the cowards: the brave ones were reckless and ended up dead. This was not exactly the Middle East, but a kind of war—whether over drugs or gangs or race—raged on these streets all the same.

The first woman he spoke to was blank; so was the next. The third had heard the name but could not place where. She recommended someone else, until one neighbor was calling out to another, and eventually Will was facing the woman who had found Howard Macrae.

African-American and in her mid-fifties, the woman was named Rosa. Will guessed she was a churchgoer, one of those black women who stop communities like this one from going under. She agreed to walk with him to the scene of the crime.

"Well, I had been at the store, picking up some bread and a soda, I think, when I noticed what I thought was a big lump on the sidewalk. I remember I was annoyed: I thought someone had dumped some furniture on the street again. But as I got closer, I realized this was not a sofa. Uh-uh. It was low down and kind of bumpy."

"You realized it was a body?"

"Only when I was right up close. Until then, it just looked like, you know . . . a shape."

"It was dark."

"Yeah, pretty dark and pretty late. Anyway, when I was standing over it, I thought, That ain't a sofa, that ain't a chair. That's a body under that blanket."

"Sorry, I'm asking you to go back to what you saw right at the beginning. Before the blanket was laid on the corpse."

"That *is* what I'm describing. What I saw was a dark blanket with the shape of a dead man underneath."

"The blanket was already there? So you were not the first to find him." *Damn.*

"No, I *was* the first to find him. I was the one who called the police. Nobody else did. It was the first they'd heard of it."

"But the body was already covered?"

"That's right."

"The police seem to think it was you who laid down the blanket, Rosa."

"Well, they're wrong. Where would I get a blanket from in the middle of the night? Or do you think black folks carry blankets around with them just in case? I know things are pretty bad 'round here, but they're not that bad." None of this was said with bitterness.

"Right." Will paused, uncertain where to go next. "So who did leave that blanket on him?"

"I'm telling you the same thing I told that police officer. That's the way I found him. Nice blanket, too. Kind of soft. Maybe cashmere. Something classy, anyway."

"Sorry to go back to this, but is there any chance at all you were not the first there?"

"I can't see how. I'm sure the police told you. When I lifted that blanket, I saw a body that was still warm. Wasn't even a body at that time. It was still a *man.* You know what I'm saying? He was still warm. Like it just happened. The blood was still coming out. Kind of burbling, like water leaking from a pipe. Terrible, just terrible. And you know the strangest thing? His eyes were closed, as if someone had shut them."

"Don't tell me that wasn't you."

"It wasn't me. Never said it was."

"Who do you think did that—closed his eyes, I mean?"

"You'll probably think I'm crazy, what with the way they knifed that poor man to death, but it was kinda like . . . no, you'll think I'm crazy."

"Please go on. I don't I think you're crazy at all. Go on." Will was stooping now, an instinctive gesture. Being tall was usually a plus: he could intimidate. But right now he did not want to tower over this woman. He wanted to make her feel comfortable. He bent his shoulders lower, so that he could meet her eyes without forcing her to look up. "Go on."

"I know that man was murdered in a horrible way. But his body looked as if it had been somehow, you know, laid to rest."

Will said nothing, just sucked the top of his pen.

"You see, I told you. You think I'm crazy. Maybe I am!"

Will thanked the woman and carried on through the projects. He only had to walk a few blocks to get into real sleaze country. The boarded-up tenements, he knew, served as crack houses; the shifty young men palming off brown parcels to each other while looking the other way were the people to ask about Howard Macrae.

Will had ditched his jacket by now—a necessary move on this bright September day—but he was still encountering major resistance. His face was too white, his accent too different. Most assumed he was a plainclothes cop, drug squad probably. Most people started walking the moment they saw his notebook.

The first crack in the ice came the way it always does—from just one person.

Will found a man who had known Macrae. He seemed vaguely shifty but, above all, bored, with nothing better to do than to while away a few daytime hours talking to a reporter. He rambled on and on, detailing long gone and wholly irrelevant local disputes and controversies as if they would be of burning interest to the *New York Times.* "You want to put that in your paper, my friend!" he would say over and over, with a bronchial smoker's laugh. *Heh-heh-heh.* Humoring folks like this was, Will concluded, an occupational hazard.

"So what about this Howard Macrae?" said Will when his new acquaintance finally took a breath during an analysis of the flawed stop-light system on Fulton Street.

It turned out he did not know Macrae that well, but he knew others who did. He offered to hook Will up with them, introducing the reporter each time with the priceless character reference: "He's OK."

Soon Will was forming a picture. Macrae was a certifiable, card-carrying lowlife. No doubt about it. He ran a brothel; had done for years. The sleaze community seemed to have a high regard for him: apparently he was good at being a pimp. He ran a functioning whorehouse, kept it looking all right—even took the girls' clothes to the Laundromat. Will got inside, to see the rooms for himself. The best he could say for it was that it was not nearly as seedy as he had imagined. It looked a bit like a clinic in a poor neighborhood. There were no needles on the floor. He even noticed a water cooler.

The whores told him the same story. "Sir, I can't tell you anymo' than what the lady already told you: he sold ass. Tha's what he did. He collected the money, gave some to us, and kept the rest for hisself."

Howard seemed to have been a contented sort of pimp. The brothel was his domain, and he was obviously a genial host. At night, Will discovered, he would put on loud music and dance.

It was late afternoon before Will found what he had been looking for all day: someone genuinely mourning the death of Howard Macrae. Standing on a street corner, Will phoned every funeral home in the area; the fourth one he tried said yes, they were "bidding farewell" to a Howard Macrae. They were waiting for the body to be transferred over from the police morgue; he could come now, they were open for another hour.

It was a rundown place that was depressing even by the standards of the rest of the neighborhood. Will wondered how many of these "garden-variety gangland killings" they had to clear up. Only the receptionist seemed to be around, a young black woman with the longest, most outstandishly decorated nails Will had ever seen. They were the only spot of brightness in the entire place.

He asked who was organizing the funeral for Howard Macrae. Was it a family member? The girl shrugged and said nothing; Will's notebook had scared her into silence.

"Look," he said. "Mr Macrae's friends or family may not even know that he's gone. If I write about this, at least they'll have a chance to come pay their respects."

Finally, she found a Post-it with a name and a phone number and passed it across the counter. A woman. Will dialed the number there and then. He said he was calling from the funeral home: he wanted to talk about Howard Macrae. "Come right over," she said.

In the cab, Will instantly reached for his BlackBerry, tapping out a quick e-mail to Beth. There was a rhythm to all this electronic communication: BlackBerry by day, when he knew his wife was near a computer terminal, text message by night when she was not.

> Quick psychology lesson needed. Need to get interview with woman who knew the victim. Have led her to believe I work for funeral company. Will now have to reveal truth: how do I do that without getting her so angry she throws me out of her house? Need yr considered opinion asap, am just few mins away.
>
> xx W

He waited; but there was no reply.

It was twilight when Will tapped on the screen door. A woman poked her head out of the upstairs window. Early forties, Will guessed; black, attractive. Her hair was straightened, with an auburn hue. "Coming right down."

She introduced herself as Letitia. She did not want to give her last name.

"Look, my name is Will Monroe, and I apologize." He began babbling that this was his first big story, that he had only lied because he was desperate not to let his bosses down, when he noticed that she was neither doing nor saying anything. She was not throwing him out, just listening to him with a faintly puzzled expression. His voice petering out now, he gave her a precooked line: "Look, Letitia. This may be the only way the truth about Howard Macrae will ever come out." But he could see it was not needed. On the contrary, Letitia seemed rather glad to have the chance to talk.

She gestured him away from the front door toward a living room cluttered with children's toys.

"Were you related to Howard?" he began.

"No." Letitia smiled. "No, I only met that man once. But once was enough."

Will felt a surge of excitement. *Letitia has the dirt on Macrae. She knows why he was killed. I'm ahead of the police!*

"When was this?"

"Nearly ten years ago. My husband—he'll be back soon—was in jail." She saw Will's face. "No! He hadn't done anything. He was innocent. But we couldn't pay the bail to get him out. He was in that prison cell night after night. I couldn't bear it. I grew desperate." She looked up at Will, her eyes hoping that he understood the rest. That she would not have to spell it out.

"Everyone knows there's only two ways to make quick money 'round here. You sell drugs or . . ."

Now Will got it. "Or you sell . . . or you go see Howard."

"Right. I hated myself for even thinking about it. I grew up singing choir in the AME church, Mr. Monroe."

"Will. I understand."

"I was raised right. But I had to get my husband out of that jail. So I went to . . . Howard's place."

Without looking down, Will scribbled in his notebook. *Eyes glittering.*

"I was going to sell the one thing I owned." Now she was tearing up. "I couldn't even go in, I was sort of hiding in the shadows, hesitating. Howard Macrae spotted me there. I think he had a broom in his hand, sweeping. He asked me what I wanted. Kind of, 'Can I help you?' I told him what I wanted. I told him why I needed the money. I didn't want him to think, you know. And then this man, who I never met before, did the oddest thing."

Will leaned forward.

"Right there and then, he marched off to what I guessed was his own room in that . . . place. He unlocked it, and straight away, he starts stripping the bed."

"Stripping the bed?"

"Uh-huh. I was scared at first, I didn't know what he was about to do to me. He put these blankets in a pile, and then he gets to work on his bedside table. Starts packing it up. Starts unplugging his CD player, takes off his watch. It all goes in this big pile. And then he begins moving all this stuff, shooing me out of the way. Now this bed is one of those really good ones, big with a deep, strong mattress, like a top-of-the-line bed. So it's heavy, but he's dragging it and lugging it, till it's outside. And then he opens up his truck, a real beat-up old thing, and he loads up the bed—pillows and all—into the back. Then all the rest of it. I swear, I had no idea what in God's name the man was doing. Then he winds down the window and tells me to meet him just around the block, on the corner of Fulton Street. "See you there in five," he says.

"Well, now I'm mystified. So I walk 'round the block, just like the man said. And I see his truck, parked outside a pawnshop. And there's Howard Macrae pointing at all the stuff, and men are coming out the shop and unloading it, and the boss is handing Macrae cash. And next thing I know, Macrae is giving the money to me."

"To you?"

"Uh-huh. You got it. To me. It was the strangest thing. I wondered why he didn't just give me some cash, if that's what he wanted to do, but no, he insists on making this big sacrifice, like he's selling all his worldly goods or something. And I'll never forgot what he said to me as he did it. 'Here's some money. Now go bail your husband out—and don't become a whore.' And I listened to what the man said. I bailed out my husband, and I never did sell my body, not ever. Thanks to that man."

There was a sound at the front door. Will looked around. He could hear several voices drifting through: three or four young children and a man.

"Hiya, honey."

"Will, this is my husband, Martin. And these are my girls, Davinia and Brandi, and this is my boy—Howard." Letitia gave Will a firm stare, silencing him. "Martin, this man is from the newspaper. I'm just seeing him out."

As they reached the front door, Will whispered. "Your husband doesn't know?"

"No, and I don't plan on telling him now. No man should know such a thing about his wife."

Will was about to say he believed the opposite, that most men would be honored to know their wives were prepared to make such an extreme sacrifice, but he thought better of it.

"And yet his son is called Howard."

"I told him it was because I always liked the name. But *I* know the real reason, and that's good enough. Howard is a name my boy can wear with pride. I'm telling you, Mr. Monroe: the man they killed last night may have sinned every day of his God-given life—but he was the most righteous man I have ever known."

CHAPTER FIVE

SATURDAY, 9:50 P.M., BROOKLYN

THAT NIGHT IN THE KITCHEN, where they did all their talking, Will followed traditional custom. Beth was cooking pasta; he was tagging along behind her, washing each pan and spoon as she finished with them. This was smart strategy, he reckoned: forward planning, prevent the washing-up mountain after dinner. Will was talking Beth through his day.

"The guy's a scumbag pimp, but when he sees this woman in distress, he sells his most personal possessions to help her. A woman he doesn't even know. Isn't that incredible?"

Beth was stirring, saying nothing.

"I'm not sure what Glenn will make of it, but this woman, Letitia, felt Macrae had saved her life. That he had saved *her.* That's something isn't it? I mean, that will make a piece."

Beth seemed far away. Will took that as a sign of success, as if his point had struck home, stunning his wife into contemplative silence.

"Anyway, enough about that. How was your day?"

Beth looked up, her stirring hand stilled. She held him in a long, cold gaze.

"Oh, Christ, I just realized—" Beth's note from this morning. *Big day today.* He had read it and forgotten it. Instantly.

Beth said nothing, just waited for him to explain himself.

"I went straight to work, and then I got stuck into this story. I must have had my phone on silent while I was interviewing that woman. Did you call?"

" 'I just realized.' How can you say that? You can't 'just realize' this, Will. That's not how it works. Not this."

She was speaking with that voice of iron calm that almost scared Will. It was reserved for when Beth was truly furious. He imagined she had acquired this kind of steel as part of her psychological training: never lose your cool. He admired it in the abstract, but could not bear to be on the receiving end.

"I've been thinking about nothing else for weeks, and you 'just realized.' You completely forgot!" Now the volume was rising. "You had all day—"

"I was working—"

"You're always working or thinking about work. You don't even remember what should be the most important thing in our lives, and I can't eat or sleep or shower or do anything without thinking about it." Her eyes were reddening.

"Tell me what they said."

"You don't get off that easy, Will. If you wanted to know what they said, you should have come to the hospital with me. You should have been there with me."

Each of those last four words were heavy as anchors. Of course he should. How could he have forgotten? It was true what she said: he had thought about nothing but this story from the moment he woke up.

He knew he needed to break out of this procedural stage of the conversation—Why had he missed the appointment?—and move fast onto the substance: What had the doctors said? But how to make the shift? There was only one person he knew who would instantly understand how to pull off such a conversational maneuver, what psychological trick to play. That person was Beth.

"Babe, I am completely in the wrong. I can't believe I missed that appointment. And I don't deserve to know what happened. But I really want to. We will talk about this whole other thing—me obsessing about work—I promise. But, right now, I think you should just tell me what happened."

She was sitting now, still holding the wooden spoon. In a barely audible whisper, as if the air had been sucked out of her, she finally spoke. "They didn't examine me; it was just a 'chat.' And they said we should keep trying for another three months before they'll consider treatment." She sniffed deeply, reaching for a tissue. "They said we are both perfectly healthy, we should give it more time before 'taking the next step.' "

"That's good news, isn't it?" said Will, half aware that this was a tactical error—the premature move into cheer-up mode before the silent, listening phase was complete. Rationally, he knew that what Beth needed most was to talk, to get it all out. Not to have to argue, explain, or defend anything. He knew that in his head, but his mouth had had different ideas, instantly wanting to make things better.

"No, as it happens, I don't think it is good news, Will. I don't think it's good news at all. It just makes it more fucking mysterious. If my eggs are so perfect, and your sperm is so fucking tip-top, why the hell CAN'T WE HAVE A BABY?"

She threw the wooden spoon at the wall, where it splattered tomato sauce into a Jackson Pollock pattern, turned, and fled for the bedroom. Will chased her, but she slammed the door. He could hear her crying.

How could he have screwed up so badly? He had promised they would go to the clinic together, that he would take an hour or two out during the afternoon. Instead he had gone to work and clean forgot about everything else for the rest of the day. He had even sent a BlackBerry message—about work—to Beth at the time of the appointment. He knew what his psychiatrist wife thought. That he was throwing himself into his career to avoid dealing with the real issue: four years of marriage, two years of unprotected sex, and one year of serious "trying"—and still Beth was not pregnant. Will knew it looked like that, but she was wrong. This was not some new phase. He had always been ambitious. Even at college, he had worked hard: when he was not editing *Cherwell*, he was trying to sell tales of university life to Fleet Street. That was what he was like.

The phone rang.

"Will?"

"Oh, hi, Dad."

"I was just calling to see if you enjoyed the concert."

"Yes, of course. I loved it," Will said, running his fingers through his hair and facing the floor. How could he have been so stupid? "I should have called. Amazing choir."

"You sound subdued."

"No, just tired. It's been a long day. Remember that thing I was called out on after the concert, that killing? I had this idea to take what everyone thinks is a bog-standard murder and see what really happened. 'Portrait of a Crime Statistic,' the life behind the death, that kind of thing."

Beth's presence behind the slammed door of their bedroom was burning up the apartment. Surely he should be going over there, talking through the door, coaxing her back out. Or at least coaxing his way in.

"That's good thinking. What did you find out?"

"That he was a lowlife pimp sleazeball."

"Well, I guess that's no great surprise. Not in that place. Still, I can't wait to read your IMF piece: much more like something you would write about, I suspect. Listen, Will, Linda's gesturing. I'm at a dinner for Habitat—you-know-who is here—and we're expected to mingle. Speak soon."

Even on his nights off, thought Will, his father and his "partner"—a word Will could not bring himself to utter except in quotation marks—were doing something morally worthwhile. Habitat for Humanity was one of his father's favorite charities. "I like the idea of a cause that asks you to give your time and your labor, not just your money," Monroe Sr. had said more than once. "They ask you to open your heart, not just your pocketbook." Hanging in the judge's chambers was a photograph of himself and the former president—"you-know-who"—each midway up a ladder, both clad in lumberjack shirts, the ex-president holding a hammer. They were taking part in one of Habitat's trademark events: building a house for the homeless in a single day. In Alabama or somewhere.

He wondered about all this great do-gooding fervor of his father's. In fact, he was suspicious of it. The most cynical reading was that it was merely a career move, designed to burnish William Monroe Sr.'s image as a man of fine character, eminently suited to a place on America's highest bench. More specifically, Will wondered if his father was trying to improve his chances with the evangelical Christian constituency that were such key players in the nomination of judges to the Supreme Court. Some of his father's rivals were committed, vocal Christians. A secular liberal like William Monroe Sr. could not match that, but if he could smooth out some of his hard, godless edges, it could only help. That, at least, was his son's guess.

Will tiptoed over to the bedroom, creaking the door open just a crack. Beth was fast asleep. He closed the door, recovered what was left of the pasta, and ate it from the saucepan. He felt as if a high wall had just appeared in their apartment—and he and his wife were on opposite sides of it.

He reached for the remote and jabbed on his default channel: CNN.

"International news now, and more trouble in London for Britain's finance minister, Chancellor of the Exchequer Gavin Curtis, today under fire from the church. The bishop of Birmingham took to Britain's House of Lords to step up the pressure.'

Will sat up to take a close look. Curtis looked harried and much older than Will had remembered him. He had come to Oxford when Will was a student. Curtis was then in opposition, shadowing the Department for Environment. He had come up to act as lead speaker in an Oxford Union debate: "This House believes the end of the world is nigh." Will was then the news editor on *Cherwell*, and he had given himself the plum assignment of interviewing the visiting politician.

He had not thought about it in years, but at the time Curtis had left quite a mark. He had taken Will seriously, treating him as a real journalist when Will could not have been much more than nineteen. The funny thing was, Curtis had not seemed like a politician at all, more like a teacher. He had constantly peppered their conversation with references to books and films, wondering if Will had read some obscure Dutch theologian or seen a new and controversial Polish movie. Will had left their conversation feeling inadequate, but also convinced Curtis was destined for oblivion: he seemed too intellectual for the blood sport of high politics. As his former interviewee had risen through the Cabinet, Will became embarrassed by his own lack of political foresight.

CNN was now showing a clip of a white-haired cleric in a gray suit with just a slice of purple showing underneath. The bishop's face, flushed with wrath, seemed to be trying to match the color of his shirt. CNN identified him as the leader of the British equivalent of America's Church of the Reborn Jesus, a fiercely moral wing of Christian evangelism. "This is a sinful man!" he was saying of the chancellor, to the murmured rhubarb of agreement and disagreement in the chamber. "If it is true that he has been embezzling from the public purse, he must be cast out!"

Will turned off the television and went to the computer. Beth would sleep till morning now. He thought about waking her up so they could talk some more. They had a rule: never go to bed on a fight. But she was so deeply asleep, he would hardly score any points by disturbing her now. He had seen how she looked. She could wear a dozen different expressions in the course of the night:

serene, brow furrowed, even ironic amusement. More than once, Will had been woken by the sound of his wife laughing in her sleep at some secret joke. But just now, even with her autumn-brown hair falling over most of her face, he spotted what he feared was a worry line in her forehead, as if she was concentrating hard. He imagined smoothing it away, with just a touch of his hand. Perhaps he should go back in and do just that. No, he thought. What if she woke up, and their row reopened? Better to leave it be.

Might as well pull an all-nighter instead, write up the Macrae story and deliver it first thing. At least that would impress Harden. And it would be an excuse not to go into the bedroom.

At the keyboard, his mind kept wandering away from Letitia, Howard, and the streets of Brownsville. He knew what Beth wanted, and biology, or something, was standing in their way. He had been encouraged by the hospital's attitude: give it time. But Beth was not used to being a patient. She liked to sit in the other chair. And she wanted clarity: a diagnosis, a course of action.

Besides, he knew, getting pregnant was only part of the story. Beth had become irritated by his professional single-mindedness, his determination to make his mark. When they first met, she would say how much she liked his drive; she found it sexy. She admired his refusal to coast along, to trade on his father's prestige. He had made things difficult for himself—he could have gone back to America when he turned eighteen and used the family name to breeze into Yale—and she admired that. Now, though, she wanted the ambition to cool down. There were other priorities.

He finally crashed out just after four a.m. He dreamed he was on a boating lake, pushing a punt like some cheesy gondolier. Facing him, twirling a parasol, was a woman. It was probably Beth, but he could not quite see. He tried squinting, determined to make out the face. But the sun was in his eyes.

CHAPTER SIX

MONDAY, 10:47 A.M., MANHATTAN

THE GOOD SINNER: The Story of a New York Life—and Death.

Will stared at it, not on B6 or B11 or even B3 but A1: the front page of the *New York Times.* He had stared at it on the subway into work, looked at it some more as he walked to the office, and spent most of the time at his desk pretending not to look at it.

He had arrived to a bombardment of congratulatory e-mail, from colleagues sitting three feet away and old friends living in different continents, who had learned of his feat via the paper's online edition. He was receiving a plaudit by phone when he felt a surge move through his little desk-pod, a silent movement of energy like the magnetic force that passes through iron filings. It was Townsend McDougal, making a rare descent from Mount Olympus to walk among the troops. Suddenly backs were stiffened, rictus smiles adopted. Will noticed Amy Grossman reflexively reaching around to the back of her head to plump up her hair. The veteran City Life columnist sought to tidy his desk with a single back-sweep of his arm, thereby sending a couple of crumpled Marlboro packets into his pencil drawer.

The high command at the *New York Times* was still getting used to McDougal: appointed as executive editor only a few months earlier, he was an unlikely choice. His immediate predecessors had been drawn from that segment of New York society that had produced so many of the city's best-known names and given it so much of its humor and language: liberal Jews. Previous *New York Times* editors looked and sounded like Woody Allen or Philip Roth.

Townsend McDougal was a rather different proposition. A New England aristocrat with *Mayflower* roots and WASP manners, he wore a panama hat in summertime and tasseled loafers in winter. But that was not what had made *Times* veterans anxious when his appointment was announced. No, what made the editor and the *New York Times* an unlikely fit was the simple fact that Townsend McDougal was a born-again Christian.

He had not yet made Bible study classes compulsory, nor did he ask reporters to link hands in prayer before each night's print run. But it was a culture shock for a temple of secularism like the *New York Times.* Columnists and critics on the paper were used to a tone that was not quite mocking but certainly distant. Evangelical Christianity was something that existed out there, in flyover country—in the vast Midwest or the Deep South between the coasts. None of them would ever say so explicitly, still less write it, but the undeclared assumption was that born-again faith was the preserve of the simple folk. "Trust in Jesus" was for the women in polyester trousers watching Pat Robertson on the 700 Club, or for recovering alcoholics who needed to "turn around" their lives and declare their salvation in a bumper sticker. It was not for Ivy League sophisticates like themselves.

Townsend McDougal unsettled every one of those presumptions. Now *Times* journalists had to check the default arithmetic that stated that secular equaled smart. From now on, religion would no longer be cast as a matter of poor taste, like big hair or

TV dinners. It was to be treated with respect. The change in articles, from the fashion pages to the sports section, became apparent within weeks of McDougal's arrival. The new executive editor had not sent out a memo. He did not have to.

Now he was walking among the Metro staff, with his gaze aimed in only one direction.

"Look, I better go," Will said into the phone in what he hoped was a low whisper. As Will replaced the receiver, McDougal began.

"Welcome to the Holy of Holies, William. The front page of the greatest newspaper in the world. A phrase your father used himself on the telephone to me this very morning." Will felt himself blush. It was not embarrassment at the compliment, nor even McDougal's klaxon of a voice, bellowing his praise all around the office in an accent that was so Brahmin as to be almost English, though that was embarrassing enough. It was the reference to his father. Will thought his dad had reached an understanding with McDougal: that there was to be no public acknowledgment of the friendship between them. Will knew he would be resented as it was—the hotshot young journo on the fast track—without his colleagues assuming he was the beneficiary of that old-fashioned career-enhancing drug, nepotism.

Now it was out there; McDougal's decibels had seen to that. The internal e-mails would be flying: Guess who's all chummy with the boss? As it happened, Will had applied for this job the same way as everyone else: sending in a letter and turning up for an interview. But no one would believe that now. He could feel his neck becoming hot.

"You've made a good start, William. Taking some unpromising raw material and turning it into something worthy of page one. I sometimes wish some of your more mature colleagues would show similar degrees of industry and verve."

Will wondered if McDougal was deliberately setting out to make his life hell. Was this some kind of initiation rite practiced by the Skull and Bones set at Yale, where he and his father had first become such pals? The editor might as well have painted a target on Will's back and handed crossbows to each of his colleagues.

"Thank you."

"I shall be expecting more from you, William. And I shall be following this story with interest."

With that, and a swish of his finely tailored gray suit, Townsend McDougal was gone. The reporters who had previously been sitting to attention now collectively slumped. The City Life columnist opened up his top drawer, reached for his cigarettes, and headed for the fire escape.

Will had an equally instant urge. Without thinking, he dialed Beth's number. After the second ring, he abandoned it. A call about a triumph at work would confirm everything she had said about him. As of yesterday morning, they were talking again; but he still had to do penance.

"Now, William." It was Walton, his chair swiveled around to face the common space that linked them with Grossman and Schwarz. He was looking upward, the lower half of his face covered with a supercilious smile. He looked like a malevolent schoolboy.

Although he was nearly fifty years old, there was something infantile about Terence Walton. He had the unnerving habit of playing high-tech computer games while he worked, rattling the keys as he zapped various alien life forms to "proceed to the next level." His fingers seemed to be in constant search of distraction; the moment he had finished one phone call, he would be onto the next. He was always fixing up extracurricular activities, a radio appearance here, a well-paid lecture there. His work from Delhi had been highly praised, and he was in fairly regular demand as an expert. His book, *Terence Walton's India*, was credited with introducing the American public to a country they barely knew.

Inside the building, Walton was held in slightly lower esteem. That much, Will had picked up. The seating arrangements alone confirmed it: a returned foreign correspondent placed alongside the Metro staff's newest recruit. It was hardly star treatment. Will did not yet know what Walton had done to deserve this slight.

"We were just discussing your front-page triumph. Good job. Of course, there will be doubters, skeptics, who wonder what greater light this tale shed, but I am not one of them. No, William, not me."

"Will. It's Will."

"The executive editor seems to think it's William. You might need to have a word with him. Anyway, my question is this: Why, I wonder, should this little story be on the front page? What larger social phenomenon did it expose? I fear our new editor does not yet fully understand the sacred bottom left slot. It's not just for amusing or interesting vignettes. It should serve as a window onto a new world."

"I think it was doing that. It was correcting a stereotype about urban life in this city. This man seemed like a sleazeball, but he was, you know, better than that."

"Yes, that's great. And well done! Tremendous job. But remember what they say about beginner's luck: very hard to pull off that trick twice. I doubt even you could find too many 'tales of ordinary people' "—he was putting on a cutesy, Pollyanna-ish voice—"that would interest the *New York Times*. At least not the *New York Times* I used to work for. Once counts as an achievement, William; twice would be a miracle."

Will turned back to his computer, to his e-mail inbox. *Grossman, Amy.* In the subject field: *Coffee?*

Five minutes later Will was in the vast *Times* canteen, all but deserted at this morning hour. He paced up and down by the glass cases that housed *Times* merchandise: sweatshirts, baseball caps, toy models of the old *Times* delivery trucks. Amy materialized beside him, clutching a cup of herbal tea.

"I just wanted to say sorry about all that just now. That's the downside of working here: lot of testosterone, if you know what I mean."

"It was fine—"

"People are very competitive. And Terry Walton especially."

"I got that impression."

"Do you know the story with him?"

"I know he used to be in Delhi and that he was forced to come back."

"They accused him of expenses fraud. They couldn't prove it, which is why he's still here. But there's certainly some trust issues."

"About money, you mean?"

"Oh no, not just about money." She gave a bitter chuckle.

"What else, then?"

"Well, look, you didn't hear this from me, OK? But my advice is to lock up your notebooks when Terry's around. And talk quietly when you're on the phone."

"I don't get it."

"Terry Walton steals stories. He's famous for it. When he was in the Middle East they called him the Thief of Baghdad."

Will was smiling.

"It's actually not that funny. There are journalists around the world who could talk all night about the crimes of Terence Walton. Will, I'm serious: lock away your notebooks, your documents, everything. He will read them."

"So that's why he writes like that."

"What?"

"Walton has this very tiny handwriting, completely indecipherable. That's deliberate, isn't it? To make sure no one reads his notes."

"I'm just saying, be careful."

When he arrived back in the newsroom he found Glenn Harden sticking a Post-it to his screen. "Come up and see me some time."

"Ah, here you are. I have a message from National. Go west, young man."

"I'm sorry?"

"To Seattle. Bates's wife is in labor, and National needs us to cover. Apparently they don't have any reporters of their own, so they've put out the begging bowl." Harden raised his voice. "I scraped the bottom of the barrel and offered them Walton, but he's come up with some lame-assed excuse and suggested you." Walton was on the phone, not listening. "Talk to Jennifer, she'll fix you a flight."

"Thank you," Will stammered, a smile beginning to break on his face. He knew this was a major break, a serious vote of confidence. Sure, it was only cover, only temporary. But Harden would not want Metro disgraced in the eyes of what he regarded as the Ivy League snobs over at National: he would want to show Metro's best face. Will gulped at the thought: that was him.

"Oh, and pack your galoshes."

CHAPTER SEVEN

TUESDAY, 10:21 A.M., WASHINGTON STATE

AND I HAVE SHOWN YOU, *Jesus Christ is the light and the way. We have seen a miracle today . . .*

Christian radio, along with country music, was the one staple you could always rely on: even the remotest backwater, where there were no other stations on the dial, would always be favored with the word of the gospel, beamed through the air. The mountain passes of Washington State were no different.

Will was getting closer to the flood scene, he could tell. The roads were becoming clogged, and soon he began to see the flashing lights of emergency teams. Then, most reassuring of all, a fleet of white, liveried satellite trucks: local TV, confirmation that he had arrived at the site of the story.

He hooked up with a photographer who seemed to know what he was doing. For one thing, he had all the right equipment. Not just the regulation photographer jacket, with enough pockets to store the possessions of a nuclear family, but industrial-strength, thigh-high rubber boots, waterproof pants, polar-ice-cap socks, and gloves that looked as if they were custom designed by NASA.

Will waded into the floodwater after him, conscious of the chill creeping up his trouser leg. Before long they had hitched a ride on a police dinghy and were ferrying from submerged home to submerged home. He saw one woman winched to safety carrying the thing she valued most: her cat. Another man was standing, sobbing, by his storefront, watching a lifetime's investment wash away like leaves in a gutter.

A few hours of that, and Will was back in the rental car, soaked and hunched over his keyboard. "The people of the Northwest are used to nature's temper—but her latest mood swing has them reeling," he began, before detailing the individual tales of woe. A couple of quotes from officialdom and a nice closing line about the fickleness of the climate, spoken by the man who had lost his stationery shop, and it was done.

Once back in the hotel room, he called Beth. She was already in bed. She talked about her day; he uncoiled the full story of his sodden journey into the flood lands. Both of them were too exhausted to restart the conversation they had never really finished.

He flicked on the local news, pictures of the Snohomish floods; Will picked out faces he recognized. His heart went out to the reporter doing the live shot: that meant he was still there.

"Next up, more on the murder of Pat Baxter. After these messages." Will turned back to his computer, only half listening to the words coming out of the TV.

The victim, fifty-five, found dead and alone in his cabin . . . police suspect a botched break-in . . . much damage, but nothing stolen . . . Baxter had been under surveillance for years . . . was briefly prime suspect in Unabomber case . . . no family, no relatives . . .

Will wheeled around. One word had leapt out. Will Googled "Unabomber," getting an instant refresher course on a bizarre case that had foxed the FBI for two decades. Someone had sent mail bombs to corporate addresses on the East Coast, leaving behind a trail of obscure clues. Eventually, the culprit released a "manifesto," a quasi-academic tract that seemed to be the work of a loner with a deep suspicion of technology. He also seemed to harbor a profound loathing for government. There was a piece on the *Seattle Times* Web site, just posted.

> *That sentiment put the Unabomber in tune with an entire 1990s movement, one in which the late Pat Baxter had been a reliable player. For this was the age of the gun-toting militias—Americans arming themselves against what they believed was an imminent onslaught by the U.S. government. They eventually spread throughout America, but they began in the Pacific Northwest.*

Will started working his way through the *New York Times'* online archive. He was struck by the first pieces that appeared: quite benign, depicting the militia men as "weekend soldiers," overweight, overgrown schoolboys huffing and puffing their way through war games. But soon the tone changed.

The 1992 standoff at Ruby Ridge, where a white supremacist lost his wife and child in a shootout with federal agents, like the siege at Waco, Texas, a year later, revealed a world that most Americans—certainly those in media offices in New York—had never heard of. This world saw Washington as the center of a shadowy new world order, embodied by the hated United Nations, which was determined to enslave free people everywhere. How else to explain the mysterious black helicopters spotted over rural America? What other meaning could there be to the numbers on the back of road signs? Surely they were coded coordinates that would one day help the U.S. Army herd their fellow citizens into concentration camps.

The more Will read, the more fascinated he became. These

civilian warriors believed the craziest theories—about Freemasons, the Federal Reserve, coded messages printed on dollar bills, mysterious connections with European banks. Some of them were so sure the jackbooted bureaucrats of the federal government were out to get them that they had retreated into the hills, hiding in mountain cabins in remotest Idaho or wooded Montana. They had severed their links with the government in all its forms: they carried no drivers' licenses, they refused to sign any official paper. Some moved, quite literally, off the grid—generating their own power, rather than living off the national electricity system.

And they were not playing games. On the second anniversary of the conflagration at Waco, the Alfred P. Murrah Federal Building in Oklahoma City had shattered into dust, broken up by a mighty car bomb, killing 169 people. The culprits turned out to be not Islamic extremists but all-American boys whose heads had been filled with loathing of their own government.

The *Seattle Times* had an archive picture of Baxter at a rally in Montana in 1994—though it looked more like a trade fair, down to the stands where exhibitors showed their wares. Baxter was pictured manning a stall that sold MREs—military-style "meals ready to eat." Apparently, he did a fairly brisk trade in dried foods, portable tents, and the like: survivalist gear that would keep the freedom-loving American in food and shelter during the coming confrontation. In the remote world of the antigovernment movement, Baxter was, if not a celebrity, then a fixture.

> *"He was a great patriot and his death is a great blow to all those who love liberty," said Bob Hill, a self-styled commandant of the Montana militia.*

Wednesday, 9:00 a.m., Seattle

Worryingly, the phone had not rung. When he finally awoke at nine—noon, New York time—he saw that his cell phone was recording no missed calls at all. He reached for his BlackBerry; just some unimportant e-mail. This was not right.

He reached for his laptop, pulling it down from the table and onto the bed, stretching its cable to breaking point. He checked the *Times* site: no sign of his story. He clicked down to the National section: links to stories out of Atlanta, Chicago, and Washington, D.C. He clicked and clicked. Here was something, datelined Seattle. But it was only an Associated Press wire story, written that morning. No sign of his own piece.

He phoned Beth. The hospital had to page her.

"Hi babe, have you seen the paper today?"

"Yes, I'm fine, thank you. How kind of you to ask."

"Sorry, it's just—have you got it there?"

"Hold on." A long pause. "OK, what am I looking for?"

"Anything by me."

"I looked this morning. I couldn't see anything. I thought maybe you were going to do more work on it today?"

Will tutted silently: of course he wasn't going to work on it today. It was an on-the-day news story, about weather, for Christ's sake: there was no more perishable commodity in journalism than a weather story.

"You checked the National section inside? Each page?"

"I did, Will. I'm sorry. Does this mean they didn't use it?"

That was exactly what it meant: his story had been spiked.

He braced himself for a call to the desk. If anyone but Jennifer, the news clerk, answered, he would hang up. He dialed.

"National." Jennifer.

"Hi, Jennifer, it's Will Monroe here, out in Seattle."

"Oh, hi. Wanna speak to Susan?"

"No! No. No need. You know that piece I filed yesterday, from the floods? Do you know what happened to it?"

Jennifer's voice suddenly dipped.

"Kind of. I heard them talking about it. They said it was very nice and all, but that you hadn't talked about it with them first. If you had, they'd have told you they didn't need a story yesterday."

"But I did speak . . ." Of course. He had only talked with Jennifer, told her his coordinates and his plans. He had assumed they wanted him to file. Had Harden not told him to pack his galoshes?

Now he realized: he was in Seattle just in case. He was keeping Bates's seat warm. All that soaking effort yesterday had been in vain. He felt embarrassed, like an overeager intern. It was a stupid mistake.

"Hold on, Susan wants a word."

Three time zones away, Will readied himself for a roasting.

"Hi, Will. Listen, I think the rule ought to be no filing unless we've talked about it first. OK? Maybe just find something that interests you, poke around a bit, and see what it's worth. As for spot news, keep your phone on, and we'll call you if we need anything."

Will ate a glum breakfast. He had screwed up, and screwed up badly. By now Jennifer would have spread the word among the tiny circle of *Times* staffers in their twenties: they would be having a good laugh at his expense. The golden boy with a big-shot daddy had come down to earth.

There was only one solution. He would have to reel in a proper story. Somehow, from this far-off patch of snow, timber, and potatoes, he would have to eke out a tale that would prove to New York that they had not made a mistake. He knew exactly where he would go.

CHAPTER EIGHT

WEDNESDAY, 3:13 P.M., WASHINGTON STATE

THE FLIGHT ACROSS WASHINGTON STATE had been brief, if bumpy, and the drive from Spokane gorgeous. The mountains were almost painfully beautiful, each cap dusted with a snow that looked like the purest powdered sugar. The trees were as straight as pencils, lines of them, so densely packed, the light almost seemed to strobe.

He was driving east, soon crossing the state line into Idaho—or at least the long, slender upper part of the state where the United States appears to be giving the finger to its northern neighbor, Canada. He drove past Coeur d'Alene, which sounded like a Swiss skiing village but which was most famous as the home of a racist movement known as the Aryan Nations. Will had seen the pictures in the cuttings: the men dressed in quasi-Nazi uniforms, the Whites Only sign at the entrance. It would make a fascinating stop, but Will did not leave the road. He had somewhere to go.

His destination lay across the Idaho finger, in the western part of Montana. The roads were small, but Will did not get frustrated. He loved driving in America, the land of the endless road. He loved the billboards, promoting furniture stores thirty-five miles away; he loved the Dairy Queen rest stops, the bumper stickers advising him of the politics, religion, and sexual preferences of his fellow drivers. Besides, he was planning his attack.

He had spoken already to Bob Hill, who was expecting him. Dutifully, Hill had conformed to the media caricature of a backwoods gun nut. He asked to have Will's full name and social security number: "That way I can check you out. Make sure y'are who y'say y'are." Will tried to imagine what Hill's research would turn up on him. Brit? That would be OK. Americans usually liked Brits. Even if they hated limp-wristed, faggot Europeans, Brits were OK: they were kind of honorary Americans. Father a federal judge? That could be problematic; federal officials were despised. But judges were not always lumped in with the rest of the hated bureaucrats who represented "the government." Some were even seen as the protectors of liberty, fending off the encroaching hand of the politicians. If Hill looked, though, he would find plenty in Judge Monroe's record that was bound to offend. Will hoped his host was not going to dig too deep.

What else? Parents divorced: that might rile the militiamen. Mind you, this wasn't Alabama; the survivalists were not the same as the Christian right. There was some overlap, but they were not identical.

The daydream ended the moment he saw the signs: "Welcome to Noxon, Population: 230." He looked down at the scribbled note perched on his lap: Hill's directions. He had to turn left at the gas station, down a road that would become a path. The SUV began rocking from side to side, over the ruts of mud, earning, or so Will liked to think, the extra charge he, and therefore the *Times*, had had to pay for it.

Soon he reached a gate. No sign. He was about to call Hill, as arranged, but he was halfway through dialing the number when a man became visible in his windshield. Early sixties, jeans, cowboy boots, old jacket; unsmiling. Will got out.

"Bob Hill? Will Monroe."

"So you found us OK?"

Will went into a hymn of praise for Hill's directions, seeking to break the ice with some shameless flattery. His host grunted his approval as he trudged up a hard mud bank, heading in the direction of what seemed to be a thick patch of forest. As they got closer, Will began to make out a glow of light: a cabin, rather brilliantly camouflaged.

Hill looked to his waist, where a thick jailer's ring of keys was weighing down one of his belt loops. He let them in.

"There's a chair there. Make yourself comfortable. I've got something to show you."

Will used the few seconds he had to look around: a metal shield on the wall, bearing a vaguely military insignia. He squinted: MoM. Militia of Montana. There were a few framed photographs, including one of his host holding the head of a dead stag. On the metal shelves, a box of leaflets. Will peered inside: "The New World Order: Operation Takeover."

"Help yourself, take a copy." Will whisked around to find Bob Hill right behind him. Ex-marine, Vietnam; of course he would know how to creep up on a mere civilian like Will. "Wrote it myself. With the help of the late Mr. Baxter."

"So he was . . . deeply involved?"

"Like I told you on the phone, a fine patriot. Ready to do whatever it took to secure the liberty of this nation—even if his nation was too duped, its brains too addled by the propaganda of the Hollywood elite, to realize its liberty was under threat."

"Whatever it took?"

"By whatever means necessary, Mr. Monroe. You know who said that, don't you? Or was that before your time?"

"It was before my time, but I do know. That was the slogan of the Black Panthers."

"Very good. And if that was good enough for them in their

struggle against 'white power,' then it's good enough for us in our struggle to keep America free."

"You mean violence? Force?"

"Mr. Monroe, let's not get ahead of ourselves. You can ask me all the questions you like, I got plenty of time. But first, I have something to show you. See if this interests the great East Coast intellectuals of the *New York Times*."

By now Hill was seated behind a battered old metal desk, one that would not have looked out of place in the office section of an auto-repair shop. He handed Will, who was still standing, two sheets of paper, stapled together.

It took a few seconds for Will to work out what he was looking at: the notes on the autopsy performed on the body of Pat Baxter.

"I demanded it under FOI." He saw Will's crinkled brow. "Freedom of information? Said it was my constitutional right to see it: Missoula faxed it over this morning." Missoula, the nearest big town.

"What does it say?"

"Oh, don't let me spoil it for you. I think you should read it for yourself."

Will felt a twinge of panic: this was the first autopsy report he had ever seen. It was almost impossible to decipher. Each heading was written in baffling medicalese; the handwriting beneath was just as inscrutable. Will found himself squinting through it.

Finally, a sentence he understood. "Severe internal hemorrhaging consistent with a gunshot wound; contusions of the skin and viscera. General remarks: needle mark on right thigh, suggestive of recent anesthesia."

"He was shot," Will began, uncertain. "And he seems to have been anesthetized before he was shot. Which does seem very odd, I grant you."

"Ah, but there's an explanation. Read on, Mr. Monroe."

Will's eyes scoured the document, looking for clues. Scribbled handwritting, sent through a fax, did not make it easy.

"Second page," Hill offered. "General remarks."

"Damage to internal organs: liver, heart and kidney (single) severe. Other viscera, fragmented."

"What leaps out at you, Mr. Monroe? I mean what word there friggin' jumps out and grabs you by the throat?"

Will wanted to say "viscera," simply because the word was so undeniably powerful. But he knew that was not the answer Hill was looking for.

"Single."

"My my, you Oxford boys are as bright as they say you are." Hill had not been kidding about his research. "That's right. Single. What do you think's going on here, Mr. Monroe? What strange set of facts do we have here that Montana's finest have so far chosen to overlook? Well, I'll tell you."

Will was relieved; the guessing game was making him sweat.

"My friend Pat Baxter was anesthetized before he was killed. And his body is found minus one kidney. Put two and two together, and what do we get?"

Will muttered almost to himself, "Whoever did this removed his kidney."

"Not only that, but that's why they killed him. They wanted it to look like a robbery, a 'break-in gone badly wrong,' they're saying on the TV. But that's all a smokescreen. The only thing they wanted to steal was Pat Baxter's kidney."

"Why on earth would they want to do that?"

"Oh, Mr. Monroe. Don't make me do all the work here. Open your eyes! This is a federal government that has been doing experimentation with bio-chips!" He could see that Will was not following. "Bar codes, implanted under the skin! So that they can monitor our movements. There's good evidence they're doing this with newborn babies now, right there in the maternity ward. An electronic tagging system, enabling the government to follow us from cradle to grave—quite literally."

"But why would they want Pat Baxter's kidney?"

"The federal government moves in mysterious ways, Mr. Monroe, its wonders to perform. Maybe they wanted to plant something inside

Pat's body, and the plan went wrong. Maybe the anesthetic wore off, and he began resisting. Or perhaps they put something inside his body years ago. And now they needed to get it back. Who knows? Maybe the feds just wanted to examine the DNA of a dissident, see if they could discover the gene that makes a real freedom-loving American and work to eradicate it."

"It does seem a little far-fetched."

"I grant you that. But we're talking about a military-industrial complex that has spent millions of dollars on mind-control techniques. You know, they had a secret Pentagon project to see if men could kill goats, simply by staring at 'em? I am not making this up. So it may be far-fetched. But I have come to learn that far-fetched and untrue are two very different things."

Eventually Will steered Hill toward saner shores, seeking the biographical details of Baxter's life that he knew he would need. He got some, including a back story about the dead man's father: turned out Baxter Sr. was a World War II veteran who had lost both his hands. Unable to work, he had grown desperate; he could barely feed his family on his GI pension. Hill reckoned Baxter was a son who grew up resenting a government that could send a young man to kill and die for his country and then abandon him when he came home. When history repeated itself with Baxter's own generation in Vietnam, the bitterness was complete.

That would do nicely, serving as the easy-to-digest, psychological key needed for all good stories, in newspapers no less than at the movies. The piece was beginning to take shape.

He asked Hill to take him to Baxter's cabin. They used Will's car, its engine revving as it climbed farther up the rutted path. Soon, Will could see color—the yellow tape of a police cordon. "This is as far as we can go. It's a crime scene." Will reached into his pocket. As if reading his mind, Hill added, "Even your fancy New York press card won't get you in here. It's sealed."

Will got out anyway, just to get a feel. It looked to him like a shed: a bare log cabin, the kind a well-off family might use to store firewood. The dimensions made it hard to believe a man had made this his home.

Will asked Hill to describe the interior as best he could. "That's easy," his guide said. "Almost nothing in there." A narrow, metal-frame bed; a chair; a stove; a shortwave radio.

"Sounds like a cell."

"Think military accommodation; that'll get you closer to it. Pat Baxter lived like a soldier."

"Spartan, you mean?"

"Yes, sir."

Will asked who else he should talk to; any friends, any family. "The Militia of Montana was his only family," Hill shot back, a little too fast, Will thought. "And even we hardly knew him. First time I ever saw that cabin was when the police had me around there. Wanted me to identify which clothes were his and which might have been left behind by the killers."

"Killers, plural?"

"You don't think someone starts performing major surgery like that on their own, do you? They would have needed a team. Every surgeon needs a nurse."

Will gave Bob Hill a ride back to his own cabin. He suspected that, though Hill's office might have been basic, his house was elsewhere—and not nearly so spare as Baxter's. The dead man was clearly an extreme kind of extremist.

They said their good-byes, exchanged e-mail addresses, and Will began the long drive on. Bob Hill was obviously a nut—DNA for dissidence, indeed—but this business with the kidney was definitely strange. And why would Baxter's killers have given him an injection?

He pulled off Route 200 to fill up the car and his stomach. He found a diner and ordered a soda and a sandwich. A TV was on, tuned to Fox News.

. . . Dateline London now and more on the scandal threatening to topple the British government.

There were pictures of a harried-looking Gavin Curtis emerging from a car to an explosion of flashbulbs and television lights.

According to one British newspaper today, Treasury records show clear discrepancies which can only have been authorized at the very top. While opposition politicians demand a full disclosure of accounts, Mr. Curtis's spokesman says only that "there has been no wrongdoing . . ."

Without thinking, Will was taking notes, not that he would ever need them: Curtis's chances of heading up the IMF were surely slim to nonexistent now. Watching the pictures of Curtis being shepherded past the baying press mob—a classic "goatfuck," as the TV guys called them—Will's mind wandered onto trivial terrain. How come his car is so ordinary? This Gavin Curtis was meant to be the second most powerful man in Britain, yet he was driven around in what looked like a suburban sales rep's car. Did all British ministers live so modestly—or was this just a Gavin Curtis thing?

Will called the sheriff's office for Sanders County and was told that, for all the federal investigations and Unabomber inquiries, Baxter had no criminal record whatsoever. He had been under heavy surveillance, but it had yielded nothing: a couple of unexplained trips to Seattle, but no evidence of illegality. He had never been convicted of anything. Will flicked back through his notebook. He had scribbled down all he could of the autopsy report, including the name at the foot of the document. Dr. Allan Russell, Medical Examiner, Forensic Science Division, State Crime Lab. Maybe this Dr. Russell would be able to tell him what Mr. Baxter's militia comrades had not. How had Pat Baxter died—and why?

CHAPTER NINE

Wednesday, 6:51 p.m., Missoula, Montana

He had got there too late; the crime lab was shut for the day. No amount of cajoling could alter that fact; the staff had gone home. He would have to come back tomorrow. Which meant he would have to spend the night in Missoula.

He was briefly tempted by the C'mon Inn, if only because the joke was too good to resist. But, Will realized, he could still tell people about it in New York: he did not actually have to stay there. So he played safe and checked into the Holiday Inn for a third night of room service, the remote control, and a phone call with Beth.

"You're making this too complicated," she said, audibly getting out of the bath.

"But it is complicated. The guy has a kidney missing."

"You need to see a medical history. Maybe—what's his name again?"

"Baxter."

"Maybe Baxter had a history of renal problems. Any reference to that or to dialysis or kidney trouble of any kind, and that will give you an explanation."

Will was silent.

"I'm ruining it, aren't I?"

"Well, if we're talking news value, the choice between the death of an old man with a past history of renal failure and an attempted kidney-snatching is very close. But, yeah, you might be right: the kidney-snatching probably just edges it." Will was relieved they were back into banter mode. Several days now stood between them and the argument; the wound seemed to be closing.

THURSDAY, 10:02 A.M., MISSOULA, MONTANA

The next morning, Will was ushered into Dr. Russell's office. He saw it straight away, a certificate on the wall carrying an emblem Will recognized: an open book, inscribed with Latin words, topped off by two crowns.

"Ah, you were at Oxford. Like me. When were you there?"

"Several centuries before you, I suspect."

"That can't be true, Dr. Russell."

"Call me Allan."

At last, a lucky break. "You know, Allan, I'm not even sure I'll write about it for the paper, but this Pat Baxter business does intrigue me, I must confess," he began, as if settling down for an agreeable chat at high table. Will noticed his own English accent had become more pronounced.

"Let me have a look here," Russell was saying, as he turned to his computer. "Ah yes, 'Severe internal hemorrhaging consistent with a gunshot wound; contusions of the skin and viscera. General remarks: needle mark on right thigh, suggestive of recent anesthesia.' "

"Now, how are you defining 'recent' there, Allan?" Will hoped his tone was saying, *Purely out of academic interest . . .*

"Probably contemporaneous."

"You see this, I have to say, is what intrigues me. Why would anyone anesthetize someone before they kill them?"

"Perhaps they were trying to reduce the victim's pain."

"Do murderers do that? It makes no sense. Unless—"

"Unless the killer was a medical man. Trained to give a shot before any procedure. Force of habit, perhaps."

"Or if he wanted to do something else before the murder. Perform some other operation."

"Like?"

"Well, I understand that Baxter was found minus one kidney."

Russell began to laugh in a way Will struggled to find funny. "Oh, I see what you're driving at." Russell was grinning. "Tell me, Will. Have you ever seen a dead body?"

Instantly, Will remembered the corpse of Howard Macrae, under a blanket on that street in Brownsville. His first. "Yes. In my work it's hard to avoid."

"Well, then, you won't mind seeing another one."

It was not as cold as he expected. Will imagined a morgue to be a giant fridge, like those cold storage rooms at the back of large hotels. This was more like a hospital ward.

The orderlies were moving a gurney into a curtained-off zone that Will took to be the examination area. With not even a moment's warning, Russell pulled back the sheet.

Will felt his stomach tighten. The body was stiff and waxy, a yellowish green. The stench was rancid, seeming to come his way in waves. For a second or two he would think it had passed, or that at least he had got used to it, and then it would strike again—inciting Will to empty his guts out on the floor there and then.

"It can take some getting used to. Apologies. Now take a look at this."

Will moved closer. Russell was gesturing toward something in the stomach area, but Will was transfixed by Pat Baxter's face. The papers had run photos, but they were grainy—"grabs" from TV footage, mainly. Now he saw the weathered cheeks, chin, eyes, and mouth of a man he would have identified as middle-aged, poor, and white. He had a longish beard that, in a different context, might have looked elegant, even statesmanlike. (The face of Charles Darwin popped into Will's head.) But the effect here was to give Pat Baxter the appearance of a homeless man, one of the winos found sleeping by trashcans in a park.

Russell was pulling back the sheet around Baxter's torso. Will could tell he was trying to conceal one thing, probably the bullet wounds, and reveal something else. "Look closely. Can you see it?"

Will leaned forward to see Russell's finger tracing a line on the dead white flesh. "That's a scar."

"In the area of the kidney?"

"I would say so."

"And that can't be from that night, right? I mean, it takes ages to form a scar."

Russell pulled back the sheet, stripped off his latex gloves, and headed for a basin in the corner of the room. He began scrubbing, talking over his shoulder. He was enjoying this.

"Well, of course, it's hard to be certain, what with the severe trauma to the skin and viscera."

"But what's your professional opinion?"

"My opinion? That scar is, at the very least, a year old. Maybe two."

Will felt his heart sink. "So it didn't happen that night? The killers didn't take out Baxter's kidney?"

"I'm afraid not, no. You look disappointed, Will. I hope I haven't spoiled your story."

But you have, asshole, was Will's first thought. All this chasing for nothing. Then he remembered what Beth had said on the phone last night.

"There is one last thing that might help. Do you have access to Pat Baxter's medical records?"

Russell went into a mini-lecture about patient-doctor confidentiality, but, Will noticed, not a denial that he had seen the records.

Back in Russell's office, Will pushed again. His instinct was right: the medical examiner had had Baxter's file sent over the previous day. Finally, and with a great show of reluctance, he pulled it out of a drawer and placed it on his lap, taking great care to prevent Will reading it, even upside down.

"OK. What are we looking for?"

"The date Pat Baxter had his kidney removed."

Russell paused, turning the pages. Finally: "That's odd. There's no record of a kidney operation."

Will perked up. He remembered Beth's briefing on the phone last night. "Anything there about a history of kidney problems, any disease, any references to renal failure, dialysis, anything?"

A longer pause now. And then, with a hint of puzzlement, "No."

Will sensed he and the doctor now had something in common. They were equally baffled. "Does the history speak of any medical problems at all?"

"Some trouble with his ankle, associated with war damage. Vietnam, apparently. Apart from that, nothing. I just assumed he was a renal patient who had to have his kidney out. This certainly appears to be a complete record. And yet there's nothing about a kidney. I've got to admit, this has me foxed."

There was a light knock on the door. A woman, introduced by Russell as the media relations officer for the crime lab, opened it.

"Sorry to interrupt, Dr. Russell. It's just we're getting a ton of calls on the Baxter case. Apparently, an associate of the deceased called a talk radio station today saying that he believed Mr. Baxter was a victim of some kind of organ-snatching plot?"

Bob Hill, thought Will. So much for his exclusive.

"Sure, I'll be with you in a minute," Russell said, his brow tensing.

Will waited for the door to close to ask what Russell would tell the press. "Well, we can't give the most simple explanation, that Baxter had a history of kidney problems. Not now." It was Will's fault: he knew too much. "We'll think of something. I'll show you out."

Will was pulling out of the driveway when he heard the pounding on his car window. It was Russell, still in his shirtsleeves and breathless.

"I just got this call. She wants to talk to you." He passed his cell phone through the window.

"Mr. Monroe? My name is Genevieve Huntley. I'm a surgeon at the Swedish Medical Center in Seattle. I saw the reports about Mr. Baxter on the news, and Allan has just explained to me what you know. I think we need to talk."

"Sure," said Will, scrabbling to find his notebook.

"I'm going to need some assurances from you, Mr. Monroe. I have a high regard for the *New York Times*, and I am relying on you to respect that. What I am about to tell you I vowed never to repeat. I only tell it now because I fear the alternative is worse. We can't have people scaring themselves senseless about some organ-snatching ring."

"I understand."

"I'm not sure you do. I'm not sure any of us do. What I ask is that you treat what I tell you with honor, dignity, and respect. For that is what it deserves, Mr. Monroe. Do I make myself clear?"

"Yes." Will could not imagine what he was about to hear.

"OK. Mr Baxter's greatest request was anonymity. That was the one thing he asked of me in return for what he did."

Will was silent.

"Pat Baxter came to Swedish about two years ago. He had come a long way, we found out later. When he turned up, the nurses assumed he was an ER case: he looked like a bum off the streets. But he said he was in perfect health, he just needed to talk to a doctor in our transplant unit. He said that he wanted to give up one of his kidneys.

"We immediately asked who he wanted to give the kidney to. Was there a sick child involved? Maybe a family member needed a transplant? 'No,' he said 'I just want you to give my kidney to someone who needs it.' My colleagues immediately assumed that, frankly, there must be some mental health issues involved. Such nondirected operations are almost unheard of. Certainly the first one we had ever dealt with.

"I sent Mr Baxter away. I told him this was something we couldn't consider. But he came back, and I sent him away again. The third time we had a long talk. He told me that he wished he had been born rich. That way—I remember his words—that way, he said, he might have known the pleasure of giving away vast amounts of money. He said there were so many people who needed help. I remember, he asked me, 'What does the word *philanthropy* mean? It means love of your fellow man. Well, why should only rich people be allowed to love their fellow man? I want to be a philanthropist, too.' He was determined to find another way to give—even if that meant giving away his own organs.

"Eventually I concluded that he was sincere. I ran the test, and there was no medical objection. We even ran psychological tests, and they confirmed he was of completely sound mind, totally able to make this decision.

"There was only one condition, imposed by him. He swore us to complete secrecy, complete confidentiality. The recipient patient was not to know where his or her new kidney had come from. That was very important. He didn't want that person to feel they owed him. And not a word to the press. He insisted on that. *No glory.*"

Quietly, almost meekly, Will asked, "And so you went ahead with it?"

"We did. I performed the operation myself. And I tell you, in my whole career there was no operation that made me prouder. All of us felt it: the anesthetist, the nurses. There was an extraordinary atmosphere in the OR that day; as if something truly remarkable was happening."

"And did all go smoothly?"

"Yes, it did, it did. The recipient took the organ just fine."

"Can I ask what kind of recipient we're talking about? Young, old, male, female?"

"It was a young woman. I won't say any more than that."

"And even though she was young, and he was old, it all worked out?"

"Well, this was the strangest thing. We tested that kidney, obviously, monitored it very closely. And you know what? Baxter was in his fifties, but that organ worked like it was forty years younger than he was. It was very strong, completely healthy. It was perfect."

"And it made all the difference for that young woman?"

"It saved her life. The staff and I wanted to have some kind of ceremony for him, after the operation, to thank him for what he'd done. It won't surprise you to hear that never happened. He discharged himself before we'd even had a chance to say good-bye. He just clean disappeared."

"And was that the last you heard from him?"

"No, I heard from him once more, just a few months ago. He wanted to make arrangements for after his death—"

"Really?"

"Don't get too excited, Mr. Monroe. I don't think he knew he was about to die. But he wanted to be sure that everything, his entire body, would be used." Huntley gave a rueful chuckle. "He even asked me what would be the optimal way for him to die."

"Optimal?"

"From our point of view. What would work best, if we wanted to get his heart, say, to a recipient. I think he was worried, because he lived so far away, that if he was killed in a road accident, for example, by the time he got to a hospital, his heart would be useless. Of course, the one scenario he didn't count on was a brutal murder."

"Do you have any idea—"

"I have no idea at all who could have wanted this man dead, no. I said the same to Dr. Russell just now. I can only think it was a completely random, awful crime. Because no one who knew him would want to murder such a man. They couldn't."

She paused, and Will chose to let the silence hang. One thing he had learned: say nothing, and your interviewee will often fill the void with the best quote of the entire conversation.

Eventually Dr. Huntley, with what Will thought was a crack in her voice, spoke again. "We discussed this when it happened and we discussed it again today, and my colleagues and I agree. What this man did, what Pat Baxter did for a person he had never met and would never meet—this was truly the most righteous act we have ever known."

CHAPTER TEN

FRIDAY, 6:00 A.M., SEATTLE

HE WOKE AT SIX A.M., back now in his Seattle hotel room. He had filed his story from Missoula and then made the long journey cross-country. As he wrote the piece, he was powered by a single, delicious thought: Eat this, Walton. What had that prick said? *Once counts as an achievement, William; twice would be a miracle.*

Will prayed he had pulled it off. His greatest fear was that the desk might find it too similar to the Macrae story, another good man among knaves. So he had played up the militia angle, thrown in lots of Pacific Northwest color, and hoped for the best. He even toyed with ditching the quote about Baxter's action being "righteous," the very same word that woman had used about Howard Macrae. It might look contrived. Still, it would be more contrived to ignore it.

He reached for his BlackBerry, whose red light was winking hopefully: new messages.

Harden, Glenn: *Nice job today, Monroe.* That was what he wanted to hear. It meant he had avoided the spike; if only he could see Walton's face. The next e-mail looked like spam; the sender's name was not clear, just a string of hieroglyphics. Will was poised to delete it when the single word in the subject field made him click it open. *Beth.* He had not even read all the words when he felt his blood freeze.

> DO NOT CALL THE POLICE. WE HAVE YOUR WIFE. INVOLVE THE POLICE AND YOU WILL LOSE HER. DO NOT CALL THE POLICE OR YOU WILL REGRET IT. FOREVER.

CHAPTER ELEVEN

Friday, 9:43 p.m., Chennai, India

The nights were getting cooler. Still, Sanjay Ramesh preferred to stay here in the air-conditioned chill of the office than risk the suffocating heat of the city. He would wait till the sun had fully set before heading for home.

That way he might avoid not only the clammy heat, but the ordeal of the stoop. Every night it happened, his mother trading gossip and health complaints with her friends as they sat outside until late. He found himself tongue-tied in such company; in most company, as it happened. Besides, September might be cool by the standards of Chennai, but it was still punishingly hot and sticky. Inside this room, an aircraft hangar of an open-plan office, filled by row after row of sound-muffling cubicles, the conditions were just right. For what he needed to do, it was the perfect environment.

It was a call center, one of thousands that had sprung up across India. Four stories packed with young Indians taking calls from

America or Britain, from people in Philadelphia anxious to pay their phone bill or travelers in Macclesfield wanting to check the train times to Manchester. Few, if any, of them ever realized their call was being routed to the other side of the world.

Sanjay liked his job well enough. For an eighteen-year-old living at home, the money was good. And he could work odd shifts to fit in with his studies. The big draw, though, was right here inside this little cubicle. He had everything he needed: a chair, a desk, and, most important of all, a computer with a fast connection to the world.

Sanjay was young, but he was a veteran of the Internet. He discovered it when both he and it were in their infancy. There were only a few hundred Web sites then, maybe a thousand. As he had grown, so had it. The World Wide Web expanded like a binary number sequence—1, 2, 4, 8, 16, 32, 64, 128—apparently doubling its size with each passing day, until it now girdled the globe many times over. Sanjay had not matched that pace physically, of course—if anything, he was a slight, skinny lad—but he felt his mind had kept up. As the Internet grew, he grew with it, constantly opening up whole new areas of knowledge and curiosity. From his upstairs bedroom in India, he had traveled to Brazil, mastered the disputed border politics of Nagorno-Karabakh, laughed at Indonesian cartoons, gazed inside the world of the Scottish caravan enthusiast, scanned the junior fencing league tables of Flanders, and seen what really motivated the tree growers of Taipei. There was no corner of human activity closed off to him. The Internet had shown him everything.

Including the images he had not wanted to see, the ones that had prompted the project he had completed just twenty-four hours earlier. He was a late developer as a computer hacker, coming to it when he was fifteen: most started before they were teenagers. He had played the usual tricks—hacking into the NATO target list, coming within one click of taking down the Indian railway's internal system—but each time he had held back from pressing the final button. Causing mayhem held no appeal for him. It would only give people a lot of grief, and, his surfing of the Web had taught him, there was plenty of that in the world already.

Now he felt the urge to laugh, partly at his own genius, partly at the joke he had played on those he had designated as his enemy. It had taken him months to perfect, but it had worked.

He had devised a benign virus, one capable of spreading through the computers of the world just as rapidly as any of the poisonous varieties hatched by his fellow boy geniuses, those whose malign purpose made them, in the argot of the Web, crackers rather than hackers.

At this moment, it was his method, rather than his objective, that delighted him. Like most viruses, his was designed to spread via ordinary desktop computers, those that were connected to the Internet all the time. While people in Hong Kong or Hannover were tapping away, e-mailing their friends or doing their accounts, or even fast asleep, his little baby was inside their machine, hard at work.

He had given it a target to look for, and just like everyone else, it used Google to find it. Invisible to the user, below the screen, it got back its results and used them to compile what Sanjay thought of as an enemies list. These would be the sites to feel the virus's wrath. All of them, like any other site, would have some bug or glitch in their software: the challenge was to find it. For that, hackers (and crackers) would devise a set of "exploits," designed to trigger the glitch. It might mean sending it a little nugget of data the software was not expecting; even one rogue symbol, a semicolon perhaps, might do the trick. You never knew until you tried. Sanjay imagined it like medieval warfare: you would fire hundreds of arrows at a castle, knowing that only one might find the slit in the stone and get through. Each castle would have a different gap in the armor, a different weakness. But if your list of exploits was long enough, you would find it eventually. And once you had, you could take down the site and the server that was hosting it. It would be gone, just like that.

And these sites certainly deserved to disappear. But Sanjay had taken his war against them a stage further. Most hackers stored their list of exploits on a single server, usually salted away in the bandit country of the Internet, a place out of the reach of the regulators. Romania and Russia were favorites. This method carried with it a fatal weakness, however: once the attacked sites realized the source of the enemy fire, they could simply block access to the server containing the exploits. The raids would stop.

Sanjay had found a solution. His virus would get its arsenal of exploits from a variety of sources, and would even carry some of this payload itself. Better still, he had programmed it to retrieve extra exploits every now and then, to improve itself. He had created a magician constantly able to replenish his bag of tricks. And *created* was the right word, for Sanjay felt he had conceived a living creature. In technical language, it was a "genetic algorithm," a piece of coding that was able to change. To evolve.

His virus would alter its list of exploits, even its method of distribution—sometimes through e-mail, sometimes through bulletin boards, sometimes through bugs in Web browsers—as it spread throughout the infinite universe that was the Internet. In this way, the virus would reproduce itself, but its "children" would not be identical either to the original virus or to each other. They would mutate, by picking up new exploits and new methods of propagation from sources all over the virtual world. Some of these sources would be servers in the Internet badlands of Eastern Europe, some would be found by scanning security bulletin boards—where people would discuss how to thwart the very tricks Sanjay was deploying. Sanjay was proud of his creation, traveling across the globe, mutating and bettering itself in a million different ways—thereby making itself all but impossible to track down and eliminate. Even if he never touched a computer again, it would continue without him. Still a teenager, he felt like a proud father, or rather a great-great-grandfather—the founder of a vast dynasty. His progeny were everywhere.

And they were engaged in noble work. Scanning the results now, he could see he had set the parameters sufficiently narrowly that only the target sites were collapsing. Within a matter of hours, every one of the world's Web sites dedicated to child pornography would dissolve. Sanjay was laughing because he could see that the final command he had programmed into the virus was also now taking effect. Each of the sites that once displayed violent and pornographic images of children was now replaced by a single picture: a 1950s Norman Rockwell–style drawing of a son on his mother's knee. Below it ran a simple, four-word message: *Read to your kids.*

Sanjay headed home, grinning at his joke—and his accomplishment. No one needed to know what he had done; he knew, and that was enough. The world would be a better place.

Even at night Chennai was a noisy city, as raucous as it had been when it was Madras. Perhaps that, and the fact that his mind was racing with his success, is why he did not hear the footsteps behind him. Perhaps that is why he saw and suspected nothing until he was walking down the side alley to his own house, when he felt a handkerchief over his mouth and heard his own muffled screams. There was a sharp pricking sensation on the side of his arm, and then a woozy slide downward into sleep.

When Mrs. Ramesh found her only son dead on the ground, she screamed loud enough to be heard three streets away. It gave her no comfort that her boy—who had dreamed of one day doing something "for children" and who had been murdered before he had a chance to do anything—had been killed by some apparently painless injection. Police admitted they were baffled by the murder; they had seen none like it before. There was no sign of violence or, God forbid, abuse. And there was the odd appearance of the body. As if it had been handled with care. "Laid to rest," was how the policeman had put it. "It must mean something, Mrs. Ramesh," he had said. "Your son's body was draped in a purple blanket. And, as everyone knows, purple is the color of princes."

CHAPTER TWELVE

FRIDAY, 6:10 A.M., SEATTLE

WILL FELT HIS FACE PALE, the blood draining from it. His head seemed light, insubstantial. He read the message again, scouring it for some clue, some indication that it was a cruel hoax. He looked to see if he had been "bcc'd," which would make this spam, sent out to millions. Maybe the Beth subject line was a coincidence. But there were no such signs. He looked for a signature at the foot of the page. Nothing but junk. His palms were sweating as he turned on his cell phone. He scrolled down to *B* and pressed *Beth*, the first one to pop up.

Please answer. Please God let me hear her voice. The phone rang and rang, with one tone suddenly shorter than the rest: it was diverting to voice mail. *Hi, you've reached Beth . . .* He crumpled as he heard her voice, surrendering as a memory floated into his head. The very first time he had asked her out, it had been via a message on her answering machine. "Unless it would be wildly inappropriate," he had begun, "I wondered whether you'd like to have dinner on Tuesday night." "Wildly inappropriate" had been his way of checking that she was single.

"Hello, this is Beth McCarthy, and the answer is no," came the reply, also left via voice mail, "it would not be wildly inappropriate for us to have dinner on Tuesday. In fact, it would be lovely." Will had replayed that message a dozen times when he had first got it. Just as he replayed it now, in his head.

He stopped the call, his hands now quivering as they punched in the number of the hospital. "Hello, please page Beth Monroe. It's her husband. Please."

Hold music by Vivaldi; he was begging it to stop, praying for it to be broken by the sound of someone picking up and for that someone to be Beth. *Please let me hear her voice.* But the music played on. Eventually: "I'm sorry, sir, there seems to be no response to that page. Is there another doctor who can help?"

A sudden realization. She might have been gone for hours. Perhaps she had been snatched from their bedroom in the dead of night. They had spoken just before twelve her time. Maybe the kidnappers broke in at five? Or six? Or just now? He was a continent away, fast asleep, when he should have been protecting his wife.

He looked at the e-mail again, his heart shrinking as he saw those words. He tried to focus, to look at the top of the message, among those strange, garbled characters. There were some numbers, today's date, and a time stamp that said 1:37 p.m., even though that was several hours away. That gave no clue.

Of course, he should call the police. But these people, these bastards, seemed so adamant—as if they really would not hesitate to kill Beth. Uttering the word, even if only as a thought in his own head, made him recoil. He regretted formulating the idea, as if expressing it made it real. He wished he could take it back.

In a moment of childish need, he realized he wanted his mother. He could call her—it would only be mid-afternoon in England now—and it would be such a comfort to hear her voice. But he knew he would not. She would panic; she might have an anxiety attack. She certainly could not be trusted not to phone the police, or at least talk to someone who would talk to someone who would. The simple truth was, she was too far away for him to manage, and his mother was a person who needed managing. (He realized that word was a Bethism. It made sense that she was one of the very few people who knew how to handle Will's mother.)

He was slowly beginning to see that there was only one person he could ask, only one person who might know what to do. His hand shook as he reached for the hotel phone, something telling him this was not a call to be made on a cell.

"The office of Judge William Monroe, please." A click. "Janine, it's Will. I need to speak to my father right away." Something in his voice cut through all social convention, conveying to his father's secretary that this was indeed an emergency. She dispensed with her usual small talk. She simply cleared out of the way, like a car making room for an ambulance. "I'll patch you through to his car now." A cell phone, thought Will, worriedly. He would have to let it pass: more important now just to get through.

It was a relief to hear his father pick up. The child in him felt glad, like a boy who persuades his dad to come kill a spider. Good, now an adult was going to take over. Doing his best to hold his voice steady, he told his father what had happened, reading the e-mail out slowly, twice.

Monroe Sr.'s voice instantly dipped; he did not want to be overheard by his driver. Even in a whisper, his voice had the deep authority that made him such a presence on the bench. Now, as he would in court, he asked all the pertinent questions, pressing his son to tell him everything he could work out about the sender. Finally, he delivered his ruling.

"It's obviously an attempt at extortion. They must know about Beth's parents. It's a classic ransom demand."

Beth's parents. He would have to tell them. How would he

even utter the words? "I want to call the police," said Will. "They know how to handle these things."

"No, we mustn't do anything too rash. My understanding is that kidnappers usually assume the victim's family will go to the police: they factor it into their planning. There must be a reason why these people are so determined to avoid the police being involved."

"Of course they don't want the police to be involved! They're fucking kidnappers, Dad!"

"Will, calm down."

"How can I calm down?" Will could feel his voice about to break. His eyes were stinging. He did not dare try speaking again.

"Oh, Will. Listen, we're going to get through this, I promise. First, you need to get back here. Immediately. Go to the airport right away. I'll meet you off the flight."

Those five hours in the air were the hardest of Will's life. He stared out of the window, his leg oscillating in a nervous tic that used to strike him during exams. He refused all food and drink, until he noticed the cabin attendants were eyeing him suspiciously. He did not want them thinking he was poised to blow up the plane, so he sipped some water. And all the time he was imagining his beloved Beth. What were they doing to her? He began to picture her tied to a chair, while some sadist dangled a knife—

It took all his strength to stop such thoughts before they had picked up speed. His guts were turning over. *How could I not have been there? If only I had phoned earlier. Maybe she called the cell phone when I was asleep . . .*

Throughout he held the BlackBerry in the palm of his hand. He hated everything about this accursed machine. Even to glance at it brought those chilling words right back. He could see them now, hovering in the air in front of him:

INVOLVE THE POLICE AND YOU WILL LOSE HER.

He looked at the device, so small, yet now containing so much poison. It was sleeping: no signal at this height. He kept watching the icon at the top right that would tell him when it was back within range. As the plane began its descent, he stole peeks at it. He did not want the flight attendants reminding him that they had asked that all "electronic devices be turned off until the aircraft has come to a complete stop."

At last he could see the sparkle of New York City in mid-afternoon. *She's down there.* The bridges, the highways, the flickering necklaces of light crisscrossing the whole vast metropolis. *She's there somewhere.*

He glanced down at the BlackBerry, moist with his own palm-sweat. The icon had changed; it was back in range. Now the red light was flashing. Will's heart began to pound. He looked at the new messages flowing in, each one taking its place like passengers in a bus queue. Some round-robin cinema listing; an internal message from work about a lost notebook. There was a news alert from the BBC Web site.

> *Tributes have been pouring in for the chancellor of the exchequer, Gavin Curtis, found dead this evening, apparently from a drug overdose. Police say he was found by a cleaner in his Westminster flat, with an excess of a sedative drug in his bloodstream. It's believed that the police are not looking for anyone else in connection with Mr. Curtis's death . . .*

Will was staring out of the window, just imagining the media frenzy back in London. He had grown up there: he knew what the British press was like when its blood was up. They had been gunning for this guy for days, and now they had got their scalp. Will could not remember the last time a politician had actually topped himself: when it came to taking responsibility, resignation was usually as far as they would go, and even that had become pretty rare. This Curtis must have been guilty as hell.

And then one more message popped into the BlackBerry: the same hieroglyphic string that refused to reveal itself. Subject: *Beth.*

Will clicked it open.

WE DO NOT WANT MONEY.

CHAPTER THIRTEEN

FRIDAY, 2:14 P.M., BROOKLYN

"IT MUST BE A BLUFF."

"Dad, you've said that three times. Tell me, what do you think we should do? Should we offer them money anyway? What should we fucking do?"

"Will, I don't blame you at all, but you must calm down. If we're to get Beth back, we need to think as clearly as we can."

That "if" stopped Will short.

They were in Will and Beth's apartment. There was no sign of a break-in; everything was how he had last seen it. Except now a chill seemed to be coming off the walls and ceilings: the absence of Beth.

"Let's think through what we know. We know that their first priority is that the police not be involved: they said it in their very first message. We also know that they say it's not about money. But if this is not about ransom, why else would they care so much about keeping the police out of it? They must be bluffing. Let's think about your e-mail address. Who has it?"

"Everyone has it! It's the same pattern for the whole *Times* staff. Anyone could work it out."

A phone rang; Will pounced on his, frantically pressing buttons, but the sound kept coming. Calmly, his father answered his own phone. *Nothing to do with this,* he mouthed silently, disappearing into another room for a hushed conversation.

His father was proving no help. The aid he was offering was defiantly of the masculine variety, practical rather than emotional, and even that was not getting anywhere. Suddenly Will realized how much he missed his mother. Ever since he had been with Beth, that sentiment had become rarer and rarer: his wife was his confidante now. But for a long while, that role had belonged to his mother.

In England they had been a team, united by what he suddenly thought of as their loneliness. In his mother's version of the story, at least, she and Will had been abandoned by his father, leaving the two of them to fend for themselves. He knew there were alternative accounts, not that his father was in too much of a hurry to share his. The fate of his parents' marriage was a long-running puzzle to Will Monroe. He had never been completely sure what happened.

One version said Monroe Sr. had chosen his career over his family: overwork broke the young marriage. Another theory cited geography: wife was desperate to return to England, husband was determined to advance through the U.S. legal system and refused to leave America. Will's maternal grandmother, a silver-haired Hampshire lady with a severe expression that frightened the young boy the first time he saw her, and for years afterward, once spoke darkly of "the other great passion" in his father's life. When Will was old enough to inquire further, his grandmother shrugged it off. To this day, he did not know if that "great passion" was another woman or the law.

Will's own memories offered little help; he had been barely

seven years old when his parents began to come apart. He remembered the atmosphere, the gloom that would descend after his father had stormed out, slamming the door. Or the shock of finding his mother, red-faced and hoarse after another fierce round of shouting. He once woke up from sleep to hear his father pleading, "I just want to do what's right." Will had tiptoed out of bed to find a place where he could watch his parents unseen. He could not understand the words they were saying, but he could feel their force. It was at that moment, hearing his British mother and American father at full volume, that the seven-year-old boy developed a theory: his mummy and daddy could not love each other because they had different voices.

Once they were back in England, his mother gave few clues as to what had brought them there. Even raising the topic carried the risk of turning her into a bitter, ranting woman he hardly recognized and did not like. She would mutter about how her husband became "a different man, utterly different." Will remembered one Christmas, his mother speaking in a way that frightened him; he could not have been much older than thirteen. The detail had faded now, but one word still leapt out. It was all "his" fault, she kept saying; "he" had changed everything. The intonation made clear that this "he" was a third party, not his father, but Will could never figure out who it was. His mother was coming off like a paranoid, raving in the streets. Will was relieved when the storm passed, and he was not brave enough to mention it again.

Friends, and his grandmother for that matter, were quick to analyze Will's return to the United States after Oxford as a response to all this. He was "choosing" his father over his mother, said some. He was trying to reconcile the two, in the manner of many children of divorce, with himself as the bridge; that was another pet explanation. If he subscribed to any theory, which he did not, it would have been the journalistic one: that Will Monroe Jr. went to America to get to the truth of the story that had shaped his early life.

But if that had been the purpose of his American journey, he had failed. He knew little more now than he did when he first arrived, aged twenty-two. He knew his father better, that was true. He respected him; he was a hugely accomplished lawyer, now a judge, and seemed an essentially decent man. But as to the big mystery, Will had gained no great insights. They had talked about the divorce, of course, during a couple of moonlit evenings on the veranda of his father's summer house at Sag Harbor. But there had been no flash of revelation.

"Maybe that is the revelation," Beth had said one night when he came back inside after one of these father-to-son chats. They were spending a long Labor Day weekend with Will's father and his "partner," Linda. Beth was lying on the bed, reading, waiting for Will to come back in.

"What is?"

"That there is no big mystery. That's the revelation. They were two people whose marriage didn't work. It happens. It happens a lot. That's all there is."

"But what about all that stuff my mother says? And that grandma used to say?"

"Maybe they needed to have some grand explanation. Maybe it helped to think that some other woman stole him—"

"Not necessarily another woman," Will muttered. " 'The other great passion' was the phrase. Could have been anything."

"OK. My point is, I can see why a rejected wife and her very loving mother would need to invent a larger explanation for the departure of a husband. Otherwise it's a rejection, isn't it?"

She had not been his wife then, just the girlfriend he had met in his closing weeks at Columbia. He was in journalism school; she was doing a medical internship at the New York Presbyterian Hospital; they had met at a Memorial Day weekend softball game in the park. (He had left the message on her answering machine that same evening.) Those first few months were bathed in his mind in a permanent golden glow. He knew that memory could play tricks like that, but he was convinced the glow was a genuine, externally verifiable phenomenon. They had met in May, when New York was in the midst of a glorious spring. The days seemed to be lit by amber; each walk they took sparkled in the sun. It was not just their lovestruck imaginations; they had photographs to prove it.

Will realized he was smiling. This daydream was the first time he had thought of Beth, rather than Beth gone. Which was what he remembered now, with the jolt of a man who wakes up to realize that, yes, his leg has been amputated, and no, it was not all a horrible dream.

His father had come back into the room and was saying something about contacting the Internet company, but Will was not listening. He had had enough. His father was not thinking straight: the moment they made any move like that, they risked alerting the police. The Internet service provider would surely take a look at the kidnappers' e-mails and feel obliged to notify the authorities.

"Dad, I need some time to rest," he said, gently shepherding his father to the door. "I need some time alone."

"Will, that's all very well, but I'm not sure rest is a luxury you can afford. You need to use every minute—"

Monroe Sr. stopped. He could see his son was in no mood to negotiate; there was a steel in Will's eyes that was ordering his father to leave, no matter how polite the words coming out of his mouth.

When the door was closed, Will sighed deeply, slumped into a chair, and stared at his feet. He allowed himself no more than thirty seconds like that before he breathed deeply, pulled his back up straight, and girded himself for his next move. Despite what he had just said, he was neither going to rest nor be alone. He knew exactly what he had to do.

CHAPTER FOURTEEN

FRIDAY, 3:16 P.M., BROOKLYN

TOM FONTAINE HAD BEEN WILL'S FIRST FRIEND in America, or rather the first friend he had made sincc coming to the country as an adult. They had met at Columbia: Tom was just ahead of Will in the line for the registrar's office.

Will's initial feeling toward Tom was frustration. The line was moving slowly enough already, but he could see the lanky guy in the old man's overcoat was going to take forever. Everyone else had their forms ready, most of them neatly printed out. But the over-coat was still filling his in as he stood. With a pen that had sprung a leak. Will turned to the girl behind him, raising his eyebrows as if to say, Can you believe this guy? Eventually the two of them started talking out loud about how irritating it was to be stuck behind such a sap: they were emboldened by the permanent presence in the sap's ears of a pair of white headphones.

Finally, Tom had rummaged in his knapsack enough times to find a dog-eared driver's licence that had lost its laminate and a letter from the university. These somehow convinced the official that he was indeed called Tom Fontaine and that he was entitled to be a student at Columbia. In philosophy.

As he turned around, he gave Will a smile: "Sorry, I know how irritating it is to be stuck behind the college sap." Will blushed. He had obviously heard every word. (Will would later discover that the headphones in Tom's ears were not connected to a Walkman—or anything else. Tom just found it useful to have headphones on: that way, strangers rarely bothered him.)

They met again three days later in a coffee shop, Tom hunched over a laptop computer, headphones on. Will tapped on his shoulder to apologize. They started talking, and they had been friends ever since.

He was quite unlike anyone Will had ever known. Officially, Tom Fontaine was apolitical, but Will considered him a genuine revolutionary. Yes, he was a computer geek—but he was also a man with a mission. He was part of an informal network of like-minded geniuses around the world determined to take on—maybe even take down—the software giants who dominated the computer world. Their beef against Microsoft and its ilk was that those corporations had broken the original, sacred principle of the Internet: that it should be a tool for the open exchange of ideas and information. The key word was *open*. In the early days of the Net, Tom would explain—patiently and in words of one syllable to Will, who, like plenty of journalists, relied on computers but had not the first idea how they worked—everything was open, freely available to all. That extended to the software itself. It was "open-source," meaning that its inner workings were there for all to see. Anybody could use and, crucially, adapt the software as they saw fit. Then Microsoft and friends came along and, motivated solely by commerce, brought down the steel shutters. Their stuff was now "closed source." The long strings of code which made it tick were off limits. Just as Coca-Cola built an empire on its secret recipe, so Microsoft made its products a mystery.

That hardly bothered Will, but for Net idealists like Tom it was a form of desecration. They believed in the Internet with a zeal that Will could only describe as religious (which was especially funny in Tom's case, given his militant atheism). They were now determined to create alternative software—search engines or word-processing programs—that would be available to anyone who wanted it, free of charge. If someone spotted a fault, they could dive right in and correct it. After all, it belonged to all the people who used it.

It meant Tom earned a fraction of the money that could have been his, selling just enough of his computer brainpower to pay the rent. He did not care; the principles came first.

"Tom, it's Will. You home?"

He had called him on his cell phone; he could be anywhere.

"Nope."

"What's that music?" He could hear what sounded like the operatic voice of a woman.

"This, my friend, is the *Himmelfahrts-Oratorium* by Johann Sebastian Bach, the *Ascension Oratorio,* Barbara Schlick, soprano—"

"What are you, at a concert?"

"Record store."

"The one near your apartment?"

"Yup."

"Can I meet you at your place in twenty minutes? Something very urgent has come up." He regretted that straight away. On a cell phone.

"You OK? You sound, you know, panicky."

"Can you be there? Twenty minutes?"

"K."

Tom's place was odd, the embodiment of the man. There was almost nothing in the fridge but row after row of bottles of mineral water, testament to his rather peculiar aversion to drinks of any kind, hot or cold. No coffee, no juice, no beer. Just water. And the bed was in the living room, a concession to his insomnia: when Tom woke up at three a.m., he wanted to be able to get straight back online and to work, falling down again when he next felt tired. Usually these quirks would spark some kind of lecture from Will, urging his friend to join the rest of the human race, or at least the Brooklyn branch of it, but not today.

Will strode right in and gestured to Tom to close the door.

"Do you have any weird gadgets attached to your computer, any microphones or cell phones or speakerphones or anything weird that might mean that what we're saying now could in some way that I don't understand get on to the Internet?"

"Excuse me? What are you talking about?"

"You know what I mean. One of your techie things that I can't even find the words for; do you have anything that could be recording our conversation and saving it as some audio file that you won't even realize has happened till later?"

"Er, no." Tom's voice and face were crinkled into the expression that says, *Of course not, you psycho.*

"Good, because what we are about to talk about is terrible, and it is also one hundred percent secret and cannot, underline *cannot*, be discussed with anyone—especially not the police."

Tom could see his friend was in deadly earnest and also desperate. Usually ashen-faced, Tom paled even more, to a shade of light porcelain.

"Is this on?" Will said, gesturing at one of several computers on the workbench, picking the one that looked most like his own. It was a silly question. When were Tom's computers ever off? "Is this a browser?" This much Internet language Will could manage. Tom nodded; he looked scared.

Will did not ask if Tom's computers were secure: he knew there were none safer. Encryption was a Fontaine specialty.

Will typed in the address to access his Web mail, then, when the page appeared, his name and password. His inbox. He scrolled down and clicked open the first message.

DO NOT CALL THE POLICE. WE HAVE YOUR WIFE. INVOLVE THE POLICE AND YOU WILL LOSE HER. DO NOT CALL THE POLICE OR YOU WILL REGRET IT. FOREVER.

Tom, who was standing, reading over Will's shoulder, almost jumped back. He let out a low moan, as if he had been struck. Only now did Will even think of it: Tom was crazy about Beth. Not romantically—he was no rival—but in an almost childlike way. Tom would often walk the few blocks over to their apartment to eat—a contrast with the sushi-in-a-box consumed in front of his screen that constituted the rest of his diet—and seemed to gain nourishment from Beth's attention. She chided him like an older sister, and he took it; he even let her buy him a stylish jacket that he wore, briefly, in place of the dead man's coat that seemed glued to his back.

"Oh, my God," he was saying softly. Will said nothing, giving him a moment to absorb the shock. He decided to short-circuit the next stage by summarizing all the conclusions he, along with his father, had drawn so far. He showed Tom the second e-mail, to establish the fact that the kidnappers seemed more interested in secrecy, and the noninvolvement of the authorities, than in any ransom. The explanation was entirely mysterious, but there could be no question of telling the police.

"Tom, I need you to do whatever it takes to work out where these e-mails have come from. That's what the police would do, so that's what you have to do."

Tom nodded, but his hands barely moved. He was still dazed.

"Tom, I know how much Beth means to you. And how much you mean to her. But what she needs from you right now is for you to be the laser-beam-focus computer genius. OK?" Will was trying to smile, like a father cheering up a toddler son. "You need to forget what this is about and imagine it's just another computer puzzle. But you have to crack it as fast as you can."

Without another word, the two swapped places. Will paced up and down while Tom started clicking and clacking at the machine.

He offered one revelation straight away. The hieroglyphics that had appeared on Will's BlackBerry now looked completely different.

"Is that—"

"Hebrew," said Tom. "Not every machine has access to that alphabet. That's why it looked weird on yours. Using obscure alphabets is an old spammer trick."

Now Will noticed something else. After the long string of Hebrew characters, he could see some English ones in brackets. It was as if they had fallen off the screen on his own computer, but here they were visible, spelling out a regular e-mail address: info@golem-net.net.

"Golem-net? Is that what their name is?"

"Apparently."

"Isn't that some *Lord of the Rings* thing?"

"That's Gollum. Two l's."

Suddenly the screen was black with just a few characters winking on the left. Had the system crashed?

Tom saw Will's face. "Don't worry about this. This is a 'shell.' It's just an easier way of issuing commands to the computer than GUI."

Will looked baffled.

"Graphic user interface." Tom could see he was speaking a foreign language, yet he had the strong feeling Will wanted him to say something. He realized his friend was like a taxi passenger in an urgent hurry: ultimately it might make no difference, but it felt better to be moving than to be stuck in traffic. Psychologically, he knew Will needed to feel they were making progress. A running commentary might help.

"I'm going to ask the computer who it was who just e-mailed us."

"You can do that?"

"Yep. Look."

Tom was typing the words "Whois golem-net.net." It always surprised Will when, amid all the codes and digits, a computer (or computer geek, which amounted to the same thing) used plain, conversational English, albeit with an eccentric spelling. Yet, it turned out, this was a bona fide computer instruction.

Whois golem-net.net

Tom was waiting for the screen to fill up. There was nothing you could do in these moments, as the lights flickered and the egg-timer graphic ticked away. You could not hurry the computer. People always tried to. You saw them at ATM machines, their hands in position, like a crocodile's mouth poised over the dispenser, waiting to catch the cash as it came out, ensuring that not even the split second it would take to move across to collect it should be wasted. You saw it in offices, where people would drum pencils or play their thighs like bongos: "Come on, come on," urging the computer or printer to stop being so damned slow—forgetting, of course, that five, ten, or fifteen years ago the task in question might have taken the best part of a working day.

"Ah. Well, that's interesting."

There on the screen was the answer, clear and unambiguous.

No match for golem-net.net

"They made it up."

"Now what?"

Tom went back to the e-mail itself and selected an option Will did not know existed: "View Full Header." Suddenly several lines of what he would have dismissed as garble filled the screen.

"OK," said Tom, "what we have here is a kind of travelogue. This shows you the e-mail's Internet journey. That line at the top is its final destination, and that at the bottom is its point of origin. Each server en route has its own line."

Will looked at the screen, each sentence beginning "Received . . ."

"Hmm. These guys were in a hurry."

"How do you know that?"

"Well, you could make up 'received lines.' But that takes time—and whoever sent this didn't have time. Or didn't know how to do it. These received lines are all genuine. OK, this is the thing we need. Here." He was pointing to the bottom line, the point of origin.

Received from netspot-biz.com

"What's that?"

"Every computer in the world, so long as it's connected to the Internet, has a name. That one there is the computer that sent you the e-mail. All right. That means there's one more move I need to make."

Will could see that Tom felt uncomfortable. This was not the way he liked to do things. Will remembered one of their earliest conversations, when Tom explained the difference between hackers and crackers, white hats and black hats. Will liked all the names; thought it might make a magazine piece.

His memory was sketchy. He remembered his surprise at discovering that *hacker* was a widely misused term. In the outside world, it was often applied to the teenage nerds who broke into other people's computers—other people being Cape Canaveral or NATO—and wrought mayhem. Among techno-folk, hacker had a milder meaning: it referred to those who played on other people's virtual lawns for fun, not malice. Those who were up to no good—spreading viruses, taking down the 911 emergency phone system—were known by aficionados as crackers. They were hackers for havoc.

The same distinction applied to white hats and black hats. The former would snoop around where they were not wanted—inside the system of one of America's biggest banks, for example—but their motives were benign. They might peek at customers' account numbers, even uncovering their PIN codes, but they would not take their money (even though they could). Instead they would e-mail the head of security at the bank with a few examples of their plundered wares. A typical white hat message, waiting in the inbox of the luckless official in charge, might read, "If I can see your data, then so can the bad guys. Fix it." If the recipient was really unlucky, the e-mail would be cc'd to the CEO.

Black hats would do the same, but with darker purpose. They would bust into a maximum security network not on the Everest principle—because it's there—but in order to cause some damage. Sometimes it was theft, but more often the motive was cybervandalism: the thrill of taking down a big target. The headline-grabbing viruses of the past—I Love You and Michelangelo—were considered artistic masterpieces in the black hat fraternity.

Of course Tom's hat was as white as they came. He loved the Internet, he wanted it to work. He had barely hacked, let alone cracked. He believed it was essential that the world grow to trust the Web, that people feel secure on it—and that meant restraint on the part of those, like him, who knew where to find the gaps in the fence. But this was an exceptional situation. Beth's life was on the line.

Will began to pace. His legs felt weak, his stomach queasy. He had eaten nothing since first sight of that e-mail, now some seven hours ago. He wandered over to Tom's fridge: multiple Volvic and a box of sushi. Yesterday's. Will took it out, smelled it, and decided it was still just about edible. He wolfed it, then felt guilty for having any appetite at all when his wife was missing. As he swallowed, Beth came back to him. The very idea of food seemed to trigger an association with his wife. The evenings together making dinner; her unabashed appetite. Whatever he imagined, warmth, hunger, or satiation, he could only think of her.

He paced some more. He flicked through the computer periodicals and obscure literary journals that Tom had in a stack by the couch.

"Will, come here."

Tom was staring at the screen. He had done a "whois . . ." for netspot-biz.com and had got an answer.

"You don't seem happy," said Will.

"Well, it's good news and bad news. The good news is, I now

know exactly where the e-mail was sent from. The bad news is, it could be anybody who sent it."

"I don't get it."

"Our path ends in an Internet café. People are in and out of those places all the time. How stupid can you get!" Tom slammed his fist on the desk. He seemed furious. "I thought we were going to get a nice, neat home address. Dumb-ass!" Will realized Tom was addressing no one but himself.

"Where is this Internet café?"

"Does it matter? New York is a pretty big fucking city, Will. Millions of people could have passed through there."

"Tom." Sternly now. "Can you find out where it is?"

Tom returned to the screen, while Will stared. Finally he spoke.

"There's the address. Trouble is, I'm not sure I believe it."

"Where is it?" said Will.

Tom looked him straight in the face for the first time since Will had shown him the kidnappers' e-mail. "It's from Brooklyn. Crown Heights, Brooklyn."

"That's fairly near here. Why don't you believe it?"

"Look at the map." Tom had done an instant MapQuest search, showing with a red star the exact location of the Internet café. It was on Eastern Parkway. "Do you realize where that is?"

"No. Come on, Tom. Stop fucking around. Tell me."

"This message was sent from Crown Heights. That's only, like, the biggest Hasidic community in America."

The red star stared at them without blinking. It looked like the X on a treasure map, the kind that used to feature in Will's boyhood dreams. What lay under it?

"Despite the location, it's possible that it's not them who sent it."

"Tom, the e-mail was in Hebrew, for Christ's sake."

"Yeah, but that could be a cover. The real name was golem.net."

"Look it up."

Tom keyed *"golem"* into Google and clicked on the first result. It brought up a page from a Web site of Jewish legends for children. It told the story of the Great Rabbi Loew of Prague, who used a spell from kabbalah, ancient Jewish mysticism, to mold a man from clay: a vast, lumbering giant they called the Golem. Will's eye raced to the end: the story climaxed in violence and destruction, with the Golem running amok. The Golem seemed to be a Hasidic precursor of Frankenstein's monster.

"All right," said Tom finally. "I admit it, it does seem to be them. But it makes no sense. Why on earth would these people take Beth?"

"We don't know it's 'these people.' It might be one psycho who just happens to be Hasidic." Will grabbed his coat.

"Where are you going?"

"I'm going there."

"Are you crazy?"

"I'll pretend I'm reporting. I'll start asking questions. See who's in charge."

"You're out of your mind. Why don't you just tell the police you've traced the e-mail? Let them handle it."

"What, and guarantee these lunatics kill Beth? I'm going."

"You can't just go charging in there, with your notebook and English accent. You might as well wear a fucking sign."

"I'll think of something." Will did not say, though he thought it, that he was getting quite good at this kind of amateur detective work. His triumphs in Brownsville and Montana had left him pumped: in both cases he had found out a hidden truth. Now he would find his wife.

CHAPTER FIFTEEN

FRIDAY, 4:10 P.M., CROWN HEIGHTS, BROOKLYN

WILL'S FIRST REACTION WAS CONFUSION. He got off the subway at Sterling Street and walked straight into what looked to him like a black neighborhood: *Ebony, Vibe,* and *Black Hair* on sale at the newsstand, murals on every other wall, knots of young black men standing around in baggy combat clothes.

But once he crossed New York Avenue, he felt his pulse quicken with a reporter's sense that he was getting nearer to the story. Signs appeared in Hebrew. Some of the words were written in English characters, though their meaning was no less opaque. "Chazak V'Ematz!" promised one, enigmatically. Another word appeared several times, on bumper stickers, on posters, even on notices collared to lampposts, like flyers seeking lost cats. Will soon learned to recognize the word, though he had no idea how to pronounce it: *Moshiach.*

Next he passed a black man the size of a large refrigerator, with a little girl in one hand and a cigarette in the other. Will's confusion returned. He was now on Empire Boulevard, noticing Indian restaurants and vans decked out in the national flag of Trinidad and Tobago. Was he in the Hasidic neighborhood or wasn't he?

He turned off, into residential streets. The houses were large brownstones or made of a firm red brick, as if once, in a long-ago Brooklyn, they had been positively posh. Each had a few steps up to the front door, which sat alongside a porch. In other American homes, Will guessed, these porches might feature a swing chair, perhaps a few lanterns, certainly a pumpkin at Hallowe'en, and very often the Stars and Stripes. In Crown Heights they looked mainly unused, though even here Will spotted that word again—*Moshiach*—on window stickers, and once on a yellow flag with the image of a crown, which Will took to be some kind of local symbol.

Directly above each porch, one story up, was a veranda, complete with wooden balustrade. Will thought of Beth, held behind one of these front doors: his legs suddenly tensed with the urge to run up the stairs of each house and knock down door after door, until he had found his wife.

Coming toward him was a group of teenage girls in long skirts, pushing strollers. Behind them were perhaps a dozen, maybe more, children. Will could not tell if these girls were older sisters or exceptionally young mothers. They looked like no women he had ever seen before, certainly not in New York. They seemed to be from a different era, the 1950s perhaps or the reign of Queen Victoria. No flesh was exposed; the sleeves of their prim white blouses covered their arms; their skirts fell to their ankles. And their hair: the older women seemed to wear it in a preternaturally neat bob, one that barely moved in the wind.

Will did not look too hard; he did not want anyone to think he was staring. Besides, he no longer needed confirmation. This was Hasidic Crown Heights, all right. As he walked, he honed his cover story. He would say he was a writer for *New York* magazine, doing a piece for its new "Slice of the Apple" slot, in which outsiders wrote dispatches from different segments of New York's wonderfully diverse community, blah, blah. He would pose as the safari-suit explorer, sent to note down the curious ways of the natives.

And this was certainly an alien landscape. Will searched desperately for something that might give him a handle—an office perhaps, where he might discover who ran this place. Maybe he could explain what had happened, and they would help him. He just needed a foothold, something in this strange place he at least understood.

But there was nothing. Every bumper sticker seemed to convey a message that might be worth decoding, but was indecipherable. "Light Sabbath candles and you'll light up the world!" There was an ad for a show: *Ready for Redemption.* Even the shops seemed to be part of this religious fervor. The Kol Tov supermarket carried a slogan: "It's all good."

He kept walking, stopping at a storefront whose window was full of notices rather than goods. One leapt out at him straightaway.

Crown Heights is the neighborhood of the Rebbe. Out of respect to the Rebbe and his community we request that all women and girls, whether living here or visiting, adhere at all times to the laws of modesty, including:

- Closed neckline in back, side and front. (Collarbone should remain covered)
- Elbows covered in all positions
- Knees covered by dress/skirt in all positions
- Proper cover of the entire leg and foot
- No slits

Girls and women who wear immodest garments, and thereby call attention to their physical appearance, disgrace themselves by proclaiming that they possess no intrinsic qualities for which they should garner attention . . .

So that explained the dress code. But the word that leapt out at Will had nothing to do with necklines or slits. It was "Rebbe." This sounded like the man Will had to meet.

He looked up to get his bearings, noticing for the first time the street sign. Eastern Parkway. He had barely walked ten yards when he saw another sign: "Internet Hot Spot." He had arrived.

His stomach heaved as he walked in. This was surely the scene of the crime. Someone had sat at one of these cheap blondwood desks, surrounded by fake wood paneling and gray floor tiles, and typed the message announcing the theft of his wife.

He stared hard at the room, hoping his would suddenly become a superhero's gaze, magically able to absorb every detail, seeing with X-ray vision the clues that must be here. But he only had his own eyes.

The room was a mess, not like the latte-serving Internet cafés he knew from Manhattan, or even his own patch of Brooklyn. There was no espresso or mocha here, no coffee of any kind in fact. Just bunches of exposed wires, peeling signs on the wall, including a picture of an elderly, white-bearded rabbi—a face Will had now seen at least a dozen times. The desks were arranged haphazardly, with flimsy partitions attempting a separation into individual workspaces. At the back were a stack of empty computer cartons, still leaking their Styrofoam packaging, as if the owners had simply bought the equipment, unloaded it, and opened for business the same day.

Will got a few upward glances as he came in, but it was not nearly as bad as he had feared. (He had visions of his occasional student forays into out-of-the-way pubs in big English cities, places so hostile the locals seemed to fall into an instinctive sullen silence the moment a stranger was among them.) Most of the customers in the Internet Hot Spot seemed too preoccupied to be interested in Will.

He tried to assess each of them. He noticed the two women first, both wearing berets. One was sitting sidesaddle on her stool, allowing her to keep one hand on her pram, rocking her baby to sleep as she typed with the other. Will ruled her out immediately: a pregnant woman could surely not have kidnapped his wife. He eliminated the other woman just as quickly: she had a toddler on her lap and wore perhaps the most exhausted expression he had ever seen.

The rest of the terminals were either empty or used by men. To Will, they all looked the same. They wore the same rumpled dark suits, the same open-necked white shirts, and the same wide-brimmed black trilby hats. Will looked hard at each one in turn—*Did you kidnap my wife?*—hoping that a guilty conscience might at least send one of them blushing or rushing out of the door. Instead they kept staring at the computer screens and stroking their beards.

Will paid his dollar and sat at a screen himself. He was tempted to log on to his own e-mail, so that anyone checking him out and reading over his shoulder would immediately know who he was. He half wanted them to know that he was here, that he was onto them.

Instead, he took time to absorb what was in front of him. Each terminal was programmed to show the same home page, the Web site of the Hasidic movement. There was a tracker on the left of the screen, scrolling birth announcements: Zvi Chaim born to the Friedmans, Tova Leah to the Susskinds, Chaya Ruchi to the Slonims. At the top of the screen was a banner, showing the same face that hung on the wall, though this time it appeared to be dissolving into a picture of the Jerusalem skyline. Underneath ran the slogan, "Long Live the Rebbe Melech HaMoshiach forever and ever."

Will read the line three times, as if trying to crack a cryptic crossword clue. He had no idea about *Melech*, but *Moshiach* was now very familiar, even if he had not seen it in this form. The word that mattered was *Rebbe*. The man in the picture that hung everywhere—an ancient rabbi with a biblical white beard and a black trilby pressed firmly on his head—was their leader, their Rebbe.

To Will, it felt like a breakthrough. All he had to do was find this man, and he would get some answers. A community like this, he was sure, would be hierarchical and disciplined: nothing would happen without the nod of the top man. He was like a tribal chief. If Beth had been taken by the men of Crown Heights, the Rebbe would have given the order. And he would know where she was now.

Will left hurriedly, anxious to find this Rebbe as quickly as he could. As he got back onto the street, he noticed that others were moving at similar speed; everyone seemed to be in a rush. Maybe something was going on? Maybe they had heard about the kidnapping?

Within a block or two he found what he was looking for: a place where people gathered to eat or drink. For reporters, cafés, bars, and restaurants were essential locations. If you needed to talk to strangers, where else could you start? You could hardly knock on people's front doors; stopping people in the street was always a last resort. But in a café, you could start a conversation with almost anybody—and find out plenty.

There were no cafés here, no bars either, but Marmerstein's Glatt Kosher would do. It was more of a dining room than a restaurant. It looked like a canteen, with hot food at a counter served by large, grandmotherly women. The customers seemed to be gaunt, pale men, wolfing down chicken schnitzel, gravy-soaked potatoes, and iced tea as if they had not eaten for twenty-four hours. It reminded Will of the refectory at his English boarding school: big women feeding thin boys.

Except this scene was much more bizarre. The men might have stepped out of a picture book of seventeenth-century eastern Europe, and yet several of them were yammering away into cell phones. One was simultaneously tapping into a BlackBerry and reading the *New York Post*. The collision of ancient and modern was jarring.

Will queued up to get his own plate. Not that he felt like eating; he just needed an excuse to be there. He hesitated over his choice of vegetable, overcooked broccoli or overcooked carrots, and was soon upbraided by one of the babushkas behind the counter.

"Hurry, I want to get home for *shabbos*," she said without a smile. So that explained the rush: it was Friday afternoon, and the Sabbath was coming. Tom had mentioned something about that as Will left, but he had not taken it in: he literally did not know what day it was. This was bound to be bad news. Crown Heights would surely close down in the next hour or two; no one would be around, and he would find out nothing. He had no choice; he would have to move fast, starting right now.

He found what he needed: a man sitting alone. There was no time for English circumlocution. He would have to deploy the instant American approach: *Hi, how you doing, where do you come from?*

His name was Sandy, and he was from the West Coast. Both of these facts caught Will by surprise. He had, half-consciously, assumed that these men with their beards and black hats would bear alien names and speak with thick Russian or Polish accents. That had been part of the culture shock of the last hour, the realization that a corner of what could have been medieval Europe lived and breathed in the here and now, in twenty-first-century New York. He felt like a novice swimmer who discovers he can no longer touch the bottom.

"You Jewish?"

"No, I'm not, I'm a journalist." Ridiculous thing to say. "I mean, the reason why I'm here is that I'm a journalist. For *New York Magazine*."

"Cool. You here to write about the Rebbe?" He pronounced it Rebb-ah.

"Yes. Well, among other things. You know, just writing about the community."

Sandy turned out to be relatively new to Crown Heights. He said he had been "a surfer dude" on Venice Beach, "hanging out, taking a lot of drugs." He had once been a student at USC, had a thing for astronomy, but the drugs had won out—and he dropped out after a couple of semesters. His life had been a mess until six years ago, when he had met an emissary of the Rebbe who had established an outreach center right on the oceanfront. This Rabbi Gershon gave him a hot meal one Friday night, and that was how it started. Sandy popped in there for the next Sabbath and the next; he stayed overnight with Gershon's family. "You know what was best, better even than the food and the shelter?" said Sandy, with an intensity Will found awkward in a man he had just met. "They didn't judge me. They just said that HaShem loves every Jewish soul, and that HaShem understands why we sometimes take a roundabout path. How sometimes we get lost."

"HaShem?"

"Sorry, that's God. HaShem literally means 'the Name.' In Judaism, we know the name of God, we can see it written down, but we never say it out loud."

Will gestured for Sandy to carry on. He explained that he had put his life in the hands of the Rebbe and his followers. He started dressing like them, eating kosher food, praying in the morning and evening, honoring the Sabbath by abstaining from all work or commerce—no shopping, no using electricity, no riding the subway—from sundown on Friday to sundown on Saturday.

"And did you do anything like that before?"

"Me? You gotta be kidding. Man, I didn't know what *shabbos* was! I ate everything that moved: lobster, crabs, cheeseburgers. My mom didn't even know what was kosher and what was *treif*."

"And what does she think about, you know, this?" Will gestured at Sandy's clothes and beard.

"You know, it's kind of a process? She found the kosher thing hard; me not being able to eat with her when I visit her in her home. And now that I have kids, that gets kind of tricky. But the toughest thing for her, without a doubt? When I became Shimon Shmuel, rather than Sandy. She couldn't get her head around that."

"You changed your name?"

"I wouldn't really call it changing my name. Every Jew has a

Hebrew name already, even if he doesn't know what it is. It's the name of our soul. So I like to say that I discovered my real name. But I use both. When I visit my mom, or when I meet, you know, someone like you, I'm Sandy. In Crown Heights, I'm Shimon Shmuel."

"So what can you tell me about this Rebbe, then?"

"Well, he is our leader and he is a great teacher and we all love him and he loves us."

"Do people do whatever he tells them to do?"

"It's not really like that, Tom." (Will had had to think quickly. In all his preparation he had forgotten to make up a pseudonym. So he had borrowed Tom's first name and his mother's maiden name: Sandy thought he was talking to a freelance reporter called Tom Mitchell.) "The Rebbe just knows what's right for all of us. He's like the shepherd, and we're his flock. He knows what we need, where we should live, who we should marry. So, yes, we listen to his advice." Will's hunch was being confirmed. This guy pulled every lever.

"And where does he live?"

"He is right here in this community, every day."

"And can I meet him?"

"You should come to *shul* tonight."

"Shul?"

"Synagogue. But it's more than that. It's our headquarters, our meeting house, our library. You'll find out all you need to know about the Rebbe there."

Will decided to stick with Sandy. He needed a guide, and Sandy would be ideal. Not much older than Will, he was not a rabbi or scholar, not some authority figure who would require ingratiation, but a burned-out hippie who, Will guessed, had simply cried out to be rescued. If the Moonies had got there first, Sandy would have gone with them; he was a man who needed someone to catch him when he fell.

They talked as they walked the few blocks to Sandy's first stop.

"Tell me something, Sandy. What's the deal with this clothing? How come you all dress alike?"

"I admit, I was pretty freaked by that at first. But you know what the Rebbe says? We are more individual because we dress this way."

"How does he work that out?"

"Well, what makes us different from each other is not the designer shirt we wear or an expensive suit, something on the outside. What makes us different from each other is what's inside: our true selves, our *neshama,* our souls. That's what shines out. If the outside becomes irrelevant, if we all look the same, then people can truly start to see the inside."

By now, they had arrived at a building Sandy referred to as the *mikve* and which he translated to Will as "ritual bath." They joined the line paying a dollar to the attendant at the door, Will handing over an extra fifty cents to get a towel, and headed downstairs into what seemed to be a large changing room.

As soon as Sandy opened the door, they were hit by a cloud of steam. The air itself seemed to be dripping; Will had to blink three or four times to adjust his eyes. When he finally regained his vision, he stepped back as if he had been punched.

The room was packed with men and boys who were either naked or about to be. There were bony teenagers, large-bellied men in their fifties, their beards frizzing in the humidity, and wrinkled geriatrics—all of them removing every last piece of clothing. Will had been to the gym enough times, but there the age range was narrower, there were fewer people, and nothing like this volume of noise. Everyone in here was talking; if they were kids, they were screaming.

"We have to be entirely unadorned when we enter the *mikve,*" Sandy was saying, "if we are to become pure for *shabbos.* Our skin must make total contact with the rainwater that's collected in the *mikve.* If we wear a wedding ring, we have to take it off. We must be as we were the day we were born."

Will looked at his own finger, at the band that Beth had given him. At their wedding ceremony, she had placed it on his finger whispering a vow that was for his ears only. "More than yesterday, less than tomorrow." It referred to the depth of their love for each other.

Now he was standing surrounded by naked men, some taking off tasseled vests—which Sandy explained were worn by order of a religious commandment: a reminder of God, even under your shirt—others putting them on, where they instantly became stained with the moisture of skin not yet dried, several muttering prayers in a language Will did not understand. How strange the world is, Will thought surveying this scene, that my love for Beth could bring me to this place and this moment.

"Coming?" Sandy was gesturing toward the pool. Something told Will that if he was going to win this man's trust, he would have to show respect and go along with whatever ritual the hour called for.

"Sure," he said, taking off his own clothes, even the wedding ring. Gingerly he followed Sandy, reminded of his school days and the walk to the communal shower after a winter afternoon of rugby practice. Then, as now, he felt self-concious, taking care to cover his private parts with his hands. The setup here looked a lot like those old school baths, down to the puddles of blackening water and the random pubic hairs on the white-tiled floor. There was a sign: "Love Your Neighbor, Take a Shower Before the Mikve." Will took his lead from Sandy, who stood under the jet of water for just a few seconds.

Then to the *mikve* itself. It was like a small plunge pool, and plunging was what you did. Down the stairs, wade a step or two, and then down—a complete dunk, so that not a hair on your head remained dry—then twice more and out. The temperature was comfortable, but no one lingered. They were not having a dip or a Jacuzzi, they were there to be purified.

As Will sank below the surface, holding his breath, he was filled with an unexpected anger. Not at the men around him, not even at Beth's captors, but at himself. His wife was missing, in who knew what kind of danger, and here he was, butt-naked. He was not where he should be, in a New York Police Department command center, surrounded by flickering computer terminals manned by kidnap specialists, each of them working round the clock to trace phone calls and decode e-mails using state-of-the-art encryption technology, until finally one officer turns around and announces to the room, "We've got him!" prompting everyone to pile into squad cars and a couple of helicopters, surrounding the criminals' den with a SWAT team of marksmen who then emerge with a trembling Beth, wrapped in a blanket, and her evil abductor in handcuffs or, better still, a body bag. All this raced through Will's mind as he held his breath in the rainwater that was meant to sanctify his body. I've seen too many movies, he thought as he came up, breathed deep, and shook the water from his hair. But the core feeling persisted. He should be hunting for Beth, and here he was instead, bathing with the enemy.

As he dried off and put his clothes back on, he could not help but see the men around him differently. What dark secrets did they carry? Were they blamelessly ignorant of this plot, or were they all in on the snatching of his wife? Was it some kind of conspiracy, starting with the Rebbe but involving all of them? He looked at Sandy, fidgeting with hairclips as he returned the black yarmulke to his head. He certainly came across as a wide-eyed innocent, but maybe that was just a skillful pose.

Will thought back to their first conversation at the diner. Will imagined he had sought out Sandy, but maybe it was the other way around. What if this "Sandy" had been following Will since he had arrived at Crown Heights, contriving to be sitting alone in Marmerstein's at just the right moment? It would not be such a hard trick to pull off. After all, weren't these people famous for their cunning . . .

Will stopped himself right there. He could see what was happening; he was panicking, allowing a red mist to descend when he needed clarity. Hoary old stereotypes were not going to rescue Beth, he told himself sternly. He needed to use his head. *Be patient, stay polite, and you will get to the truth.*

They popped in briefly to Sandy's house, which, Will guessed, had simply been allocated to him. It was decorated in a style that belonged to their grandparents' generation: white Formica cupboards that would have looked modern in 1970, a linoleum floor that seemed to hail from the Kennedy era. The kitchen had two sinks, and there was a large, industrial-looking urn of boiling water, complete with its own dispensing tap, in the corner. On every wall, in varying expressions, were photographs of the man Will now knew to be the Rebbe.

The living room provided the only clue that young people were in residence. It was dominated by a playpen and cluttered with the bright red and yellow plastic of children's toys. A toddler sat amid the toys, wheeling a dump truck. Close by, sitting in the corner of a very basic couch, was a woman bottle-feeding her baby.

Will was gripped by a feeling he had not expected: envy. At first, he thought he was envying Sandy for having his home intact, his wife still safe. But that was not it. He was envious of this woman for having children. It was a new sensation, but now, as if on Beth's behalf, he coveted this baby and toddler: he saw them through Beth's eyes, as the children she wanted so badly. Perhaps for the first time he understood his wife's need. No, it was more than that. He *felt* it.

The woman's hair was covered by a small white hat that was singularly unflattering. Underneath was a dark, thick bob—the same style worn by every woman in Crown Heights, as far as Will could see.

"This is Sara Leah," Sandy said distractedly, heading for the stairs.

"Hi, I'm Tom," Will said, leaning forward to offer a hand. Sara Leah blushed and shook her head, refusing to offer a hand of her own. "Sorry," Will said. Clearly, these rules about women and modesty went beyond the simple matter of clothing.

"OK, we're going to *shul*!" Sandy was shouting as he raced back downstairs. He sized up Will. "You won't need that," he said, gesturing toward the bag Will had slung over his shoulder.

"No, that's OK, I'll just keep this with me." Inside were his wallet, his BlackBerry, and, crucially, his notebook.

"Tom, I don't want you to be uncomfortable in *shul*, and it's *shabbos*, and we don't carry on *shabbos*."

"But this is just keys, money, you know."

"I know, but we don't have those things with us in *shul* or anywhere on Friday night."

"You don't carry house keys?"

Sandy pulled up his shirt to reveal the waistband of his trousers. Around it was a string, threaded through the belt loops, carrying a single silver key. Will needed to think fast.

"You can leave your bag here. You're having *shabbos* dinner with us, I hope: you can pick it up then."

Will could agree, dump the bag, and just hope that Sara Leah did not take a peek: one glimpse at his credit cards, and she would know that he was no Tom Mitchell. She would discover that he was Will Monroe, and it would not take much detective work to know that he was the husband of the kidnapped woman, of whose fate all these people were surely aware. She would alert the Rebbe or his henchmen, and Will would doubtless be hurled into a dungeon just like Beth.

Calm down, that's not going to happen. Everything's going to be OK. "That's fine. I'll leave it here." Will took off his bag, placed it alongside the pileup of shoes and strollers by the front door, slipped his notebook into his breast pocket, and followed Sandy out the front door.

They walked just a few blocks to reach the synagogue. Clusters of men in twos and threes, friends or fathers with sons, were heading in the same direction.

The building had a kind of piazza in front of it but was entered by walking down a couple of stairs. Just outside, a man sucked heavily on a cigarette. "Last one before *shabbos*," Sandy explained, smiling. So even smoking was banned for the next twenty-four hours.

Inside was what Will would have described as the very opposite of a church: it resembled a high school gym. At the back were a few rows of benches and tables, backing onto bookshelves. In this area, like a large schoolroom, every seat was taken and the noise was rising. Will soon realized this was not a single class, but rather a cacophony of different conversations. Pairs of men were debating with each other across the tables, each man hunched over a Hebrew book. They seemed to be rocking back and forth, whether they were speaking or just listening. Next to them might be an eavesdropper or, more likely, another pair engaged in equally intense dialogue. Will strained to listen.

It was a mixture of English and what he took to be Hebrew, all delivered in a singsong rhythm that seemed to match the rocking motion, beat for beat. "So what are the *Rabonim* trying to tell us? We learn that even though we might wish we could study all the time, that this is the greatest *mitzvah* and greatest pleasure we could ever know, in fact HaShem also wants us to do other things, including working and making a living." That last word was on a down note. Now the tune was about to go up again. "Why would HaShem want this? Why would HaShem, who surely wants us to be full of wisdom and *Yiddishkeit*, why would He not want us to study all the time?" The voice was getting high-pitched. "The answer"—raised finger, pointing at the ceiling emphasized the point—"is that only by experiencing darkness do we appreciate the light."

Now it was the turn of his friend, his study partner, to pick up the thread—and the tune. "In other words, to fully appreciate the beauty of Torah"—*Toy-ra*—"and learning, we have to know life *away* from learning. In this way, the story of Noach is telling every Hasid"—*Chossid*—"that he cannot spend his whole life in the yeshiva, but must fulfill all his other duties, as a husband or father or whatever. This is why the tzaddik is not always the most learned man in the village; sometimes the truly good man is the simple cobbler or tailor, who knows and really understands the joy of Torah because he knows and understands the contrast with the rest of his life. Such a Jew, because he is one who knows darkness, truly appreciates the light."

Will could barely follow what he was hearing; the style of it was so unlike anything he had ever heard before. Perhaps, he thought, this was what monasteries were like back in the Middle Ages, monks poring over texts, frantically trying to penetrate the word of God. He turned to Sandy. "What are they studying? I mean, what's the book they're looking at?"

"Well, usually in the yeshiva, you know, the religious academy, people will study the Talmud." Will looked puzzled. "Commentary. Rabbis debating the exact meaning of each word of the Torah. A rabbi in the top left of a page of Talmud will pick a fight with one at the bottom right, over the two dozen meanings of a single letter of a single word."

"And is that what they are reading now?" Will indicated the two men whose teach-in he had been following. Sandy craned his neck to check what book they were using.

"No, these are commentaries written by the Rebbe." The Rebbe, thought Will. Even his words are studied with the fervor of holy writ.

While they spoke, the room was filling up, people arriving in great numbers. Will had been at a synagogue once before, for the bar mitzvah of a schoolboy friend, but it had been nothing like this. On that occasion, there had been a single central service and a degree of quiet (though not the pin-drop silence he was used to in church). Here there seemed to be no order at all.

Strangest of all, he could only see men. There seemed to be thousands of those white shirts and dark suits, unbroken by so much as a splash of female color.

"Where are the women?"

Sandy pointed upward, at what looked like the balcony of a theater. Except you could see no one sitting down, because the view was blocked by an opaque plastic window. You could just make out the outline of the people behind, like glimpsing a projectionist in his booth. But they seemed to be shadows, revealed only in the small gap below the Perspex window. Will stared hard, trying to make out a face. Giving up, he realized that he had been searching for Beth.

It gave him the creeps. He felt as if he were being watched, as if these blocked-off, unseen women were spectral spectators, observing the antics of the men below. He imagined their vantage point: he would stand out in an instant. The one man not in black and white, but in chinos and blue shirt.

From nowhere, a handclap began. Rows of men were forming into two lines, as if clearing a path for a procession. The rhythm became faster as the men started singing.

Yechi HaMelech, Yechi HaMelech

Sandy translated: Long live the King.

Now people were stamping their feet, some were swaying, others were actually jumping in the air. It reminded Will of that old archival footage of screaming girls waiting for the Beatles. But these were grown men, working themselves into a frenzy of anticipation. One man, his face flushed, was jerking from side to side, inserting two fingers in his mouth to make a wolf whistle.

Will took in all the faces crushed into the crowd before him. They were not identical after all. He guessed several were Russian; a few more, their clothes somehow less formal, were dark and looked Israeli. He noticed one man, his beard wispy, whom he took to be Vietnamese. Sandy followed Will's stare.

"Convert," he explained concisely, his voice rising to be heard above the din. "Judaism doesn't exactly encourage conversion, but when it happens, the Rebbe is really welcoming. Much more than most Jews. He says any newcomer is as good as someone born Jewish, maybe even better because they chose to be a Jew—"

Will missed the rest, as he was squeezed between two men pressing forward, part of a large, surging huddle that, without cue or instruction, was now turning. The children seemed to be pointing the way. Several boys, who could not have been more than eight years old, were on their fathers' shoulders, waving their fists in the same direction, again and again. They looked like underage football hooligans, pointing the finger at a reviled ref. But they were not looking at a person. Their energies were directed instead at a throne.

That was the word that came to mind, without prompting. It was a large chair, covered in plush red velvet. In a spartan room like this, it stood out as an item of lavish luxury. There was no doubt; this seat was being venerated.

Yechi Adoneinu Moreinu v'Rabbeinu Melech HaMoshiach l'olam va'ed.

The crowd were singing this one line, over and over, with a fervor Will found both exhilarating and terrifying. He leaned into Sandy's ear, shouting to be heard. "What does it mean?"

"Long live our master, our teacher, the Rebbe, King Messiah forever and ever."

Messiah. Of course. That's what this word daubed everywhere meant. *Moshiach* was "Messiah." How could he have been so slow? These people regarded their Rebbe as nothing less than the Messiah.

Now Will was desperate to raise himself to full height, to see above the crowd who were all staring so intently at the throne, their voices hoarse with anticipation. Surely the Rebbe would make his entrance any second now, though how his followers would top their current levels of ecstasy to mark his arrival, Will could not imagine.

The noise was becoming deafening. Will tried to find Sandy's ear again, but he had been shoved forward in the mêlée. Will's face was now uncomfortably close to a different man, who smiled at him, recognizing the humor of their sudden intimacy. What the hell, thought Will.

"Excuse me, can you tell me, when does the Rebbe come in? When does everything begin?"

"Excuse me?"

"When does everything begin?"

At that moment, and before the man had a chance to respond, Will felt a hand clamp tightly on his shoulder. In his ear, a deep, baritone voice.

"For you, my friend, it all ends right here."

CHAPTER SIXTEEN

FRIDAY, 8:20 P.M., CROWN HEIGHTS, BROOKLYN

THE HAND LEFT HIS SHOULDER, only to be replaced by two more on each of his arms. He was flanked by two men who he guessed were no older than twenty but were both taller, and stronger, than he. One had a reddish beard, the other just a few wisps of chin hair. Both looked straight ahead as they frogmarched him away through the crowd. Will was too shocked to shout; no one would have heard him anyway. In the crush, he knew, people would barely take a second look at a trio of men jammed together, especially since two of them were now singing along with enthusiasm.

He was being led away from the throne, back toward the library area, where the crowds were marginally thinner. Will was no good at guessing numbers—not enough experience covering demos—but he reckoned this room must have had two or three thousand people crammed into it, all of them chanting so furiously that his captors could have killed him there and then and nobody would have noticed.

Suddenly his handlers turned behind some shelves and down a narrow, scuffed corridor. The redbeard opened one door, then another until finally they were in what seemed to be a small classroom: more of those dark wood benches and tables, more shelves lined with leather-bound books, titled in gold-lettered Hebrew. He was deposited firmly in a stiff plastic chair in the middle of the room, the Hasidic heavies planting him to the spot by taking a shoulder each.

"I don't understand what's happening," Will said weakly. "What's going on here? Who are you?"

"Wait."

"Why have you brought me here?"

"I said wait. Our teacher will be here soon. You can talk to him."

The Rebbe. At last.

The noise from next door was still throbbing. Maybe the Rebbe had finally made his entrance; perhaps he was working the room before he came in here to work over Will. The clamor was certainly thumpingly loud; the ground was moving like the walls of a club, shaken by bass. But whether it had suddenly got louder, as if the Rebbe had arrived while Will was dragged out of the room, he could not tell.

"OK, let us begin."

That same baritone voice, again from behind. Will tried to turn around, but the hands came down to clamp his shoulders tight.

"What's your name?"

"Tom Mitchell."

"Welcome, Tom, and good *shabbos.* Tell me, why do we have the pleasure of your company in Crown Heights?"

"I'm here to write a story for *New York* magazine about the Hasidic community. It's for a new slot: 'Slice of the Apple.' "

"Cute. And why have you come here this weekend of all weekends?"

"They only commissioned me to do it this week, so I came the first weekend I could."

"You didn't call ahead, you didn't want to make an arrangement, maybe?"

"I just wanted to look around."

"See how the natives live in their natural habitat?"

"I wouldn't put it like that," Will croaked. The force of two men pressing their hands down on his shoulders was starting to take its toll. "I hope I'm not being rude, but why are you holding me like this?"

"You know, Mr. Mitchell, I'm glad you asked me that, because I wouldn't want to give you the wrong impression of Crown Heights or its people. We welcome guests here, we really do. We invite visitors into our homes. We are not even hostile to the press; reporters have come here often. We have had no less than the *New York Times* pay us an occasional visit. No, the reason for this"—he paused—"unusual reception is that I don't believe you're telling us the truth."

"But I *am* a reporter. That *is* the truth."

"No, the truth, Mr. Mitchell, is that somebody has been prying into what is strictly our business, and I am wondering if that somebody is you." The voice, briefly raised, paused to recover its equilibrium. "Let's relax a bit, shall we? It's *shabbos*, we've all had a hard week. We've worked hard. Now we rest. So let's take it slow and calm down. Back to my question. You've been talking to Shimon Shmuel for a while, so I'm sure you've picked up a few things about our customs already."

They've been following me.

"You're an intelligent man. You've realized by now that observance of the Sabbath is one of our strictest rules."

Will said nothing.

"Mr. Mitchell?"

"Yes, I understand that."

"You know we are forbidden from carrying on the Sabbath, don't you?"

"Yes, Sandy told me. Shimon Shmuel." He regretted that late

addition of Sandy's Hebrew name: it sounded like an attempt at ingratiation.

"He may not have mentioned that on the Sabbath, we are forbidden to carry but not only to carry: we are also barred from using electricity of any kind. The lights that are on now were switched on before *shabbos* began, and they will stay on all day until after *shabbos* ends tomorrow night. Those are the rules: no Jew is allowed to turn them on or off. Moreover, you'll have noticed that there were no cameras out there just now. And there have never been cameras out there, not on *shabbos.* What you saw just now has never been photographed or filmed. Never, and that's not through lack of requests. Do you see where I'm heading, Mr. Mitchell?"

Now that he had heard the voice speaking for longer, he began to form a picture of the speaker. He was an American, but his accent was not the same as Sandy's. It was more, what, European? Something. Will could not quite identify what it was: certainly more New York, almost musical. It contained a kind of shrug, a recognition of the absurdity of life, sometimes comic, usually tragic. In split, fractional seconds he saw the face of Mel Brooks and heard the voice of Leonard Cohen. He still had no idea what the man speaking to him looked like.

"Mr. Mitchell, I need to know whether you understand what I'm saying."

"No, I don't have a camera, if that's what you're asking."

"As it happens, I wasn't thinking about that. More on the lines of a recording device."

Again, Will was in the clear. Despite his age, he did things the old-fashioned way: notebook and pen. This was due not to some technophobic Luddism on his part, but to sheer laziness. Transcribing recordings was just too much hassle: you did an interview for half an hour, then spent an hour writing it up. The mini-disc recorder was saved only for set-piece interviews where every word was likely to count: mayors, police chiefs, that kind of thing. Otherwise he opted for paper and ink.

"No, I haven't recorded anyone. But why would it be a problem—"

He suddenly felt himself jerked forward and then up, the darker, younger man at his left side apparently taking the lead. The pair of them had looped their arms under Will's armpits and levered him upward, ensuring he did not turn around. Next, the dark man swung around to face him, avoiding Will's eye while he first stretched Will's arms up and out, then reached under his jacket, moving his hands over Will's shirt, around his back, and under his armpits. He was like a zealous airport security guard.

Of course. *Recording device.* They weren't looking for a reporter's Dictaphone. They were looking for a wire. They were worried that he was the police or the FBI. Of course they were: they were kidnappers, and they feared Will was an undercover cop—the questions he had been asking, the snooping around with no warning.

"No wire," the dark man was saying, in an accent that confirmed him as at least Middle Eastern, if not Israeli.

"But there is this." It was the redbeard, whose task during this two-man body search, which had continued up and down Will's legs when it was not focused on his back, had been to examine the captive's every pocket—including the one on the inside left of his jacket. His secrets offered little resistance: his Moleskine notebook always made a neat bulge in his left breast pocket. Redbeard took it out and offered it to the unseen hand behind. Will, shoved back down into his seat, could hear the pages being turned.

The blood seemed to drain from him. His mind rewound back to Sandy's house, when his host had urged him to leave his bag behind. And Will thought he was being so clever. He had left his bag behind, all right—but only after he had slipped out his notebook and zipped his wallet into what he liked to think was a concealed compartment. He had not wanted Sara Leah prying. Now the book was in the Rebbe's hands. What a fool!

Will girded himself for the explosion. The longer the silence lasted, punctuated only by the sound of turned pages, the slicker the moisture on Will's palms.

His mind was racing, trying to remember what was in that book that might give him away. Luckily, he was not organized enough to have written his own name on the first page, or anywhere else. Walton did that, a neat inscription on the cover of each pad he used. Some reporters even used those nerdy address labels. On that score at least, Will was saved by his own inefficiency.

But what about the reams of words inside, including the copious notes he had taken today, right here in Crown Heights? Maybe those would be OK; they would at least confirm his Tom Mitchell cover story. But had he not scribbled down all that computer stuff at Tom's earlier? Surely he had written down something about the kidnappers' e-mail?

The seconds lurched by, like a record playing at the wrong, too-slow speed. A hope took root. Could it be that his bastard shorthand, his unique speedwriting scrawl, was about to rescue him? He had developed this hybrid non-system of note taking first at Columbia and then at the *Record*. It worked for him, though he always feared the day he was asked to produce notes for the editor, or worse still, a judge in court. He imagined a defamation trial, turning on the accuracy of his written account of a conversation. He would need teams of graphologists to verify that he was as good as his words. The upside, at least at this moment, was that Will knew his notes would be all but indecipherable.

"You've broken our rules, Mr. Mitchell. I don't mean our rules, as in us, the people of Crown Heights. What do we matter in the great scheme of things? We are ants! But you've broken HaShem's rules."

A sentence surfaced that instant in Will's head. *Thou shalt not bear false witness.* It was, Will realized, as if he were the mere recipient of the thought rather than its source, one of the Ten Commandments. He knew that Jews and Christians had those in common—and that was surely what the Rebbe had in mind. This was the preamble to an accusation of lying. He was undone.

"I think you know that we're serious about these rules: no carrying on the Sabbath. No carrying. No wallets, no keys. No notebooks."

"Yes."

"We take these rules very seriously, Tom. They apply to our

guests as much as they apply to us. I'm sure you understand that. Yet here you are, with a notebook."

"Yes, but that's the only thing I took. I left the rest of the stuff behind; I left my bag." Will was addressing a bookcase: his interrogator was behind him, his captors at his side. "Besides, I'm not Jewish. I didn't think, you know, that these rules applied to me." That sounded much more lame out loud than it had in Will's head. It sounded like schoolboy special pleading: The dog ate my homework. But it was the truth. Sure, he should be respectful to others while he was in their community, but this was crazy. They could not be this angry about a Sabbath infraction, could they? He was almost relieved: if this was the charge, it meant the Rebbe had found nothing to pursue in the notebook.

"You're not Jewish?"

"No, I told Sandy—Shimon—that already. I'm not Jewish. I'm just a reporter."

"Now that surprises me. I've got to admit, that I did not expect."

Will was baffled, but also distracted. Redbeard had vanished. Will's sole custodian was now this Israeli: he looked young. The *Times* magazine had run a piece about the Israeli army only a couple of weeks back. With a half memory of that as his source, Will knew that an Israeli man needed only to be twenty-one to have done a full three years in the Israel Defense Forces. God knows what he had learned there: this guy might look like a kid, but chances were he had steel in his veins. Why else had the Rebbe picked him to turn the screws on Will? He vaguely remembered from the same piece that many ultra-Orthodox eighteen-year-olds were given exemption from army service so that they could devote their lives to studying the Torah. But not all of them: something told him this was one of the guys who swapped his prayer book for a rifle.

"You know, Mr. Mitchell—or should I call you Tom?—I'm not sure we're making that much progress here. Something is missing from this encounter."

There it was again, that sardonic, world-weary inflection, as if there was humor in every situation, even this one. Will could not get the measure of this man at all: his voice was warm, avuncular even. Yet the room was humid with menace, and it was all coming from him, from behind Will's back.

"I propose that we relocate."

Clearly he had given some kind of nod, because the Israeli swiftly placed a blindfold on Will; not like the childhood variety, where some light always leaks through, but a complete cover, one that seemed to choke the eyelids, stopping them from breathing. He felt himself being yanked upward again, out of the chair. Except this time it was not for another standing search, but to be led away.

Will decided he would not panic. He would not give in to the feeling that, with each step, he was leaning into a dark, empty space, plunging off a cliff into an abyss. He would focus on the ground beneath his feet; each time he lifted one leg, he would remember how near the ground remained. Perhaps he should scrape his shoes along, to maintain constant contact? Maybe that was why you always saw handcuffed prisoners shuffling: it was not because they were depressed, but because they needed the reassurance that the earth was still there, right under their shoes.

He was aware of passing through another corridor, getting farther away from the clamor of the synagogue, which, Will realized, had begun to fade into a loud hubbub a while back. He chided himself for not having noticed exactly when; that detail was surely important in tracking the Rebbe's movements.

What was truly strange, though, was the feeling of dependency on the Israeli now gripping his right arm with painful force. Will was relying on him as a guide, aware that he must now look the way blind men always look: Stevie Wonder or Ray Charles, his head moving randomly, untethered to logic. This man was his captor, but, Will thought, he was also his carer.

Now he felt the cold. They had moved outside, but only for a few steps. He heard the creak of a swing door, like a garden gate, and then felt the change of temperature. As if they were in an enclosed space, not quite outdoors. There was an echo.

"No one likes this, I'm afraid, Mr. Mitchell. Tom. But I'm going to have to take a look at you."

It was in the next few seconds that Will decided that this was not some ghastly incident that would soon resolve itself, but actually something rather terrifying. Until now, he had clung to the idea that this might be an error or even an ironic sendup of the interrogation scene from a thousand movies. He had been hoping that it would all be revealed as a hideous mistake; or at least that he would soon know the identity of his inquisitor, or that he would make progress, or that this would simply stop. Now he felt sure these strange people who had stolen his wife were about to torture and kill him, probably in a way so sadistic as to chill the blood. Worse than that—and this thought turned his bowels to mush—they had doubtless already done whatever they were going to do, or worse, to Beth.

"No!" Will shouted, but it was too late. He felt his arms being pinned back while someone unbuckled his trousers. There was a hand over his mouth, too. This could not be the work of the Israeli, all alone. But where were these extra hands coming from? Who did they belong to? And then, without warning, his underpants were down.

"Stop." He heard the word, and was shocked to discover the voice was not his own. The Rebbe had spoken. "You're telling the truth. You're not Jewish."

Will could only guess what was happening: the Rebbe must have been standing in front of him, looking at his penis and concluding, rightly, that it was not circumcised.

"You're not Jewish," the Rebbe repeated. And then, to his assistant or assistants: "Cover him up." A pause. "Well, this is good news, Mr. Mitchell. I now believe that you are not a federal agent or a law enforcement official. I suspected you were, prowling around with all your questions. But I know those people, and first, they would have had you wired, and second, they would have sent a Jew. Not only that, but they would have considered themselves very smart for doing that. Oh, yes, regular geniuses for giving Agent Goldberg a call and saying, 'This is a job with your name on it.' That's how they think. Send an Arab to infiltrate a Muslim terrorist gang, send a Jew to us. But you're not a Jew, so you're not working for them. That I now believe."

Will's trousers were back on, his belt was buckled up, and he was off *a* hook, if not *the* hook: he was not an undercover federal agent. All that combined to reduce the terror of a few moments ago. His body, the pounding of his heart, the moisture on his palms, was at code orange, rather than red, where it had been seconds earlier.

"You look relieved, Mr. Mitchell. I'm glad. The trouble is, if you're not a fed, you must be working for someone else. And that, I fear, is infinitely more serious."

CHAPTER SEVENTEEN

FRIDAY, 9:22 P.M., CROWN HEIGHTS, BROOKLYN

WILL DID NOT HAVE LONG TO BE CONFUSED. After the Rebbe had spoken, perhaps a beat passed before Will felt his back pushed forward, making him buckle at the waist. His arms were now gripped like levers, pushing his head and shoulders down.

His nose felt it first, as it filled with water; then his scalp, as it shrank from the cold. His throat gurgled and gagged. He was choking and gasping at the same time.

Will's head and neck had just been submerged in freezing cold water, the blindfold still on. He could feel his chest contract with the shock of it, his heart racing. He had been shoved with some force, in the darkness and therefore without warning, into that icy liquid. He was there for five or six seconds, his shoulders held down to prevent him coming up for air. It was long enough to fill his nostrils, for the water to travel down his sinuses and into his brain. Or that's how it felt—like asphyxiation.

Once out, he gulped in air even as he coughed, a double reflex like vomiting. But then the hands were pushing again, and he was under once more.

This time it was the temperature. His eyes seemed to shrivel in their sockets, recoiling from the cold; he was sure he could hear his whole system, veins, arteries, and blood vessels, screaming with the trauma of the sudden radical change in temperature.

What was this? A pond? An icebox? The edge of a river? A toilet? The blindfold was soaked but not loosening; if anything it seemed now to be welding itself onto Will's eyelids, sealed in by ice.

"Now, Tom," the voice was saying, its timbre distorted by the frozen water in Will's ears. "Shall we start talking honestly?"

By way of response, Will spat out a mouthful of the water, emptying himself for the next, inevitable dunk.

"I believe this is your second time at the *mikve* today. You're becoming a regular *frummie*, aren't you, Tom? And I'm sure Shimon Shmuel explained to you the purpose, the meaning, of the *mikve*. This is a place of purification, a place of sanctification. We enter coated in the sins of our regular lives and emerge *tahoor*, pure. And in this state we are untainted by any sins, be they lies or deceits. Do you follow me, Tom?"

Will was now shivering. His shirt was soaked, and he could feel rivulets of liquid chill running down his back and chest. His teeth were about to start chattering.

"What I am saying is that I now insist on the truth. And if two or three dips in this outdoor *mikve*, filled only by purest rainwater, cannot find the truth in you, then maybe four or five or six or seven submersions will. We are patient men. We will keep plunging you into that water until you deal with us plainly and straightforwardly. Do you understand?"

There must have been a silent nod, because down Will went again. The cold was now biting into him, seeping below his skin and into his bones. They too seemed to contract, as if they could hide from the cold by making themselves smaller.

"Who do you work for, Tom? Who sent you here?"

"I'm a journalist," was all Will could manage, in a voice he hardly recognized, querulous with cold.

"You've said that, but who wants you here? Why are you here?"

"I've told you."

And down he went again, this time shoved so that his whole upper body was submerged. He felt the water travel below his waist, trickling into his shorts, spreading an icy damp around his groin.

He had no idea what to say. He wanted desperately for this to end, but what could he do? If he told the truth, he would endanger himself and Beth. The kidnappers had been clear: no involvement of the police. That surely extended to vigilante rescue missions as well. These were serious, violent people, and he would be admitting he had defied their instructions. He would also be confessing that he had indeed been lying. As for Beth, they had kidnapped her for some purpose—which he could not fathom—but one thing he knew: his presence here was not part of their plan. If they had not already done great harm to her, his appearance would all but guarantee it.

Yet to carry on insisting that he was Tom Mitchell seemed doomed. He could not give them any more information, because there was no more; Mitchell was a fiction. On this the Rebbe's instincts were right. Even if Will had the strength to withstand this weight, he would eventually crack because his story would crack: it had to. These were his thoughts as the weight on his hands and shoulders came again, plunging his body deep into the cold.

"Enough," Will said. "No more."

"Maybe I need to explain a little about Judaism," the voice was saying as he was finally allowed back up for air.

He could hardly make out the words, so loud was the explosion generated by his own lungs as he gulped for oxygen.

"Judaism holds the harshest possible view of murder. 'Thou

shalt not kill' is the sixth commandment. It means that murder is never allowed." There was a long pause, as if the Rebbe expected Will to react. Will could not; he was still drawing in loud, urgent breaths.

"I don't know if you're familiar with one of our most famous teachings, Mr. Mitchell. 'To save a single life is to save the whole world.' Really, the whole world. That's how much each life matters to HaShem. In each individual person is contained the whole world. Because we are all created in God's image. This is the meaning behind the phrase 'sanctity of life,' Mr. Mitchell. Now it is a cliché. People just say it without even thinking. But what do those words really mean?" The voice had a hint of the music he had heard before, back in the synagogue—that singsong, up-and-down rhythm, by turns questioning and answering, all in a single monologue. "They mean that life is sacred, because it is part of the divine. To kill a human being is to kill an aspect of the Almighty. Which is why we are forbidden to kill. Except in the most exceptional circumstances."

Will felt the cold bite deeper into his flesh.

"Self-defense is the obvious example, but it is not the only one. You see, in Judaism we have a beautiful concept known as *pikuach nefesh*. This refers to the saving of a soul. Now, there is no more sacred duty than *pikuach nefesh:* almost anything is allowed if it will save a soul. Rabbis are often asked, 'Can a Jew ever eat pork?' The answer is yes! Of course he can! If he is on a desert island, and the only means to survive is to slay a pig and eat it, then not only is the Jew allowed to do that, he *must* do it! He must. It is a religious commandment: he must save his own life. *Pikuach nefesh.*

"Let's take a more difficult case." The man was speaking as if this were a tutorial at Balliol College, a one-on-one class with Will as his pupil. The fact that Will was kneeling, his hands now tied, his body drenched and frozen, barely broke his stride.

"Would we be allowed to kill, if that would save a life? No. The rules of *pikuach nefesh* prohibit murder, idolatry, and sexual immorality even to save a life. If someone tells you to commit murder, just to save your own skin, you cannot do it. But let's say a known killer is on the loose. He is on his way to murder a family of innocents. We know that if we kill him, their lives will be saved. Is it right to kill in that situation? Yes, because such a man is what we call a *rodef*. If there is no other way to stop him, he can be killed with impunity.

"But let's sharpen the dilemma. What if the man we are discussing is not necessarily a killer, but if he stays alive, one way or another, innocent people will die? What should we do then? Can we hurt such a man? Can we kill him?

"This is the sort of question our sages discuss at great length. Sometimes our Talmudic debates can seem to be obsessed with detail, even trivia: how many cubits in length should an oven be, that kind of thing. But the heart of our study is reserved for what you would call ethical dilemmas. I have thought about this particular one in great depth. And I have reached a conclusion that, in fairness, I think I ought to disclose to you. I believe that it is permissible to inflict pain and even death on a man who may not himself be a killer—but whose suffering or death would save lives. I think there is no other way of understanding our sources. That is what they are telling us.

"To get to the point, Mr. Mitchell, if I conclude that you are, in effect, a *rodef*, and that to end your life would save others, I would not hesitate to see that it ended. Perhaps you need a moment to reflect on that."

The pressure came a half second later, as if, once again, the Rebbe had given his silent cue. The cold bit deep, still shocking. Will counted, to get himself through. Usually he was lifted out after around fifteen seconds under. Now he counted sixteen, seventeen, eighteen.

He flexed his shoulders, to give his captors a signal that it was time to let him breathe. They pressed down harder. Will began to struggle. Twenty, twenty-one, twenty-two.

Was this the meaning of the Rebbe's little lecture? Something not abstract or complex, despite the convoluted exposition, but rather simple: We are now going to kill you.

Thirty, thirty-one, thirty-two. Will's legs were kicking, as if they belonged to someone else. His body was panicking, sent into a survival reflex. Did not the movies always show this, as the murderer smothered his victim with a pillow or tightened a stocking around her neck, the legs moving in an involuntary dance?

Forty, forty-one. Or was it fifty? Will had lost count. His head seemed to flood with dull color, like the patterns you detect under your eyelids just before sleep. He wanted to weep for the wife he was about to leave behind and wondered if it was possible to weep underwater. Thought itself grew faint.

At last they let go, but Will did not burst out of the water with the gasping energy of before. Now the men had to pull him out, letting him collapse onto the ground. He lay there, his chest rising and falling fast but as if unconnected to the rest of him. He heard distant breathing and could not be certain if it was his own.

Slowly he felt his ears unblock and strength return to his arms and legs. He stayed slumped on the ground, unable to face hauling his body upright. If they wanted him to sit to attention, they would have to drag him up themselves.

Lying there, he detected a change, another person in the group around him. There was new activity, whispered exchanges. The new member of the circle seemed to be breathing heavily, as if he had just been running. He could hear the Rebbe's voice, though he seemed to be distracted, his voice aimed downward, as if he was looking at something, reading.

"Mr. Mitchell, Moshe Menachem, who was with us a few moments ago, has just completed an errand." *Redbeard.* "He ran from here to Shimon Shmuel's house. And, as a matter of *pikuach nefesh*, he is allowed to carry something that he found there in order to bring it here. I am speaking of a wallet. Your wallet."

They had rummaged through his bag; now it was surely over.

His wallet would give him away. What was in there? No business cards; he was so new at the *Times* he did not have any yet. No credit cards either; he kept those in a separate wallet, zipped into a pocket of its own in his bag. He had left them in there, calculating that even if Sara Leah could not resist a peek at his belongings, she would hesitate before doing a full probe.

What else was in there? Tons of cab receipts, but anything with his name on it? He had kept all the hotel bills and credit card slips from the Northwest in a separate envelope, for a later expenses claim. Maybe he would be OK. Maybe he would get away with it.

"Take the blindfold off. Let go of his hands. Lead him back into the Bet HaMidrash." Will could feel the confusion in his own adrenal gland: Was this a cue to produce yet more adrenaline, ready for the ordeal to come or, at last, a sign that the danger was receding? Was this good news or bad news?

He could feel hands fussing behind his head and then an increase in light as the sodden cloth covering his eyes was removed. Instinctively he shook off the drops as he opened his eyes. He was outside, in a small area surrounded by a wooden fence—the kind of space large buildings use to keep their trash. There were a few pipes and, at his feet, the glint of water. He barely had a chance to look; his two handlers were already turning him away. But he guessed that this was the housing for some kind of outdoor storage tank, a big vat used to collect rainwater.

Now he was heading through a door and back inside, though something told Will this was not the way they had come out. It seemed to be quieter, for one thing, away from the crowds. Will guessed that this was a separate building, perhaps a house adjoining the synagogue.

Inside it did not look that different: the same functional floors and rabbit warren of classrooms and offices. With red-beard, Moshe Menachem, and the Israeli flanking him, they headed into one of them, and Will heard the door shut behind him.

"Let him sit down. Untie his hands and give him a towel. And find a dry shirt."

The Rebbe's voice; still behind him. The blindfold was off, but clearly Will was not going to see everything.

"OK, we should begin again."

Will braced himself.

"We need to have a talk, Mr. Monroe."

CHAPTER EIGHTEEN

FRIDAY, 7:40 P.M., RIO DE JANEIRO, BRAZIL

IT WAS THE END OF AN EXHAUSTING WEEK; Luis Tavares could feel the fatigue spreading through his joints. Even so, he would climb one more level: there were other people to see.

Some money had just come in. He could see that all around him. Suddenly this street was paved, the asphalt fresh enough to smell. Kids were buzzing around a TV set, visible through the open, doorless entrance to a shack. Luis smiled: his pestering of the authorities had worked. Either that, or someone had bribed the power company to connect this row of huts to the city grid. Or a few people had clubbed together to find a cowboy electrician who would do it for a few *reais*.

Luis felt a familiar spasm of ambivalence. He knew he was meant to advocate respect for the law and condemn all forms of theft. Yet he could not help but admire these outlaws, these entrepreneurs of the favelas, who did whatever it took to provide for their communities. He applauded their determination to provide a stretch of road or desks for a classroom. Could he condemn them for breaking the law? What kind of pastor would deny people who had next to nothing the little that makes life bearable?

He wanted to rest, but he knew he would not. Even the briefest pause made Luis feel guilty. He felt guilt when he awoke: how much more work could he have done if he had not slept? He felt guilt when he ate: how many more people could he have helped in that half hour he had spent feeding his face? And in Favela Santa Marta there was never any shortage of people needing help. The poverty was unstoppable, insatiable, like waves on a beach. And Luis Tavares was the local Canute—standing on the shore, raging at the sea.

He continued upward, heading for the view he knew would stun him, even after all these years. From that vantage point, he would be able to see both the city and the ocean, stretching out ahead. On nights like this, he liked to gaze at the glittering carpet of light, the sparkle of other favelas in the distance. Best of all, he was close to the sight that had made Rio de Janeiro famous: the giant statue of Jesus Christ, watching over the city, the country and, as far as Luis was concerned, the whole world.

As he climbed, the pastor noted for the thousandth time how the housing deteriorated with the altitude. At the bottom of the hill, there were homes that were recognizable as homes. The structures were solid; they had walls, a roof, and glass in the windows. Some had running water, a phone line, and satellite TV. But as you moved up the hillside, such sights became rarer. The places he passed now barely qualified even as shelters. They were thrown together, perhaps a wall made of rusty steel, a sheet of corrugated plastic serving as a roof. The door was a gap; the window a hole. They were jammed together, one leaning on the other like a house of cards. This was one of the main shantytowns near Rio's wealthy beach district, and it was abject.

He had been here for twenty-seven years, ever since he first graduated from divinity school. Baptist clergy were always meant to see some searing deprivation early in their career, but not all became transfixed by it as he had. He would not learn its lessons and move on. He would stay and fight it, no matter how unequal the struggle. He knew poverty on this scale was like a garden weed: you might banish it today, but it would be back tomorrow.

Even so, he refused to feel that what he had done here was futile. There were close to ten thousand people crammed on this hillside, each one of them a soul created in the image of God. If even one had a meal, he would otherwise not have eaten, or slept under a roof rather than in a tiny, fetid alleyway—there was no room for anything so grand as a street—then Luis's entire life's work would have been justified. That was how he saw it, at any rate.

He felt frustrated that he was not engaged in that kind of activity this evening: the direct business of care—ladling out soup to a hungry woman, draping a blanket over a shivering child—where a change is made every second. No, his task tonight was to gather evidence for a report he had been asked to submit to a government department.

That they even wanted to see a report counted as an achievement, the result of nine months of Luis's lobbying. Government—federal, state, and municipal—had given up on places like Santa Marta years ago. They did not visit them, they did not police them. They were no-go areas where the writ of the state did not apply. So if people wanted something—a hospital, say, or a yard where the kids could play football—they either organized it themselves, or they had to harangue and nag government until it finally paid attention.

Which is where Luis came in. He had become Santa Marta's advocate, lobbying the state bureaucracy one week, a foreign charity the next, demanding they do something for the people of the favela, for the kids who grew up sidestepping sewage in the alleys or scavenging food from the trash mountains nearby. His favorite tool was shame. He would ask people to look at Lagoa, the neighborhood just over the hill which was proud to be one of the wealthiest districts in Latin America. Then he would show them a Santa Marta child who ate less in a week than a Lagoa chihuahua nibbled in a day.

Tonight he was gathering testimony, talking to residents of one of the favela's toughest stretches. They would explain to him why they needed a clinic, what it should provide and where it should be, and he would pass that information on to officialdom as part of his submission. These days Luis even used a video camera, ensuring that the people of the favelas could speak for themselves.

Now he was at the first address, not that there were any numbers on this or any other house. He went inside and was surprised to see several unfamiliar faces: all young men. Perhaps Dona Zezinha was not around.

"Should I wait?" he asked one of the group. But there was no reply. "Is this your home?" he said to another, a wolf-faced boy who seemed nervous, avoiding Luis's gaze. Finally, "What's going on?"

As if to answer the pastor's question, the wolf-boy produced a gun. Luis's instant thought was that the weapon looked vaguely comic; it was too large for the lad's hand. But then the gun was aimed at him. Before he had a chance to realize he was going to die, the bullet had torn his heart wide open.

Luis Tavares died with a look of surprise rather than terror on his face. If anything, it was his killers who looked scared. They hurriedly covered the corpse with a blanket, just as they were instructed, then ran through the streets, agitated, rushing to meet the man who had ordered this job done. They took the money from him quickly, their eyes feverish. They did not listen as he thanked them. They barely heard him as he praised them for doing the Lord's work.

CHAPTER NINETEEN

FRIDAY, 10:05 P.M., CROWN HEIGHTS, BROOKLYN

"I SEE THAT WE HAVE BOTH MADE A MISTAKE HERE. Your mistake is that you have lied to me and lied consistently, even under immense pressure. Under the circumstances, I now understand that and even find it admirable." Will could hardly hear the words over the sound of his own heart throbbing. He was scared, much more terrified than he had been outside. The Rebbe had discovered the truth. Something in the wallet had betrayed him, doubtless one loose credit card receipt or a long-forgotten Blockbuster membership card. God only knew what pain lay in store for him now.

"You are here to look for your wife."

"Yes." Will could hear the exhaustion in his own voice. And the anguish.

"I understand that, and I hope that I would do the same in your position. I am sure Moshe Menachem and Tzvi Yehuda agree." Now both the thugs had names. "It is a duty for all husbands to provide for and protect their wives. That is the nature of the marriage commitment.

"But I am afraid the usual rules cannot apply in this case. I cannot let you come charging in here, no matter how heroically, and rescue your wife. I cannot allow it."

"So you admit that you have her here?"

"I don't admit anything. I don't deny anything. That is not the purpose of what I am saying to you, Mr. Monroe. Will. I am trying to explain that the usual rules don't apply in this case."

"What usual rules? What case?"

"I wish I could tell you more, Will, I really do. But I cannot."

Will was not sure if he had just been ground down by the ordeal of the last few—what was it: hours, minutes?—or whether he was simply relieved that it was over, but he was sure he heard something different in the Rebbe's voice. The menace had gone; there was a sadness, a sorrow in it that Will heard as sympathy, maybe even compassion for himself. It was ridiculous: the man was a torturer. Will wondered if he was succumbing to Stockholm syndrome, the strange bond that can develop between a captive and his captor: first depending on the Israeli as if he was a guide dog for the blind rather than a violent brute, and now detecting humanity in his chief tormentor. This was surely an irrational reaction to the end of the ducking-stool treatment: rather than feeling anger that it had happened at all, he was feeling gratitude to the Rebbe for ending it. Stockholm syndrome, a classic case.

And yet, Will rated himself a good judge of character. He reckoned he had always been perceptive, and he was sure he could hear something real in that voice. He gambled on his hunch.

"Tell me something that I have a right to know. Is my wife safe? Is she . . . unharmed?" He could not bring himself to say the word he really meant—*alive*—not because he feared the Hasidim's reaction so much as his own. He feared his voice would crack, that he would show a weakness he had so far kept hidden.

"That is a fair question, Will, and yes, she will be safe—so long as no one does anything reckless or stupid, and by 'no one' I am referring chiefly to you, Will. And by 'anything reckless or stupid' I am speaking chiefly of involving the authorities. That will ruin everything, and then I can make no guarantees for anyone's safety."

"I don't understand what you could want from my wife. What has she done to you? Why don't you just let her go?" He had not meant to, but his mouth had taken the decision for him: he was begging.

"She has done nothing to us or anyone else, but we cannot let her go. I'm sorry that I cannot say more. I can imagine how hard this is for you."

That was the Rebbe's mistake, that last line. Will could feel the blood rushing to his face, the veins on his neck rising.

"No, you fucking CANNOT imagine how hard this is. You have not had your wife kidnapped! You have not been grabbed, blindfolded, shoved into freezing water, and threatened with death by people who never so much as show their face. So don't tell me you can imagine anything. You can imagine NOTHING!"

Tzvi Yehuda and Moshe Menachem almost sprang back, clearly as shocked by this outburst as Will himself. The anger had been brewing since he got to Crown Heights—in fact, long before. Since the moment that message popped into his BlackBerry: *We have your wife.*

"You said it was time for plain dealing. So how about some plain dealing? What the hell is this about?"

"I can't tell you that." The voice was softer than it had been, almost dejected. "But this is about something much bigger than you could possibly know."

"That's ridiculous. Beth is a shrink. She sees kids who won't talk and girls who starve themselves. What bigger thing could involve her? You're lying."

"I'm telling you the truth, Will. The fate of your wife depends on something much larger than you or her or me. In a way it hangs on an ancient story, one that no one could ever have imagined would have turned out this way. No one ever predicted this. There was no contingency plan. No preparation in our sacred texts, or at least none that we have found so far. And believe me, we are looking."

Will had no idea what this man was talking about. For the first time, he wondered if these Hasidim might simply be delusional. Had he not seen them earlier this evening, swept up in an ecstatic frenzy in adoration of their leader, worshiping him as their Messiah? Was it not possible that they had fallen into a state of collective madness, with this man, their leader, the maddest of all?

"I wish I could say more, but the stakes are too high. We have to get this right, Mr. Monroe, and we don't have long. What day is it today? *Shabbos shuva?* We have just four days. That is why I cannot afford to take any risks."

"What do you mean, the stakes are too high?"

"I don't think it will be helpful for me to say any more on this, Will. For one thing, my guess is you won't believe a word I say."

"Well, if you mean I'm unlikely to trust a man who's nearly killed me, you're right."

"I see that. And one day, and I suspect it will be very soon, you'll understand why we had to do what we just did. All will become clear. That is the way of these things. And I meant what I said. I feared you were a federal agent, and when I confirmed that you were not, I feared you were something much worse."

"What would you have to fear from a federal agent? And what would you fear even more than that? What are you up to here?"

"I can see why you're a journalist, Will: always asking questions. You'd do well in our line of work, too: that is what Torah study is all about, asking the right questions. But I'm afraid I think we have done all the Q & A we're going to do tonight. It's time for us to say good-bye."

"That's it? You're going to leave it at that? You're not going to tell me what's going on?"

"No, I cannot risk that. So I'm going to leave you with a few things for you to remember. You can write them down later if you like. The first is that this is much bigger than any of us. Everything we believe in, everything you believe in, hangs in the balance. Life itself. The stakes could not be higher.

"Second, your wife will be safe unless you endanger her life by your recklessness. I urge you not to do that, not just for your own sake, but for the sake of all of us. Everybody. So even though you love her and want to protect her, I plead with you to believe me that the best thing you can do for her, as a loving husband, is to stay away. Back off and don't meddle. Interfere, and I can offer no guarantees, not for her, not for you, not for any of us.

"And third, I don't expect you to understand. You have wandered into all this quite by accident. Perhaps it's not an accident, but a series of steps fully understood only by our Creator. But this is the hardest thing of all. I'm asking you to believe things that you cannot comprehend, to trust me just because I ask you. I don't know if you're a man of faith or not, Will, but this is how faith operates. We have to believe in God even when we have not the barest inkling of what he has in mind for the universe. We have to obey rules that seem to make no sense, simply because we believe. Not everyone can do it, Will. It takes strength to have faith. But that is what I need from you: the faith to trust that I and the people you see here are acting only for the sake of good."

"Even when that means nearly drowning an innocent man like me?"

"Even when the price is very high, yes. We are determined to save lives here, Will, and in that cause almost any action is permitted. *Pikuach nefesh.* Now I must say good-bye. Moshe Menachem will give you back your things. Good luck, Will. Travel safely and, please God, all should be well. Good *shabbos.*"

At that moment, as Will imagined the Rebbe lifting himself up out of his chair and shuffling toward the door, he heard an interruption. Someone else had come into the room; barged in, by the sound of it. He seemed to be showing the Rebbe something; there was muttered conversation. The new voice was highly exercised, a raised whisper. They need not have worried: even at that volume, all Will could establish was that they were not speaking English. It sounded like German, with lots of phlegmy *ch*'s and *sch*'s. Yiddish.

The exchange ended; the Rebbe seemed to have gone. Redbeard, Moshe Menachem, now left his sentry position at Will's side and stood in front of him. His eyes were sheepish as he handed to Will the bag he had left at Shimon Shmuel's. "I'm sorry about, you know, before," he mumbled.

Will took the bag, seeing that his notebook had been put back inside, too. His phone was still there, and his BlackBerry, untouched. He took out his wallet, faintly curious to see which stub or ticket had given him away. It was as he expected, full of anonymous cab receipts. He opened up the series of slots made to carry credit cards, a feature he never used. In one, a book of standard U.S. postage stamps; in another, a business card of a long-forgotten interviewee. In the third, a passport-sized photograph—of Beth.

A bitter smile passed across Will's face: it was his bride who had betrayed him. Of course they would recognize her. She had given him this picture about six weeks after they met; it was summer, and they had spent the afternoon boating off Sag Harbor. They passed a photo booth, and she could not resist: she mugged for the automated camera there and then.

Will turned the picture over, and there it was, the message that had left no doubt. *I love you, Will Monroe!*

Will looked up, his eyes wet. Before him was a new face; he guessed it was the man who had briefly clashed with the Rebbe a few moments ago. His face was soft and round, his cheeks chipmunk-full, framed by a jet-black beard. He was tubby, with a round head atop a round tummy. Will guessed he was in his early twenties.

"Come, I'll show you out."

As Will got up, he saw at last the chair where the Rebbe had sat during the inquisition. It was no throne, just a chair. Next to it was a side table, the kind a lecturer might use to keep his notes and a glass of water. What was on it made Will jolt.

It was a copy of that day's *New York Times*, folded, very deliberately, to highlight Will's story about the life and death of Pat Baxter. So that was what the round-faced man had shown the Rebbe; that was what they had argued about. Will could guess what the young man had been saying: *Remember, this guy's from the* New York Times. *He's never going to keep this quiet. We should keep him here, where he can't shoot his mouth off.*

By now they were outside, Will holding the clean white shirt the Hasidim had given him but which he was not yet wearing: he had not wanted to undress in front of his inquisitors. He had been humiliated enough already.

They stood on the street, outside the shul. Men were still coming in and walking out. Will looked at his watch: 10:20 p.m. It felt like 3:00 a.m.

"I can only repeat our apologies about what happened in there."

Yeah, yeah, thought Will. Save it for the judge when I sue your Hasidic asses for false imprisonment, assault, battery, and the whole fucking shebang. "Well, better than an apology would actually be an explanation."

"I can't give you that, but I can give you a word of advice." He looked around, as if making sure that he was not being watched or overheard. "My name is Yosef Yitzhok. I work to bring the Rebbe's word into the world. Listen, I know what you do, and here's my suggestion." He lowered his voice into a conspiratorial whisper. "If you want to know what's going on, think about your work."

"I don't understand."

"You will. But you have to look to your work. Go on, leave."

This Yosef Yitzhok seemed agitated. "Remember what I said. Look to your work."

CHAPTER TWENTY

FRIDAY, 11:35 P.M., BROOKLYN

TOM ANSWERED HIS PHONE WITHIN ONE RING. He told Will, who had been stumbling through the streets of Crown Heights looking for the subway, to hail a cab and head straight over to his apartment.

Now Will lay on Tom's couch, fit to pass out with tiredness, kept awake only by a kind of fever. He was wearing nothing but three thick towels. Tom had shoved him in a hot shower the minute he walked through the door, determined that his friend not succumb to a cold, a fever, or even pneumonia. He knew they had no time to waste on illness.

Will did his best to tell him what had happened, but most of it was too bizarre to take in. Besides, Will spoke like a man just awakened, trying to remember a dream: new bits of information, new characters, new descriptions and phrases, kept popping up. There were so few items of normality for Tom to cling to, he gave up making sense of it after a while. Bearded men, a near-drowning, a sign telling women to cover their elbows, an unseen inquisitor, a leader worshiped as the Messiah, a rule preventing people from carrying even keys for twenty-four hours. He wondered if Will had gone to Crown Heights at all, rather than to the East Village to score some particularly strong acid and embark on one of the more surreal trips in recent hallucinogenic history.

Harder to resist was the urge to say, "I told you so." This was precisely the outcome Tom had feared: Will charging into Crown Heights, underprepared and out of his mind with anguish, clumsily walking into the hands of his enemies.

Not only did Will expect Tom to follow his account of the last, baffling few hours, he also wanted his help in trying to decode it. What was that reference to his work? What did the Rebbe mean about an ancient story, about saving lives, about having just four days to go?

"Will," Tom said after his friend had spoken for nearly fifteen uninterrupted minutes, trying to break his flow. "Will." No luck; he kept on talking. Finally, Tom had to break with his own iron rule and raise his voice. "WILL!"

At last, he stopped.

"Will, this is too serious for us to keep flailing around like amateurs. We need expert help now."

"What, the police?"

"Well, we should think about it."

"Of course I've fucking thought about it. I thought about it when I had my head in the deep freeze. But I don't think I can risk it. I saw these people, Tom. They were ready to kill me tonight, on some hunch. Because I wasn't wearing a wire and because I do have a foreskin. Or some such crazy nonsense. They were going to drown me. The guy gave me the full, theological justification—all this stuff about Peking Nuff-said or whatever it was. Essentially, you can take a life if it will save lives—and the life they were thinking of taking this evening was mine. And maybe Beth's. So yes, I've thought about it, but what I think is, the risk is too great. From the very beginning they've said it: if we go to the police, she's not safe. And now, having seen them—or not seen them—I think they mean it. They're serious people. They're not messing around."

"OK, so we need some other kind of help."

"Like what?"

"Like Jews."

"What?"

"We need to talk to someone Jewish who can begin to make sense of everything you saw and heard. We know nothing. All we've got is what you heard underwater and what we can get off the Internet. It's not enough."

Will recognized the logic. It was true. He had been bluffing his way through in that typically English way. They taught it in the best schools: bullshit studies. Learn to get by on native wit and charm. Never be anything so boring as a qualified expert; be the gifted amateur. That's what he had done by marching into Crown Heights in his bloody chinos with his bloody notebook. As if it would all fall into his charming English lap. They needed help.

"Who?"

"What about Joel?"

"Joel Kaufman?" He had been in the journalism program with Will at Columbia; he was now writing for the sports pages of *Newsday.* "He's Jewish, but only technically. He barely knows more than I do."

"Ethan Greenberg?"

"He's in Hong Kong. For the *Journal.*"

"This is pathetic. We're in New York. We must know some Jews!"

"I actually know plenty of Jews," Will said, thinking suddenly of Schwarz and Grossman in the pod at work, which in turn reminded him that he had made no contact with the office all day. He had ignored Harden's e-mail. He would have to do something; he couldn't just go AWOL. But it was too much to think about; he shoved the thought aside, telling himself he would deal with it as soon as he left Tom's apartment.

"The trouble is, I can't start blabbing about this situation to just anyone. The risk is too great. It has to be someone who is not just Jewish but who's smart enough to know Jewish things, who might know about this world"—he gestured toward the screen, still flickering with the map of Eastern Parkway—"and who we can trust. I can't think of anyone who falls into that category."

"I can," said Tom, though his face registered no pleasure at the fact.

"Who?"

"TC."

"You can't be serious. TC? To help Beth?"

"Who else can do it, Will? Who else?"

Will fell back onto the couch, clenching his jaw, the muscle inside his cheek tightening on and off as if pulsing with an alternating current. Once again, Tom was right. TC checked all the boxes. She was Jewish, smart, and would never betray a secret. But how could he make that phone call? They had not spoken in more than four years.

For nearly nine months, from the start of Columbia to that Memorial Day weekend, they had been inseparable. She was a fine art student, and Will had fallen for her before either of them had said a word. He could not lie: it was lust. She was the woman on campus everyone noticed, from the diamond stud in her nose to the ring that pierced her belly button; from the flat, constantly exposed midriff to the tint of blue running through her hair. Most women over the age of sixteen could not carry off that look, but TC had enough natural beauty to get away with it.

They had started dating straight away, becoming virtual recluses in his tiny apartment on 113th and Amsterdam. They would have sex in the daytime, eat Chinese food, see movies, and have more sex until it was morning again.

Appearances were misleading. People saw the blue hair and the navel ring and assumed TC was a wild, free spirit—one of those girls in movies who leap onto the roof to dance in the moonlight or take spontaneous rides to the shore to see the fishing boats. Despite the piercings and torn jeans, TC was not like that. Underneath that neo-hippie exterior, Will soon discovered a precise, analytical brain that could be terrifying in its demand for exactitude. Conversation with TC was a mental workout: she let Will get away with nothing.

She seemed to have read everything—citing plot lines from Turgenev one moment, the central doctrinal tenets of Lutheranism the next—and have absorbed it all. The only crack in her armor, again defying all expectations, was popular culture. She could get by on the most recent stuff, but dip into the childhood memories she and Will were meant to share, and she would become clueless. Mention *Grease*, and she assumed you meant Greece; refer to Valley Girls, and she would ask, "Which valley?" Will found it endearing; besides, it was reassuring to know there was one area where the human database he was dating had a defect. He concluded the two facts were related: when kids like him were watching mindless TV and listening to trashy pop, TC had been reading, reading, reading.

Mind you, all that was a guess. TC only spoke about her childhood in the vaguest terms. (Even her name remained a mystery: a nickname she had got as a toddler, she said, its origins forgotten.) He had never met her parents or siblings: that would be impossible. Despite her own aggressively irreligious life—she made a point of ordering jumbo shrimp and sweet and sour pork—she explained that her family were still fairly traditional, and they would just not accept a gentile boyfriend. "But we're not getting married!" he would say. "It doesn't matter," would be the reply. "Even the theoretical possibility that one day we might, that we are together at all, is bad enough. For them."

They went through all the arguments. He would accuse her unseen parents—and he never even glimpsed a photograph of them—of racism, as bad as the prejudice of any anti-Semite who would bar his daughter going out with a Jew. She would then walk him through the long, bloody course of Jewish history. Knowledgeable as ever, she would tell how, across continents and down the centuries, Jews had been tormented, clinging only perilously to their lives and the civilization they had created. Jewish culture could not survive, people like her parents believed, if it gradually dissolved, through intermarriage and assimilation, into the general population—like a drop of blue hair dye in an ocean of clear water. "So that's what your parents believe," Will would say. "What about you? What do you believe?"

Her answers were never clear enough, not for Will. The arguments became too tiring. And while the forbiddenness of their romance had been a thrill at first, making them coconspirators in the Manhattan winter, by the spring it had begun to pall. He did not like feeling that their fate was being decided by a vast, external force—five thousand years of history—of which he knew so little and over which he had no influence. By the time he met Beth, he knew he and TC had run out of road.

It ended very badly. He had been a coward and started seeing Beth before breaking off properly from TC: she had found a digital picture of the new girlfriend on his computer. That was bad enough, but she was furious that what they had come to call "the Jewish thing" had proved so decisive. She was angry with him for allowing that to be an obstacle—for rejecting her because of "a fact about myself I cannot change"—but he always had the feeling the fury was not only directed at him. He could see she was raging at a heritage, a culture, that she had mostly abandoned but which had pulled her apart from a man she had loved. Their last conversation was a shouting match. His last image of her was a face raw with tears. Occasionally, he wondered who had won out: the uptight parents or the blue-streaked world of art and adventure that had so enthralled the girl he had fallen in love with.

Now Tom was suggesting he get in touch. Tonight, at nearly midnight. He still remembered her cell phone number; but what would he say? How would he explain that the only reason he was making contact was because he needed something—and that was for the sake of the woman who had stolen him from her? How would he make that call? And why would she do anything but slam the phone down, vowing never to speak to him again?

And yet he was desperate, and Tom was right. She was the closest thing to the expert they needed. He would have to do it. He would have to put aside his own emotions, including his cowardice, and dial that number. Now.

He paced up and down the room for a while, mentally scripting his opening. It was like writing for the paper: once he had his first line, he had the courage to plunge in, hoping instinct would take care of the rest. To increase his chances for success, or at least to prevent immediate failure, he also played a cheap trick.

He reckoned that if TC's number was still stored on his phone, there was at least a possibility that his lived on in her SIM card, too. He imagined the sight of his name flashing up on her screen. So he called from Tom's line, knowing his number would be wholly unfamiliar. It was an ambush call.

"Hello, TC? It's Will." Loud noise in the background. A club? A party?

"Hi."

"Will Monroe."

"I don't know any other Wills, Will. Not before, not since. What's up?"

He had to hand it to her: as an instant response, with barely a second's thinking time, that was not bad. And entirely typical: the hint of a put-down, the reference to their past, the rapid-fire formulation. The only bum note was that "What's up?" It was not her kind of phrase, the lightness in it too forced. In those words, he heard the strain of speaking to a man whom she had loved and who had rejected her.

"I need to see you very soon. You know I wouldn't trouble you like this unless it was very important. And this is very important. I think it's a matter of life and death." He swallowed on that last word, and he knew TC had heard him.

"Is something wrong with your mom? Is she OK?"

"It's Beth. I know—" He could not complete that sentence: he was not sure what came next. "I need to see you right away."

She did not ask any more questions. She just gave him her address. Not her home, but her work: a complex of artists' studios in Chelsea. She said it would be nearer, but Will suspected there was another motive. Maybe she was with someone else; perhaps she was ashamed still to be alone; or maybe she just could not face the intimacy of having Will in her apartment.

Artists' studios. Even in that nugget of information, there was a whole story. It meant she had made good her promise: she had dreamed of being an artist, they talked about it through those long, bed afternoons. But he, and even she, had wondered whether she had the nerve to go through with it. She had surprised them both.

Less than an hour later he found himself stepping out of a service elevator, an old-style one complete with concertina iron gate. He emerged on the fourth floor, silent and dark. He could just make out a corner reserved for a sculptress who seemed to specialize in female bellies. He turned past what looked like a metal workshop, but was in fact the workspace of a man who created installations using neon. Finally he saw a photocopied notice: "TC." Just those two letters, no first or last name. Smart branding, Will thought as he knocked lightly on the partition door.

He had only a second or two to take it all in: walls covered with paintings, three more on easels, yet more covered in bubble wrap, leaned up against the walls. A plain, battered table covered with clutter. On a counter that ran the length of the back wall, artists' materials—bottles of white spirit; oil paints in bent, metal toothpaste tubes; glue; knives; various rusty scrapers; string; and, unaccountably, a cookbook that seemed to have lost all its pages.

Toward the back of the room, on a threadbare red velvet couch,

TC. She was smaller than he remembered, but nothing else was diminished: she was still a woman who made you stare. Her hair was now shoulder length, where once it had been punkily short. Most of it was a natural brown but for that trademark streak of blue, still there. Taking in her flimsy, vaguely vintage shirt above tight jeans, torn at the knees, he could see the shape that had once made him weak. In the semi-dark he spotted a glint of metal: the navel ring, still in place.

This had been the moment he was most uncertain of: should he hug her, kiss her on the cheek, shake hands, or do nothing? But she made the decision for him, standing up and opening her arms as if welcoming back a prodigal son. He fell into a hug and tried, through the positioning of his arms and hands, to make it somehow—what was the word—*fraternal*.

"What's the problem, Will?"

He told her as methodically and briefly as he could: the e-mail, Tom's tracing of it to Crown Heights, Will's visit, the interrogation, the trial by *mikve*.

"You've got to be kidding," she said when that last detail dropped, her face giving a smirk that was either disbelief, nervous tension, schadenfreude, or a little bit of all three. The semi-smile vanished when she saw Will's reaction. She could see this was deadly serious. "Will, I feel for you, I really do. And my heart goes out to Beth's family." *Beth.* He had never heard TC say her name before. "But what exactly do you need from me?"

"I need to know what you know. I need you to explain to me what I heard. I need you to *translate* for me."

She responded with a small, wan smile that somehow made her look older. At that moment, Will realized aging was not chiefly about lines or wrinkles, though those things played their part. The years really showed in expressions like the one he had just seen. Suddenly TC's was a face of years; of knowledge.

"OK. Very slowly and with as much detail as you can remember, you have to tell me everything that happened. Every street you walked, every person you met, every word they used. I'll put some coffee on."

Will fell back in the wicker chair TC had pulled up for him. For the first time in sixteen hours, he let his muscles relax. He was so relieved: TC was on his side. He was filled with a sentiment he had never had when they were together; he felt that TC was going to look after him.

She was, Will soon realized, a skillful interviewer, patient but methodical, demanding that he be precise about each detail, going back over episodes to ensure he had not missed anything. She pointed out contradictions too, in that old forensic way of hers. "Hold on, you said there was only you and two others in the room. Who is this new person?" "What did he say exactly? Did he say, 'I will' or 'I might'?"

Her precision exhausted him. By way of a break, he let his eyes wander toward her work, scattered around the room, large canvases depicting classic Americana—naturalistic paintings of a yellow cab or a vintage diner. Much as he admired their technical skill, he found himself wondering if TC was not in the wrong line of work. She had too clear a mind, too linear and logical, to be an artist. Surely with a brain like hers, she should be a scholar or a lawyer or, on current form, a police officer? Wisely, Will did not say any of this.

By the time he had got to the end, he realized TC had so far explained nothing. Each time she had opened her mouth, it was only to seek clarification from him or to ask supplementary questions. He knew no more now than he had when he left Crown Heights. He began to feel impatient. But he did not dare voice his frustration; he had to keep TC as an ally. Besides, he was nearly faint with fatigue; his words were starting to slur.

He woke when his elbow slipped off the chair arm. He could tell from the taste in his mouth that he had fallen into a brief but deep sleep. He had dreamed of chants and dances, with Beth at the center, surrounded, like a tribal queen, by men in white shirts and black suits.

Will looked at his watch; two-thirty a.m. So this was not a

nightmare, just a terrifying long day and night that seemed never to end. It had begun when he powered up his BlackBerry some eighteen hours ago. And now, incredibly, he was half-asleep in TC's wicker chair, and it was still going on.

"Hi, you're back," she said, suddenly looking up from an artist's sketchpad that rested on her knees. Her forehead was crinkled in a way, Will remembered, that meant she had been concentrating hard. "Here's what we've got. The first fact is, they say Beth is safe—so long as you back off. Second, they seem to admit that she's done nothing wrong and maybe even nothing at all, but they cannot let her go. They acknowledge that this seems baffling now, but they promise it will all become clear. We know from their e-mailed notes to you that they don't want money. They just want you to go away. That's it.

"What this adds up to is one very weird kind of kidnapping. It's like they somehow want to *borrow* her for some unspecified time and some unspecified reason—and they expect you just to take it. We need to work out why." Will found that *we* comforting, even if the rest of the puzzle—and the fact that TC had not instantly cracked it—was anything but.

"So what do we have on motive? A clue is surely that they feared you were a fed. The charitable explanation for that is that they feared the feds were coming after them simply because of the kidnapping. The uncharitable view is that their fear was separate from the kidnapping, that they are involved in some other criminal activity and had long worried that the authorities were onto them. Kind of like those weirdo cults who lie in wait for the feds to come and take their guns away."

Will had a flash of memory back to Montana, Pat Baxter and his chums. Christ, that was only a few days ago; it felt like years.

"But then they rule that out, for fairly rational reasons. I don't know about the wire, but I reckon they're right about the undercover Jew thing: that is what the feds would do. Yet, your not being a federal agent does not reassure them. Quite the opposite. It's once they've ruled that out that they get really heavy, nearly drowning you. That also makes some sense: they wouldn't dare mistreat you if they thought you were law enforcement. Once you weren't, they felt free. The question, though, is why? What could be, to use their phrase, 'infinitely worse'? A rival Hasidic sect? A rival kidnapping cartel?"

Will detected a glint of mischief in TC's eye, as if she was still taken by the humor of Hasidim up to no good. It irritated him; and she still had not come up with anything he did not know already.

"What about all the Jewish stuff I heard, what does that all mean?" He wanted to get her back on track.

"Well, the phrase you heard as 'Peking Nuff-said' is actually *pikuach nefesh*. The safeguarding of a soul. It is usually used benignly, to forgive various infractions of religious law in order to do good. You know, you'll hear the Israelis invoke *pikuach nefesh* to explain why ambulances are allowed to run on the Sabbath. But by mentioning it alongside all that stuff about a *rodef*, they were obviously using it to threaten you—to imply that Jewish law might allow them to kill you. Or Beth."

Will winced.

"As for '*shabbos* something,' that's real. What you heard was *shabbos shuva*, the Sabbath of repentance, the most important Shabbat of the year. That's today, as it happens. It's the one between Rosh Hashanah, the New Year, and Yom Kippur, the Day of Atonement. We're in the middle of the Ten Days of Penitence, the Days of Awe. This is a big time for Jews. For the ultra-Orthodox especially. But what did your questioner mean by 'we have only four days left'? It's true there are only four days till Yom Kippur, but, judging from what you said, he meant it as some kind of deadline. He can't mean just four days left to repent, though they would think that. This must be connected to the wider thing he mentioned: you know, 'everything hangs in the balance,' 'the stakes could not be higher,' 'the ancient story.' "

"And as far as all that stuff is concerned, we haven't got a clue, have we?"

TC had her head down, consulting her sketchpad. He could see she was desperate to find something that would unlock this mystery. She had corralled all the facts as best she could, organized a coherent set of questions. But that's all she had: questions. "No," she said quietly. "We haven't."

"What about the Rebbe?"

"Ah, yes. Now, I need you to think hard on this one. Did he ever say his name to you? Did he ever introduce himself to you?"

"I told you, he never let me see his face."

"So why are you so certain he was the Rebbe?"

"Because they were all chanting and stamping and waiting for him inside the synagogue. Then I get led away. These thugs say they can't talk to me until their 'teacher' arrives. Then, when he does, they do whatever he tells them to do. He was obviously the boss."

"When you were in the synagogue and you felt a hand on your shoulder, and the voice said, 'For you my friend, it's all over' or whatever he said, that voice was the same one who interrogated you later?"

"Yes, same voice."

"So if that was the Rebbe, how come the crowd was not facing in that direction, looking toward him? If that were him, surely every face in the room would have been looking just past your shoulder, going nuts for the guy who is within whispering distance of your ear. But they weren't, were they?"

"Maybe he was just hidden from view, crushed in that huge crowd."

"Come on, Will. You said it yourself: they worship this guy as if he's the Messiah. They're not going to just let him wander around, getting mashed by the foot soldiers. Think hard, did he ever announce himself as the Rebbe?"

Will realized with embarrassment that his tormentor had never said any such thing. Now that he thought about it—

"Did you ever address him as Rebbe?"

TC had read his mind. Throughout the ordeal, Will had assumed he was speaking to the Rebbe. Inside his own head, he referred to him as Rebbe. But had he ever used the term out loud?

"So you're sure that man who nearly had me killed tonight was not the Rebbe?"

"I know it."

"How? How can you be so certain?"

"I'm certain, Will, because the Rebbe of Crown Heights has been dead and buried for more than ten years."

CHAPTER TWENTY-ONE

SATURDAY, 6:36 A.M., MANHATTAN

THEY WERE IN A BAKING HOT COUNTRY, on a wide bed covered by a vast white net. It was a suite in an old colonial hotel. Sounds were floating up from the street below, car horns and traders; a mosquito buzzed lazily. It was the afternoon, and he and Beth were making fevered love, their bodies slick with sweat . . .

Will's heart thumped; the shock of waking from a dream. He looked down to see a bed that was narrow—and empty. Except it was not quite a bed. He had fallen asleep in TC's studio, on her red velvet sofa. It turned out she had a camp bed of her own behind a partition at the side of the studio. "Sometimes I work nights," she had said.

He reached instantly for his BlackBerry. Nothing more from the kidnappers; two e-mails from Harden; several from his father, begging him to get in touch and complaining of his desperate worry. His phone would not switch on: the battery must have died when he was at Tom's.

He tiptoed over to TC's workbench, where he was relieved to see she had the same brand of phone as him. There would be a charger here somewhere. While looking, he spotted the sketchpad from last night. He turned it the right way up and saw that TC had not been taking notes, but doing what seemed to be an elaborate doodle. It formed a geometric pattern: circles linked by straight lines, like one of those molecular diagrams. Was TC an expert in chemistry on the side? It would not have surprised him.

Seeing her Hebrew doodles brought back with a thud the night's biggest, and most baffling, revelation. The Rebbe was dead. Despite the pictures on every wall in Crown Heights, the Web sites covered with his face, the constant references to him in the present tense, the fervor aroused by the mere sight of his chair—despite all this, TC had been adamant that the Grand Rabbi of the Hasidic sect, the Rebbe, was deep in the ground.

He had died in his sleep a decade earlier, plunging his entire community and thousands of followers worldwide into abject grief. In the last years of his life, the belief had grown that the Rebbe was not just an extraordinary leader but something more. "Judaism holds that each generation includes one person who is the candidate to be the Messiah," TC had explained. "That doesn't mean he actually is the Messiah. But if God decided the time had come, that it was time for the messianic era to begin, then this person, this candidate, would be the one. He would be revealed as the Moshiach."

"And so they started thinking the Rebbe was the candidate?"

"Exactly. That's how it began. Just that he was the candidate for this age. But then things started getting more intense. People started saying this was not some remote, abstract possibility but that the messianic days were imminent, that the moment was approaching. Truth be told, I think the Rebbe encouraged it. He whipped up this fervor."

"What, was he on some major ego trip?"

"I don't know if it was that. He was an amazingly modest man in most ways. He lived frugally, in a few spartan rooms in Crown Heights. After his wife died, he confined himself to his study. He'd sleep in there, but only for an hour or two at night; the rest of the time, the light would be on and he'd be working, working, working. Dictating letters mostly; offering advice to his people all over the world. You've got to realize, this is a billion-dollar, global organization. They have centers in almost every city of the world, even in really obscure places where there are hardly any Jews, just in case there are Jewish travelers nearby who might feel the urge to have a Sabbath meal. He would tell one of his emissaries, 'You're needed in Greenland,' and they'd go to Greenland. The Rebbe was like a cross between the CEO of some huge multinational corporation and the commandant of a revolutionary army." TC grinned. "He was Bill Gates and Che Guevara, all rolled into one. And aged ninety-something."

Will thought back to the picture of the twinkling old man with the snow-white beard. An unlikely revolutionary.

"Anyway, then he died and most people assumed that would be the end of that. After all, he couldn't exactly be the Messiah if he was dead, could he?"

"I guess not."

"Well, you guess wrong. The hard-core devotees started camping out at the graveside. When people asked them what on earth they were doing, they said, 'Waiting.' They wanted to be ready to welcome the Rebbe when he rose from the dead."

"Are you sure these guys aren't Christians?"

"I know; it's weird, isn't it? There's some serious debate going on about that, in fact. There are plenty of Jews who say Crown Heights is effectively taking itself outside Judaism, that it is becoming another faith. The argument is that Christianity was once just a form of Judaism that believed the Messiah had come; now Crown Heights is making the same move."

"The difference is they're still waiting. Mind you, Christians are still waiting for the second coming. Everybody's waiting."

"This lot certainly are. They're waiting for their leader to reveal himself, for him to rise from the dead and tell them it's all going to be OK. Look, theologically speaking, they might be right. It is quite true that, in the messianic age, Judaism says the dead will live again. And there's nothing written that says the Messiah can't be one of them; you know, one of the dead. So they might be right. It's just, I don't know, it just seems kind of sad to me. Like this is a group of children who've lost their daddy or something. As the therapists would say, 'they're hurting.' "

Will tried to square TC's account—a cult traumatized by the loss of their leader, stirring themselves to a Friday-night fury as if desperately summoning him back from the dead—with the gang who had nearly killed him a few hours earlier. He found sympathy did not come easily. "How come you know so much about them?"

"I read the papers," she said quickly; an instant scold. "It's all been in the *Times*."

Will kicked himself. His haste at Tom's meant he never did the thorough Google search that would have told him all this—or at least that the Rebbe was dead. More galling was the certain knowledge that all this had, just as TC said, been in the paper but that he had skimmed over it: weirdo religious news, not relevant.

That was last night. This morning's thunderbolt came once he finally found the phone charger, near the coffee pot. He plugged it in, and his mobile came silently to life. (He always set his to silent: you never knew when a loud, synthetic chime would embarrass you.) The voice-mail messages declared themselves first: four from his dad, three increasingly sarcastic ones from Harden, the last saying, "You better be on a story so good that I win a Pulitzer for running it," before telling him he would be on "the first boat back to Oxford" if he did not report for duty soon. Two others that Will skipped after a few words, deeming them nonurgent.

Next came the texts. One from Tom, wishing him luck.

And then:

DON'T STOP, A FRIEND

He pressed the button marked "Details," but the phone yielded nothing. For number, it said "Withheld Private Caller": new software that allowed cell-phone users to keep their identity discreet. For the time, it uselessly gave the hour, minute, and second Will had switched on the phone. He had no idea who had sent it or when.

By now, TC was up, emerging from her mini-bedroom with a sleepy stretch. Even in man's-style boxer shorts and a thin-strapped white vest, she looked sumptuous. The navel ring was fully exposed now. Will felt a tremor of movement in his groin, followed by a thump of guilt. To lust after your ex-girlfriend was appalling under any circumstances. To do so when your wife was a hostage in fear for her life was contemptible. He gave TC only the merest acknowledgment, looked back at his cell phone, and reflexively tucked in his pelvis—as if to staunch the flow of erection-threatening blood before it passed the point of no return.

To his relief, TC kept some spare clothes behind that partition, and she now disappeared to put them on. When she emerged, Will handed her his phone. "Now this," he said.

TC fumbled for her glasses; it was too early for lenses. "Hmm," she said, staring at the words.

Will briefed her on his early lines of inquiry. "I reckon this must be from them, the Hasidim. They obviously got my number off the phone when they had my bag."

"No, they wouldn't have done that. It breaks Shabbat. And they wouldn't send a text message for the same reason. Both violate the Sabbath."

"What, and dunking an innocent man into freezing water is OK?"

"Technically, yes. They didn't use any electricity, any fire. They didn't write anything down, didn't use any machinery."

"So what they did to me was all perfectly kosher."

"Look, Will, don't give *me* a hard time. I don't make up these rules. All I'm saying is, they would only break the Sabbath if there was no alternative. So far they avoided that."

"But what about *pikuach nefesh*, you know, the saving-a-soul thing?"

"You're right. If they felt it was justified, they would do it. OK, so it could be them. It's strange, though. Not many people send text messages by phone like this."

"Brits do."

"Yeah, but most Americans don't. And it would have been just as easy to communicate by e-mail. But they didn't do that. Why not?"

"Because they know that we can trace their e-mails. They must know that I worked out where their last one came from."

"Sure, but that might not be a bad thing, from their point of view. They might want you to know it was a message from them. No, they chose a different method for a reason. Can you pass me your phone?"

She stared at it some more. Will could smell her hair and had to fight the urge not to breathe deeply: in an instant, her scent had carried him back to those long, hot afternoons together.

That in turn jogged another sense memory, the perfume of Beth. He liked it best when it was strongest: when she dressed up to go out for the evening. She might have got her outfit just right; he would want to rip it all off, to ravish her there and then. Later, at the party, he would spot her across the room and find himself looking at his watch: he wanted to get her back home. He was suddenly flooded with memories, of TC and of Beth, and they were arousing him. He felt confused.

"Don't stop, a friend." She began circling, staring at the floor. "Who would want to stiffen your resolve now? Who would think there was a chance you would give up?"

"The only people who even know about this are you, my father, Tom, and the Hasidim themselves."

"You're sure there's no one else? No one who's aware this is happening?"

With a stab, Will thought of Harden and the office: he would have to do something about that eventually.

"No. No one knows. And since neither you, nor Tom, nor my Dad need to contact me anonymously, that leaves the Hasidim themselves. I think we may have a bit of a split on our hands."

"What do you mean?"

Will enjoyed the novelty of TC being a pace behind him for once. Politics never was her strongest suit.

"A split. A split in the ranks of the enemy. The only person who could have sent this would be somebody who heard the Rebbe, I mean the rabbi I spoke to yesterday, telling me to back off. They must want me to ignore that advice. They must disagree with what the rabbi's doing. This person doesn't want me to stop. And I think I can guess who it is."

CHAPTER TWENTY-TWO

SATURDAY, 8:10 A.M., PORT-AU-PRINCE, HAITI

THESE DAYS HE CAME DOWN TO CHECK only once a week. The Secret Chamber now seemed to run itself, needing only the lightest supervision. These visits of his were less practical than sentimental: it gave him pleasure to see his little invention working so well.

He had designed things before, of course. Down at the docks, he had come up with a new roll-on, roll-off method for unloading the boats that came in from Latin America and went on to the United States. He had not planned it this way, but his new system was said to have revolutionized the country's drug trade. He had only been trying to improve the efficiency of import-export. But thanks to him, cocaine could come in from Colombia and be bound for Miami with the shortest possible turnaround. From there, and in a matter of hours, the parcels of white powder would spider out to America's cities—Chicago, Detroit, New York. Haiti's drug bosses boasted that if ten lines of coke were snorted into the nostrils of a U.S. citizen at any given moment, it was certain that at least one had passed through Port-au-Prince.

In his social circle, that gave Jean-Claude Paul prestige. Among the well-heeled dollar millionaires of Petionville, each in his armor-fenced, high-walled villa, no one fussed too much as to the ethical origins of one's wealth. That you could drive a Mercedes and send your wife to Paris to replenish her wardrobe and retint her high-lights was enough. When the Americans invaded in 1994, they called the mansion-dwellers of Petionville MREs—morally repugnant elites—and Jean-Claude was classed among them.

Maybe that was why his brain had come up with the Secret Chamber, as a way to make amends. He could not imagine where else the idea could have come from: it seemed to arrive in his head fully formed, nothing to do with him.

The chamber was, in fact, a single-story building, painted white. It looked like a glorified hut, no more noticeable than a bus shelter. Crucially, there were entrances on all four sides, which were open at all times.

The system was simple. At any moment, the rich could come in and leave money inside the chamber. And, also at any moment, the poor could come in and take what they needed.

The beauty of it was its anonymity. The doors operated on an automatic locking system that ensured only one person could be inside the chamber at any one time. That way a giver and a receiver were guaranteed never to meet. The wealthy would not know who had benefited from their largesse; the deprived would not know who had helped them. Port-au-Prince's well-off would not get the chance either to lord it over their beneficiaries or to judge them insufficiently needy. And the city's impoverished would be spared the sense of indebtedness that can make charity so humiliating.

The four doors were the finishing touch. It meant that there could never arise, not even informally, a givers' entrance or a receivers' entrance; it was too random for that. And so, if you saw someone walking in or out, you had no idea what kind of errand he was on.

There was only one more thing Jean-Claude had to do to make it work. He had to exploit a Haitian national trait, one that applied as much to the SUV drivers of Petionville as the searingly poor of Cité Soleil: superstition.

He spoke to the healers and voodoo priests whose writ ran among the MREs, slipping a few dollars to those with a knack for spreading the word. Before long the wealthiest folk in Port-au-Prince came to believe that they would be cursed if they did not visit the Secret Chamber and do the right thing.

So Jean-Claude smiled as he stood inside the chamber now, looking at a bowl filled with U.S. dollars as well as local currency and even the odd item of jewelry. Those outside assumed he was another visitor; his own role in setting up the chamber had remained unknown to all but the handful of holy men whose PR skills he had enlisted.

He was picking up a discarded food wrapper from the floor when the lights flickered and went off. With all four doors closed, the room was now in complete darkness. Jean-Claude silently cursed the electric company.

But it did not stay dark for long. Someone struck a match, just behind him. The power failure must have short-circuited the automatic locks, allowing this man to gain access.

"I'm sorry, sir. Only one at a time, that's the rule."

"I know the rule, M. Paul." The voice was unfamiliar; speaking French, not Creole.

"Well, perhaps I'll leave, and then you can do what you need to do."

"For that I need you here."

"No, no. It's all private and confidential, my friend. That's why we call this the Secret Chamber. It's secret."

The match had burned out now, shrouding the chamber once more in perfect black.

"Hello? Are you still here?"

There was no answer. Not a sound, in fact, until the gasp of

Jean-Claude's own breath as he felt two strong hands on his neck. He wanted to protest, to ask what he had done wrong, to explain that this man could take all the money he needed—there were no restrictions, no maximum. But the air would not come. He was rasping, a sandy, dry exhalation that barely sounded human. His leg was trembling, his hand clinging to the forearm of this man who was strangling him.

But it was no good; darkness came upon darkness. He slumped to the floor. The stranger lit a new match, crouched down, and closed the dead man's eyes. He murmured a short prayer, then straightened himself up and shook the dust off his clothes. He headed for the door he had used to come in, taking care to reconnect the circuit he had broken a few minutes earlier. And then he stepped out into the night, anonymous and unseen, just as Jean-Claude Paul had intended.

CHAPTER TWENTY-THREE

SATURDAY, 8:49 A.M., MANHATTAN

WHEN THEY TALKED IN THE NIGHT, TC had not been that interested in Yosef Yitzhok. She was focused on the rabbi and on everything that happened inside the classroom and later at the *mikve*. Now, though, she trained the full beam of her intellect on the encounter that had concluded Will's brief and unhappy stay at Crown Heights.

"You're wrong about one thing," she told Will rapidly. "It doesn't make sense for Yosef Yitzhok to have brought in the paper just to make the point that you work for the *New York Times*, and therefore they've got to be careful. They already knew you worked for the *Times*. They sent that very first e-mail to your *Times* address. That much they had worked out. So as soon as they realized you were not Tom Mitchell but were Will Monroe, they knew exactly who they were dealing with. Beth's husband. A reporter for the *Times*."

"So why did they have a copy of my story laid out? Why had Yosef thingy brought it in?"

"You don't know he brought it in. Might have been in there throughout."

"No, I definitely—" Will stopped himself. After the Rebbe fiasco, there was nothing he knew definitely. He thought he had heard the arrival of a new person in the room, the rustling of paper, and a row—but he had not seen that. He might have just got it wrong.

"So what did Yosef Yitzhok—we'll call him YY, it'll save time. What did YY say to you outside?"

"He apologized for what had happened inside. At the time I thought that was bullshit, and I ignored it. But maybe that was his way of telling me he disagreed with what was happening. Maybe he's a dissenter! Perhaps he can help. You know, from the inside."

"Will, I know you're stressed out, but we really have to keep it cool and calm. This is not the movies. Just tell me what he actually said."

"OK, so there's the apology. And then there's this stuff about my work. 'If you want to know what's going on, look to your work.' "

"Hmm." TC began pacing, stopping by a painting she had done of the Chrysler Building, apparently melting in the twilight rain. "So he's seen your story in the paper; he knows what you do. It's possible he didn't know that until that moment."

"I thought you said they knew the moment they e-mailed me."

"That's true. *They* knew. The rabbi and whichever one of his techie helpers sent you the e-mail knew. But this guy might not be inner circle. It may have been news to him."

"So it's possible that he was steaming in there, warning them that I was a reporter and could make trouble."

"It's possible. But something about it doesn't feel right. If he's in the room, he must be trusted enough to know what's going on. It must be something else. But OK, let's say you're right. He doesn't like what's happening, and so he breaks Shabbat to tell you urgently that you must not give up. And I suppose the thing he said to you last night—'look to your work'—is related. Perhaps he's telling you to do what you do in your work: to keep looking, keep asking questions."

"I reckon that's it. Don't stop, keep probing."

"Good. So that's what it is. OK." Will could see she was only partly persuaded. "What do you want to do now? Are you going to reply?"

Will had not even thought of that, but she was right. He should just hit reply—presuming the privacy software allowed him to—and send a message of his own and see what happens. *Who are you?* That might scare YY off. *What do you want me to do?* He needed to get this right. "What do you think?"

"I think I need some coffee." She flicked on the machine and, clearly out of habit, flicked on the radio at the same time. It was big, old-fashioned, and splattered with paint; a builder's radio. Except hers was not programmed to KROC or Kiss FM, but WNYC, New York's public radio station.

Will fell back into the sofa, willing himself to have a brainwave. He had to think of something that would end this ordeal. Beth had now spent a night as a captive. God only knew where she was, and in what kind of conditions. He had seen how hard these men could be, nearly freezing him into unconsciousness. What pain were they inflicting on Beth? What strange rules would allow them to hurt a woman who, they admitted, had done nothing wrong? He imagined how frightened she was. Think, he urged himself. Think! But he just stared at the cell phone, bearing its message of bland encouragement—*Don't stop*—and at the BlackBerry that had, so far, brought only bad news. One in each hand, they yielded nothing.

The radio was burbling with a signature tune, announcing the top of a new hour. Will looked at his watch: 9:00 a.m.

> *Good morning, this is Weekend Edition. The president promises a new initiative in the Middle East. The Southern Baptist Conference gets under way with a promise to make war on what it calls "Hollywood sleaze." And in London, more revelations on the scandal of the year . . .*

Will spaced out for most of it, but he caught the latest on Gavin Curtis. It turned out that the red-faced cleric Will had seen on TV the other night was right: Curtis *had* been siphoning off colossal amounts of public money. Not just millions, which would have made him fantastically rich, but hundreds of millions at a time. Apparently the money had been diverted into a numbered account in Zurich. The humble Chancellor Curtis, riding around the British capital in a modest sedan car, had made himself one of the richest men in the world.

In his current mood, Will found even this news depressing. It was confirmation on a grander scale of everything the last twenty-four hours had been saying. You could trust no one; everyone was up to no good. Then, as if to reproach himself, he thought of Howard Macrae and Pat Baxter. They had both done something good—but they were the exceptions.

"Will, listen."

TC had turned the volume all the way up. Will recognized the voice: WNYC's anchor, giving the local news.

Interpol has made a rare trip to Brooklyn this morning, with the mainly Hasidic neighborhood of Crown Heights the scene. Officials from the NYPD say they are working with police from Thailand on a murder inquiry. NYPD spokesperson Lisa Rodriguez says the case relates to the discovery in the Hasidic sect's Bangkok center of the body of a leading Thai businessman. He'd been missing for several days, believed kidnapped. The rabbi in charge of the Bangkok center is now under arrest, and the Thai authorities requested, via Interpol, that the NYPD investigate the world headquarters of the Hasidic movement, here in New York, to further their inquiries.

The weather: in Manhattan, another chilly day . . .

* * *

TC looked pale. "I need to get out of here," she said suddenly. She seemed choked, claustrophobic. She moved across the room, picking up essentials—purse, phone—until Will realized this was not a negotiation. They were leaving.

Watching her frightened him. There was no mistaking TC's reaction: she thought Beth had either been murdered or was about to be. He had not realized it, but TC's earlier calmness, almost insouciance, had been a comfort as well as an irritant. Now, with TC slamming the steel concertina door of the elevator after her, jabbing the buttons to make the damn thing go faster, he was robbed of that illusion. He felt his palms grow damp: while he had been dicking around playing amateur sleuth, his beloved Beth, his partner in life, might have been strangled or drowned or shot. . . . His eyes closed in dread. *More than yesterday, less than tomorrow.*

They were outside, TC grabbing him by the wrist, not so much walking alongside him as leading him, like a mother escorting a reluctant child to nursery school. "Where are we going?" he asked.

"We're going to play them at their own game. See how they like it."

They had only walked a couple of blocks when she strode into NetZone, an Internet café which actually served coffee. There were copies of the *New York Times*, including the Sunday magazine and Arts and Leisure section, traditionally released twenty-four hours in advance, piled up invitingly by the fashionably shabby armchairs. The Internet Hot Spot on Eastern Parkway felt very far away.

TC was not here to sip cappuccino. She was on a mission, first handing cash over and then planting Will at a free terminal.

"OK, log on."

Will suddenly remembered what going out with TC had been like. He had always felt as if he were somehow the junior partner, and she the person in charge. He used to think that was because she was the native New Yorker while he was the outsider, that he deferred to her because she knew her way around what was for him a foreign land. But he had been in America for six years now, and she was still at it. He realized TC was plain bossy. "Hold on," he said. "Let's talk about this first. What exactly are you suggesting I do?"

"Log on to your e-mail, and I'll show you."

"Why do we have to do this here? Why don't we just use the BlackBerry?"

"Because I can't think using my thumbs. Now come on. Log on."

He relented, typing in the string of letters that enabled *Times* staffers to access their e-mail remotely. Name, password, and he was in: his inbox. There were no surprises, just the same list of messages he had already seen on his BlackBerry.

"Where's the last message from the kidnappers?"

Will scrolled down until he found it, the string of garble in the "name" field and the subject: Beth. He opened it, seeing the unblinking words anew.

WE DO NOT WANT MONEY

The news from Thailand made this sentence look positively cruel. If it was not money they were after, what motivated them: the simple, sick pleasure of killing? Will could feel his blood rising in anger—and desperation.

"OK, hit reply."

Will did as he was told before TC nudged him aside and shared the seat with him, so that their bodies touched from their knees to their shoulders. She grabbed the keyboard and began two-finger typing furiously.

I am on to you. I know you must be guilty of what happened in Bangkok because I know you are doing the same here in New York. I plan to go to the police and tell them what I know. That will implicate you in at least two very serious crimes, to say nothing of your assault and false imprisonment of me. You have till nine pm tonight to give me my wife back. Otherwise I talk.

Will read the words twice over, stopping once to look at TC, whose face stayed fixed on the computer screen. Her profile was just inches away from his, a minute diamond stud sparkling in her nose. He had seen this face from this angle so many times before; it seemed strange not to be kissing it.

"Christ," he said eventually. "That's pretty strong." He wondered if it was too explicit, mentioning his treatment the previous night. He remembered a slew of recent trials, in the United States and in Britain, where journalists' e-mails had been produced. What would they make of this one, issuing direct threats and proposing obstruction of justice—and all from a *New York Times* address? *Fuck it*, was all he could think. His wife was in dire danger; anything was permitted. TC's note was sharp and hit the target directly. He was about to press send when something caught his eye.

"Why till nine pm? Why's that the deadline?"

"They might not read this till after the Sabbath is finished; we've got to give them time to reply."

The insanity of the situation had not faded with time. The notion of pious killers, happy to murder but queasy about turning on a computer before the appointed hour, was too bizarre for Will to get used to. TC had explained that the Sabbath did not officially conclude until a specific minute on Saturday evening. Nothing so imprecise as "sunset" or "once it's dark." It was 7:42 p.m. If you did not have a watch, you could check by looking outside your window: tradition held that once you could see three stars, you knew the Sabbath was over and the normal working week had resumed.

Will had no idea how the Hasidim would respond. TC had moved so fast, her desire for action meshing perfectly with his fury at the kidnappers who, he now knew, were capable of murder, that he had barely thought through the consequences of what they had just done. Surely these were strange, unpredictable people; who knew how they would react? Will's tone of angry defiance might push them over the edge: they could decide this was provocation enough to finish Beth off. They could kill her, and it would be his fault—for following the whim of, of all people, his ex-girlfriend. He imagined the pain of future years, learning to live with such a weight of guilt.

And yet, what had he got to lose? Playing nice had brought no results. He had to get their attention, force them to realize that there would be a price to pay for killing Beth. This e-mail told them they needed his silence—and that they should spare her life to buy it.

He pressed send. He had done something at last; he had made his move.

The urge to fall into one of the café's roomy armchairs was strong; Will was exhausted. But TC was already chivvying him to get up and out. She was not just edgy, Will realized; she was making a calculation. *Of course.* TC was worried that Will himself could be a target for the Hasidim. If she had had her initial doubts, now she was convinced: the men of Crown Heights were not to be messed around with. It was the news from Bangkok that had converted her. Once a skeptic, she was now a believer.

As they left, Will's mobile stirred. He waited till they were outside before he even looked at it: DadHome. Poor guy, he'd been calling for hours, and Will had not sent him so much as a text message.

"Hello?"

"Thank God for that. Oh, Will, I've been worried sick."

"I'm fine. I'm exhausted, but I'm OK."

"What the hell's been happening? I've wanted so much to call the police, but didn't dare until you and I at least had a chance to talk. Really, Will, I was this close—but I held off. It's such a relief to hear your voice."

"You haven't told anyone, have you? Dad?"

"Of course I haven't. But I've wanted to. Just tell me, have you heard from Beth?"

"No. But I know where she is, and I know who's got her."

TC was gesturing at Will's phone, then wagging her finger across her face like a schoolmistress. Will got the message.

"Dad, maybe we should talk about this when I'm on a landline. Can I call you later?"

"No, you have to tell me now! I'm going out of my mind here. Where is she?"

"She's in New York. She's in Brooklyn."

Will instantly regretted his revelation. Cell phones were notoriously leaky: he knew that much from the scanners on the Metro desk, where police radio transmissions were easier to get than NPR. For those who knew how, plucking cellular calls out of the air was a breeze.

"But, Dad, I'm serious. There can be no vigilante rescue attempts here. No calls to the police commissioner who you knew at Yale. I mean it: that would truly fuck everything up and could cost Beth her life." His voice was wobbling. Will could not tell if he was about to scream at his father or break down and cry. "Promise me, Dad. You're not going to do anything. Promise."

His father gave a reply but Will could not hear it. A word went missing, drowned out by the sound of a beep on the line.

"OK, Dad, I'm going to say good-bye. We'll speak later." There was no time for niceties; he needed his father off the line so he could take this incoming call.

Will pressed the buttons as fast as he could, his thumbs trembling with tiredness, but there was no call. The beep he had heard had announced instead the arrival of a text message.

Will could feel TC leaning on his upper arm, straining to see his phone as they stood together on the street.

"Read message?" the phone asked dumbly. *Of course I want to read it, idiot!* Will hit the Yes button, but found the keypad was

locked. Damn. More buttons to press, forcing him to go the long way around, choosing text messages, then his inbox, then a long wait while the display promised that it was "opening folder." Finally, the message appeared: five words, short, simple—and utterly mysterious.

CHAPTER TWENTY-FOUR

SATURDAY, 11:37 A.M., MANHATTAN

TWO DOWN. MORE'S TO COME.

IT TOOK TC TO BREAK THE SILENCE. "Listen, I'm cold." They were still standing on the street. "There." She pointed at a McDonald's.

With a bacon breakfast bun in one hand and a pencil in the other, she began doodling. "Let's think this through," she said. "What did you say in your reply to him?" Will, his mouth now full, froze just as his hands were about to claw a clump of fries. "I didn't."

"Sorry?"

"I meant to. I was about to. But then we heard the news from Bangkok, and everything got forgotten."

Will was almost waiting for TC to pick him up on that lapse into what she used to call the cowardly passive. "Everything got forgotten" was the cowardly way of saying that Will himself had forgotten. (TC coined the term in honor of an old roommate who, despairing at the state of the kitchen they shared, but too meek to accuse TC directly, announced, "Dishes have been left." Hence, and thereafter, the cowardly passive.)

"Well, that makes this even more intriguing," TC said, letting Will off despite his error. "It's not a reply. It's a second message, sent voluntarily. It suggests Yosef Yitzhok felt a degree of urgency: two messages in one morning."

"The first one could have been last night. But, OK. Why would this be urgent? I think he's playing games with us," said Will. "Right, 'you've deciphered two of my messages; I'll send more.' So long as we do . . . what?"

"We need to let him know we understand, but we need more information. We don't want to piss him off. If he's trying to help, we need to keep him happy. Send another message back."

Will took the phone, glancing up at TC with eyes that said, I hope you're right about this.

Thank you. I won't stop. And I want to hear more. Can you tell me anything? Please.

All they could do now was wait. TC was convinced that McDonald's made a sufficiently anonymous hiding place. Will suspected there was another motive: TC did not want Will in her home. It was one thing having him in her studio, sleeping on her couch; but to see him in her own apartment, that would be an intimacy too far. He understood that; in a way, he shared her fear.

But they had to wait somewhere. If the Hasidim were not going to reply till sundown, or when the three stars appeared, or whatever way these jokers had of telling the time, there was nothing else to do—save waiting for Yosef Yitzhok to give them another tantalizing veiled message.

It came nearly an hour later. As he read it, Will felt his stomach churn. TC was craning to look, and once she saw it, she gasped.

YET MORE DEATHS SOON

CHAPTER TWENTY-FIVE

SATURDAY, 11:53 A.M., MANHATTAN

EVERYONE WAS EITHER STARING AT THEM directly or pretending not to look. TC was attempting to calm Will, who had just pounded the table and then thrown a cup of coffee at the wall. A cleaner had appeared with a mop.

"We've got to try and think straight," TC was saying.

"How can I think straight? It's a fucking death threat."

"He might be trying to warn us."

"Warn us? He's saying they're going to kill Beth." Will looked up, his eyes red.

The phone buzzed again. TC grabbed it first, before Will had a chance. For the first time, a straight sentence.

He who hesitates is lost

TC looked at it for only a second before trying out the text alternative. It made no sense. No, she concluded, this was a different kind of clue. Maybe it was not even a clue. Perhaps it was merely a warning. Hurry, there is no time to waste. She turned the display to Will for his inspection. It somehow calmed him: there was no direct menace here. It sounded more like a call to action.

TC peered at it a while, then wrote it down on the top page of her sketchpad, just below the first three messages. Will saw that she had neatly written the first, coded version on the left and then the second, deciphered one on the right. For an instant, Will imagined TC at school: the kind of girl who always kept a clean, well-stocked pencil case.

While TC chewed her pen and did her best to stare the latest riddle into submission, Will tried to while away the afternoon. He picked at junk food, bit his nails, drummed his fingers on the table; tried reading the paper but could not concentrate. He could hear a couple arguing. "I don't believe you," the woman was saying to the man. The instant he heard the words, he sat bolt upright, remembering that night in the Salonike diner. Beth had said a beautiful sentence to him without irony, even if he had tried to pierce the moment with a joke. "I believe in you and me," she had said. He suddenly wished he had repeated the words back to Beth. For it was true. She was his faith.

The cell phone beeped.

He that knows nothing doubts nothing

This time Will read it out loud. He knew the answer to his next question, but he asked it anyway: "Did you work out the first one, *He who hesitates is lost*?"

"Not yet. *He that knows nothing doubts nothing*. What could that mean?" TC was penciling the words down in the corner of a page already covered with drawings.

"I don't get it," Will said, chiefly for the sake of saying something. "It's a contradiction. In the first message, he's telling us not to hesitate. Just to get on with it. Now he's saying that it's good to doubt. You know, only a moron doesn't experience doubt."

"Doubting's not the same as hesitating."

"What's the difference?"

"I don't fucking know. I'm trying to think. He wants to tell us something. You know, *Move it.* Or *Think things through.* I don't know. But he sounds like he wants to help."

"No. If he was trying to help, he wouldn't be talking in fucking riddles." Another beep.

OPPORTUNITY SELDOM KNOCKS TWICE.

As soon as Will read it out, TC began murmuring, "Twice is interesting. Perhaps he's telling us to multiply something. Maybe we're looking at this all wrong. Maybe he wants us to look at the letters as numbers!"

"What?"

"You know, text messages are letters and words formed from numbers. Maybe this is the reverse. We're meant to take the letters and think of them as numbers."

"What are you talking about?"

"Well, one thing could be to count the number of letters in each clue. That number could be significant. Or perhaps each letter has a numeric value. You know, A is one, B is two."

Will was baffled, but TC was ignoring him. She was scribbling away frantically on her sketchpad, wildly computing one sum after another.

More beeping; perhaps a minute after the previous one.

A friend in need is a friend indeed

Will was becoming more irritated with each message. If this was help, why did it have to be so damned opaque? Will felt like shaking young Yosef Yitzhok by his lapels: *If you want to help, then just help!* "What is this, Cliché Night? *A friend in need is a friend indeed.* What the hell is that? How on earth does he expect us to solve these so fast?"

"Look, cool down Will. Right now this is all we have. *He's* all we have. Maybe he's suddenly in a place where he can text without being seen; he might want to get all his messages out while he can."

It was plausible; Will bit his lip. He did not want to set off a whole row with TC now, not while she was concentrating so hard on her role as unofficial cryptographer.

Will began to pace around, letting his pores fill up with the fat and grease of a burger joint—which this place was, even if it did now sell salads. He strode into a seating area where a single TV monitor was playing. Set to NY1, the local news channel, it now flashed pictures of the Bangkok arrest of a Brooklyn rabbi on murder charges. The suspect was in the trademark garb—beard, white shirt, black suit, trilby hat—as he was handcuffed and led away by two young, scowling Thai policemen. His face seemed to be determinedly aimed downward, in shame or to avoid recognition, Will could not tell. Altogether, the sight could not have been more incongruous. That sequence was followed by footage of NYPD officers arriving on foot in Crown Heights, eschewing their usual squad cars in a gesture of "sensitivity" apparently ordered by the mayor's office.

Those pictures renewed an argument Will and TC staged several times that long afternoon.

"I should go back there, right now."

"And do what? Get dunked again?"

"No. I would tell them what I, what you, wrote in that e-mail. That I know what they're up to and that they should cut a deal."

"Too risky. You might say just the wrong thing and escalate the whole situation. The virtue of e-mail was that we could control exactly what was said." Was said, the cowardly passive again. TC was obviously reluctant to admit that she had put those words in Will's mouth.

"I can't just leave Beth there. Who knows what they might do now that they're under siege? They might panic. One of those thugs could tighten the screw a bit too hard, or keep her head in water ten seconds too long—"

"You're doing it again. Getting into a panic. I told you, this is like climbing a mountain: you mustn't look down. You mustn't think about any of that. Besides, the place is crawling with police today: they wouldn't dare do anything while they're around. The whole vibe of those text messages from Yosef Yitzhok is that everything's still to play for. Nothing has changed, nothing terrible has happened."

"Except you don't think they're from Yosef Yitzhok."

"I'm not sure, that's all."

That's how it went, several times over, ending inconclusively with both TC and Will falling into a sullen or drained silence. Afterward, Will would reflect on the fact that Beth and he never bickered. They argued but never bickered; he and TC had turned it into an Olympic sport.

Interruption came whenever a message landed. These texts, which once made Will's chest pound with nervous anticipation, were becoming routine. Even boring. Will clicked to see the latest.

To the victor the spoils

That sounded menacing, as if the Hasidim were registering a claim on Beth: *If we win, we will keep her.* Will felt his hatred rising. "Now they're threatening us."

"To the victor the spoils," TC repeated slowly once Will had read it out, as if she were taking dictation.

Will glimpsed what looked like a grid on TC's sketchpad, neatly filled in with each new line from YY. "What have you got?"

"The numbers thing didn't work out, so I've been looking at anagrams for each one. And I can get something, but nothing that hangs together. There's no pattern. I've tried running it as an acrostic—"

"A what?"

"An acrostic. Where the first letter of each sentence provides a letter of the hidden word. You know, 'Roses are red' gives you R, 'Violets are blue' gives you V. There are some psalms laid out like that. Put together the first letter of each line, and you get another line of prayer. It was a trick: a twelve-line poem with an invisible thirteenth line."

"I get it. So what do we get if we do that?"

"So far? We have H, H, O, A, T. If we skip the indefinite article—so it's 'Friend in need,' not 'A friend in need'—we get H, H, O, F, T. Not much better."

"What the hell is he playing at? Hang on." Another one was coming through.

Goodness is better than beauty

Will was beginning to feel swamped. TC was having to think like a grandmaster at one of those chess exhibitions, moving around the room, playing a hundred games on a hundred different boards at once. It had taken a long time to decode just one message. Now she had six.

"Look, Will. There's no way to work out what this is till it stops. Whenever I try one theory, it's blown out by the next message. We need to have the full set and then see what this guy's trying to say."

"YY."

"If it's him, yes."

"Who the fuck else could it be?"

"Leave me alone, Will."

He couldn't blame her for being exasperated. He knew he was being insufferable, taking out his rage, grief, and sheer fatigue on her. She didn't have to take this from him. She could walk away—and he would be stranded.

He wanted to say sorry, but it was too late. She had turned her back on him, wisely preventing any escalation in hostilities. Pity neither of them had ever been so shrewd when they were lovers.

No more than two minutes later, another message arrived:

A man is known by the company he keeps

Was this some way of urging Will to think about the people around the rabbi who had interrogated him last night? Forget about him, start thinking about his henchmen. Was that what this clue was trying to say?

And then, perhaps thirty seconds later:

From little acorns, mighty oaks grow

Christ, this guy was annoying. What was this, some oblique reference to fathers and sons? The effort he was putting into these messages, hammering out long texts when all he had to do was send a few simple words: the address where Beth was held. The ire was rising through Will's body, reaching the veins in his neck.

He had not even shown TC the latest message when he began texting back:

Enough of these horseshit games. You know what I need.

The instant he had sent it, Will regretted it. What if he scared Yosef Yitzhok off? TC was right: he was all they had. Worse, what if Will's message was somehow intercepted by the Crown Heights hardliners, who would instantly realize what YY was up to, that he was in communication with the enemy, and punish him? Will imagined YY in an alleyway just off Eastern Parkway, huddled over his cell phone, maybe using his prayer shawl as a canopy, when two men grab him from behind, snatch away his phone, and drag him off for an impromptu meeting with the rabbi.

And yet Will felt a release of cathartic energy flow through him. He could not stand the passivity of his situation, sitting there, hands outstretched, waiting for clues to fall like crumbs from the Hasidim's table. It felt good to fight back.

Finally the sky began to darken. Will started pacing, his right hand gripping the BlackBerry, turning it clammy. At 7:42 p.m.

exactly TC nodded, telling him that the Sabbath had now ended. Will glanced down immediately, expecting a red light to flicker on within seconds. No, no, advised TC: they should give it at least thirty minutes before expecting a reply. There were things to do after the Sabbath, including the Havdalah ceremony that uses wine, spices, and a braided candle to bid a final farewell to the day of rest. Then there was the walk back from synagogue to make Havdalah at home. Most men would probably want to freshen up after that. Even if the Hasidim read Will's message on a computer in a home or office, they would not want to reply from there: too traceable. Not by Will of course, but by the police in some future investigation. So they would have to go back to the Internet Hot Spot—all of which could take at least an hour. Even this scenario was optimistic, TC warned. Will knew he had sent them an e-mail, but they did not. They were not expecting one, so why would they rush to check?

On the other hand, maybe today was different. Crown Heights was crawling with detectives investigating a murder under instruction from Interpol. The rabbi who had grilled Will would not be able to stick to his usual ritual. He would be answering questions, and they would not be about the correct dimensions of a Talmudic stove. He would be under interrogation—and under pressure. (The thought of that role reversal pleased Will.) If that was the atmosphere, Will reckoned they would have a hundred reasons to check e-mail as soon as they could. Even if they were not waiting for word from him, they would need to communicate with their people in Bangkok. Will guessed they would be powering up their laptops the moment it was theologically decent.

At eight o'clock Will's hunch was confirmed. Twenty minutes after sundown, the red light on his BlackBerry blinked. Will clicked the track wheel and saw that same, hieroglyphic script, the characters he now knew to be Hebrew. Re: *Beth*.

You are out of your depth. Do not drown.

CHAPTER TWENTY-SIX

SATURDAY, 8:01 P.M., MANHATTAN

HE HAD NO TIME FOR A SEMINAR with TC. He replied instantly, his thumbs working furiously.

I could call the police right now. What do I have to lose?

He waited, while TC sat opposite him, curled into a ball, rocking herself backward and forward. Will wondered if he had ever seen her in this position, so nervous she was fetal. The crowd at McDonald's had changed, the bums and homeless mutterers now mostly replaced by twenty-something men about to fuel up before a night hitting the bars. The red light came on.

You have everything to lose. You could lose her.

Again, Will did not wait. This, he realized, was what he had wanted since that first message: a direct confrontation with the kidnappers. When they had met last night, Will was pretending to be someone else. He had had to be polite. Now it was out in the open, he could take them on.

You touch her, and you'll be guilty of two murders. My evidence will send you down. Release her, or I start nailing you.

The delay was longer this time, excruciating. The red light flashed, Will pouncing on the little blue machine.

Low price pharmacy for all your medical needs. We deliver.

Spam.

More minutes and then:

Call now on 718-943-7770. Do not use a recording device. We will know if you try.

Will imagined how this was working at the other end. Doubtless, one of the monkeys, Moshe Menachem or Tzvi Yehuda, was at the Internet Hot Spot, reading and typing the e-mails, taking direct instruction from the boss on the end of a phone. Now the boss had something to say that he did not want committed to e-mail, even one as disguised as this. Good, thought Will, sensing his opponent was weakening a little. He looked at TC: having consumed her nails, she was now gnawing at her cuticles.

He pulled out his cell phone, dialing the number slowly, as if he was performing surgery. His hands were trembling. He realized that this man frightened him.

It rang only once. He could hear the phone had been answered, but no one spoke: he was going to have to make the first move.

"This is Will Monroe. You asked me to call."

"Yes, Will, I did. First, let me apologize for what happened yesterday. A bad case of mistaken identity, partly compounded by the fact that you made the mistake of concealing your identity." Will wondered if he was meant to laugh at this little bit of wordplay. He did not. "I think it's right that we talk about the current situation."

"You're damn right we need to talk about it. You need to give me back my wife, or else I will implicate you in a double murder."

"Now calm down, Mr. Monroe."

"I'm not feeling very calm, Rabbi. Yesterday you nearly killed me, and you have abducted my wife for no reason. The only reason I have not gone to the police so far is because of your threats to kill my wife. But now I can go to them and confirm your guilt in the Bangkok case by saying you have already performed a kidnapping right here in New York City. If you kill her then, that will only compound your guilt." Will was pleased with how that had come out; it was more coherent than he had expected.

"All right, I am going to make a deal with you. If you say nothing and talk to no one, we will do our best to keep Beth alive." *Beth.* It sounded strange coming from this baritone voice, whose timbre had only barely altered in the metallic compression of the phone.

"What do you mean, 'do our best'? Who else is there? You've done this, you should take responsibility for it. Either you will guarantee her safety, or you won't." That sentence, unplanned, prompted a thought, one he voiced out loud before it was fully formed in his own mind. "I want to speak to my wife."

"I'm sorry."

"I want to speak to her right now. I want to hear her voice. As proof that she is still . . . safe."

"I don't think that's a good idea."

"I don't care what you think. As I'm only too happy to explain to the police. I want to hear her voice."

"That will take some time."

"I'm calling you back in five minutes."

Will put the phone down and exhaled as if he had been holding his breath; the blood seemed to be pounding through his veins. His own firmness had taken him by surprise. And yet it had seemed to work; the rabbi had not refused.

Will counted the minutes, staring at the second hand as it swept across the face of his watch. TC could say nothing.

A minute passed, then two. Will felt an ache in his forehead; the muscles of his face had been tensed so long, they hurt. The top of the plastic pen he had been chewing came apart in his mouth.

Four minutes gone. Will stood up and stretched, tilting his head toward one shoulder, then the next. It made a loud crack. He looked down at the phone and, four minutes and fifty-five seconds after he had hung up, he redialed the number.

"It's Will Monroe. Let me speak to her."

There was no reply, just a series of clicking sounds, as if his call were being transferred. The sound of breath and then: "Will? Will, it's Beth—"

"Beth, thank God it's you. Oh, my love, are you OK? Are you hurt?"

Silence, and then three more clicks. "Beth?"

"I'm afraid I had to cut off the line. But now you have heard her voice; you know she is—"

"For God's sake, you barely gave us a second." Will smashed the table with his fist, making TC leap back in fright. He felt himself flood with emotion. For less than a second he had felt such relief, such joy: it was Beth's voice, no mistaking it. Just the sound of it made him weak. And then it had disappeared, cut short before he had even had a chance to tell her he loved her.

"I couldn't risk any more time. I'm genuinely sorry. But I did what you asked: you have heard your wife's voice."

"You have to promise me NOW that nothing is going to happen to her."

"I tried to explain this to you last night, Will. This is not entirely in our hands, not in mine, not in yours. Much bigger forces are in play. This is something mankind has feared for millennia."

"What the hell are you talking about?"

"I cannot blame you for not understanding. Not many would,

which is why we cannot explain this to the police, much as all of us might like to. They would certainly not understand. For some reason, HaShem has left this in our hands to resolve."

"How do I know you're not tricking me to stay quiet? How do I know that you don't plan to kill my wife the way you killed that man in Bangkok?"

A pause. Then: "Ah, nothing grieves me more than what happened there. Every Jewish heart will cry out in despair at the pity of what happened there." He paused again. Will let the silence hang. Wait for the interviewee to fill the void . . . "I am going to take a risk, Mr. Monroe. I hope you take it as it is meant, as a gesture of good faith on my part. I am going to let you into a secret that you could easily use against me. By revealing it to you, I will be showing a degree of trust in you. As a result, I hope you will feel better able to trust me. Do you understand?"

"I understand."

"What happened in Bangkok was an accident. It is true that we wanted to take Mr. Samak into custody, just as we have with your wife, but we certainly had no intention of killing him. God forbid." TC had moved around to sit next to Will, pressing her ear against the back of his cell phone.

"What we did not know, what we could not have known, was that Mr. Samak had a weak heart. Such a strong man, but a terribly weak heart. The . . . steps we had to take to bring him into custody were, I'm afraid, more than he could take."

For a brief moment, Will thought like a journalist: he had wrung a confession from this man. Not of murder, perhaps, but of manslaughter. In a spasm of professional pride, Will guessed that, despite hours of intense questioning, New York's finest had not yet achieved quite so good a result.

"That is what happened, Mr. Monroe, and though it will amaze you to hear it, I have only told you the truth in all our encounters so far. I repeat that I have taken a great risk in speaking so candidly. But something tells me you will take my gesture the right way, and you will not spurn me. I have trusted you, and now, I hope, you will trust me. Do it for your own reasons, Will. Do it because I have told you that I will do my best to keep your wife alive. But do it also because of what I told you yesterday and repeat again today: that an ancient story is unfolding here, threatening an outcome mankind has feared for thousands of years. Your wife matters to you, Mr. Monroe, of course she does. But the world, the creation of the Almighty, matters to me."

Now the rabbi was leaving the silence, waiting for Will to fill it. He knew what was happening, but he could not help himself.

"What are you asking me to do?"

"To do nothing, Mr. Monroe. Nothing at all. Just to stay out of this and to be patient. There are perhaps a couple of days left, and then we will all know our fates. So even though you are desperate to see Beth again, I urge you to wait. No meddling, no amateur detective work. Just wait. I hope you will do what's right, Will. Good night. And may God turn his face to shine upon all of us."

The phone clicked off. Will looked at TC, who seemed to be trembling with him.

"It's so strange to hear his voice," she was saying, in little more than a whisper. "After we've talked about him so much, I mean."

Will had scribbled the odd note while the rabbi was talking so that he and TC could deconstruct his meaning. But it was the tone that was most striking. If Will was briefing Harden on the conversation he had just had, that would be his headline. The rabbi had sounded conciliatory but something else, too—almost regretful.

The silence was not allowed to last. The cell phone had another text to disgorge.

A chain is no stronger than its weakest link

And then, a moment later:

Safety in numbers. No more.

Will read them out, pausing as TC demanded clarification of

the location of the period in that sentence. There were two full stops, Will replied. Was he sure? He was sure. He was having trouble concentrating. He was hearing Beth's voice, over and over: *Will? Will, it's Beth.*

"OK," TC was saying. "Let's assume that he means what he says, that there will be no more. This is the full set."

In front of her, laid out on the table, were ten neat squares of paper, one message written on each.

He who hesitates is lost
He that knows nothing doubts nothing
Opportunity seldom knocks twice
A friend in need is a friend indeed
To the victor the spoils
Goodness is better than beauty
A man is known by the company he keeps
From little acorns, mighty oaks grow
A chain is no stronger than its weakest link
Safety in numbers. No more.

TC was glaring at them, her sketchbook on her lap, surveying the pattern she had arranged. The messages were in three groups. Encouragement, warnings, enigmas.

TC now laid the pad onto the table, alongside the scraps of paper. It was almost dark with ink: she had filled the page. All over it were words or half-phrases crossed out, written backward or in diagonals. She had written out the messages in every possible order, each time underlining the first letter of each line: attempting the acrostic. Will could see the results: HHOATGAFAS followed by a list of random variations using the same letters. All of them spelled gibberish.

As if reading his mind, TC turned the page of her sketchbook to show the one underneath, its surface no less covered with calculations and abortive anagrams. She peeled that away to show the one below and the one below that. She had been breaking her head to solve this puzzle for hours.

Will felt a surge of gratitude: he knew how lonely he would have been without her. But there was no getting away from it. Despite all her efforts, despite their combined intellect, they still had not cracked this riddle in ten parts. It had defeated them.

"I can't believe I am that dumb."

"What?" Will looked up from the table to see TC leaning back in her chair, hands on her head and eyes fixed on the ceiling.

"I cannot believe I am so stupid." She was smiling, shaking her head in disbelief.

"Please tell me precisely what you're talking about," Will said, in a voice that even he recognized as excessively polite and English, a voice he often used when trying to stay calm.

"It was so obvious, and I made it so complicated. How many hours have I spent on this thing now?"

"You mean, you've worked it out?"

"I've worked it out. What has he sent us? 'A friend in need.' 'From little acorns.' He's sent us proverbs. Ten proverbs."

"Right, so . . . Sorry, you're going to have to tell me. I can see he's sent us ten proverbs. The trouble is, we don't know what they mean."

"They don't mean anything. They're not meant to mean anything. He's sent us ten proverbs. Because that's where we're meant to look. Proverbs 10."

CHAPTER TWENTY-SEVEN

SATURDAY, 8:27 P.M., MANHATTAN

HE HAD BEEN THERE AS LONG as they had, and had been muttering just as loudly. He was on his own, middle-aged and no doubt homeless, with a face that seemed swollen through exposure to the elements. In the course of the afternoon Will had seen him eat half an apple pie, handed to him by a guy wearing an iPod (who did not take the earphones out), and perhaps a bag and a half of fries; and at intervals he had read aloud from the plastic-bound black Bible he held in his right hand.

Will had found these random sermons an irritation during the afternoon, as had the succession of customers who took pains not to sit too near. Now, though, he could not have been more grateful. With a hot cup of coffee in his hand, he approached gingerly.

"Sir, I wonder if perhaps you'd like a cup of coffee. It's freshly made."

The man looked up, his eyes watery. The whites were yellow.

"If it had not been the Lord who was on our side—let Israel now say—if it had not been the Lord who was on our side, when our enemies attacked us, then they would have swallowed us up alive, when their anger was kindled against us—"

"Yes, sir, I'm sure that's quite right," Will tried, in the short moment the man drew breath. But it was no good; he was off again.

"Then the flood would have swept us away, the torrent would have gone over us; then over us would have gone the raging waters."

"Sir, I'm sorry to trouble you, but I wondered if I could borrow your Bible."

"Blessed be the Lord, who has not given us as prey to their teeth. We have escaped like a bird from the snare of the fowlers; the snare is broken, and we have escaped."

"That's truly what I pray for, too, sir. But if I could just take a peek at your Bible." Will bent down and tried to take the book from the man's hand, but his grip was surprisingly strong. He would not let go.

"Our help is in the name of the Lord, who made heaven and earth."

"Yes, yes, that's what I think too. So if you'd just let me glance at the holy book." The man's hand gnarled itself even more tightly. Will tugged, but the man tugged back, still muttering.

Will looked up; TC had arrived. By now he was almost sitting next to the tramp, pulling horizontally at the book. He knew he looked ridiculous: he was mugging a tramp for his Bible.

"Sir," TC said softly. "Do you think we could pray together?" Suddenly the man stopped talking. TC continued, her voice a gentle stream of pure reason. "Can I suggest we take as our text the book of Proverbs, chapter 10?"

Without complaint, the man opened up the book, thumbing through its tissue-thin, closely printed pages. Within a few seconds, he began his recitation: "The proverbs of Solomon. A wise son maketh a glad father: but a foolish son is the heaviness of his mother."

Will tried to peer over his shoulder, to skim the rest of the ancient text at top speed. To him, it looked like the usual biblical mix of profundity and obscurity. Scripture always had this effect on him: the words might make stirring music, but their precise meaning only ever became clear through great effort. Most of the time, in church or at morning prayers at school, the sounds just washed over him. As they did now, in this odd, spontaneous prayer meeting.

Their leader was onto verse 2: "Treasures of wickedness profit nothing: but righteousness delivereth from death."

Eyes down, Will was racing ahead. Confronted now with verse after verse of the stuff, he found his eye lighting upon anything either immediately intelligible or, better still, familiar. One word stood out, again and again. It had appeared in verse 2 and was there again in verse 3. *The Lord will not suffer the soul of the righteous to famish: but he casteth away the substance of the wicked.*

And again in verse 11. *The mouth of a righteous man is a well of life: but violence covereth the mouth of the wicked.*

And in verse 16. *The labour of the righteous tendeth to life: the fruit of the wicked to sin.*

Verse 21 had it too. *The lips of the righteous feed many: but fools die for want of wisdom.*

Wherever Will looked, the word seemed to jump off the page. In his sleep-deprived state, he could almost hear voices, angry male voices, shouting the word at him. There it was again, in verse 24. *The fear of the wicked, it shall come upon him: but the desire of the righteous shall be granted.*

Listening to the rambling murmur of the homeless man, he pictured the rabbi of Crown Heights swaying as he read verse 25, his bearded disciples swaying along with him. *As the whirlwind passeth, so is the wicked no more: but the righteous is an everlasting foundation.*

The word refused to let go. Verse 28 had it—*The hope of the righteous shall be gladness: but the expectation of the wicked shall perish*—and so did verse 30: *The righteous shall never be removed: but the wicked shall not inhabit the earth.*

It was even there at the very end, in the final verse. *The lips of the righteous know what is acceptable: but the mouth of the wicked speaketh perversity.*

The tramp now had his eyes shut, incanting the words from memory. But Will had heard enough. He stood up and moved around, so he could whisper in TC's ear.

"I'm going."

He knew they could have discussed it for hours, parsing every clause for multiple meanings like a pair of the sharpest Talmudic scholars. But sometimes you just have to go with your first instinct. Journalism was like that. You would be at a press conference, handed some voluminous document, and somehow you would have to whip through it in five minutes, decide what it was all about, ask your question, and go. In truth, the document could not be read properly in less than four or five hours, but journalists liked to think such strictures were for lesser mortals.

So Will trusted his judgment. Besides, he was sick of talking, deciphering, and interpreting. He wanted to move, to go somewhere. He had been inside for hours, inhaling air made sweet and sickly by fast food.

He had heard what he needed to hear. He knew exactly where he had to go—and he knew he would have to go there alone.

CHAPTER TWENTY-EIGHT

SATURDAY, 9:50 P.M., MANHATTAN

A LONG LINE OF ELEVATORS, maybe ten of them, and barely a soul to elevate. All big offices were probably like this on the weekends: still functioning, still with a guard at the front desk and lights on in the canteen, but skeletal versions of their weekday selves.

The lobby of the *New York Times* building looked especially bereft. On Monday at 10:00 a.m., this space would be jammed, as circulation managers jostled with graphic designers to cram into elevators, half of them clutching steaming cups of overpriced coffee. Now the same space was empty and silent, with only the rarest *ping* to announce that an elevator had moved up a few floors and come back home again.

Will nodded a hello to the guard on duty, who gave him the merest glance. He was watching a ball game on a TV monitor that Will was sure was supposed to be turned to closed-circuit pictures of the fire escape or rear entrance or something. Will swiped his card and headed to the newsroom.

He was glad to be here. He had not worked at the *Times* for long, but this office felt familiar. And he could not face going home. Just the thought of closing the front door and hearing the silence made him shudder. The pictures on the wall; Beth's clothes in the closet; her smell in the bathroom. Even imagining it scared him.

Besides, was this not what Yosef Yitzhok had told him to do in person, before he began communicating by texted riddle? *Look to your work.* Now, via Proverbs 10, he had been more specific.

Will's pace quickened as he walked into the newsroom, deliberately avoiding eye contact with anyone who might spot him. At this time of night it was mainly production staff, not friends of his, but still Will kept his peripheral vision switched off, focused only on reaching his desk.

As he got nearer, glimpsing something over the flimsy partition wall, his heart thumped. There was a box, placed on his seat. Could this be what YY had been talking about? Had he been perfectly literal? *Go to your office, it's all there waiting for you.* A box containing all the answers?

Will knew it was pure fantasy, but he could not help himself. He sprinted the last yard or two, grabbed the box, feeling its weight and tearing it open all at the same time. It was much lighter than its size had suggested, and hard to open too. Finally the two top leaves came apart. Will stuck his arm inside and felt something soft and fleshy, like a fruit. What the hell was this? He dug in deeper; it felt moist. He hooked his fingers through some kind of opening and, using it as a handle, pulled up the entire object.

A Halloween pumpkin. Will had poked his fingers through an eye socket.

Attached was a card.

The Better Relations Company invites you to a special evening . . .

Some bullshit PR freebie. Invitations for promotional events in New York had become increasingly absurd and excessive: FedEx packages arriving at great expense, containing a silver key that turned out to be the ticket for the launch of the new Ericsson cell phone. The English Puritan in Will balked at such conspicuous waste. He picked up the pumpkin and hurled it across the pod toward a dustbin; it landed and split open by Schwarz's desk. *He'll hardly notice.*

He glanced at the rest of the mail: circulars and press releases. A few seemed to be new deposits—an invitation for a party at the British Consulate in New York; a flyer for a convention hosted by some evangelical outfit, the Church of the Reborn Jesus; a notice about the *Times* healthcare scheme—otherwise, the pile of paper was just as he had left it on Monday, the last day he had been in the office.

That was nearly a week ago; it felt like a lifetime. It seemed like an earlier, golden era—life before the kidnap. How lucky he had been, flying out of New York, then bombing down the backroads of Montana with nothing more grave on his mind than the fickle tastes of the National desk. Of course he had not appreciated it: he had even been idiotic enough to feel glum about the hash he made of the flood story. As if any of that mattered.

Will could feel his eyes stinging. He wanted very badly to cry, to give in to this memory of his wife that had caught him unawares. He wanted to fall into a chair, make a pillow of his arms, and prolong the memory, to hold on to it the way a child wants to catch a bubble, never letting it burst.

Instead he began searching for the notebook he had left here five days ago, the one he had filled up in Brownsville, writing on both sides of the pages.

It was not under the press release pile, nor in the stack of magazines and papers Will had already begun to accumulate, waiting to be clipped. (A job he liked in theory but never got around to doing.) He checked the drawers, which he had loaded on his first day with Post-its, a handful of contacts' business cards, batteries, and an old tape recorder in case his mini-disc recorder broke down. Not there. He looked back at the desk-chair and on the floor and then rummaged through the papers all over again.

He looked around the pod, his eye stopping on the photo of Amy Grossman's toddler son apparently wrestling with his mother, pushing her over from the side. They were both smiling, Amy wearing an expression of relaxed joy that neither she, nor anyone else, ever displayed in this newsroom.

Suddenly he heard Grossman's voice in his head. *My advice is to lock up your notebooks when Terry's around. And talk quietly when you're on the phone.*

Will turned himself around slowly. Neat as ever, Walton's desk seemed to carry no excess paper. Just the single yellow legal pad.

Will inched closer, his eyes instinctively darting left and right to check no one was around. He ran his hands along the desk, as if to confirm through touch that it really was as clear and empty as it looked. Nothing there. He checked below the yellow pad, to see if there was another stashed underneath. No.

Now his hand was moving toward the desk drawer. Still scoping the room, he began to pull. It was locked.

Will sat himself in Terry Walton's chair, ready to mount the search for the key. He was sure it would be here somewhere: no one kept the key to a desk drawer on a ring, did they? Will ran his hand underneath the desk, hoping to find it taped in place. Nothing.

He sat back in the chair. Where could it be? The desk held only the yellow pad and a couple of lame mementos of Walton's glory days as a foreign correspondent: a bust of Lenin and, most bizarre, a snow dome in which the winter scene was not children sledding or reindeer riding but a fatherly-looking Saddam Hussein, his arms outstretched, reaching out to a young boy and girl running toward him. Ba'athist kitsch, doubtless picked up when Walton covered the First Gulf War. Without thinking, Will picked it up to give it a shake, to watch the blizzard fall on the great Iraqi tyrant. As the first flakes fell, he saw it. Stuck to the underside of this plastic bauble—a thin, silver key.

"Good evening, William."

Will could feel his muscles seize up. He had been caught. He swiveled his chair around.

The man was barely visible, standing in the half-light. Still, Will recognized his profile before he could even make out the features. It was Townsend McDougal, executive editor of the *New York Times.*

"Oh, hello. Good evening." Will could hear the nerves, the exhaustion, and the panic in his own voice.

"I've heard of eagerness and dedication, William, but this is surely beyond the call of duty: spending Saturday night toiling not only at your own desk, but at that of a colleague. Most industrious."

"Ah, yes. Sorry. I was . . . I was looking for something. I think I might have left my notebook here. On Terry's desk, I mean."

McDougal made a show of craning his neck and peering at the desk, as if searching it was a difficult task, when in fact it was uncluttered and visibly empty.

"Doesn't seem to be here, does it, William?"

"No, sir. It doesn't." Will was embarrassed by that "sir." He was also aware of sitting so far back in his—Walton's—chair, he risked falling over. Like a man held at gunpoint.

"We didn't see you in the office yesterday, William. Harden wondered if you had been kidnapped."

Will felt a feverish chill run along his neck, as if he was fighting a severe flu. He was so tired. "No, I was . . . I've been working on something. On a story."

"What kind of story, William? Do you have another unlikely hero for us? Another 'diamond in the rough' like your saintly crack dealer? Another organ-giving gun nut?"

Will had a dread thought. The editor was either mocking him or, much worse, voicing skepticism. The paper had been burned before by young men in such a hurry to make their mark that they had written works of short fiction rather than journalism, which the *New York Times* had swallowed whole and published on page 1.

People still spoke of the Jayson Blair scandal, which had toppled one of Townsend's predecessors.

Will realized what he now looked like. Unshaven and twitchy—and, unaccountably, in the newsroom late on a Saturday night at someone else's desk. "It's not what you think, sir." Will could hear his own voice slurring with fatigue. His mouth was dry. "I just wanted to check something about the Brownsville story. I was looking for my notebook, and I thought maybe Walton—"

"Why would Walton want your notebook, William? Be careful not to believe everything you hear in the newsroom. Remember, journalists don't always tell the truth."

There it was again, another coded dig at Will and his stories. Was he accusing him of faking the Macrae and Baxter tales, albeit in the genteel language of a New England Brahmin? He may have had the accent and erect posture of a Massachusetts aristocrat, but McDougal's unblinking expression was the poker face of a consummate office politician.

"No, I was not believing anything. I just want to go through my notes."

"Is there something about the story you're not sure of, William?"

Damn. "No, I've just been wondering if there's more there than I first realized."

"Oh, I would certainly assume that."

Another dig.

"You need to be very careful, William. Very careful. Journalism can be a dangerous business. Nothing more important than the story, that's what we always say. And that's almost true. But not completely. There is always something far more important than the story, William. Do you know what that is?"

"No, sir." He was back in the headmaster's study.

"It's your life, William. That's what you have to look out for. So, mark my words. Be very careful." He left a long pause before speaking again. "I'll tell Harden you're getting some rest."

With that, the editor withdrew back into the semi-darkness and began his stately glide toward the National desk. Will fell back into Walton's chair and let out what he knew was an audible sigh. The editor thought he was a junkie, about to go off the rails and ready to take the *New York Times* with him.

And now he was "getting some rest." It sounded like a management euphemism for suspension, while they investigated the veracity of the Macrae and Baxter stories. Was that why the notebook was missing? Had Townsend taken it as evidence?

His fingers were still balled around the Saddam snow dome, now misted over with clammy hand moisture. He had held it tight throughout the entire conversation with Townsend. That would have looked great: not only wild-eyed, but his hand a permanent fist. As his fingers uncurled, he saw it again—the plain, thin key that would surely open Walton's desk drawer. He knew it was madness to try it, having received an all but formal warning from the most senior man in U.S. journalism. But he had no choice. His wife was a hostage, and that notebook surely held the clue to getting her back.

Will glanced left and right and back again to see if anyone was nearby. He turned a complete circle, mindful that Townsend had surprised him from behind. Then, in a single rapid movement, he ripped the key from its sticky tape, ducked down, and slid it inside the lock. One jiggle, and it turned.

Inside were multiple neat, fawn-colored files. Between them, hardly concealed, was the telltale white metal spiral of a reporter's pad. Will pulled it out and saw the scribble on the thick front cover.

Brownsville.

Jesus. Grossman was not kidding: Walton had stolen his notebook. God only knew why. The story had already been published. There was no scoop to be scooped. What possible use could it be to him? Will put it out of his mind: there were enough puzzles to be solved without adding Walton's bizarre strain of journalistic kleptomania to the pile.

Will wanted to start flicking through it right away, but he knew he had first to close the drawer, lock it, replace the key, and return to his own desk—all without being spotted. Exactly what possibility he was guarding against, he was not sure. He had already been caught by the editor; the damage was done.

Even so, Will made sure he was hunched over his own desk before he so much as opened the book. He devised a method. First, a rapid-fire search for something alien: a note stashed inside that he had failed to see, a scrawled message in a hand other than his own. Perhaps, through some sorcery that remained utterly opaque, Yosef Yitzhok had smuggled a message onto these pages. *Look to your work.*

Will moved through it fast, scanning the lines in search of the unfamiliar. There was nothing, just his own scrawl. The newsroom was so quiet, he could hear the pages turn. He could hear his own brain.

Briefly, he became excited by a couple of lines that leapt out, clearly written by someone else, but they turned out to be contact details for Rosa, the woman who had found Macrae's body, scrawled onto the page in her own hand. Will now remembered that he had promised to send her a copy of the piece once it was published.

There was no mystery phone number, no smuggled message—not that there could have been with this notebook stashed in Walton's filing cabinet since who knew when.

Instead he would have to stare very hard at the one clue he knew this book did contain, the thing that had brought him here. There it was, on one of the last pages, boxed and ringed with asterisks: the quote that had made the piece, from Letitia, the devoted wife who had contemplated prostitution rather than let her husband rot in jail. *The man they killed last night may have sinned every day of his God-given life—but he was the most righteous man I have ever known.*

In an instant, Will was back in Montana, talking to Beth on the cell phone. It was, he realized, the last conversation they had had before she was taken. He was telling her about his day spent reporting the life and death of Pat Baxter. He could hear his own voice, speaking animatedly, before realizing that Beth was miles away.

"You know what's weird. It hit me straight away because no one uses this word, or hardly ever: the surgeon who operated on Baxter used the same word as that Letitia woman. *Righteous*. They even used it the same way: 'the most righteous person,' 'the most righteous act.' Isn't that strange?"

He had not pursued the point. He had rapidly realized Beth was elsewhere, preoccupied with the issue that should have been preoccupying him: their failure to have a baby. He felt his throat go dry: the thought that Beth might die never having known motherhood.

He pushed the notion away, staring down at his own handwriting on the page. *The most righteous man I have ever known.*

He had flirted with pointing out this uncanny echo when he wrote up the Baxter story, but had ruled it out almost immediately. It would seem too self-regarding, noting a similarity between two stories whose only real common link was his own byline. Baxter and Macrae lived at opposite ends of the country; their deaths were obviously unrelated. To notice a reverberation between one random murder and another only made journalistic sense if both cases were well known, their details lodged in the public mind. That was emphatically not the case here, so Will had dropped it. He had not thought about it again until that evening, as he and TC stood on either side of the homeless preacher in McDonald's. Every verse of Proverbs 10 he had incanted seemed to contain this same word, repeated too often to be a coincidence. *Righteous*.

But these murders could not possibly be connected. Black pimps in New York and white crazies in the Montana backwoods did not mix in the same circles or have the same enemies. They had lived and died worlds apart.

And yet, there was something oddly similar about these two eccentric tales. Both involved men who seemed suspect and yet had done a good deed—or rather, an extraordinarily good deed. Righteous. And both had been murdered, with no suspect yet arrested in either case.

Will swiveled around to face the computer screen. He logged on to the *Times* Web site and found his own story on Macrae. He would read it forensically, looking to see if there was anything else to go on.

> *Police sources spoke of a brutal knife attack, with multiple stab wounds puncturing the victim's abdomen. Local residents say the style of the killing fits with the latest in gangland fashion, as in the words of one,* "knives are the new guns."

The method of killing was entirely different. Baxter had been shot: Macrae stabbed. Will opened another window on the screen, allowing him to call up his Baxter story. He scrolled down, looking for the paragraphs with the forensic detail, time, and method of death. Finally he came to the line he was looking for.

> *Initially, Mr. Baxter's militia comrades suspected that a macabre act of organ theft lay behind the murder. Unaware of his earlier act of philanthropy, they assumed Mr. Baxter lost his kidney on the night of his death. As if to add weight to that theory, there were signs of recent anesthesia—a needle mark—on the corpse.*

Will read on, looking for more, as if he had never read the story before. Now he wanted to curse whoever had written it: there was no more on the mystery injection. It had just been left hanging.

He dug into his bag to retrieve his current notebook, the one he had taken to Seattle. He riffled through the pages to find the interview with Genevieve Huntley, the surgeon who had removed Baxter's kidney. He remembered the conversation, sitting in the front seat of his rental car, cradling a cell phone to his ear. He had just let her talk, wary of interrupting the flow. According to the scrawl in front of him, he had not even asked about the recent needle mark. Looking back, he knew why. He had dismissed the whole business once the surgeon had told him about Baxter's kidney op.

The story had changed, from organ-snatching gore to righteous man, and that inconvenient detail had got forgotten. *He* had forgotten it. Besides, Huntley had said there had been no more surgery, so the recent injection idea did not fit.

Yet now he flicked a few pages back in the notebook to see his encounter with the medical examiner and Oxford man Allan Russell. "Contemporaneous" was his verdict on the needle mark. It was strange but inescapable: Baxter's killers had anesthetized him first.

Will clicked back on to the Macrae story. No talk of injections there. Just a frenzied stabbing. He sat back in his chair. Another hunch was evaporating. He had thought he was going to prove these two deaths were somehow connected. Not just by the odd coincidence of the word *righteous*, but by something physical. A real tie that might suggest a pattern. But it was not there. What had he got? Two deaths that had good-guy victims in common. That was it so far. In one case, Baxter's, there had been a weird twist: he had been sedated before he was killed. That was not true of Macrae.

Or rather, Will had no idea if it was true or not. The police had never mentioned it—but he had never asked. He had not seen Macrae's body; he had not met the coroner. It had not been that kind of story. And if he had not asked, then no one had. After all, the Macrae death had hardly been a big deal. Apart from a few briefs written on the night, no paper had run much on it—until Will's story in the *New York Times,* of course.

Will reached instantly for his cell phone, punching at the internal phonebook. There was only one person who could help. He hit J for Jay Newell.

CHAPTER TWENTY-NINE

SATURDAY, 10:26 P.M., MANHATTAN

"THIS IS JAY."

"Jay, thank God I got you." Newell was the member of Will's Columbia set who had taken the least likely career route. He was a fast-tracker at the New York Police Department, leapfrogging over all the old doughnut-munchers on his way to becoming a big city commissioner before he was forty. Jay was as resented by the old-guard cops as Will was by the aged newsmen.

"It's Will. Yeah, I'm fine. Well, I'm in a bit of a jam but I can't explain it now. I need you to do me a very large favor."

"OK—" But the word was drawn out.

"Jay, I need you to check out something. I wrote a piece in the paper this week—"

"About that pimp guy? Saw it. Well done on making the front page, big fella."

"Yeah, thanks. Look, I never checked autopsy reports or anything. Do you have access to those?"

"It's the weekend, Will. I'm kind of, you know."

Will looked at his watch. It was late on a Saturday night; Jay was a single guy with a lot of girlfriends. Will guessed he had called at a spectacularly inconvenient moment. "I know. But I bet you have the authority to see whatever you want, whenever you want." The old flattery maneuver. Jay would not want to admit that, as it happened, he did not have that kind of access.

"What do you want to know?"

"I want you to see if there were any unusual marks on the victim's body."

"I thought the guy was stabbed like a million times."

"He was, but he was still in one piece. I want you to see if there was anything like a needle mark on him."

"Some pimp scumball from Brownsville, you kidding? The amount of drugs these guys are whacking into their veins, he probably looked like a pincushion."

"I don't think so. None of the people I spoke to said anything about injecting drugs. In fact, no one said he used drugs at all."

"OK, my man. Whatever you say. I'll check it out. This the right cell for you?"

"Yeah. And I need whatever you've got really fast. Thanks, Jay. I owe you."

Suddenly he could hear voices, followed by a burst of laughter. It seemed to be a knot of men, walking in this direction. And then, louder than the others, the unmistakable intonation of Townsend McDougal, talking newsroom talk.

"Can we hold it for twenty-four hours? Do we have this to ourselves?"

Clearly a big story was cooking, one big enough to bring in the top brass on a Saturday night. But why were they heading toward this barren part of the third-floor landscape? They had no shortage of meeting rooms at their end. Oh, God. Maybe McDougal was looking for Will, coming with a posse of senior executives this time, to begin the inquisition right away.

He could not risk that, not now. At top speed, with too little time to check what he was doing, Will shoved the essentials—cell phone, notebooks, pen, BlackBerry—off his desk and into his bag, wheeled around, and headed away from the McDougal ambush. The only perk of this faraway corner of the office, Will realized at that very moment, was its proximity to the back stairway. He had never used it before, but now was the time.

Once outside, Will gulped in the Saturday-night air. He let his eyes close in relief, leaning backward against the wall, the Times clock just above his head.

It was late, and quiet. In normal circumstances, Will liked this vibe—working at a time when the rest of the city was not; leaving a half-empty office and walking into the Manhattan evening. It was such a contrast with the usual throng that bustled down this street in the day. No one around, save a lonely tourist in a sleeveless down vest and baseball hat peering into one of the *Times* display windows, doubtless looking at an antique printing press or a framed photograph of the late Mr. Sulzberger shaking hands with Harry Truman or something. He must be cold, standing around outside. But Will was in a hurry to get away. He barely saw him.

CHAPTER THIRTY

SATURDAY, 11:02 P.M., MANHATTAN

TC'S ROOM WAS JUST HOW HE WOULD HAVE IMAGINED IT, and, he realized now, he had indeed imagined it. Perhaps a dozen times since his marriage to Beth he had thought about TC, not just for a second or two, but in long, extended sessions. Daydreams, really, in which he had brought back to himself her face, her voice, her smell.

The room was less bohemian than the studio just a few blocks away where he had seen TC the previous night. Much of the furniture was vaguely ethnic—dark wood tables that Will guessed were from India or Thailand; a pair of Moroccan shutters in distressed blue wood, not attached to a window but hung on the wall, like a painting. Mementos, Will guessed, from some serious traveling: TC had been a fearless explorer, even when he knew her.

He knew that TC had been reluctant to let him in here, but when Will phoned from outside the *Times* office, she explained that she had grown tired of café-hopping. She needed to shower, to sleep in her own bed—and to hell with the risk. Will, who had earlier fired off a text accusing YY of "horseshit games," knew exactly how she felt. He simply asked for her address and said he would come straight over. He reckoned it was easier on both of them if she had no chance to say no.

When he came in, she tried to pretend it was no big deal. She let him find her kneeling on the floor in the main room surrounded by yellow Post-it notes. On each one was written a biblical verse. Will recognized them: chapter 10 of the book of Proverbs.

TC was in the middle of them, her sketchbook on her lap, surveying the pattern she had arranged. He crouched down to look at the ink-covered page, and at the Post-its arranged around the hardwood floor, and felt a sudden powerful surge of gratitude for this woman who was offering not only emotional sustenance but a razor-sharp intellect. He felt as if she was saving him.

In a gesture that was almost involuntary, he reached out to touch the back of TC's neck, so that his palm touched her skin and his knuckles brushed against her hair. Her head was down, as if she was a coy schoolgirl receiving a prize, but now it came up to meet his gaze. Again without conscious thought, a pulse of energy went through Will's hand, pressing slightly on TC's neck as if to bring her closer toward him.

She moved and he moved, and now their lips were touching in the lightest of kisses. He could smell her skin, an aroma that made his muscles weaken and his blood race at the same time. It was a familiar feeling, one he had known with TC a thousand times before. His innards seemed to melt, even as his loins hardened.

She stopped suddenly, gripping his arm with an urgency he knew was not lust. Her mouth was away from his.

"Shhh. What's that?"

It was a metallic rattle, now repeated. It seemed to be coming from inside the apartment. They froze, neither risking movement. Will saw his hand still cupping the back of TC's head, his fingers in her hair, and caught himself. What the hell was he doing? Beth was a hostage in some godforsaken jail, and he was making out with his ex-girlfriend on the floor of her apartment. The shame seemed to congeal somewhere in his guts; he sickened himself.

He pulled his hand away and pushed back out of the embrace. He was exhausted, he told himself, his spirits sunk. It was a reflex, a cry for help, the act of a desperate man, a grasping for human comfort; it was gratitude for all TC had done, it was the familiarity of a former lover, it was a lapse, a moment of madness, the unhappy byproduct of a crisis. All these explanations coursed through his mind, and he knew they were all true. But they would not convince anybody, least of all him.

TC tensed again, gripping Will's arm tighter. The buzzing had returned, a grinding, jangling sound. Was someone inside this flat, carrying an electric saw, attempting to muffle it inside a blanket?

Will now leapt to his feet, striding over to the couch by the front door where he had dumped his coat. He shoved his hand into the side pocket and held up his phone for TC to see: set on silent, it had vibrated against his keys.

"Damn, we missed a call."

Will dialed his voice-mail. *You have one new message.* His chest began pounding. What if it was some vital clue? What if it was Beth herself, having wriggled out of her chains and somehow crawled on hands and knees to a phone, only for her husband not to answer—because he was too busy necking with his ex-girlfriend? Will appalled himself.

At last the message was playing.

"Hey, big fella." It was Jay Newell. "Don't know what this is all about, and my ass would be in the wringer if anyone knew I had so much as farted in your direction, so this stays strictly in the vault, OK. *Capisce?* All right, here is the news. Turns out the autopsy report on your friend Howard Macrae found, cue drumroll, a 'puncture on the right thigh, consistent with'—get this—'a tranquilizer dart.' " Newell was beginning to chuckle. "Can you believe that? A tranquilizer dart? Like they use to stun elephants in the zoo. Apparently, they fire 'em from some big safari gun. Anyway, blood tests confirm the guy had a shitload of sedative in his system at ToD as well. Sorry, time of death. I'm going native, Will! I'm talking like a cop! Help! OK, hope that works for you. Give me a call sometime. We should hook up. And send love to your gorgeous wife from me."

Will almost fell into the couch, as if knocked off his feet. He realized now that he had never expected this theory of his to stack up; a Brownsville hustler and a wing-nut from Montana were almost mathematical opposites. He had contacted Newell to confirm that the deaths of Macrae and Baxter could not possibly be linked. With that proved, he could start looking in more likely directions.

But Yosef Yitzhok had told him to look to his work, and so he had. In the lead-up to Beth's abduction, his work had consisted of two bizarre stories at opposite ends of the continent. And yet now Will had proof that they were connected. In life these two victims had both performed an unusually good deed; in death, they had both been anesthetized before the act of murder. The method of sedation was radically different, just as the killings had been. But it was too much of a coincidence.

Will began to feel elated. At last he had made progress; a hunch had been vindicated. Somewhere in the events of the last week lay the key to Beth's kidnapping and, therefore, her freedom. He had come this far; all he had to do was work out the rest. He was closing in.

Will jumped to his feet, about to stride over to TC and trumpet his breakthrough. Instead he halted after two paces. First, he was hit anew by the memory of a few minutes ago. Now, to add to the shame and self-disgust at his betrayal of Beth, was embarrassment. He had made a pass at TC, and both of them would have to act as if it had never happened.

Then another thought struck him. It surely meant something that Baxter and Macrae had been killed in a similar fashion, but what exactly? Just because these two deaths were apparently related, what did that have to do with Beth's kidnapping? Baxter and Macrae might have lived thousands of miles from each other, but they both lived in different worlds from Beth—and from the Hasidim, for that matter. So YY had told him to look to his work, but what possible connection between these three events could there be?

As he began to pace around the room, he wondered: Could his stories have served as a trigger for the Hasidim to take Beth? She had gone missing on Friday morning, just as his Baxter story had appeared in print. Could something in that story have set off the plot to kidnap his wife? Was there something in the combination of the two, Baxter and Macrae, that spurred the Hasidim to abduct Beth?

Will spooled back to last night in Crown Heights. His story on Baxter had been marked and laid out in the room where he had been interrogated. The Hasidim had been discussing it. It was not the byline that interested them: they already knew he was a reporter for the *Times.* They had e-mailed him at the *Times* address. No, it was the story itself. Or, thought Will for the first time, the *stories.*

He reached for his cell phone, finding the inbox of messages and scrolling through the batch from YY. He counted ten, making sure he got past the latest riddles. There it was. Decoded, it read. "Two down: More's to come."

At the time, both he and TC thought it was a mere confirmation message. Like one of those computer games: *Well done, you have reached Level 2, the Castle of Doom. Next, prepare to enter the Sanctum of Fire . . .*

Now Will saw it differently. *Two down* referred to Macrae and Baxter. But who were the rest?

CHAPTER THIRTY-ONE

SATURDAY, 7:05 P.M., CAPE TOWN, SOUTH AFRICA

HE USED TO COME HERE WHEN IT WAS ALL-WHITE. This beach, with its gentle curve of fair sand, was one of his favorite spots. When he was a student, he would come to ogle the girls and drink beers by the crateload. Back in those days, outsiders thought his country was in flames, consumed by a race war. But it did not feel like that; at least not to him. He was white and well-off and having the time of his life. He knew a couple of guys who had signed a petition, but otherwise politics did not intrude. Besides, as an Afrikaaner who had grown up in the rural heartland of the Transvaal, he was raised to believe the separation of the races, apartheid, was not offensive but natural. On the farm, rabbits and cows had their own places and did not mix, so why should blacks and whites be any different?

Now the beach looked as beautiful as ever, the water glittering in the moonlight. As he faced the Atlantic Ocean, he could hear the buzz of the bars behind him: a more mixed crowd now, black, white, and what he had grown up calling colored. He tried to tune out the noise; he wanted to listen to his own thoughts.

Was he elated by what he had just done? He was not sure. Relieved, certainly. He had been planning this moment for months. Each day, taking a different document home—sometimes a diagram, sometimes a string of algebraic numbers—until he had built up the full set.

He breathed out heavily. He remembered those years at the university, followed by more years in graduate school, most of them spent in a lab. He had become a research pharmacologist by the time he was twenty-seven and had spent the next fifteen years working on a single project, code-named Operation Help. It was his boss's little joke, playing on *help* as a synonym. For Andre van Zyl belonged to a team searching for a cure for AIDS.

They were just a part of it, of course. The headquarters of the research effort was in New York, with satellite teams in Paris and Geneva. The South Africa field office was smaller still, chosen for what the corporate literature called its "clinical resonance." Translation: South Africa had a handy supply of AIDS sufferers.

They had been testing out new remedies on groups for years now. Andre had been at some of the trials, clinics out in the sticks taking one hundred sick men and women, marking fifty of them as a control group and handing new tablets to the rest. Andre had been at his computer when the results came through. Time after time his reports had had the same conclusion: *No impact; statistically negligible results; needs further work.*

But nine months ago, a set of data had come back that could not be ignored. The sample group had shown an improvement unlike any seen before. The symptoms were not just held at bay; they were becoming nonexistent. The medication seemed not only to pacify the virus but to chase it out of the system altogether.

Within a week, scientists from the Geneva team had flown in to see the patients for themselves. A few days later the head of the entire project arrived from New York. He ordered the control group be put on the new drug immediately, on "humanitarian grounds."

Andre had to laugh at that. For he knew what would happen next. The head honcho from America would publish a paper in *Nature*, hailing his breakthrough and bidding for the Nobel Prize that was surely his, while the U.S. Food and Drug Administration would start testing the new tablet. Once they had given the seal of approval, it would go on sale and make the company they all worked for one of the richest in the world. They had found the holy grail of twenty-first-century medicine: they had found a cure for AIDS.

The only trouble was people like Grace, the woman Andre had met on one of the earliest trials, too poor to get the antiretroviral medicine she needed. AIDS was a death sentence for her—not a condition that could be lived with, as it was in Europe or the United States. This cure would be no cure for her or for the millions of women, men, and children like her, all over the world. The new drug would never reach them because it would be too expensive. The company had a patent on the new medicine that would last twenty years: until then, they had a monopoly and could charge what they liked.

So he had gone to the FedEx office earlier that day with a large box addressed to a man he had never met in Mumbai, India. Revered and reviled as the king of the copycats, this man had made a fortune making bootleg copies of the latest Western drugs and selling them to the Third World for a tenth of the price. He had done it with some of the early AIDS medicines. Now, in the next day or two, he would receive a full blueprint for the cure. Andre's note issued a clear demand: "Make this drug and distribute it to the world. Now."

The sun was beginning to set; he could hear the waves more easily than he could see them. He would go to a bar and chug back a beer. Who knew when he would get another chance. Tomorrow the company might discover his theft, his treachery, and have him arrested on a dozen counts. With this much money at stake, they would have to make an example of him: he could be in jail for years.

So he decided to savor this night. He drank, he flirted. And when one beautiful girl, with long bronzed legs and a skirt that barely stretched over her bottom, came on to him, he rose to the occasion. She laughed at his jokes; he rested his hand on her smooth, naked thigh.

The ride in her open-topped car was punctuated by long, open-mouthed kisses at each traffic light. They fell into her apartment, her clothes falling willingly to the floor. And when she went to fix him a drink, he gulped it down gratefully, not even noticing the powdery residue still undissolved at the bottom of the glass.

He coughed a little; he grew dizzy and resolved to drink less next time. As he lost consciousness and fell toward death, he could hear the girl's voice, gently reciting what sounded like a poem. Or perhaps a prayer.

CHAPTER THIRTY-TWO

SATURDAY, 11:27 P.M., MANHATTAN

IF IT HAD NOT BEEN FOR LUST AND GUILT, Will might never have seen him. He had not yet had a chance to tell TC of his breakthrough, the phone call from Jay Newell, when she stood on tiptoes to reach for a book from one of her highest bookshelves. As she stretched, her thin shirt pulled away from her jeans, revealing the taut, unmarked skin of her lower back. For all the feelings of shame, he was at it again, noticing the shape and curve of TC's body. He turned away.

To dispel any impression that he was ogling, he made a point of looking elsewhere, starting with a glance down at her desk. It was piled high with papers, cuttings from magazines, fine art journals mostly, but with the odd piece from the *New Yorker* and the *Atlantic Monthly* too. And what he could see was a handwritten letter.

At a job interview he would have called his next impulse professional curiosity, but the simpler truth was that he was nosy. He tugged at the paper, sandwiched between an edition of the *New York Times* Sunday magazine and a seasonal guide to Lincoln Center, until he could glimpse the top half of the first sheet.

Will jumped. The letter was written in a series of symbols that looked like gibberish. Yet it was definitely a letter, on personal notepaper, with a date at the top right in conventional numbers. He frowned. Surely he would have remembered if TC was fluent in another language. Indeed, he distinctly recalled that one of her few areas of academic deficiency was linguistic. She always said she regretted that she had never learned French or Spanish; despite her supercharged education, she had never found the time.

Movement outside caught his eye. A couple were getting out of a just-parked Volvo: perhaps they had been at the movies or at a dinner party with friends. They might have been himself and Beth, enjoying a normal life.

He dragged his gaze away. Farther up the street there was a pair of teenage boys in oversized jeans and a middle-aged woman carrying a single flower.

Directly below, on the opposite sidewalk, was the man in the baseball cap.

Will did not recognize him straight away. Even when he saw the blue vest, he did not make an immediate connection. But something in the man's stance, a certain relaxation of posture that suggested he was not on his way somewhere else, but needed to be right here, sparked a memory.

Will instantly snapped back the curtain and took a step away from the window. He had seen that man this very evening; he had thought him a lonely tourist, admiring the headquarters of the *New York Times*, peering into the window as if he had nothing better to do. Now this same man was pacing around outside TC's building. It was too much of a coincidence.

"TC, how many exits are there out of here?"

She looked up from the King James Bible she had just taken off the shelf. "What? What are you talking about?"

"I think we've been followed, and I think we're going to have to leave right now. Except we can't walk out the front entrance. Any ideas?"

"You're kidding. How would any—"

"TC, we don't have time for a discussion."

"There's a fire escape at the back; it comes out onto the alleyway, I think."

"Too risky. There could be someone at the back as well. Does this building have a caretaker?"

"A what?"

"You know, a super?"

"Oh, yes. Sweet guy. Lives down in the basement."

"Do you know him? Please tell me he has a soft spot for you."

"Kind of. Why? What are you thinking?"

"You'll see. Pack up everything you might need."

"Might need for what?"

"For a night away from here. I don't think we can risk coming back."

Planning their exit, Will made one hurried call, then rounded up TC's scattered Post-it notes, his mobile, and his BlackBerry and shoved them all into the voluminous pockets of his coat. He could hear TC rifling through drawers.

At the open front door they surveyed the apartment one last time. Out of habit TC reached for the light switch; Will gripped her forearm just in time.

"We don't want to advertise our departure, do we?"

That gave him an idea. Like plenty of security-conscious New Yorkers, TC had several time-switch gadgets attached to her light fittings. Most people used them when they were away, timing them to act as phantom occupants, turning on lights in the evening and off in the morning. Now, without asking, Will found the one in the living room and set it to go off at midnight. No, too neat. Ten to midnight. Next, he went into TC's bedroom—taking care not to look around too closely—and set the light to go on in there five minutes earlier and then to go off again twenty minutes later. With any luck, the peeping Tom outside would conclude that Will and his female friend had turned in for the night.

With that done, they headed for the basement. Overheated and marked by a series of handleless doors, it seemed an inhuman place to live. But this was home to Mr. Pugachov, the Russian super. TC knocked lightly on the door, from behind which, Will was delighted to note, floated the sounds of late-night TV. Finally the door creaked open.

To Will's surprise, the super was not some crabby old man in a holed cardigan and worn-out slippers like the school caretakers of Will's youth. Instead Mr. Pugachov was a handsome man in his thirties bearing an uncanny resemblance to the onetime chess champion Garry Kasparov. And given the migration patterns from the former Soviet Union, it would be no great shock if this man, whose job was to sign for daytime deliveries of mail and fix busted water pipes, turned out to be a grandmaster.

"Miss TC!" Pugachov's expression flicked from pleasure to disappointment the moment he caught sight of Will, though.

"Hello, Mr. P."

Flirtatious, thought Will. Good.

"What can I doing for you?"

"Well, it's a funny situation, Mr. P. My friend and I have been planning a lovely surprise for his wife's birthday."

Nice touch, establishing that I'm not the boyfriend.

"Which is due to begin"—TC made a show of looking at her watch—"any minute now, in fact. At midnight!" She was sounding breathless, too eager.

"So the thing is," Will said, taking over, "we need to leave here without her seeing us. We left her outside the building, you see. Now, I know this is going to sound crazy, but I wondered if there might be a way for you to somehow hide us in, oh, I don't know, some kind of wagon or trolley and take us out the back way."

Will could see that the chess champion was stumped. He was staring, baffled, at both of them. TC was laying on a smile you could have seen from space, but it was no good. The super was utterly confused. Will decided to speak the international language.

"Here's fifty dollars. Take us out of here in one of those trash cans." He pointed at a row of oversized plastic bins on wheels lined up just outside the back door.

"You want me to put Miss TC in Dumpster?"

"No, Mr. P. I want you to put both of us in there and just wheel us down the street. One hundred dollars. OK?"

Will decided the negotiation was over. He stuffed the money in the super's hand and headed over to the back door. Still shaking his head, Mr. P opened up. Will pointed at the blue bin marked "Newspapers," gesturing for the janitor to wheel that as close to the door as he could. It was too risky to step outside: he might be seen. Next, Will reached out, grabbed the handle, and tilted the bin, flipping open its lid and emptying its contents onto the floor. Magazines, listings guides, and free inserts selling home computers came tumbling out, spreading themselves on the ground. When he saw the janitor's face fold into a grimace, Will dug into his pocket and took out another twenty.

Once he had got the bin almost horizontal, its top resting on the stoop, it was not too hard to crawl in. Will did it in a crouch, as if entering a tunnel. Then he curled himself up, lay on his side, and gestured for TC to follow until the pair of them sat like two halves of a walnut in a blue plastic shell.

Will gave the nod and Garry Kasparov closed the lid. Then, with a mighty effort and a deep, low grunt, he lifted the bin so that it was vertical, tilted it, and began to push. With panic, Will realized they had never discussed either a route or a destination.

Inside, TC and Will rattled and bounced, but knew better than to let out even a squeal. Their knees were touching and their faces were just an inch apart, and as they tossed upward when Mr. P hit a rut in the alleyway, the urge to giggle was strong. Their situation was so ridiculous. But the smile only had to form in Will's mind for his plight to come pressing back in. *Beth.*

They could feel themselves slowing down; Mr. P was obviously tiring. Will lightly tapped on the side. The bin tilted back down, allowing them to creep out. The janitor had done a good job: he had covered nearly three blocks, staying with the narrow alleyway behind the apartment buildings. They were surely unseen.

They said good-bye, TC giving Mr. P a brief hug that, Will suspected, was more valuable than twice his cash fee. They watched him lope back, a Russian emigré pushing an empty wheelie bin through the streets of New York at midnight. That was the beauty of a big city: nothing was ever out of the ordinary, so nobody paid attention.

"OK," Will said, looking around and getting his bearings. "Now all we need to do is head north about six blocks. We should jog." And off he went.

Finally TC had a chance to speak. "What the hell is going on here, Will? You see a guy in a baseball cap, and suddenly we're shoving ourselves in a trash can? And now we're running? What is this?"

"I've seen that guy before. Outside the *Times* building."

"You're sure? How could you tell from six flights up? You only saw him for a second."

"TC, believe me. It was the same man." He was about to explain his posture theory, but realized it would sound unhinged. And take up too much oxygen. "His clothes were the same. He was there to watch me. Or us."

"You reckon the Hasidim sent him?"

"Sure. He might even be one of them. All he'd have to do is change clothes, then he could pass for normal."

TC shot him a look.

"You know what I mean. He could disappear into the crowd. What I saw at Crown Heights last week—Christ, it was only yesterday. What I saw *yesterday* is that plenty of these blokes were born into ordinary American backgrounds." He was beginning to pant. "It wouldn't be hard for them to shed all the garb and go right back into it, if that's what the mission required."

They had arrived at their destination, Penn Station, and had only five minutes to wait for what Will called the "milk train," a Britishism referring to the sleepy services that ran after midnight. They had the carriage all to themselves, but for an unshaven man apparently snoozing into his neck, obliviously drunk.

"This is the train I used to catch visiting my dad's place, before we got the car." He regretted that "we": it felt somehow unkind to rub his married-coupleness into TC's still-single face. And that regret instantly reminded him that he and TC had never once spent a weekend at Sag Harbor. He had taken his cue from her, keeping their relationship a virtual secret. TC had met Will's father just once, and they had never spent any proper time together. Beth, on the other hand, had fitted in straight away; it was one of the things that made it feel so right.

A silence fell. It was TC who broke it, digging into her bag to produce the item she had been holding before they left her apartment. The Holy Bible. "Christ, I nearly forgot." She thumbed through the pages at top speed. "There. The book of Proverbs, chapter 10."

"Haven't we been through this already? We found what he wanted us to see: righteous, righteous, righteous."

"I know, but I'm a nerd. I want to study it some more."

"What are you looking for?"

"I don't know. But something tells me I'll know it when I see it."

CHAPTER THIRTY-THREE

SUNDAY, 3:08 A.M., SAG HARBOR, NEW YORK

THE HOUSE IN SAG HARBOR, at least, sprung no surprises. The key was under the flowerpot, as always; the place was even quite warm, testament to the efficiency of the local couple Will's father hired to keep things ticking out of season.

He moved around rapidly, turning on lights, putting hot water on the stove, making tea. Clutching a packet of Oreos, he finally sat himself opposite TC, facing her across the vast, aged oak table that dominated Monroe Sr.'s stylishly rustic kitchen.

Instantly, the memories flooded back. The long winters at school, when Will could feel every one of those three thousand miles that separated him from his father. The joy when a parcel arrived in the mail, often containing a delicious slice of exotic Americana—perhaps a packet of bubble gum or, never forgotten, a leather baseball. And then the thrill as he was put on a plane during the summer vacation, "an unaccompanied minor" on his way to see his dad. Those August weeks in Sag Harbor, spent crabbing on the beach or eating clams on the deck, were the highlight of Will's year. He could still feel, even now, twenty years later, the hollowness in his stomach when September loomed and he would be taken back to the airport—away from his father for another year.

Will forced himself back into the moment. They had gone over it half a dozen times on the train, and again in the cab from the station, but he wanted to talk it through once more: the phone message from Jay Newell. Now it was TC's turn to explain what it all meant.

"OK, we know Baxter and Macrae were both drugged before they were killed; they were both deemed righteous by people who knew them; and, according to YY and Proverbs 10, if your reading of it is right, it's this righteous thing that is significant. Which somehow explains the wider Hasidic plot. Why they've taken Beth, why they killed the guy in Bangkok, why they had someone follow you, or us, tonight. That's essentially the theory here, isn't it?"

"It's a bit more than a theory now, TC. 'Two down: More's to come.' 'Yet more deaths soon.' That's what he said. He was addressing me directly! He's read the stories in the *Times*, and he's telling me, 'OK, you've cracked two of them, but there are going to be more.' Meaning we have to link this with everything else that's going on! Don't you see?"

"No, no, I do see." She chose her words carefully. "I do see that this must all be linked. The trouble is . . . rather, my problem is, I personally cannot quite see how we get from the Macrae/Baxter/righteous thing—which I admit is fascinating and incredible—to the 'more' that are supposed to be coming."

Will slumped in his chair.

"No, Will. Don't be like that. This is great progress. We're nearly there, I'm sure of it. Look, let's get some sleep, and then we'll think this last bit through," she said, placing her hand on his shoulder, sending a pulse of memory through them both. "Come on, we can do this."

Suddenly Will leapt up, walking out of the kitchen. TC chased after him.

"Will! Will! Come on, don't do this."

She found him standing in his father's study, a room filled from floor to ceiling with books. Row after row of leather-bound legal texts, collected case reports, volumes of Supreme Court judgments going back to the nineteenth century. On another wall, there were more contemporary works, lines of hardcover texts on politics, the Constitution, and of course, the law. They seemed to be arranged with a librarian's zeal for order: grouped by theme and then, within each category, rigorously alphabetized. TC's eye landed on the Christianity section: *Documents of the Christian Church* by Henry Bettenson, *The Early Church* by Henry Chadwick, *From Christ to Constantine* by Eusebius, *Early Christian Doctrines* by I.N.D. Kelly, all lined up in perfect order.

But Will was ignoring the books, instead powering up the computer on his father's desk. He scrolled down an Associated Press story, barely reading the words, looking for something.

He moved his cursor over the text to define two words: the name of the Hasidim's kidnapping victim in Bangkok: Samak Sangsuk. He moved up to the Google window at the top right of the screen, pasted in the name, and hit return.

Your search—"samak sangsuk"—did not match any documents

He was about to curse, but he was silenced. Not by TC, but by the distinct sound of a creak in the hallway. Not just one, but several in quick succession. There was no doubt about it. Someone else was in the house.

CHAPTER THIRTY-FOUR

SUNDAY, 12:12 A.M., MANHATTAN

HE HAD WAITED LONG ENOUGH. It was the lights going out that had made him suspicious. He was told this man was desperately searching for his wife: it did not make sense that he would happily go to sleep at midnight.

Besides, he feared he was arousing suspicion, pacing around outside an apartment building for hours on end. This might be Manhattan, where no one seemed to notice anything, but it was a risk.

He telephoned his superiors, asking for permission to make his move.

"All right. But keep it clean. Do you understand?"

"I understand."

"And may the Lord be with you."

He waited for the next new arrival at the building, a woman apparently returning from a late-night convenience store with a bag full of groceries. It took him a second to jog the few yards to the entrance, as if catching up with her.

"Oh, let me get that," he said, holding the door once she had opened it. He followed her in.

While she checked her mailbox, he headed downstairs for the basement, pausing only to cover his face with a ski mask.

He could hear the sound of a television, seeping out from under the door. He knocked and waited, checking once again the cold steel of the revolver he would reveal the instant the door opened. This would not take long.

Mr. Pugachov jumped back in fright, raising his arms in an instant surrender.

"Good. Now, you need to stay nice and calm. We need to do this nice and easy. All you gotta do is take me to the apartment on the sixth floor. The one that looks out onto the street. The one where the pretty girl lives. You know the one I mean. Mighty pretty girl."

Pugachov had never heard such an accent before; this man did not sound like the New Yorkers he knew. It took him a while to work out what he was saying. Guessing, he reached with his right hand behind the door.

"Hey! Hands in the air! What did I say just now, mister?"

"Excuse, excuse," Pugachov sputtered. "I was getting key. Key!" He gestured behind the door, where the man in the ski mask could see a series of numbered hooks: spare keys for every apartment in the building.

He shoved Pugachov out of the door and toward the back stairway. It was late; no one was around. But it was still too risky to take the elevator. Those were his orders: he must not be seen.

The super opened TC's door tentatively, calling out a meek hello. He felt the gun at his back.

The man in the ski mask flashed on a flashlight, searching out the bedroom door. He pushed his hostage toward it.

"Open it."

Pugachov turned the handle slowly, but the gunman reached over him and pushed the door hard.

"Freeze!" he shouted, shining a flashlight onto the bed. Seeing nothing, he wheeled around, anticipating an ambush from behind. Nothing. Now grabbing Pugachov by the collar, he started flinging open closet doors, training his revolver on each new opening of dark space. When he came to the bathroom door, he gave it a firm kick and jumped in before turning around to ensure no one could pounce.

He searched the rest of the apartment, beaming the flashlight into every corner.

"Well, there's a moral to this story. Trust your hunches. I thought they'd gone, and they have."

He put on the lights and started looking around more closely, never letting Pugachov out of his sight—or out of range.

He flipped open TC's computer, instantly opening up her Internet browser. He asked for a history, generating a long list of the sites she had looked at most recently. He took out a silver pen and a black notebook and began writing down what he saw. Pugachov noticed for the first time that he was wearing tight black leather gloves.

Next he saw a half-finished pad of Post-it notes. The top sheet was blank, but he held it up to the light all the same. Sure enough, as so often, he could see the trace of words and numbers indented from the page above. It amazed him that people still made this elementary mistake: he would have thought Will Monroe would know better.

Next he picked up the phone, pressing the "last number" button: 1-718-217-54771173667274341. So many digits could only mean one thing: Monroe had dialed some kind of automated service, offering a series of numerical options, rather than a personal number. The gunman wrote down the full string of numbers and hit redial.

Thank you for calling the Long Island Railroad . . .

After that it was simple; he only had to punch in the sequence of numbers he had written down: 1 to use touchtone, 1 for schedule information, then, when asked to enter the first five letters of his starting station, 73667, and so on. It was easy. Obligingly, the automated female voice told him the times for the next three trains from Penn Station to Bridgehampton, the nearest station for Sag Harbor.

He ran his flashlight over the floor one more time, noticing a yellow piece of paper that he had missed: "Verse 11. The mouth of a righteous man is a well of life: but violence covereth the mouth of the wicked."

He tucked that into his pocket and turned once again to face Pugachov.

"OK, son. It's time to shape up and ship out." He used his revolver to gesture toward the front door.

As Pugachov made for the handle, he turned his back slightly, so that he was sideways to the gunman. Now, he decided, remembering the training he had received as a long-ago conscript in the Red Army, was the moment. In an instant, he grabbed the masked man by the wrist and looped his own arm under his shoulder, bringing him quickly to the ground.

The gun had fallen, and Pugachov reached for it, only to be kicked, hard, in the balls. He doubled over and felt an arm around his neck. He tried to jab back with his elbows, but there was no movement. He was in a headlock, and the man holding him seemed to have superhuman strength. He could feel his breath around his ear.

Somehow, and only with supreme effort, Pugachov managed to wriggle his right arm free and aim it at the man's head. But it did not connect. His fingers were flailing until they finally grabbed something. It took him a second to realize it was not hair. Out of the corner of his eye he could see what he was holding: he had removed the gunman's mask.

Suddenly the grip was loosened. Pugachov slumped, panting heavily. He was no longer the fit fighting machine of his youth;

that stint of military duty in Afghanistan was in the faraway past. Perhaps the masked man had realized that; maybe he understood that Pugachov could inflict no serious damage and was about to let him go.

"I'm afraid you've just made a big mistake, my friend."

Pugachov looked up to see a much younger man than he was expecting. Now that the mask was off, he could see that his eyes were of the most exceptional blue, almost feminine in their beauty. They seemed to cast beams of sharp, bright light.

He did not have long to stare into them because his view was soon obscured—by the mouth of what he recognized to be a silencer, aimed right between his eyes.

CHAPTER THIRTY-FIVE

SUNDAY, 4:14 A.M., SAG HARBOR, NEW YORK

TC WAS STARING AT WILL, STOCK-STILL. The sound was too regular to be the music of an old house, the creaking of aged timber. There was no doubt about it: these were footsteps. Will grabbed the heaviest poker he could find from the fireplace, placed his finger over his lips to hush TC, and edged out of the study.

He crept down the corridor, toward the kitchen. The sound seemed to have moved there. As he got closer, he could hear a rustling, as if the intruder was rifling through papers. He inched closer, until he could see the shadow of a tall man. His heart was pounding; his throat was parched.

In a single movement, Will swung around the corner, lifted the poker above his head—

"Christ, Will! What the hell are you doing?"

"Dad!"

"Will, you scared me out of my wits. I thought someone had

broken in. Jesus." Monroe Sr., clad in striped pajamas, collapsed into a chair, clutching at his chest.

"But Dad, I didn't—"

"Hold on, Will. Give me a second to catch my breath here. Hold on."

When Will called out to TC, his father's bewilderment was complete. "What on earth is going on here?"

Will did the best he could, talking his father through the events of the last few hours: the text messages, Proverbs 10, the visit to the office, the stalker, the dash for Penn Station. He listened patiently, nursing the hot tea TC had made for him, the great judge now a dad.

"I should have told you I was here. I came yesterday evening. I hadn't heard from you, and I was climbing the walls with worry. I thought it might help to hear the ocean, breathe in the sea air. Beth is your wife, Will, but she's also my daughter-in-law. She's family." He glanced toward TC, whose face turned hot.

"I'm sorry we woke you," she said, as if trying to change the subject. Then, yawning, "I could really use some sleep."

"Motion granted. Will, the garden room is made up."

That peeved Will. Was his father giving his son an order, instructing him that he must sleep separately from TC—as if suspecting that, left to their own devices, they would share a bed? Did his father really believe that Will was cheating on the daughter-in-law he loved so dearly?

Perhaps his father suspected something much darker. Was it even possible? Could he imagine his son had somehow engineered this whole episode as a way to get back with his ex? Will realized how economical with information he had been, barely letting his father in on the quest for Beth. How insistent he had been that the police remain uninvolved. It had been nearly thirty years since Will Monroe Sr. had practiced criminal law—but he would have forgotten none of it.

What was worse, Will knew he could feel no righteous indignation. After all, a matter of hours earlier he had pressed his lips to

TC's, their eyes closed, in a kiss. And not a fleeting brush either; it had been a real kiss.

He was too exhausted to say any more. He surrendered mutely to his father and headed upstairs, joining TC, who was waiting for him on the landing. The way she stood, as if she were hiding herself, suggested she felt it, too: the suspicion radiating from his father and the guilty admission that it was not entirely groundless.

SUNDAY, 12:33 A.M., MANHATTAN

"Good work, young man. And your enthusiasm is a joy to me, it really is." The voice was clear and distinct, even on the telephone. "No, your best move now is to hang back. I'm not worried about Sag Harbor. That's not going to be a problem. We need you there, in the city."

"So where do you want me to post myself, sir?"

"Well. They're not going to stay in Long Island long, are they? He's going to have to come back. And that means Penn Station. Why don't we make sure you're there to greet him?"

CHAPTER THIRTY-SIX

SUNDAY, 9:13 A.M., SAG HARBOR, NEW YORK

HE HAD LEFT HIS PHONE ON and placed it right by his ear. But his exhaustion was so deep, the short trill of a newly arrived message barely woke him. Instead, it insinuated itself into his dream. He was putting the key in the lock of his front door; he walked in to find Beth standing in the kitchen, clasping a child to her waist. She seemed fierce, as if she was protecting this little boy—or girl, Will could not tell—from an intruder about to do terrible harm. *Get back,* her eyes seemed to say. She looked wild; feral. Oh, I see, thought the Will of the dream. That's Child X. And, right on cue, as if heralding this realization, a bell started to toll . . .

Like a winch pulling a diver up to the surface, his conscious brain dredged him up and out of sleep. Reflexively, he grabbed the phone and brought it to his face.

1 new message

fOrtY

He leapt out of bed and marched down the corridor to TC's room, one of the few denied a view of the ocean, backing onto a large English-style garden instead. The sun was streaming into the hallway, accompanied by the sound of the waves. There was no getting away from it: his father had chosen a gorgeous spot.

His father. Only now did Will remember their nighttime encounter. He had very nearly bludgeoned his dad. He might have killed him. But there was no time to dwell on that.

"OK," he said, once he had shaken TC awake and she was propped up on one of the dozen or so pillows his father's housekeeper routinely provided for each bed. "There's another one. *Forty.*" He was holding up the phone.

"Forty messages?" she croaked, eking the sleep out of one eye.

"No. That's the message. Look."

"Why's he written it so weirdly?"

"I don't know. Get cracking on that, can you? I have a phone call to make."

He looked at his watch: 9:30 a.m. He checked the BlackBerry: nothing new from Crown Heights. They surely did not believe he had acceded to the rabbi's demand in yesterday's phone call—that he back off and sit tight. It was obvious they believed no such thing: after all, they had sent a man to follow him precisely because they knew he would keep probing.

Nine thirty. Someone from the foreign desk would be in by now. Besides, he could not afford to leave it much later. As he dialed the number, he scrunched his face up in virtual prayer. *Please let it be Andy.*

There were at least four assistants who worked on the *New York Times* Foreign desk; Will struggled to name three of them. But one he had got to know. Andy was probably four years younger than Will, and ever since they had chatted in the line for the canteen one lunchtime, he had latched on to him as a kind of mentor. He was from Iowa and had a dry, unsmiling humor that Will liked instantly; a surrogate for the sensibility he missed from home.

"Foreign."

"Andy?"

"No less."

"Thank God."

"Will, is that you?"

"Yeah. Why?"

"No, nothing. Just—"

"What?"

"Dude, if I believed every evil rumor that I heard—"

"What evil rumor?"

"Word is, you got pounded by the big guy yesterday. That he found you rifling through someone else's desk? I told people, 'Hey, investigative journalism's a tough business.' "

"Thanks, Andy."

"Is it true?"

"Put it this way, it's not entirely untrue."

"Hmm. Well, it's a novel approach to career development, I'll say that for ya."

"Look, Andy. I need a favor. I need you to give me the number for the *Times* correspondent in Bangkok."

"John Bishop? Everyone's on his case today, man. He's run ragged."

"How come?"

"Don't you watch the news? The police are all over Brooklyn. Apparently the black hats tried to kill some guy in Thailand. It's a Metro story: Walton's on it."

"Walton?" That was all Will needed: more needling from the notebook thief. He would have to speak to Bishop behind his back.

"Yeah. I hear Walton tried to wriggle out of it, being the week-end and all. Apparently he nominated you for the story: until the desk told him you were, you know—"

"I was what?"

"You know, not available for work just now."

"Is that how they're putting it?"

"Something like that. Listen, Will, what's the deal? Are you sick or something? You smoke some bad weed?"

He knew Andy was trying to mock the heaviness of it all, sending up, in particular, the absurdity of the hardworking, married Will Monroe under suspicion as some Freak Brothers drug fiend. But it did not make Will laugh. Instead his friend's banter merely confirmed his worst anxieties: that he was indeed effectively suspended from the *New York Times* and that he had become precisely the office talking point, the topic of water-cooler conversation, he had dreaded. The fact that this was a trivial matter, barely worthy of consideration alongside his other worries, only emphasized the desperation of his situation.

"No, Andy. No bad weed, no weed at all as it happens. But I can see how it must look. Excellent. Tip-top. Bloody marvelous."

"I'm sorry, dude. Is there anything I can do?"

"Yeah, that number will be a huge help. Cell phone, if you have one."

"Sure. And remember, they're twelve hours ahead there. It's like nearly ten at night now."

Will did not allow himself a moment to digest the call with Andy. As he dialed the multiple digits to reach Bangkok, he imagined how the *Times*'s interns and young reporters would be burning up New York's cellular system, updating each other on the rise and dramatic fall of Will Monroe at this very moment, but that was all. He tried to put it out of his mind and focus on the sound of a telephone ringing that was now in his ear.

"Hello."

"Hello, John? This is Will Monroe from the Metro desk. Is this a bad time?"

"I've just been up for about thirty-six hours, and I'm about to file a story. Why would it be a bad time? How can I help?"

"Sorry, I'll try to keep it really brief. I know you're liaising with Terry Walton, so I don't want to cut across anything he's doing—"

"Uh-uh."

"But I'm working on a piece at this end—" Terrible lie, and one that Bishop could so easily expose, but Will figured he was up to his neck already, a few more inches would not make much difference. "I'm trying to get more of a handle on the victim. Mr. Sangsuk."

"Mr. Samak. His name was Samak Sangsuk. In Thailand, the family name comes first; you know, like Mao Tse-Tung. Anyway, I filed all that already. Foreign will have it."

Shit. Should have asked Andy to send everything over first.

"I know, and that's all great. It's just a bit of a steer I've been getting from some of the Hasidim here."

"Oh, yes? That's great, Will. What's the steer?" The tone had changed. The prospect of useful information always improved journalists' manners.

"I know this sounds odd, but I've been told to look closely at the victim's biography."

"Just some rich guy. In business."

"Well, I know. But my informer"—a notch above "source" and therefore much more tantalizing—"suggests if we dig a bit deeper, we might find something useful. And relevant."

"What, was he a crook? There's a ton of corruption in this town. That wouldn't be news."

Now Will would have to take his chance. "No, what I hear is the opposite. I'm told that if we look hard enough, we'll find something very unusual about this man—and I don't mean unusually corrupt."

"Well, what do you mean? What 'very unusual' thing will we find?"

"I don't know, John. I'm just telling you what the Hasidim told me. Look for it, and it will explain everything. That's what my guy said. Just wanted to pass the tip on."

"It's ten o'clock."

"I know. But maybe some relatives of the victim, of Mr. Samak, are still awake? Perhaps his friends?"

"I've got a couple of numbers I can call. I'll file whatever I get to Foreign."

They said good-bye, and Will let out a lungful of air in relief. Now he was wasting senior foreign correspondents' time. He would be back at the *Bergen Record* within a week. If they would have him . . .

He phoned Andy, instructing him to e-mail any new files from Bishop the second they came in. He had no idea what the *Times*'s man in Bangkok would find out.

"Well, thanks for breakfast."

"Shit, sorry. I've been on the phone." TC was holding a piece of paper. "Have you done it?"

She showed him. It just read *fOrtY.*

"Yeah?"

"At first I thought it was just a typing error. But this guy is very neat and precise. Everything is deliberate."

"And?"

"And he's emphasized two letters: the second and the fifth. I started trying to say it out loud. I thought maybe it was 'forty O-Y,' but that makes no sense."

"TC—"

"Anyway, it's even simpler. It's forty, second and fifth. Or, put another way, Forty-second and Fifth."

"That's the public library."

"Exactly, which means—"

Suddenly TC tensed up. Will looked around. His father had come in, wearing Sunday-morning chinos.

"Is there some news?"

"Yeah, we just got another text message. Sending us to the public library."

"Is this man suggesting he meet you there? Be careful, William, please."

"No, he hasn't said anything yet. Just the address. Forty-second and Fifth. That's all we've got."

"Well, let me at least give you a ride to the station."

There was another buzz. Another message.

* * *

Dare to be a Daniel.

Will showed it to his father and then to TC.

"Oh, I think I know what that is," said his father, a matter of seconds later. "What did Daniel do?"

"He entered the lions' den."

"And the New York Public Library—"

"—is guarded by two lions. Of course. The statues."

"Patience and Fortitude. That's what they're called. Maybe that's what he's saying you need."

"No, I think it's simpler than that." It was TC. "I think he's just saying go into the library. Dare to be a Daniel, enter the lions' den. That's it."

The phone buzzed once more.

1 New Message

Will fumbled to press the right buttons. All three of them were watching and waiting.

Primers' domain discovered in the orchard of fruit

"Christ. What the hell's that? Just when I thought we were getting somewhere."

"It's worded like a crossword clue. Or perhaps there's a room in the library that has a painting of an orchard?"

"TC, what do you reckon?"

"Your father's right. It's a cryptic crossword clue. But I can't quite see—"

"Come," said Monroe Sr., calling a halt to proceedings. "You can make the next train if you hurry."

Once on board, Will watched as TC got to work. She bit her nails, then twitched her leg before finally stroking her eyebrow with her right index finger, over and over. She borrowed Will's notebook and made a series of scribbled attempts at code breaking—trying to write the words backward, forward, and broken up into pieces. Nothing.

Occasionally she broke off for more of the conversation that had consumed them since their unscheduled reunion on Friday night. They tried to untie the logical knot that events and the succession of riddles had handed them. They went back and forth, trying to tease out any clues they might have missed, again and again.

Finally, as they clattered past Flatbush Avenue and Forest Hills, TC had a breakthrough.

"It works like a clue for those crosswords I used to like doing whenever you bought the British papers. When it says 'discovered in,' that's code for an anagram. Like when they say 'messed up' or 'hidden in.' So the fruit orchard is somehow 'discovered in' *primers' domain."*

"In those two words?"

"Yep. *Primers' domain* is an anagram."

"For what?"

"For *Pardes Rimonim.* It means 'Garden of Pomegranates' in Hebrew; an orchard of fruit." She was smiling.

"OK, but what on earth is it?"

"We're about to find out."

CHAPTER THIRTY-SEVEN

SUNDAY, 2:23 P.M., MANHATTAN

PATIENCE AND FORTITUDE WERE GAZING ELSEWHERE, as always. Apparently uninterested either in the volumes of learning behind them or the hordes of knowledge-seekers marching toward them, they maintained their poses: stone sentries, silent guardians of the house of wisdom.

On their way in, Will's phone had buzzed once more. The message: *3 times I kiss the page.* It seemed obvious that this was the final instruction they needed. *Pardes Rimonim* was the name of the book; that much TC had worked out. This was telling them where to look, perhaps even the page.

TC fairly galloped up the two flights of stairs to the Dorot Jewish Division. She told the librarian which book she wanted to see, prompting a sharp intake of breath. "You mean the 1591 manuscript of *Pardes Rimonim?*" TC and Will looked at each other. "You do appreciate that that is an extremely rare and precious book.

Only the manager of the reading room or her deputy is authorized to bring out that manuscript. Could you come back tomorrow?"

"I really need to see it right away."

"I'm afraid a book such as this needs special permission. I'm sorry."

"Who's that woman there? The one drinking coffee." TC was nodding toward a back office.

"That's the deputy manager. This is her lunch break."

"Hello! Hello!"

Will could have cringed with embarrassment. TC had all but shoved the librarian aside and was leaning across the counter, shouting and waving to catch the deputy manager's attention—here, in the solemn quiet of a library. Scholars at the reading room's five tables were craning to see the cause of the commotion. If only to restore order, the woman in the back office put down her mug of coffee and came over.

It worked. TC was asked to write her name and address in the visitors' book, fill in a form, and leave ID. Still huffing, the woman disappeared to retrieve the manuscript from a locked cabinet inside a locked room—twenty long minutes in which Will paced, studying the faces of the weekend researchers all around him.

"Here it is," said the woman eventually, standing over the table where Will and TC had pitched camp. She did not hand them the book, nor did she lay it on the table. Instead she propped it up on a pair of wedge-shaped black Styrofoam blocks, so that the spine did not fully open. TC pulled out her notepad and reached for a pen.

"Pencils only, I'm afraid. No pens near a book of this quality."

"I'm sorry. Pencils it is. Thanks very much. I'm sure we won't be too long."

"Oh, I'm not going anywhere. I'm staying right next to this book until it's back in its cabinet. Those are the rules."

TC began turning the pages with slow deliberation. The manuscript was a relic from a vanished era, handcrafted in Kraków; its pages were thick with four centuries of history. TC was wary even of touching it.

Will sat at her side, staring at the latest text message. Mindful of the woman watching over them, he whispered, "Is that some religious thing, to kiss the page?"

"Jews do kiss their prayer books when they're closed, or if they drop them on the floor. But not three times. And not specific pages." TC was speaking without looking away from the book. She seemed to be in awe of it.

Will took out his notepad. Maybe this was an exercise in mathematics; perhaps if it was expressed as arithmetic. Will wrote "3 times" as "3 ×." Perhaps *I* was the figure 1. What would that give him? 3 × 1 = 3. No good.

Then he took a second look at what he had written. *Hold on.* Will's mind suddenly went back to the Wednesday afternoons he had spent as a nine-year-old boy, in Mr. McGregor's Latin class. McGregor was an old-school schoolmaster, all black gown and hurling the blackboard eraser, but every word he taught had stuck. Including the games he used to play with the Lower Remove to teach Roman numerals.

Hurriedly now Will wrote out "3 times" as three *x*'s in succession: xxx. Now for "I kiss." Of course. The *I* was an *i*. And how did you denote a kiss, except with the letter *x*?

Now he wrote it out: *xxx* for "3 times," *ix* for "I kiss": xxxix.

"Turn to page thirty-nine."

TC was slow, handling the text before her with solemn care. Will wanted to tear at the pages so that he could just see whatever they were meant to see *right now.*

"OK," said TC finally. "This is it."

Before them was a page dominated by a graphic: ten circles arranged in geometric fashion and linked by a complex series of lines. Will had a faint memory of such drawings, and it took him a while to place it. This reminded him of the chemistry textbooks of his youth, depicting molecular structures in two dimensions.

Except each circle had a word written inside it. Will had to squint to see that the script was Hebrew. It was jarring, geometry and scientific neatness in a drawing that was medieval.

"What are we looking at?"

He could see TC did not want to answer. She was hunched over the image, her shoulder all but blocking Will's view. "I'm not sure yet. I need to look."

"Come on, TC. I know you know what this is." Will was shouting in a whisper. "Tell me."

Self-consciously, and aware of the hovering librarian, TC started to point and talk. "This is the key image of kabbalah."

"Kabbalah? As in Madonna? Red string and all that?"

"No. That's just some bullshit celeb cult. It's about as close to real kabbalah as, I don't know, the Easter Bunny is to Christianity. Just listen."

"Sorry."

"Kabbalah is Jewish mysticism. It's a very arcane form of Jewish study, closed off to most people. You're not meant to look at it until you've reached the age of forty. And it's for men only."

"What about this picture?"

"It's like the starting point of kabbalah. It contains everything. They call it the Tree of Life."

"My God."

"That's sort of what they think this is. It's a diagrammatic representation of the key qualities of God. Each of these circles is a *sefirah*, a divine attribute." She pointed at the lowest circle.

"See, it starts at the bottom with *malchut*, that means 'kingdom.' That refers to the physical realm. Then it branches off into *yesod*, 'foundation,' *Hod*, 'Glory,' and *Nezah*, 'Eternity.' Then it progresses into *tiferet*, 'Beauty,' *gevurah*, 'judgment,' and *hesed*, 'mercy.' And finally, at the top of the tree, there is *binah*, which is kind of like intellectual understanding. And on the right, *hochmah*, which is wisdom. And at the summit, *keter*, the Crown. Something like the divine essence."

"So we're looking at the image of God."

"Or the closest we're ever going to get to it."

Will could not say anything. A shiver had run down his spine as TC had spoken. Maybe it was all just crankish hokum, but this series of lines and circles, drawn so many hundreds of years ago and taught down the generations only to those deemed able to cope with its secrets, seemed to radiate a kind of power.

TC spoke again. "It's funny talking about the 'image of God.' The mystics believe that the whole reason for existence is that God wanted to behold God."

Will looked bemused.

"Until then, there was just God. Nothing else. Just a limitless, infinite God. The trouble was, there was no room for anything else: there was no room for God's creation, for the physical world that would mirror him. So he had to shrink a little. He had to contract, leaving a space so that a kind of mirror could exist—to reflect God back to himself. See, it says it here." She picked up another book, one she had ordered while waiting for the manuscript, rapidly flicking through the pages until she found what she was looking for.

"Until the moment of *zimzum*, contraction, 'Face did not gaze upon Face.' God could not see himself."

Will was fascinated by this image and even more so by the explanation TC was supplying, but he was dispirited by it, too. This was deep theological water: how deep would he and TC have to dive before they found the connection to the here and now, to the Hasidim, to their victims, and to Beth?

Once again, he felt a rising indignation with Yosef Yitzhok. Why could he not just give it to them straight?

It had failed once before, but he decided to try a direct appeal again. While TC pored over the drawing, sometimes cocking her head to one side to read the text on the opposite page, he rummaged in his bag and, away from the prying eyes of the librarian, texted YY.

We're in the library. We see the drawing. We need more.

He noticed the time on the phone display: 3:30 p.m. Which meant it was the dead of night in Bangkok. Will looked at the BlackBerry; nothing from the Foreign desk.

"Listen," he whispered to TC. "I'm going outside to call the paper. I'll be back in a few minutes."

"Bring me a soda."

As soon as he was out of the main reading room, he started dialing the Foreign desk number. Andy picked up before Will got out of the building.

"Yo, Will. How you doing? Shit, I was meant to send you that stuff, wasn't I? Sorry, been crazy here all afternoon."

"Andy! I told you I needed it right away!"

"I know, I know. Sorry. I fucked up. Anyway, here it comes."

"Just read it out to me now, will you? I can't wait for the Black-Berry."

By now Will was outside the main entrance, pacing up and down at the top of its vast staircase.

"Will, we are *slightly* on deadline here." The word was delivered in a mock-English accent; Andy was sending him up, which was a good sign. "OK. Here goes. I'll have to be quick, and I'll skip over the funny names, OK? From John Bishop, Bangkok. Samak Sang-suk was mourned yesterday by those who knew him best—and by a few who hardly knew him at all.

"Mr. Samak, who fell victim to what appears to have been an international kidnapping plot Saturday, was a member of Thailand's financial elite, earning top-dollar fees on real estate and through the burgeoning Thai tourist industry."

Get on with it, Will was thinking.

"But he was also known to the Bangkok underclass as the man they called Mr. Funeral. Mr. Samak, it seems, had a strange side-line, one he ran not for profit but for its own sake. He organized funerals for the poor.

" 'Mr. Samak would be in touch with all the mortuaries, all the hospitals, all the funeral homes,' recalled one associate Sunday. 'If a corpse came in with no family or friends, with no one to bury them, they would call Mr. Samak. If there was no money to pay for a proper burial, they would call Mr. Samak.' "

Will could feel the blood in his veins pumping harder.

"Will? You still with me?"

"Yeah, just keep reading."

"In the past, Bangkok's poorest would end their days in a pauper's grave, sometimes buried a dozen at a time, without a coffin between them. Mr. Samak is credited with putting an end to the practice—almost single-handedly. Not only would he pay the burial costs, locals say he would also round up a congregation for the ceremony, often by paying 'mourners' a few dollars to show up. 'Thanks to Mr. Funeral,' said one doctor, 'no one was buried like a dog and no one was buried alone.' "

Will had heard enough. He hung up and galloped down the stairs, enjoying the sun on his face. First Macrae, then Baxter, and now Samak. Not just good men, but unusually, strangely good men. This was no longer a coincidence.

He found a store, bought a couple of bottles of iced tea, and headed back up toward the library: he would have to tell TC the news and work out the connection with the drawing. Surely this was about to slot together.

Except now he noticed a figure who until then had only lurked in his peripheral vision. Darting out of view, as if frightened that he had been seen, was a tall man, wearing jeans and a loose gray hooded sweatshirt. His age, his color, his expression, were all impossible to discern: his face was entirely obscured by the hood. Only one thing was clear: he was stalking Will.

CHAPTER THIRTY-EIGHT

SUNDAY, 3:51 P.M., MANHATTAN

WILL HEADED STRAIGHT FOR THE STEPS, taking care not to look over his shoulder. Once inside, he walked just as briskly. But he felt them before he heard them: the *click, click* of footsteps behind his, clacking along the cold stone floor. He headed for the first staircase he could find, daring, as he moved up another flight, to take a glance down. As he had feared, the gray hood was right behind him.

Now he broke into a jog, taking two more flights up. Once he hit a landing, he broke off, taking an instant decision to seek refuge in a room full of card catalogs. He dashed in, slowing to an immediate walk: even then, and silent, he felt too noisy, too sweaty for the hushed concentration of the room. He turned around: the hood.

He walked faster, under a vast painting showing a trompe l'oeil sky. Dark clouds were gathering. Spotting an opening on the back wall, Will went in, only to discover it was not an exit but a small photocopying room. He darted back out, but now the hooded man was just a few yards away.

Will saw the double doors out and ran for them. Once through, he was in a throng of people enjoying a midwork break. He weaved through them to get to the staircase on the other side and, clutching the handrail, galloped down, two at a time. A woman carrying a computer monitor was in his way, and he had to dodge to get past her. He moved to the left, and so did she; he moved to the right, and so did she. He leapt to her side to get past, but she let out an involuntary yelp—followed by a thud and a cymbal crash of broken glass. She had dropped the machine.

Now Will was in the main foyer, facing a large cloakroom. This was where regular readers began their day. There were lockers for bags and a long rail for coats that snaked around the room, as if in a dry cleaner's shop. He could hear a commotion: the woman with the computer was calling over a security guard. At the same time, the man in the hood was walking toward him. Calmly.

Will had to move fast. While the attendant was looking the other way, he vaulted over the wooden counter and plunged into the thickness of the coats. Squeezing between a heavy anorak and a shaggy afghan jacket, he pressed himself against the back wall. He could sense his stalker had stopped; Will guessed he was by the cloakroom, peering over the counter, searching. He tried to still his breathing.

Suddenly he felt movement. The attendant was handling the coats, pushing whole bunches of them aside, looking for a number. Will held in his cheeks to make no sound. But the man was getting closer, closer, closer—until he stopped, less than a foot away. Will felt him pull out a jacket and return to the counter.

Then a flash of gray. Will was sure the stalker had walked past. He allowed himself an exhalation; perhaps he had not been seen. He would wait five more minutes, then come out, find TC, and get the hell out of here.

But the hand got him first—thrust in before he had seen a

face, like the robotic arm on a space probe. It grabbed his shirt by the collar, in an attempt to drag him into the daylight. Even in the dark, he could see the gray sweatshirt fabric that covered the arm. Twice Will locked onto it with both hands, pulling it off himself. But each time the hand came back, eventually smashing Will's chin in the process. Crammed behind the coats, Will just could not get the space he needed to reach beyond this single, flailing arm—and hit the man behind it.

The struggle was soon over. Will was pulled out of his hiding place like the meat from a sandwich. Now he came face to face with the man in the hood. To his complete surprise, he recognized him immediately.

CHAPTER THIRTY-NINE

SUNDAY, 3:56 P.M., MANHATTAN

"WHY DID YOU RUN AWAY? I just want to talk."

"Talk? You just want to talk? So why were you bloody stalking me? Christ!" Will was bending over, one hand on his knee, the other tending to his chin.

"I didn't want to approach you while you were with, um, that woman. Upstairs. I didn't know who she was. I didn't know if it was safe."

"Well, it would have been safer for me, believe me. Jesus *Christ*."

Will could see two security guards striding in his direction; trailing behind was the woman who had dropped the computer. Will ducked down as if to tie his shoes, his back turned; the men passed him. Finally he found a bench and all but fell onto it, trying to catch his breath. "So what the hell's this about, Sandy? Or is it Shimon?"

"Shimon Shmuel. But call me Sandy, it'll be easier."

"Gee, thanks."

"I'm sorry. I didn't mean to hit you, I really did not. But I couldn't let you run away. I have to talk to you. Something very bad has happened."

"You're telling me. My wife has been kidnapped; I've practically been tortured; your rabbi killed some guy in Bangkok; and now you've spent a weekend stalking me, before the grand finale of a whack on the chin."

"I haven't spent a weekend stalking you."

"Save it, Sandy, really. I saw you from the window last night: the baseball cap nearly threw me, but I got it in the end."

"I promise you, I came to find you today. Not last night. I was in Crown Heights last night."

"Well, someone was waiting for me outside the *Times* building yesterday evening. They followed me to my friend's house and waited there too. And so far the only person I know who does that kind of thing is you."

"I swear that wasn't me, Will. It wasn't. I had no need to come then."

"What do you mean, no need?"

"It hadn't happened last night. Or at least we didn't know about it till this morning."

"What hadn't happened?"

"It's Yosef Yitzhok." The voice faltered enough to make Will look, for the first time, at Sandy's face. He still had not removed his hood—a substitute skullcap, it was doing the religious duty of covering his head—but even in the shadow it cast, Will could see. Sandy's eyes were red raw. He looked like he had been weeping for hours.

"What's happened to him?"

"He's dead, Will. He was murdered, brutally murdered."

"Oh, my God. Where?"

"No one knows. They found him dead in an alleyway near the

shul. It was early this morning, probably on his way to *shacharis.* Sorry, morning prayers. His *tallis*, his prayer shawl, was red with blood."

"I don't believe this. Who would do such a thing?"

"I don't know. None of us know. That's why Sara Leah—you met her, my wife—said I should find you. She thought this was somehow connected with you."

"With me? She blames me?"

"No! Who said blame? She just thinks this might be connected to whatever happened on Friday night."

"You told her about all that?"

"Only what I knew. But Yosef Yitzhok's wife is her sister. We're family, Will. He's my brother-in-law. *Was* my brother-in-law." The redness of his eyes was about to deepen again.

"And Yosef Yitzhok said something to his wife?"

"Not much, I don't think. Just that he had spoken to you on Friday night. He said you were caught up in something very important. No, that wasn't the word. He said you were caught up in something catastrophic. That was the word he used, *catastrophic.*"

"Did he say anything else to his wife?"

"Just that he hoped and prayed that you understood what was happening. And that you would know what to do."

At that moment, Will could not have felt more helpless. The rabbi had said it first, and now Yosef Yitzhok was repeating it, from the grave. *An ancient story is unfolding,* that's what the rabbi had said. *Something mankind has feared for millennia.* Now YY was telling him the stakes were so high that he was praying that Will would know what to do. And yet Will felt as confused as ever. If anything, more confused—his head swirling with the bizarre coincidence of Macrae, Baxter, and Samak, three noble men, all dying horrible deaths; the blustering rhetoric of the book of Proverbs; and, most recently, the impenetrable, mystical geometry of the diagram he and TC had found in this very library.

"Shit! TC! She's still upstairs. Come with me. Hurry!"

Will was scolding himself at every step as he bounded up stairs and along corridors, Sandy behind him, returning to the reading room. How could he have left her alone?

Will marched toward the desk he and TC had shared nearly an hour earlier. As he got nearer, his heart sank. A woman was sitting there—but it was not TC. She had gone.

Will punched the desk with his fist, sending a bolt of pain through his arm—and a look of terror across the woman's face. *How can I have been such a fool!* These kidnappers had now taken two women from under his nose. He was meant to have protected them both, and he had failed them. Both.

Sandy was standing by him, but Will could not see him or hear him. Only one thing stirred him out of his torpor: the steady, persistent vibration he now felt on his thigh. It was his phone.

2 New Messages

He pressed the first one.

Where are you? Had to leave. Call me. TC.

Will sighed out a chestful of air. Thank God up above for that. He opened the next message, sure it would be TC, suggesting the place they should meet up. What he saw made him take two steps back in amazement.

Fiftieth and Fifth.

Yosef Yitzhok might have been dead—but the riddles lived on.

CHAPTER FORTY

Sunday, 4:04 p.m., Manhattan

"And when did it arrive?"

"Just now. This second."

"Well, the first conclusion we can draw is that Yosef Yitzhok was not our informant after all."

"We can't be certain of that, TC. His killer may have grabbed his phone and carried on sending messages." As he said it, Will saw the absurdity of his suggestion. What were the chances that an assailant would steal a phone, check the "sent" file, and carry on sending perfectly coded messages in the same vein? Besides, there was an easy way to check.

"Sandy, can you do me a favor? Call home and find out if anyone took Yosef Yitzhok's phone when he was killed." Now talking back into the mouthpiece, to TC, he offered another theory. "What if someone stole his phone in the first place?"

"Well, then it wouldn't have been YY sending the messages at all, would it?" TC was getting exasperated. Fearful of returning to her own apartment, she had fled to Central Park. To her great relief, she had run into some people she knew: married friends, with plenty of kids. As Will could hear through the phone, she had stuck herself in the middle of the group. The strollers, toddlers, and picnic blankets would, she reckoned, serve as a security cordon, keeping the stalkers and kidnappers at bay. Listening to the sounds of childhood chatter, of softball games and a mother handing out cake, Will felt a pang of envy or, rather, longing—longing for a Sunday afternoon of relaxed, sun-kissed normality. TC was still talking.

"YY is dead, but the messages have not stopped. Ergo, he wasn't the one sending them."

"So why would they kill him?"

"Who?"

"The Hasidim."

"We don't know it was the Hasidim who killed him. That's just another conclusion you're jumping to. The truth is, Will, we *know* hardly anything. We can guess and speculate and theorize, but we know very little."

"What about the drawing in the library? Did you see anything?"

"I think it's probably telling us something very simple. It's saying, 'Think kabbalah.' The image is so complex, full of so many component parts, it can't be about any one bit. It's just the general idea. That diagram is the fundamental building block of all kabbalah. It's almost like a logo."

"Hang on. There's another one coming now. I'll call you back."

He walked as he pressed the buttons to reveal the latest message, one that he willed to be clear. Now that he did not have TC at his side, he desperately needed a little simplicity.

Behold the lord of the heavens but not of Hell.

They only had to walk eight blocks north to find the junction that the earlier message had directed them to: Fiftieth Street and Fifth

Avenue. That was where they stood now. Looming over them was the Gothic fortress of St. Patrick's Cathedral, where, little more than a week ago, he had sat rapt, listening to *The Messiah* with his father. A week ago, but a different lifetime.

His father. A spasm of guilt passed through Will: he had barely included him in this search. It was obvious he wanted to help; he had made that clear last night and again this morning, even doing his bit to decipher the text messages. Yet Will had been impatient, happy to use his father as a glorified chauffeur and not much more. Perhaps for all the effort of the last few years, the two of them were not as close as Will liked to believe. Most men would probably have looked to their fathers as their chief ally in a crisis like this, but Will was not most men. He had lived the bulk of his childhood, his formative years, a continent away.

What could it mean? Beckoning Sandy to follow him, he waded through the tourist throng and stepped inside, enveloped immediately in the deferential hush vast houses of worship wreathe around themselves like fog. Will marched forward, his eyes scanning for anything that might fit that message. Who was lord of the heavens but not of hell?

He looked over his shoulder. Sandy was still standing at the door, apparently reluctant to go any farther. Gawping at the impossibly high ceiling, he seemed startled by the rebounding echo. Clearly, he had never been in such a building before. The contrast with the lino-and-fake-paneled gymnasium that served as the Hasidim's synagogue had overwhelmed him. Will remembered something his father had once said, that religious people had much in common, even when they did not share a faith: "The same magic works on all of them." There was no doubt about it: Sandy was moved to be here.

Will, who had gone to school and college in buildings older than this one, was not overawed by the cold stone floors or medieval architecture. He was on a mission, to find a lord of heaven but not of hell. He faced the Grand Organ and then the smaller Chancel Organ. He checked out the altar and the pulpit, raised like the crow's nest of a ship. He examined the narrow shelves holding glass jars for the lighting of candles, and the boxes of new ones, available free of charge. He had a look at the small, private chapel, apparently closed off for private ceremonies. He looked upward to see two flags: the first belonging to the United States, the second to the Vatican. He had no idea what he was looking for.

He walked the length of the nave, studying the blocks of pews. He glanced up at the loudspeakers and screens attached to the pillars. There were tapestries with inscriptions, but no reference that might fit the message. There were stained-glass windows with pictures of saints, shepherds, and the odd serpent. Will thought he saw an angel or two.

Hold on. Directly above, dominating the space around, was a huge crucifix with a sculpted Jesus. It was picked out in strobing white light, as tourists lined up to photograph it.

Was this the lord of the heavens but not of hell? After all, the underworld was the realm of Lucifer rather than Jesus. Maybe it was as simple as that. Maybe he was meant to look at Jesus. But then what?

He wished TC was with him, another pair of eyes, another brain. Sandy was nice enough, but he did not have the kind of laser observation or brainpower Will was sure he needed right now.

Will headed for the exit, shoving a dollar bill in the glass box marked for donations—and filled with what seemed to be the coins of a thousand nations.

Outside, he dialed TC's number. "Look, we've been inside the cathedral. I'm meant to be finding the lord of the heavens but not of hell. There's nothing that seems to connect with that. Nothing I can see. Yeah, I've walked up and down. It's just pews, crucifix—"

He could feel Sandy tugging at his elbow. He tried to shake him off, but the tug was persistent.

"What is it? I'm talking to TC."

"Look." Sandy was pointing, not back at the cathedral but directly across the street.

"TC, I'll call you back."

They were facing Rockefeller Center, Sandy breaking into a semi-jog so they could get a closer look. Barely checking the traffic, he crossed the street, Will behind him, until they were standing before it.

Or, rather, him. Even in shimmering metal, his stomach rippled, the lines of a perfect, mythic abdomen. His thighs were enormous, each one as thick as a bison. One leg was placed before the other, in the manner of a weight lifter steadying himself. Except this was no ordinary weight.

His arms were fully outstretched at his sides,. curving slightly upward to mold themselves around his load. For there, on his shoulders, was nothing less than the universe itself, rendered as an intersecting series of circles, like the lines of latitude and longitude that girdle the globe. On each of the metal arcs were marked the names of the planets. They were looking at Rockefeller Center's largest sculpture, the two-ton statue of Atlas.

"Behold the lord of the heavens but not of hell." Sandy was murmuring the words almost to himself.

"I can see why he's the lord of the heavens," said Will. "But what's the hell thing?"

Sandy was struggling to get the words out. He was panting with exhilaration. "It's a famous thing about this statue. When they did it—"

"Yes?"

"—they hadn't discovered Pluto yet. So there's no Pluto on here."

"And Pluto's the god of the underworld," whispered Will. *Behold the lord of the heavens but not of Hell.* This was the right spot. He dialed TC's number and instantly described what he could see.

"OK, you need to pick me up," she said. "Then we can lose Sandy and go to your apartment."

"Why?"

"Because I think I finally know what's going on. And Atlas has just confirmed it."

CHAPTER FORTY-ONE

SUNDAY, 5:50 P.M., BROOKLYN

THERE WAS NO TIME TO BE SELF-CONSCIOUS. Even so, he could tell TC felt strange to be in this place, the home of the man she had once loved and the woman he had made his wife. He saw her stealing glances at the photographs, especially the wedding collage—perhaps two dozen pictures, pressed under glass—that hung in their kitchen.

If it was odd for TC, it was horrible for Will. He had not been back since the day Beth went missing, visiting here only in his mind. Now he saw the calendar, covered in Beth's handwriting. He saw a cardigan of hers, slung over a chair. He felt her absence so strongly, it made his eyes sting.

"TC, you have to tell me what's going on." Throughout their journey from Central Park, from the moment they had ditched Sandy, he had been pressing her to talk. But she was adamant.

"Will, I'm not sure I'm right. And I know you: the moment I start talking, you'll run off and do something, and it could be a big mistake. We have to get this right. One hundred percent right. There's no room for guesswork."

"OK, I promise I won't run anywhere. Just tell me."

"You can't make that promise. And I don't blame you. Trust me, Will. Please."

"So when am I going to find out?"

"Soon. Tonight."

"You'll tell me tonight?"

"You'll find out tonight. It won't be me who tells you."

"Look, TC. Seriously. I've just about had it with riddles. What do you mean, it won't be you who tells me?"

"We're going to Crown Heights. That's where the answer is."

"We? You mean, you're coming with me?"

"Yes, Will. It's about time."

"Yeah, that's true. I mean, it makes sense—" Will stopped himself. TC was staring at him expectantly. It took him a while to realize what her expression meant. She was waiting for him to ask another question.

"What do you mean, 'it's about time'?"

"Haven't you guessed, Will? This whole weekend, everything we've been doing? You really haven't guessed?"

"Haven't guessed what?"

She was turning away, avoiding his gaze. "Oh, Will. I'm really surprised."

His voice rising: "What are you surprised at? What are you talking about?"

"This is very hard for me, Will. I don't quite know how to say it. But it's about time I went, you know, back."

"Back? To Crown Heights?"

"Yes, Will. Back to Crown Heights. I thought you'd guess ages ago. And I've been meaning to say something, but the moment never felt right. There's been so much to think about, so much to work out. The Hasidim, the kidnapping, and . . . Beth. But you have a right to know the truth.

"So here is the truth. My name is Tova Chaya Lieberman. I was born in Crown Heights, Brooklyn. I am the third of nine children. There's a reason I know this world, Will. I've always known it, inside out. It's my world. These crazy Hasidim? I'm one of them."

CHAPTER FORTY-TWO

SUNDAY, 6:02 P.M., BROOKLYN

WILL COULD SAY NOTHING. He sat pressed against the back of the sofa, as if pinned there by a fierce wind. He listened hard, his mind trying to absorb everything TC was saying. But it was also racing, rewinding wildly through the events of the last forty-eight hours, seeing each moment in a new light. And not just the last forty-eight hours, but the last five or six years. Every experience he and TC had shared now looked utterly, entirely different.

"You saw those families with a dozen children. That's what my family was like. I was number three, and there were six more after me. Me and my older sister, we were like mini-moms: cleaning and preparing meals for the babies from the day we were old enough to do it."

"And did you, you know, look like that?"

"Oh, yes. The whole business: long dresses brushing the floor, mousy hair, glasses. And my mother wore a wig."

"A wig?"

"I never explained that to you, did I? Remember, the women with 'unnaturally straight' hair you saw, and how they all seemed to wear their hair in the same style? Those were *sheitls*, wigs worn by married women as an act of modesty: they're only meant to show their real hair to their husbands."

"Right."

"I know you think it's weird, Will, but what you've got to realize is, I loved it. I lapped it all up. I would read these folktales in the *Tzena Urena*, old legends of the Baal Shem Tov—"

Will turned his face into a question mark.

"The founder of Hasidism. All these stories of wise men journeying through the forest, paupers revealed as men of great piety and honored by God. I loved it."

"So what changed?"

"I must have been about twelve. I would doodle in my exercise books a lot. But at that age I started surprising myself with what I could do. Even I could see the drawings were becoming more elaborate and, you know, quite good. But there were so few pictures to look at. You see, ultra-Orthodox Jews are not that big on graven images. There were hardly any around. And then, one day at sem—sorry, seminary; kind of the girls' school—I found one of those 'Introduction to the Great Painters' books. On Vermeer. I stole it and hid it under my pillow. I'm not kidding, for months I would wait till my sisters were asleep, and then, under the covers, I'd stare at these beautiful pictures. Just stare at them. I knew then that's what I wanted to do."

"You started painting."

"No. There was never any time. At sem, it was just study, study, study. Holy texts. At home I had to clean, cook, change diapers, play with the baby, help the younger ones with their homework. I shared my room with two sisters. I had no time and no space."

"You must have gone out of your mind."

"I did. I'd dream every day how I could get out. I wanted to go to the Metropolitan Museum. To see the Vermeer. But it wasn't just the painting."

"Go on."

"I know this sounds funny, given what I'm like now, but I was really good at religious studies."

"No, sorry, I don't find that surprising at all."

"I was top of my class. I found it *easy.* The texts, all those multiple meanings and cross-references, they just seemed to open up to me. Once a rabbi told me I was as good as any boy."

"Oh, dear."

"I was furious. It was like, girls are only meant to go so far. Once you're seventeen or eighteen you become a woman—and that means getting married, having babies, keeping house. Men could carry on at the yeshiva forever, but girls were only allowed to acquire the basics. Then we had to stop. Those were the rules. Five books of Moses, a bit of Gemara maybe. That's a kind of rabbinic commentary. But that was it."

"So all this kabbalah, you never studied that."

"Wasn't allowed. Only men over forty can even look at it, remember."

"Christ."

"Exactly. You know me, if there's a forbidden zone, I want to go there. I found the odd book among my father's things, but I knew I couldn't do this on my own. I needed a guide. So I asked Rabbi Mandelbaum."

"Who?"

"The one who told me I was as good as a boy. I told him I wanted to study. I came to him with all the relevant texts that proved I had the right, as a woman, to know what was in those books."

"And did he agree? Did he teach you?"

"Every Tuesday evening. He told my parents of course, but no one else in the community. It was a secret class at his house. The only other person who knew about it was his wife. She would bring a glass of lemon tea for him, a glass of milk for me—and *rugelach*, little pastry cakes, for both of us. We did that for five years." She was smiling.

"What happened?"

"He got worried. Not for his sake—he was too old to care what people thought—but for me. I was approaching 'the age of marriage.' He told me, 'Tova Chaya, it would take a very strong man not to feel threatened by so learned a wife.' I think he was worried that he had ruined me: that, thanks to him, I would not be happy keeping house. I wouldn't be a good wife like Mrs. Mandelbaum. He had lifted my sights. In a way he was right.

"But he needn't have worried; by then I had planned my escape. I applied to Columbia; I gave a P.O. box address so that no one would see the correspondence. I applied for tons of scholarships, so that I could afford a room. It was hard: I had to get transcripts and SATs from school; I had to make up all kinds of stories. I had to get an official document, to prove I was an independent adult. I'm ashamed to say I told some terrible lies. As far as the college was concerned, I had no parents.

"So when the day came, I gave the kids breakfast, as always, called out good-bye to my mother, as always, and I walked to the subway station."

"And you never went back."

"Never."

Will's mind was speeding, spilling with questions. But he was also overrun with answers. Suddenly, he saw so much that had been hidden. "TC" was no toddler nickname, its origins forgotten. It was a vestige of Tova Chaya's former life. And no wonder TC's parents were such a mystery: they were from a past she had abandoned. Of course there were no pictures: that would have betrayed her secret.

"Do they even know you're alive?"

"I speak to them by phone, before the major festivals. But I haven't seen them since I was seventeen."

In an instant, TC made sense. Of course she was brilliant but knew nothing of pop music and junk TV: she had grown up without them. Of course she spoke no French or Spanish: she had devoted her time to Yiddish and Hebrew instead.

Will suddenly thought of TC's eating habits—the fondness for Chinese food, studded with jumbo prawns, the fry-up breakfasts, with generous rations of bacon. She loved all that stuff. How come? "The zeal of a convert," she said wryly.

Now that he had been to Crown Heights himself, Will realized the scale of TC's rupture from her upbringing. He looked at her now: the tight top revealing the shape of her breasts; the exposed midriff; the navel stud. He thought back to the notice he had seen in Crown Heights:

> GIRLS AND WOMEN WHO WEAR IMMODEST GARMENTS, AND THEREBY CALL ATTENTION TO THEIR PHYSICAL APPEARANCE, DISGRACE THEMSELVES . . .

Her break from Hasidism could not have been more complete. And he was forgetting the biggest rebellion of all: him.

People from her world did not have sex outside marriage. They rarely married people from outside their own sect of Hasidism, let alone non-Jews. Yet she had had a long, physical relationship with him—not her husband, and not a Jew. For him it had been a wonderful romance. He now understood that for her it had been a revolution.

He suddenly saw TC differently. He imagined her as she would have been: a bright, studious girl of Crown Heights groomed for a life of modesty, child-rearing, and dutiful observance. What a journey she had made, crossing this city and centuries of tradition and taboo. He stood up, walked over to her, and gave her a long, warm hug.

"It's a privilege to meet you, Tova Chaya."

CHAPTER FORTY-THREE

SUNDAY, 6:46 P.M., BROOKLYN

HE WANTED TO INTERROGATE TC FOR HOURS, about her life, about the secret she had kept for so long. Lots of Jewish people became Orthodox; they were known as *chozer b'tshuva*, literally "one who returns to repentance." She had gone the other way: *chozer b'she'ela*. She had returned to question.

But they had no time for that conversation, no matter how much they wanted it. They had to get to Crown Heights. Yosef Yitzhok had been murdered, though neither of them had any idea why. The last messages Will had received—directing him to Atlas at Rockefeller Center—had been sent after YY's death, proof that he had not been the informer after all. So why would anyone want him dead? Will was baffled. All he knew was that things were turning steadily more vicious. The rabbi had not been exaggerating: time was running out.

Just as pressing was TC's promise. All would become clear, she had said, once they were in Crown Heights. She could not tell Will herself what was going on. But the explanation lay there. They just had to find it.

"I'm going to need to use your bathroom. And I'm going to need to borrow some of Beth's clothes."

"Sure," Will said, trying hard to shrug off the potential symbolism of that request. He led TC to Beth's closet and, steeling himself, pulled back the sliding door. Instantly his nostrils filled with the scent of her. He was sure he could smell her hair; he could think himself into the aroma of that patch of skin below her ear. He breathed in deeply through his nose.

TC pulled out a plain white blouse, one Beth wore for formal work meetings, usually under a dark trouser suit. It was cut high, Will noticed. *We request that all women and girls, whether living here or visiting, adhere at all times to the laws of modesty . . .*

She turned to Will. "Does Beth have any really long skirts?"

Will thought hard. There were a couple of long dresses, including a particularly beautiful one he had bought for his wife on their first anniversary. But they were evening wear.

"Hold on," he said. "Let me look at the back here." He wondered if Beth had gotten around to throwing it out; he knew she planned to. It was a long, drab, dark velvet skirt that Will had mocked mercilessly. He called it Beth's "spinster cellist number." She put up a mock defense, but she could see his point: it did make her look like one of those silver-haired lady players spotted in every orchestra. But she felt attached to it. To Will's great relief at this moment, she had never gotten rid of it.

"OK," said TC, moving toward the bathroom. "These will have to go." She cocked her head to one side to take off her earrings. Then she pressed her face closer to the mirror and began the complex maneuver of removing her nose stud. Finally she gazed down at her middle and unscrewed the ring that pierced her belly button: no one would see it, but she would know it was there. It would not feel right. She now had a small pile of metal in her hand, which she placed by the basin.

"Now for the toughest job of all." She reached into her bag to produce a newly purchased bottle of shampoo, one specially designed for the task at hand. She started running the tap, grabbed a towel, and slung it around her shoulders. As if bracing herself for a nasty ordeal, she bent down and lowered her head toward the water.

As Will watched, she began to lather up and rinse. She had to scrub hard, but soon her effort was paying off. The water in the sink began to turn a bluish purple. The dye was coming out, a stream of it swirling around the white porcelain and away. Will was fascinated by the colored water. It was not only removing a chemical from TC's hair; it seemed to be washing away the last decade of her life.

He left to collect a few things of his own. What had the rabbi said? "All will become clear in a few days' time." That was two days ago. Perhaps he was about to close in on the truth, at long last. What would it be? What was this "ancient story" into which he and his wife had somehow fallen? Once he knew, would he be back with her? Would he hold her again? Would that be tonight?

"So, what do you think?"

Will wheeled around to see a different woman. Her hair was now dark brown, brushed straight and long. She wore sensible black shoes, a long black skirt, and a white blouse. She had borrowed a thick, quilted jacket of Beth's that, in other circumstances, might have been fashionable but which now looked only practical. Standing there in his apartment was a woman who could have passed for any of the young wives and mothers he had seen in Crown Heights two days earlier. She looked like Tova Chaya Lieberman.

"I'm so glad for the shoes. Thank God, they fit me, and that's all that counts . . ."

It took Will a moment to realize what TC was doing. She was trying out the singsong, Yiddish-inflected accent of a New York Hasidic woman. It came to her so easily, it persuaded Will immediately.

"Wow. You sound . . . different."

"This was the music of my youth, Will," she said, sounding like TC once more. Except there was a wistfulness in her voice he had never heard before. Then, snapping out of it: "Now, what about you?"

"Me?"

"Yes, you. We're going there together. Tova Chaya wouldn't be seen with some *shaygets.* You need to look the part, too. Now, come on: black suit, white shirt. You know the drill."

Will did as he was told, finding the plainest outfit he could. He had to reject a suit with a pinstripe and a white shirt with a Ralph Lauren polo player on the chest. Plain, plain, plain.

He looked in the mirror, hoping his transformation would be as convincing as TC's. But his face gave him away. He might have passed for American, but Jewish? No. He had the coloring and bone structure of an Anglo-Saxon whose roots lay in the villages of England rather than the steppes of Russia. Still, that need not be a problem. Had he not seen the faces of Hanoi and Helsinki among the faithful on Friday night? He would say he was a convert.

He only needed one last thing. "TC, where am I going to get a skullcap from at this time of night?"

"I already thought of that." With a flourish, TC held up a large black disc of material. "I borrowed it from your friend Sandy when we were in the park."

"Borrowed?"

"Well, I knew they always carry spares. And I just happened to be glancing into one of his jacket pockets. Here, put it on."

As if in a ceremony, TC stretched onto tiptoe and placed the yarmulke onto Will's head. She dashed into the bathroom and came back with a hairclip. "There," she said, attaching it just so. "Reb William Monroe, it's a pleasure to meet you."

Once in the cab, Will felt himself begin to twitch with excitement—and nerves. He had never so much as attempted an undercover assignment, and that's what this had become. He was in costume, trying to pass himself off as somebody else. His protective armor—chinos, blue shirt, notebook—was gone. He felt exposed.

In a bid for reassurance, he reached for his cell phone—a memento of his regular life. A new message, apparently from the same unknown sender he had once thought was Yosef Yitzhok:

Just men we are, our number few

Describable in digits two

We're halved if these do multiply

If we few perish then all must die.

He had no idea what it meant, but it hardly mattered now. According to TC, everything was about to be explained. Habit made him check his BlackBerry next. The red light was blinking: a *Guardian* news alert. Nostalgia had made him an electronic subscriber to the paper he used to read back home. Ordinarily, he rapidly deleted these e-mail updates: he had enough to do, keeping up with the news in New York and America. But that "alert" did the trick: what breaking news might justify its own bulletin? He clicked it open.

The Robin Hood of Downing Street

Britain's hottest political scandal in decades took its most bizarre turn yet today.

The former chancellor of the exchequer, Gavin Curtis, who police believe took his own life last week, seems set to be transformed overnight from a disgraced hate figure into a posthumous folk hero. Treasury officials, who earlier revealed that Mr. Curtis had diverted large chunks of the UK's budget into a private Swiss bank account, have this morning disclosed where that money ended up—in the hands of the world's poorest people.

Instantly hailed by the tabloids as a "real-life Robin Hood," it seems Mr. Curtis spent much of his seven years at Britain's exchequer robbing from the rich to give to the poor.

"Our government grant doubled, then tripled under Mr. Curtis," said Rebecca Morris, a spokeswoman for Action on Hunger, a leading relief agency. "We thought it was just—government policy."

It was nothing of the kind. Instead, such generosity to those fighting the wars on poverty, HIV/AIDS, and famine was the personal decision of Mr. Curtis himself—made possible by taking money out of dormant bank accounts that had lain unnoticed and unclaimed for years and then burying the details in a bafflingly complex labyrinth of Treasury data.

Some observers speculate that the chancellor went further in recent months, finding extra funds by raiding subsidies earmarked for Britain's arms exporters. "They got less so that the starving of Africa and the sick of the Indian Ocean could get more," explained a ministerial ally last night. One report suggested it was this move that led to his eventual exposure.

"He must have known the risks he was taking," Ms. Morris told the Guardian. *"And yet he was prepared to do all that, just so the hungriest and weakest would have a better chance. I can't tell you how many lives Gavin Curtis must have saved. Some will call this a scandal, but I think this was the action of a truly righteous man."*

CHAPTER FORTY-FOUR

SUNDAY, 8:16 P.M., CROWN HEIGHTS, BROOKLYN

TC DID NOT WANT TO RUN THE RISK OF A PHONE CALL. She feared that Rabbi Mandelbaum would be too shaken by the sound of a voice from his past. She feared, too, that he would instantly call her parents. It was likely he had been plagued by guilt during these long years: he was bound to have blamed himself for encouraging young Tova Chaya's rebelliousness when he should have curbed it. All this she imagined.

So she would turn up at his front door instead, leaving him no option. She looked at her watch: with any luck, he would be back from synagogue by now. She remembered the address, and once she saw that the lights were on inside, she told the cab to wait. "Sorry, Will. I just need a second." She was staring out of the window, as if unable to move. "It's been nearly ten years. I was a different person."

"You take your time."

Will looked out at streets that were preternaturally quiet. Theirs was the only car; no one was out walking. The only sound came from the radio, playing a song.

Finally, TC gave the signal to get out of the car. They paid the driver and walked toward the house. Will adjusted his skullcap. Again. TC knocked on the door. It took a while, but Will could hear activity. A slow shuffle to the door, and then a hunched, gray-bearded old man. He could have been no younger than eighty.

"Rabbi Mandelbaum, it's Tova Chaya Lieberman. Your pupil. I've come back."

The eyes spoke first, brightening and moistening in an instant. He looked and looked, without uttering a word. Then he nodded gently and waved them in. He walked ahead of them, allowing his left arm to lift as he passed the door to the dining room: his way of saying, *Go in there.* He carried on in the direction of the kitchen.

Will was hit immediately by the smell of old books: the room was crammed from floor to ceiling with the leather-bound, gilt-edged volumes he had seen in the interrogation room on Friday night. Holy texts. The surface of the dining-room table was invisible: covered first by a tablecloth, then a plastic sheet, and finally dozens of open books. It was hard to see; the room was lit by one weak electric light. But even with a cursory scan, Will could tell: barely a word was in English.

There were no paintings on the wall, only photographs. Perhaps a dozen of them, maybe more, all displaying a single subject. The Rebbe. Dead more than ten years, he stared out from every angle, sometimes smiling, sometimes with an arm aloft, but always gazing intently. In one photograph the Rebbe stood with Rabbi Mandelbaum in a group. The others seemed to be commercially produced, specially mounted on tacky, log-style slices of fake wood. It reminded Will of the souvenirs you could buy in small Italian villages, depicting the local saint.

Rabbi Mandelbaum was back, holding an unsteady tray with a single glass of water.

"Sit, sit," he insisted as he offered the tray to Will. He was puzzled. Why was he the only one to have anything to drink? TC leaned over and whispered: "Yom Kippur has already begun. This evening. No food or drink."

"So why has he given me water?"

"He's a smart guy."

TC had positioned herself facing her old teacher.

"Mrs. Mandelbaum?" she said in a voice at once hesitant and gentle.

"Haya Hindel Rachel, aleyha hosholom."

"I'm sorry. *HaMakom y'nachem oscha b'soch sh'ar aveilei Tzion v'Yerushalayim."* May the Lord comfort you amongst all those who are mourning for Zion and Jerusalem.

Will could only watch and listen, but he knew enough body language to know TC was giving condolences.

"Rabbi Mandelbaum, I've come here after all these years on a matter of life and death. I believe there is a *sakono fur die gantseh breeye."* A risk to the whole of creation. She paused, before remembering herself.

"This is my friend, William Monroe." The rabbi made the slightest movement with his eyebrow, a tiny reflex that said, "Don't think I'm naive, young lady. I understand the ways of the world. I understand that a man named William Monroe is not a Jew, no matter how he is dressed. And I also understand that a word like 'friend' has multiple meanings."

"His wife has been kidnapped. She is held hostage, here in Crown Heights. Will has spoken to a rabbi—I believe it must be Rabbi Freilich." She glanced over at Will, who was glaring at her in surprise: *Why didn't you tell me you knew his name?* She carried on. "He doesn't deny that he has taken her. But he has never explained why." No shock registered on Mandelbaum's face. He just nodded, encouraging TC to continue.

"We have been getting various messages, delivered by telephone. Text messages." She enunciated the phrase, as if it might be unfamiliar to the aged rabbi. But he did not seem fazed by it.

"We do not know who these messages are from. But they do

seem to indicate some kind of explanation for events here and beyond. I can't be sure what they mean. But I have an idea. Which is why we're here."

"Fregt mich a shale." Ask your question.

"Rabbi Mandelbaum, will you explain to Will the idea of a tzaddik?"

For the first time, the rabbi conveyed an emotion. He looked quizzically at TC, as if wondering what he was about to get into.

"Tova Chaya, you know well what is a tzaddik. This much we learned together already. For this you came back?"

"I want him to hear it from you. Will you tell him?"

The rabbi stared hard at TC, as if trying to work out her motives. Finally and hesitantly, he turned to Will and began. "Mr. Monroe, a tzaddik is a righteous man. The root of the word is *tzedek*, which is justice. A tzaddik is not just wise or learned. For that we have different words. A tzaddik is a man of special wisdom. He embodies justice itself. The English word *righteous* is the closest you have."

William had never heard a voice like it. The rabbi who had interrogated him so forcefully—whom he now discovered was called Freilich—had spoken with an unusual intonation, a musical lilt that bobbed up and down. But it was still a recognizably American accent. This was something else. Not German, not Eastern European exactly, perhaps a blend of the two. Was it the accent of *Mittel Europa*? Or was it, in fact, the voice of a place that no longer existed—the voice of Jewish Europe? In that sound, Will could recognize the pictures he had studied in history books of World War II: the Jews of Poland or Hungary or Russia, their dark eyes staring out of black-and-white photographs, on the brink of a terrible fate they did not know. He heard the sorrowful, wry violins of the klezmer music he had occasionally caught on New York radio. In this one man's voice, Will Monroe imagined he could hear a lost civilization.

He pulled himself back into the present, determinedly concentrating on what the rabbi was saying.

"Our tradition speaks of two kinds of tzaddikim, those who are known and those who are hidden. The hidden are understood to be on a higher plane than those whose holiness is public. They are righteous, and yet they seek no fame or glory. They have none of the conceit that comes with public life. Even their closest neighbors have no idea of their true nature. Often they are poor. Tova Chaya will remember the folk stories she read as a child: tzaddikim who lived as if in secret, working with their hands. They might be poor or do very humble jobs. In folktales, they are often blacksmiths or cobblers; maybe a janitor. And yet these men perform deeds of the highest goodness. Holy deeds."

"But no one knows who they are?" The question just popped out of Will's mouth.

"Precisely. Indeed"—and at this the rabbi allowed himself a smile—"the tzaddik will often go to great lengths to put people off the trail, so to speak. Our writings are full of stories of tremendous paradox: the holiest men, found in the unholiest places. It's deliberate: they want to conceal their true nature behind a mask, so they disguise themselves as crude, even unpleasant, men. Tova Chaya might remember the story of Rabbi Levi Yitzhok of Berditchev?"

"God's Drunkard."

"I'm glad. You have not forgotten all we studied together. *God's Drunkard* is indeed the story I have in mind. In that story, the holy Rabbi Levi Yitzhok finds that when it comes to divine grace, he is outshone by Chaim the Watercarrier—an ignoramus who is *shicker* from morning till night." TC and the rabbi chuckled together.

"So some of the most righteous men appear in the very opposite form?"

"Yes. Consider it a kind of divine joke. Or proof that Judaism is a profoundly democratic philosophy. The holiest are not those who know the most, or who have the most letters after their name. Nor is this group made up of those who pray most energetically, fast most assiduously, or observe the commandments most diligently.

The measure of holiness is the just and generous treatment of our fellow human beings."

"So this man, this drunkard, he was good to his fellow man?"

"He must have been very good." The three of them sat in a brief silence, punctuated by the sound of the old man breathing noisily.

"There is a story. One of the oldest." Again the beginning of a smile was playing on his lips. Will suddenly saw behind the beard and the accent; he saw a rather charming man. Now elderly and hunched, in his youth he would, Will realized, have been quite a charismatic teacher.

Rabbi Mandelbaum was out of his chair, shuffling around the table to reach the bookshelf just behind Will's head. "Here, this is from *Talmud Yerushalmi*, from the tractate dealing with fast days. Tova Chaya, did we study this together?"

Will was getting lost. "Sorry, where is this from?"

TC stepped in. "It's from what's known as the Palestinian Talmud: the book of rabbinic commentary written in Jerusalem."

"When?"

Rabbi Mandelbaum, now back in his seat and flicking through pages, answered without looking up. "This story comes from the third century of the common era." *The common era.* A euphemism for *anno domini*, the year of our lord, referring to Jesus Christ—a phrase no believing Jew could use. "This is probably the oldest story of its kind." His eyes were scanning the text. "OK, so we don't need all the details, but in this story, Rabbi Abbahu notices that when a certain man is in the congregation, the community's prayer for rain gets answered. When he's not there, no rain. Anyway, it turns out this man works in, of all places, a whorehouse! Excuse me, Tova Chaya, to speak of such things."

"You mean," said Will, "he's a pimp? And yet he is one of the righteous men?"

"That's what the Talmud says."

Will felt an ice shard slide down his back. He shuddered, his shoulders trembling. He could not hear what TC or the rabbi were saying. In his head there was room for only one voice. It belonged to Letitia, the woman he had met in Brownsville. He could hear her words loud and clear. *The man they killed last night may have sinned every day of his God-given life—but he was the most righteous man I have ever known.* She had said that about Howard Macrae, who, like the man in that third-century congregation, earned his living as a pimp.

". . . the stories almost seem to delight in this kind of paradox," the rabbi was saying. "Good men disguised as humble men or even as great sinners."

Will's head was throbbing. Pat Baxter, the militia crazy mixing with gun-toting fanatics, yet who had never been arrested and had given one of his own organs to a total stranger. Gavin Curtis, despised as a corrupt politician, yet funneling money to the world's poorest people. Samak Sangsuk, just another high-rolling Thai businessman, yet quietly ensuring that the Bangkok underclass found dignity in death.

Will could hardly keep up with his own thoughts. He remembered Curtis's curiously humble car as he fled the press truck. And what had Genevieve Huntley said about the kidney donor? *Mr. Baxter's greatest request was anonymity. That was the one thing he asked of me in return for what he did.* All of these men had done noble deeds—and all had done them *in secret.*

"How many of these righteous men are there?"

The rabbi instantly looked at TC. "This you don't know? This you've forgotten?"

"I didn't forget, Rabbi Mandelbaum. But I wanted Will to hear it from you. To hear it all."

"There are thirty-six tzaddikim in each generation. You know perhaps that in Hebrew, each letter also has a numerical value? In Hebrew, thirty-six is expressed by the Hebrew characters *lamad*, which is like an English *l*, and *vav*, which is equivalent to the letter *v* in English. *Lamad* is thirty, and *vav* is six. In Yiddish, these righteous men are known as the *lamadvavniks*: the thirty-six just men who uphold the world."

Will jolted, his antennae twitching the way they did when he heard the words that would make a news story.

"Excuse me, what do you mean by 'uphold the world'?" He saw TC was nodding, a half smile on her lips that seemed to say, At last we're getting to the heart of the matter.

"Ah, well, this is the whole point of the story. I am sorry, Mr. Monroe, I'm getting old. I should have mentioned this at the start. Please, let me get past." The rabbi was reaching for yet another book; one of the few in the room in English. *The Messianic Idea in Judaism*, by Gershom Scholem. "Someone gave this to the seminary. I think it tries to explain these matters to the general reader—"

Will was almost scratching at his own skin in frustration. He nodded politely, his eyes wide, doing all he could to encourage the rabbi to cut the academic footnotes and get on with it.

"Ah yes, here we are. Scholem says that Jewish tradition 'speaks of thirty-six tzaddikim, or just men, on whom—though they are unknown or hidden—rests the fate of the world.' " He was skimming farther down the page. " 'Already in the biblical Proverbs of Solomon, we find the saying that the just man is the foundation of the world and therefore, as it were, supports it.' "

"Hold on, Rabbi Mandelbaum." It was TC, suddenly on the edge of her seat. "Where in Proverbs is that reference?"

Slowly, the rabbi turned back a page. "Chapter 10, verse 25."

Instantly, TC reached into her bag and pulled out her pile of Post-it notes, written after the text message clues had led them to Proverbs 10. She thumbed through them until she found the one she wanted. She smiled and passed it to Will.

Verse 25: As the whirlwind passeth, so is the wicked no more; but the righteous is as an everlasting foundation.

"A foundation," said TC quietly. Now looking at Will: "The righteous men are the foundation on which the world stands. Without them, the world collapses."

"Tova Chaya has summarized it well. There is some discussion about the origin of the idea. Some scholars think it dates back to Abraham's argument with the Almighty over the people of Sodom."

TC could tell Will did not know of any such argument, and that Rabbi Mandelbaum was not about to explain it. She stepped in. "Basically, God was about to destroy the entire city of Sodom because they had become sinful," she said in a semi-whisper, keen to get this out of the way rather than opening up a new discussion with her old teacher. "Abraham tries to make a deal, proposing that if he, Abraham, can find fifty good people in the town, then God should spare it. God agrees, and then Abraham starts negotiating. In that case, he says, if you'd save it for fifty, then what about forty? God agrees to that, too. They keep haggling until finally Abraham has beaten God down to ten good men. OK, God says, find me ten good people, and I'll save Sodom. So that establishes the principle that, so long as there are some truly righteous people around, the rest of us are OK. We're saved because they are in the world."

Rabbi Mandelbaum picked up the thread. "There is some dispute about the exact numbers. Some say thirty, some say forty-five. But from the fourth century or so, the number becomes settled on thirty-six. As Rabbi Abaye writes, 'There are in the world not less than thirty-six righteous persons in every generation upon whom the Shekhina rests.' "

"Sorry. What was that word?"

"My apologies. The Shekhina is God's radiance, the Divine Countenance."

Still in a semi-whisper, TC said, "It refers to the outward appearance of God. It's kind of like a divine light," adding with what Will felt sure was pride, "It's feminine."

"I want to be sure I understand this correctly," Will began, haltingly. "Jewish teaching holds that there are thirty-six people alive at any one time who are truly righteous. They may be hidden away in obscurity, doing humdrum jobs, living flawed, even sinful lives. But, quietly and in secret, they perform acts of extraordinary goodness. And so long as they're around, we're all OK. They keep the world afloat." Will finally understood the last clue: the statue of Atlas at the Rockefeller Center, carrying the whole universe on his shoulders.

"Which means," he said, his voice slowing, "that if they were not around, for whatever reason, it would, literally, be the end of the world."

Heavily and slowly, the aged rabbi nodded. "I'm afraid that's exactly what it means."

CHAPTER FORTY-FIVE

SUNDAY, 8:46 P.M., CROWN HEIGHTS, BROOKLYN

SO THIS WAS WHY PEOPLE WERE DYING. For nothing more than a bizarre, quasi-biblical legend. The waste of life struck Will with new force: what insanity, what cruelty, for Howard Macrae or Pat Baxter to be murdered in the name of a lunatic fantasy. The end of the world indeed! It was obviously nonsense. Who could seriously believe thirty-six people kept the world alive? Will had not breathed in the empirical, skeptical air of Oxford for nothing. He had been taught to dismiss such bunkum out of hand: it made more sense to believe in fairies at the bottom of the garden.

And yet what *he* thought was surely irrelevant. Someone obviously did believe it—with an intensity that made them ready to kill wholly innocent men, all over the world. If this was the killers' motive, what did it matter whether it was rational or not?

That was what Will told himself. But still something nagged.

Something about this man and his books; something about the respect TC had for him. Something about TC, Tova Chaya, herself. These people were not bug-eyed maniacs. They were keepers of an ancient tradition that had endured since the city of Sodom. The story of the thirty-six had been passed down quietly, generation after generation, from the days of Abraham through centuries of wanderings from Babylon to eastern Europe and, now, to America. Jews were not cranks, latching onto fantasies; not as far as he knew. His conversations with TC had always projected the same impression: that Judaism was not concerned with the supernatural so much as with the way real human beings treated each other in the here and now. They did not seem to believe in flying saucers or cripples throwing away their crutches. They were more grounded than that. So if they believed in the hidden presence of thirty-six good men, maybe there was a reason.

Something else dulled Will's usually skeptical instincts. If he had not discovered it for himself, he would never have believed it. But Macrae and Baxter, Samak in Bangkok, and Curtis in London, had fit the rabbi's description perfectly. They had indeed performed acts of uncommon goodness, and had done so entirely in private. They had shunned publicity, just as the legend demanded. (Will's strong hunch was that, until he started digging, the righteous acts of Baxter and Macrae, at least, had been entirely unknown.) The four people he knew about had even been considered sinners, people who would be reviled rather than revered. A pimp and a politician, for heaven's sake!

What if he accepted the existence of these *lamadvavniks*, just for the sake of argument? That allowed a new thought to encroach. Until that moment, his sole interest had been in discovering how this strange, ancient story might lead him back to his wife. Now he felt his hands go moist at a different notion. If this myth had any grounding in reality, then the pursuit of the righteous men was not just a cruel crime. It would also bring disaster upon the world. For the first time he understood Rabbi Freilich's words to him on the telephone the previous evening. *Your wife matters to you, Mr. Monroe, of course she does. But the world, the creation of the Almighty, matters to me.*

Thirty-six, thought Will. It was so few. Just thirty-six people on the whole of this crowded, cramped planet, teeming with, what, six billion people? Four men were dead, he knew that. Did that mean there were another thirty-two dead, or dying, in far-off corners of the world, all but unnoticed?

He remembered again his conversation with Rabbi Freilich. *An ancient story is unfolding here, threatening an outcome that mankind has feared for thousands of years.* So this is what he meant. The ancient story was the legend of the *lamad vav*, the thirty-six righteous men. The outcome feared for so long was nothing less than the end of the world.

Whoever had been sending those text messages knew all this, Will now realized. While Rabbi Mandelbaum stretched for another book, Will stole a glance at his cell phone, to look at the last message he had received. A four-line poem, a quatrain.

Just men we are, our number few
Describable in digits two
We're halved if these do multiply

If we few perish then all must die.

Just men . . . describable in digits two. The two digits were three and six. *If these do multiply.* Three times six was eighteen, half of thirty-six: *We're halved*. And the texter understood what was at stake. *If we few perish then all must die.*

Will tried hard to compose himself. He wanted desperately to produce his notebook, to start ordering all this information. Still, he had to ask some questions.

"These thirty-six? Are they all Jewish?"

"Usually in Hasidic folklore the tzaddikim are Jewish. But this is more sociology than theology: who else did these *yidden* know?

They knew only Jews. That was their entire world. In the early rabbinic writings, there are different views on the identity of the tzaddikim. Some believed they all lived in the land of Israel; some said that a portion lived outside it; others said that the righteous men emerged from the goyim, the gentiles. There is no settled view. It could be all Jews, all non-Jews, or a mixture."

"But they're always men?"

"Always. On that the sources all agree. No doubt about that at all. The *lamadvavniks* are all men."

TC could read Will's mind. *So why are they holding my Beth?*

The truth was, Will was disappointed. Since the rabbi had first started talking, Will had been trying to trace a path back to his wife and her abduction. Even before he came here he had accepted that Macrae and Baxter were connected, but he could not fathom their link to Beth. This theory of the thirty-six seemed bizarre and far-fetched, if not completely loopy, to Will, but at least it might explain what was in the Hasidim's mind. Perhaps for some deluded reason, they had decided Beth was one of the righteous ones. Now he knew that could not be true: she was the wrong sex. He was as mystified as ever.

A new question surfaced.

"Who would want to do such a thing? Who would want to bring about the end of the world?"

"Only one who was in thrall to the Sitra Achra."

Will's brow furrowed.

Rabbi Mandelbaum realized he needed to say more. "I'm sorry, I'm forgetting. The Sitra Achra means literally 'the other side.' In kabbalah, it is the phrase used to refer to the forces of evil. Unfortunately, these are present all around us, every day and in everything."

"A bit like the devil, like Satan?"

"No, not really. Because the Sitra Achra is not some external force we can blame for everything that goes wrong. The power of the Sitra Achra derives from the actions of human beings. It is not Lucifer who brings evil into the world. I'm afraid, Mr. Monroe, it is us."

"Why would religious people, men of God who clearly know and believe in this idea of the thirty-six, why would they want to do such a thing—to kill the righteous men?"

"I cannot imagine why. You know, we Jews say that if you save a life it is as if you have saved the whole world. So to kill any human being is a great crime. The ultimate crime. To kill a tzaddik? That would be a further desecration of the name of the Almighty. To kill more than one? To aim to kill all of them? I cannot even contemplate such wickedness."

"No motive we can think of?"

"I suppose it's conceivable that someone very misguided might want to test this belief to its limits. To see if it's really true, that the *lamad vav* maintain the world. If the *lamad vav* are all gone, all not here, well, then we will know, won't we?"

"Or they could believe it already," said Will. "Believe it so much that they want to bring about the end of the world."

In the silence that followed, Will was struck by something he had half noticed but had not thought about properly till now. For someone who had just been confronted with such news, Rabbi Mandelbaum looked remarkably calm. He remained in his chair, thumbing his books. As if this was a purely theoretical problem.

Now it was the rabbi's turn to read Will's mind.

"Anyway, no one could ever do it," the old man said, sighing as he adjusted himself in his seat. "Because no one ever knows who the *lamadvavniks* are. That is their power."

Will was ashamed to realize that this was the one thing he had never thought of. Thirty-six people, living in humble obscurity across the globe: How would anyone know who they were? How had the killers of Macrae and Baxter found them?

"The tzaddik is hidden, sometimes even from himself; he may have no idea of his own nature. If a man does not know himself, who else can know him?"

"So no one has any idea who the thirty-six are? There's no secret list?"

The rabbi twinkled. "No, Mr. Monroe, there's no list. Tova

Chaya, behind you, can you pass me the book by Rebbe Yosef Yitzhok?"

Will started. He had heard so few familiar words since he had arrived in this room, but this was a name he knew. TC caught his expression and whispered a clarification.

"That's the name of a previous rebbe. YY was named after him. He died fifty years ago."

"All right," the rabbi said, now fallen back into his chair. "This is a kind of autobiography of the rebbe. Here he describes the tzaddikim as if they were a secret society. He doesn't refer to them explicitly as the *lamadvavniks*, but that's what he's talking about. He suggests these people, each stationed in a different city, were somehow the founders of Hasidism." He turned away from the book, his eyes closed, as if reading a text written inside his eyelids. Will realized he was dredging something up from his memory. "There is also the great Rabbi Leib Sorres. From the eighteenth century. It was said of him that he was in secret contact with the hidden just men, that he even made sure they were fed and clothed. They said the same about the Baal Shem Tov, the recognized founder of Hasidism." His eyes opened. "But these are the exceptions. Generally, it is understood that the hidden tzaddikim remain hidden. There are stories of near misses, of tzaddikim about to meet another of their own kind, only to miss out. And it's assumed that one righteous man would have the wisdom to recognize another. You know, he would somehow 'feel the glow.' " The rabbi cracked the smile Will had seen earlier, the one that belonged to the playful, mischievous young man it seemed Rabbi Mandelbaum had once been. "But generally these men are out of view, from themselves, from each other, from the rest of us."

"How would anyone work out where to find them?"

"Now, this is the kind of question Tova Chaya used to ask—a question Rabbi Mandelbaum cannot answer!" The two exchanged warm smiles, like an old man with a favorite granddaughter. "I wish I knew, Mr. Monroe, but I don't. For this, you would need to talk to others. Those who have penetrated the deepest secrets of the kabbalah."

Will could see the rabbi was getting tired. And yet Will did not want to let their conversation end. In the last thirty minutes he had got more answers than he had had in the previous forty-eight hours. At last he not only understood the barrage of clues that had arrived by text message but now could see the wider picture, the ancient story unfolding. Surely this wise old man held the key to why Beth was a captive. If only Will could think of the right question.

There was a buzzing sound, the low vibration of a cell phone. TC, so used to wearing combat trousers with multiple pockets, seemed flummoxed by the realization she was now in a long, pocketless skirt: she did not know where to look. Eventually she remembered. She had borrowed a smart leather handbag of Beth's—more grown-up than anything TC owned herself. The phone was in there. Blushing a deep crimson, and muttering a garbled apology to the rabbi, she stepped out of the room to answer it. Will took a moment to understand her embarrassment: using the telephone on Yom Kippur was strictly forbidden.

He was scrambling to absorb everything he had just heard. Wild theories about the end of the world, dire warnings of a cataclysm foretold. He put his head in his hands. What on earth was he caught up in here?

Suddenly there was a hand on his shoulder.

"It is a terrible thing for a man to be without his wife. Mrs. Mandelbaum has been dead three years, and I carry on with my life. I still study, I still pray. But if, occasionally, I dream of her at night—ahhh, now that's a *shabbos*."

Will felt his eyes soaking with tears. To break the spell, he cleared his throat and collected himself to ask a question. He did not know if it would help him find Beth, but he wanted to know everything he could. "What counts as good? What counts as such a good deed that it marks you out as righteous?"

"I'm not sure it's as simple as this. One has to think of the soul of the tzaddik. This is a soul of such purity, of such goodness, that it cannot help but express itself. The deeds are merely the outward manifestation of a goodness that is within." The rabbi began to haul himself out of his chair as if on a book-hunting expedition. "One of our key texts is known as the Tanya. In that book, there is a definition of the tzaddik. It explains that in each person there are two souls: a divine soul and an animal soul. The divine soul is where we have our conscience, our urge to do good, our desire to learn and study. The animal soul is where we have our appetites, for food, for drink; lust. This is all from the animal soul.

"Now, these two souls are usually in conflict. A good person works hard to control his animal soul. To restrain his desires, not to give in to every longing. That's what it is to be a regular, good person—to struggle!" He gave a creased smile, as if in recognition of the frailty of man. "But a tzaddik is different. A tzaddik does not just tame his animal soul. He *transforms* it. He changes his animal soul into something else, turning it into a force for good. Now he is firing on two cylinders, so to speak! It's as if he has two divine souls. This gives him a special power. It equips him to save the world."

"And would one act be enough?"

"How do you mean?"

"Well, if a man had performed one act of extraordinary goodness, would that be enough to say he was a tzaddik."

"Perhaps you have some example in mind, yes? My answer is that it may seem to us as if the tzaddik performed just one holy act. But remember, these men hide their goodness. The truth may be that this is the only act we *know* about."

"And what might such an act look like?"

"Ah, this is a good question. You know, in that story about Rabbi Abbahu and the man in the whorehouse—"

"The story from the third century?"

"Yes. In that story, the tzaddik has done something very small. I forget the details, but he makes some small sacrifice to preserve the dignity of a woman."

Will heard himself gulp. *Just like Macrae.*

"And this seems to be the common thread. Sometimes it is an

act on a very large scale"—Will thought of Chancellor Curtis in London, diverting precious millions to the poor—"perhaps a tzaddik will save an entire city from destruction. Sometimes it is a tiny gesture to one individual: a meal when they are hungry, a blanket when they are cold. In each case, the tzaddik has treated a fellow human being justly and generously."

"And in that way, even a small gesture might redeem a whole life?"

"Yes, Mr. Monroe. The tzaddik may have lived as if he was drenched in sin. Think of Chaim the Watercarrier, drinking himself into oblivion. But those acts of righteousness, they change the world."

"So goodness is not about rules. Or wearing a hair shirt. Or praying hard. Or knowing every word in the Bible. It's about how we treat each other."

"*Bein adam v'adam.* Between man and man. That is where goodness, even divinity resides. Not in the heavens, but right here on earth. In our relations with each other. It also means we have to be careful. We have to treat everyone we meet with great respect because, for all we know, this man driving a cab or sweeping the streets or begging on a street corner, he might be one of the righteous."

"That's pretty egalitarian, isn't it?"

The rabbi smiled. "The equal value of every human life. This is the preoccupation of Torah. This is what Tova Chaya studied each day at the seminary. And what she studied here with me, before . . ." The rabbi looked wistful and, suddenly, very old. He did not finish his sentence.

Will felt guilty. Not personally—he knew he was not to blame for TC leaving all those years ago. But he felt guilty as—he struggled to articulate it—as a representative of the modern world. That was it. It was modernity, America, that had lured young Tova Chaya away from the routines and rhythms that had shaped Jewish lives for centuries, whether in rural Russia or Crown Heights. Modern America had seduced her.

And yet, Will could see that TC had lost something by leaving. He could hear it in Rabbi Mandelbaum's voice, and he had seen it in TC's eyes. He had experienced it for himself in those few hours before he was grabbed and grilled on Friday night. This place had something Will had hardly known, either growing up in England or living as an adult in America. The bland word for it was *community.* People fantasized about that often enough. Back home, the myth of the English village, where everyone knows everyone else, still exerted a powerful hold, though Will had never seen it for real. In America, suburban picket-fence neighborhoods liked to think they were communities—with their carpools and block parties—but they did not have what Will had seen in Crown Heights.

Here, people were as involved with each other as one large, extended family. An elaborate welfare system meant that each provided for the other as if they were drawing from a common pot. Children were in and out of each other's houses. No one seemed to be strangers. TC had explained that the claustrophobia could be choking: she had had to get out to breathe. But she also described a warmth, a shared life, she had never known again.

Rabbi Mandelbaum had his head down, turning the pages of yet another book. "There is one more thing. I don't know if this will be useful or not. According to several legends, one of these thirty-six men is even more special than the others."

"Really? What kind of special?"

"One of these thirty-six is the Messiah."

Will leaned forward. "The Messiah?"

" 'If the age were worthy of it, he would reveal himself as such.' That's what the scholars say."

"The candidate," Will said softly.

"Someone explained this to you already?"

"TC told me that in every generation there is a candidate to be Messiah. If now were the messianic time, then that man would be it. If it's not the time, then nothing happens."

"We have to be worthy. Otherwise, the opportunity is lost."

Almost involuntarily, Will looked at the photographs of the

Rebbe, gazing out from every wall and every angle. Dead more than a decade, his eyes still shone.

"Exactly," said Rabbi Mandelbaum, following Will's eyes. And the two men looked at each other.

The door opened. TC was standing there, clutching her phone. There was no color in her face; her eyes were glassy, like the eyes of an animal stunned for slaughter.

She bent down and whispered in Will's ear. "The police are after me. I'm wanted for murder."

CHAPTER FORTY-SIX

MONDAY, 2:20 A.M., DARWIN, NORTHERN AUSTRALIA

THE MUSIC HAD STOPPED; that was why he had gone in. He kept this up throughout his shift, whether it was day or night—tiptoeing into the room to take out the finished CD and replace it with a new one. The bedside cupboard was full of them, Schubert mainly, left there by the old man's daughter. The family had not asked Djalu to do it, but he knew it was what they wanted.

He put on the record. He could hear wailing from the next room along; he would have to be there in a second. But he wanted to stay a while with this resident, Mr. Clark, the man who loved music. Djalu had only seen him awake for an hour or two each day; the sedative kept him asleep the rest of the time. But in those conscious minutes, Mr. Clark seemed healed by the sounds of violins and cellos that uncoiled from the CD and into the room like skeins of fine thread. His aged lips parted as if to taste the melodies; his mouth sometimes made the same tiny movement even when he was in deep slumber.

Djalu would seize on those moments to take the small sponge, mounted on a stick, dip it into the bedside glass of water, and brush it onto Mr. Clark's mouth. The old man, nearly eighty-five, could no longer eat or drink, not without vomiting. So this was the only way to give him sustenance. He was dying, like so many of the people in this place, not from the disease that had assailed him for months but of starvation and eventual dehydration. Once it was clear that the patient could never be cured, the organs would be allowed to pack up, one by one, until death finally arrived.

It seemed a cruel way to let a person die. Djalu's father denounced it as typical of white man's medicine, all science and no spirit. Sometimes Djalu thought he was right; after all, he had seen some terrible things in this place. Old women lying in pools of their own urine; men crying out for hours to be helped to the toilet. Some of the nurses quickly lost patience, shouting at the residents, telling them to shut up. Or addressing them by their first names, as if they were babies.

In his first few months, Djalu had gone with the flow. He did not want to draw attention to himself, one of only two aboriginal care assistants in the home. His position was hardly secure, not with a résumé that included two spells in jail—one for burglary, the other for shoplifting. So he said nothing when the senior staff, hearing moans or screams from down the corridor, would turn up the TV to drown out the noise.

Even now he said nothing. He made no complaints to the matron or the manager; he wanted no fuss and no hassle. Sometimes he even joined in the jokes about the "crinkly old buggers." But he did what he could.

So when he heard a resident crying out, he ran. He was part of what the nursing home called Team Red, responsible for about two dozen beds. But if he saw a light flashing for a resident in Blue or Green, he went anyway—often sneaking in, hoping none of the staff would see him. He made sure Mr. Martyn sipped some water or that Miss Anderson was turned over. And if they had soiled themselves, he would clean them up, wiping them gently, afterward stroking their hair, trying to soothe away their shame.

He heard how some of the residents referred to him. "Matron, I don't want that boong touching me," one had said when Djalu first appeared at his bedside. "It's wrong." But Djalu put that down to their age. They did not know any better.

Mr. Clark had not been much friendlier. "Which one are you?" he had asked.

"Which one, Mr. Clark?"

"Yes, there's that other abo, whatsisname? Which one are you?"

But Djalu could not feel angry, not with a man who was in the last days of his life. So he brought tea and biscuits when Mrs. Clark visited; brought her a tissue when he found her quietly sobbing; and when she fell asleep in the chair by the bed, he draped a blanket over her.

Maybe his father was right that European medicine was a cold, metallic discipline. So he, Djalu, would give it a warm, human face—even if that face seemed to scare so many of these dying white folks.

This was his favorite time to work, late at night when he could have the corridor to himself. He would not need to explain his presence in the rooms, would not need to make up excuses for why he was reading the newspaper out loud to a woman on the second floor, not on the Red list, or simply holding the hand of a man who craved the touch of another human being.

So he jumped when he saw the door to Mr. Clark's room creak open. The woman who came in had her finger to her lips, hushing Djalu. Her eyes were smiling, as if she were planning on giving Mr. Clark a surprise and did not want Djalu to ruin it.

"Good evening, Djalu."

"You gave me a fright. I didn't realize you were working tonight."

"Well, you know death. It never sleeps."

Djalu leapt to his feet. "Did someone die tonight?"

"Not yet. But I expect it."

"Who? Maybe I should—"

"Djalu, don't get excited. OK?" Calmly, the woman bent down and pulled out several of the CDs in the bedside cabinet, letting them fall to the floor.

"Hey, miss. That's Mr. Clark's music. I'm looking after it—"

"Here it is." She had reached behind the discs for what looked like a bandage. Now she lay it on the bed, on the square of mattress next to Mr. Clark's chest, which was rising and falling like a set of bellows. The old man was fast asleep.

She opened up the bandage, pulling one flap of material to the left, the other to the right, to reveal a hypodermic needle alongside a vial of clear serum.

"Is the doctor coming? No one told me."

"No, the doctor is not coming." She snapped on a pair of latex gloves.

"You giving Mr. Clark a shot? What you doing?"

"I'll show you if you like. Come closer."

"Don't hurt him."

"Relax, Djalu. Now come over here, and you can see. A bit closer."

The woman held the needle up to the window, where it made a silhouette against the moonlight. "Now, Djalu, if you can place your hands on Mr. Clark's shoulders. That's it, just bend slightly."

Cleanly, the woman jabbed the needle into Djalu's neck, her thumb pushing the plunger hard, sending the drug swimming into his veins within an instant. Djalu had a second to turn around, his face frozen in astonishment. A second later, he fell forward, landing heavily on Mr. Clark's heaving chest.

His killer had to use all her strength to haul Djalu off and lay him smoothly on the floor. She laid a blanket over him, stopping only to close his eyes with the palm of her hand.

"I apologize, Djalu Banggala, for what I have done. But I have done it in the name of the Lord God Almighty. Amen."

She packed the needle and the empty vial back into the bandage, tucked it into her pocket and headed out, noiselessly. Mr. Clark did not stir. If he heard anything, it was only music—the insistent strings of one of Schubert's most famous pieces. *Death and the Maiden.*

CHAPTER FORTY-SEVEN

SUNDAY, 10:10 P.M., CROWN HEIGHTS, BROOKLYN

TC WAS LEADING THE WAY, FAST AND DETERMINED. She was not to be diverted. She had last walked these streets a decade ago, but she had not forgotten where Rabbi Freilich lived.

Rushing to keep up, Will was firing off questions. But TC was staring straight ahead. "They found the body a couple of hours ago. On the floor of my apartment. Apparently no one realized he had gone missing till this morning."

"Christ. How long do they think he'd been dead?"

"Since last night. He was killed in my apartment, Will." TC's voice wavered for the first time.

Will thought of the super's face: the Garry Kasparov of the basement. If he had been killed last night, it could only have been minutes after he had helped Will and TC escape. That was surely why he had been murdered. An image jumped into Will's mind. *The man in the baseball cap.*

First Yosef Yitzhok, now Pugachov. Two people who had come to Will's aid had paid for it with their lives. Who would be next? Rabbi Mandelbaum? Tom Fontaine?

Ever since Friday morning Will had felt as if he was falling down a mineshaft, getting farther and farther away from the light. He could see nothing clearly. The rabbi had explained what was surely going on, but how on earth did it involve him and Beth? What had they got to do with this mystical prophecy, a kabbalistic legend that now appeared to be fuelling an international killing spree? He was falling and falling.

And just when he thought he had hit rock bottom—hearing of the killing in Bangkok or of YY's death—he would fall some more. Now Pugachov was dead, and TC was in dire trouble.

"Janey says the police knocked on every door, asking after the occupant of Apartment 7. Thank God she was in. She told them my name and said she hadn't seen me since yesterday afternoon, which is good. Luckily, she was smart enough to say she didn't know my cell number. They just left and she phoned me right away, to give me a heads-up."

"And they definitely regard you as the suspect?"

"Janey says she got that impression. Why else was the guy in my apartment? He went in there alive, and now he's dead. I'm gone. What else does it look like?"

TC was still striding forward, her breath forming instant clouds. Her cheeks were beginning to glow. "Apparently, they asked lots of weird questions."

"What kind of weird questions?"

"About me and Pugachov. Did we have a sexual relationship? Was he obsessed with me? Was he a stalker?"

Now Will understood what the police were thinking. Pugachov, the psycho super, gets himself into TC's apartment after midnight. Tries to rape her. TC reaches for her gun, kills him, and flees the scene.

"It won't take long for them to get your cell number. The police must have access to all that."

"Hence this." TC held up the carcass of a cell phone, minus its battery. Once the police had her number, they would doubtless be able to track it. Will had covered a couple of investigations where detectives reconstructed someone's movements using phone records. These not only revealed the numbers the suspect had dialed, but each time they had come within range of a transmitter. Police could draw a map showing where someone had been and when—unless the phone was completely without power: no signal, no trace.

"When did you last have it on?"

"Mandelbaum's."

"It won't take them long to get there. Will he talk?"

TC slowed down and turned her eyes to meet Will's. "I don't know."

They had come to Rabbi Freilich's house, no grander than any of the others in Crown Heights. The paint was peeling on the front door, but that was not what Will noticed. Rather it was the bumper sticker that had been placed just above eye level: "Moshiach is coming."

If these were student digs, it would not have looked incongruous. But this was the home of a grown-up, a man of standing. The sticker sent a tremor through Will. It said one thing: fanatic.

TC had already knocked on the door, and now Will could hear movement. Through the opaque glass, he could see the outline of a man's head and shoulders.

"Ver is? Vi haistu?"

Yiddish, Will imagined.

"*S'is Tova Chaya Lieberman, Reb Freilich.* I've come because of the great *sakono.*"

"Vos heyst?" What do you mean?

"Reb Freilich, a sakono fur die gantseh breeye." The same warning she had given Rabbi Mandelbaum: a threat to all creation.

The door opened to reveal the man Will had talked to at some length but had never seen. He was neither tall, nor physically commanding, but his face had stern, firm features that, Will could see, conveyed a quiet authority. His beard was brown rather than white or gray, and it was short and well-kept. He wore neat, rimless glasses. In a different context, Will could see him as the CEO of a moderate-sized American company. As he saw and recognized Will, he hesitated, then gave a dip of the head, a gesture Will chose to interpret as contrition.

"You'd better come inside."

They were ushered in once again to sit around a dining table—white tablecloth, plastic sheet—in a room filled with holy books. This room, though, was large, airy, and tidy. In a corner, Will spotted a pile of editions of the *New York Times.* He could also see a magazine rack stuffed with the *Atlantic Monthly*, the *New Republic*, and a variety of Hebrew newspapers. Making the instant assessment that was part of his trade, Will wrote a four-word headline in his head to describe Rabbi Freilich: "Man of the World."

"Rabbi, you know Will Monroe."

"We've met."

"I know how strange this must seem, Rabbi Freilich, me turning up like this after all these years. I promise you, I never thought I'd come back, truly I didn't. But Will is an old friend of mine. And he asked for my help when his wife went missing. He didn't know about my . . . my background." She paused to collect herself. "But now we know what's going on. We've pieced it together. It's taken some time and it's not been easy, but we are certain."

Rabbi Freilich held TC's gaze and said nothing.

"Good men are dying. First it was Howard Macrae in Brownsville, then Pat Baxter in Montana. Then Samak Sangsuk in Bangkok. And now this British politician. Someone is killing the *lamadvavniks*, aren't they, Rabbi? Someone is killing the righteous of the earth."

"Yes, Tova Chaya. I'm afraid they are."

Will drew breath, a tiny gasp. He had expected a battle with Freilich, a round of game playing as the rabbi played dumb, forcing TC and Will to produce all their evidence. But he was denying nothing. A dread thought surfaced. What if the rabbi had already realized that these two had indeed exposed his murderous plot and had therefore decided there was no alternative but to silence them? They would have walked straight into his hands! No need for the man in the baseball cap, Pugachov's killer: Will and TC had done his job for them. How could they have been so stupid? They had not even planned a strategy for this encounter. TC had just stormed over there . . .

"A plot is indeed under way to murder the thirty-six hidden just men. For some reason, this plot is taking place now, during the Ten Days of Penitence—the holiest time of the year. The killing started on Rosh Hashanah, and it has not stopped. Whoever is behind this must have decided that these are the judgment days, that a righteous man murdered in this period will not be instantly replaced by the birth of another. Perhaps they have seen something in our texts we never saw, the existence of a kind of limbo period between the New Year, when people are inscribed in the Book of Life, and the Day of Atonement, when the Book of Life is sealed. During these ten days maybe the world is especially vulnerable. Whatever their reasoning, they have set out to kill the *lamad vav*, and they seem determined to do it by sunset tomorrow, by the end of Yom Kippur." He faltered. "I didn't think anyone else would find out." He turned toward Will, though not quite meeting his eyes. "Tova Chaya was always an exceptional student. And you, you have shown admirable persistence."

Thanks for nothing, thought Will.

"We have known about it only for a few days. But I tremble for the world at the very thought of it. Some will say this is only a legend, only a fairy story. But it has deep roots, ones that go back to Avraham Avinu, to Abraham our father. It has endured for millennia. What if it is anything but a story? What if it is a true statement about the way the world has worked since the beginning of time? Whoever is doing this is testing the idea to destruction. It will be the destruction of everything." The rabbi was drumming his fingers on the table. If he was faking anxiety, thought Will, he was doing a very good job.

"You keep saying *they*," Will said suddenly, his confidence taking even himself aback. "But I'm not sure there is a *they.* I think there's a *you.*"

"I don't understand."

"Oh, I think you do, Rabbi Freilich. So far there are no suspects in any of these cases, except you and your, your . . . followers." He knew it was the wrong word. The only leader these people followed was the man whose photograph hung on every wall. And he was dead. "You more or less admitted killing Samak Sangsuk to me." The muscle around the rabbi's left eye gave a slight twitch. "And I know you are holding my wife, though what she has to do with any of this, still no one has explained to me." On those last words, he had raised his voice, betraying an anger he could not conceal. He stopped, to bring himself back under control. "The only people we *know* have been engaged in criminal activity are you and the people who work with you."

"I can see how it looks."

"So can I. And I'm sure the police, who have you in their sights already, would get the picture very quickly if they knew half of what we know. I don't think I need to mention Mr. Pugachov, the super at TC's, sorry, Tova Chaya's, building, do I? Killed last night by that goon in a baseball cap you had chasing us?"

"I'm sorry, I don't know what you're talking about."

"Oh, come on. We really can't play these games much longer, Rabbi. Don't you see? We know what's going on."

"Will, that's enough." It was TC, speaking in her normal accent.

"I have no idea about any Mr. Pugachov. And I know nothing of any man in a baseball cap."

"I don't believe this. This is ridiculous! You sent a man to follow me yesterday. We saw him, we got away, and the man who helped us is now lying dead in her apartment." He could hardly bring himself to use the name Tova Chaya again. It sounded strange enough the first time.

"Will, please." TC was imploring him to stop. But he could not help himself. The pressure of the last few days had been coiled up for too long.

The rabbi's face was tensing. "I promise you, I know of no man in a baseball cap. I did not send anyone to follow you. I have not lied to you. Not once. When you confronted me about the man in Bangkok, I did not deny it. I told you that a terrible mistake had occurred. When we"—he paused for the right word—"met on *erev shabbos*—excuse me—when we met on Friday night, I even conceded that we are indeed holding your wife. I have not lied. And I am telling you the truth now: what you tell me happened in Tova Chaya's building was nothing to do with me."

"So who do you think did it, then? Eh? If you didn't kill that man, who did?"

"I don't know. Which should worry you infinitely more. It suggests that whoever is behind this dreadful scheme is now aware of you."

"Rabbi Freilich, I think you have to tell us what's going on." TC was sounding like Tova Chaya again. "You know things, we know things. We all know time is running out. It is already the Day of Judgment. Whoever is doing this wants to finish the job before the Ten Days of Penitence are over. We don't have time to fight each other. So far, handling this alone, what have you done? Have you stopped the killing?"

The rabbi had his head bowed, his right palm flat on his forehead. It moved up onto his scalp, tucking under his yarmulke, and back down again. Whatever TC was saying, it was striking a nerve. The man looked weighed down with worry. He muttered a barely audible no.

TC sat forward, trying to close the deal. "The killing is still going on. In twenty-four hours they might have killed the last of the *lamadvavniks*. And who knows what will happen then. You can't do this alone. We can help you and you have to help us. You must do it. For the sake of HaShem."

For the sake of the Name, for the sake of God himself. It was the ultimate argument, the one no believer could refuse. Was TC deploying it because she knew which buttons to press? Or was Tova Chaya speaking sincerely, genuinely fearing for the sake of the world if they did not act? Will was not sure. But if he had to guess one way or the other he would, to his great surprise, declare for the latter. For all her skepticism, for all her ten years away from Crown Heights, for all her bacon breakfasts and body piercings, she was not acting merely to find Will's wife, nor even for the sake of the remaining righteous men. At that moment Will realized that TC was driven by nothing less than fear for the fate of the world.

"Tova Chaya, we have so little time." Rabbi Freilich was looking up. He had removed his glasses, revealing a face etched in anguish. "We have tried everything. I don't know what more there is you can do. But I will tell you what we know."

Unexpectedly, he rose to his feet and made for the front door. He put on his trilby and his coat and, without another word, gestured for TC and Will to follow him.

Outside was a quiet Will had never experienced in a city. The streets were desolate. No cars were on the streets because the Yom Kippur restrictions prohibited all driving. A few knots of young men walked together, wearing their prayer shawls. Even though the evening was warm and people were out together, the atmosphere was not festive. Instead Crown Heights seemed to be under a blanket of contemplation and silent thought; it was as if the whole neighborhood was a single, roofless synagogue. Will felt grateful for his costume, so that he could move through this extraordinary atmosphere without breaking the spell.

They were, Will now understood, moving toward the synagogue. Once again, he wondered if he and TC were walking voluntarily into the wolf's lair—with the wolf as their guide.

But they did not go in through the main entrance. Instead they entered a building next door, one that seemed entirely out of place in this neighborhood. It looked like a red-brick annex to an Oxford college, ancient by New York standards. Outside were crowds of men, spilling out from the lobby. They did not have to wade through the throng: people stepped out of the way the moment they recognized the rabbi. Will could see some raised eyebrows. He assumed they were directed at him, a face they did not know. But when he saw TC looking down at her feet, he understood: they were shocked to see a woman in this usually male terrain.

TC managed to whisper an explanation. They were entering the Rebbe's house. This was the home the late leader had lived in and which had doubled as his office.

Will stared. He had been here before, forty-eight hours earlier.

Soon they had reached a staircase. The crowds were thinning now. They moved up another flight, to a corridor empty of people. Straight into his trap, thought Will.

Rabbi Freilich led them through one door, which revealed another. But he did not go in. Instead he turned around, to offer an explanation to TC.

"I want you to know that what you are about to see is a mark of our desperation. It is a violation of Yom Kippur that has never before occurred in this building and, please God, will never happen again. We are doing it for—"

"Pikuach nefesh." TC had interrupted him. "I know. It is a matter of saving lives."

The rabbi nodded, grateful to TC for her understanding. Then he turned around, breathing in sharply through his nostrils as if bracing himself for the secret he was about to reveal. Only then did Rabbi Freilich dare open the door.

CHAPTER FORTY-EIGHT

Sunday, 11:01 p.m., Crown Heights, Brooklyn

THIS PLACE, WILL REALIZED, would normally be still on such a holy evening: no lights on, no machines in use, no phones answered, no eating, no drinking. Even Will could tell that the scene before him was an act of mass sacrilege.

It looked like the control room of a police station. Perhaps a dozen people at computers, surrounded by in-trays spilling over with paper and, on a back wall, a large whiteboard, covered with names, phone numbers, addresses. Down one side, Will could see a list of names. In a quick scan, he spotted Howard Macrae and Gavin Curtis—a line through each of them.

"No one knows about this room apart from the men working in it—and now you. We have been working in here day and night for a week. And today we lost the man who knew it best, the man who set it up."

"Yosef Yitzhok," said Will, noticing a pile of maps—one of them for Montana—and a stack of guide books, for London, for Copenhagen, for Algiers.

"All of this was his work. And today he was murdered."

"Rabbi Freilich?" It was TC. "Do you think you could start at the beginning?"

The rabbi led them to the front of the room, where a desk had been set out as if for a teacher to supervise an exam. The three of them sat around it.

"As you know, the Rebbe in his later years spoke often about Moshiach, about the Messiah. He gave long talks at our weekly *farbrengen* touching on this theme. Tova Chaya will also know how we preserved those talks for posterity."

TC took her cue. "Because he spoke on the Sabbath, the Rebbe could not be tape-recorded or filmed. That's not allowed. So we relied on an ancient system. In the synagogue would be three or four people chosen for their amazing memories. They would stand just a few yards away from the Rebbe, usually with their eyes closed, listening to every word, memorizing what he said. Then, the minute the Sabbath was over, they would gather together and kind of spew out their memories, while one of them would scribble it all down. They would get it out of their heads as quickly as they could. While they were doing it, they would check what they remembered against each other, adding a word here, correcting a word there. I can still picture it: these guys were incredible. They could listen to a three-hour speech by the Rebbe and recite it off by heart. They were called *choyzers*, literally 'returners.' The Rebbe would say it, they would play it back. They were human tape recorders."

"And, Tova Chaya, do you remember who was the most brilliant *choyzer* of them all?"

TC's eyes suddenly widened, as a long-buried memory came back. "But he was just a boy."

"It's true. But he became a *choyzer* soon after he had reached the age of bar mitzvah. He was just thirteen when he began relaying the words of the Rebbe. He had a special gift." Freilich faced Will. "We are speaking about Yosef Yitzhok."

"He could memorize whole speeches, just like that?"

"He always said he could not memorize whole speeches. Only the words of the Rebbe. When the Rebbe spoke, he would make himself, his own thoughts, disappear. He would try to insert himself into the mind of the Rebbe, to become an extension of him. That was his technique. No one else could do it the way he could. The Rebbe had a special—affection for him." Rabbi Freilich rolled back into his seat, his eyes closed. Will could only guess, but this grief looked genuine.

"As I said, in his last years, the Rebbe began to speak more and more about Moshiach. Telling us to prepare for the coming of Messiah, reminding us that Messiah was a central belief in Judaism. That it was not some abstract, remote point of theology but that it was real. He wanted us to believe it, that Moshiach could be with us in the here and now.

"No one knew this teaching of the Rebbe's better than Yosef Yitzhok. He heard it week after week. But it was more than hearing. It was *absorbing*. He was ingesting this material, taking it into himself. And then, long after the Rebbe was gone, Yosef Yitzhok—who was now a brilliant scholar in his own right—noticed something.

"He thought back to all the talks the Rebbe had given on the theme of the messianic age, and he discerned a pattern. Very often the Rebbe would quote a *pasuk*—"

"A verse."

"Thank you, Tova Chaya. Yes, the Rebbe would quote a verse from Deuteronomy. *Tzedek, tzedek tirdof*."

"Justice, justice shall you pursue," TC murmured.

"The English translation the books give is, 'Follow justice and justice alone, so that you may live and possess the land the Lord your God is giving you.' But it was that word, *tzedek*, that caught Yosef Yitzhok's attention. To use it so often, and always in the same context. It was as if the Rebbe had been reminding us of something."

"He wanted you to remember the tzaddikim. The righteous men."

"That's what Yosef Yitzhok thought. So he went back through the texts, examining them intensely. And that's how he saw something else, something even more intriguing."

Will leaned forward, his eyes boring into the rabbi's.

"In close proximity to the quotation—*tzedek, tzedek tirdof*—he would offer another quotation. Not the same one every time, but from the same two sources. Either he would cite the book of Proverbs—"

"Chapter ten?"

"Yes, Mr. Monroe. Chapter ten. That's right. You knew all this already?"

"Think of it as an informed guess. Don't let me interrupt you; please, continue."

"Well, as you say, the Rebbe would either quote a verse from Proverbs, chapter ten, or he would quote from the prophets. Specifically, Isaiah, chapter thirty. Now that got Yosef Yitzhok very excited. Because kabbalists know one important thing about Isaiah, chapter thirty, verse eighteen. It ends with the word *lo*, the Hebrew for 'for him.' The full phrase is 'blessed are all they who wait for Him.' But the real significance of the word—"

"—is the way it is spelled."

"Tova Chaya has beaten me to it. The word *lo* is made up of two characters, Mr. Monroe. *Lamad* and *vav.* It spells thirty-six. Now the Rebbe was a careful speaker. He did not say things by accident. He did not pull quotations out of the air. Yosef Yitzhok was convinced there was a deliberate intent.

"So he went through every transcript. And, sure enough, the Rebbe spoke of *tzedek*, followed immediately by a verse from one of those two chapters, thirty-five times. By that method, he left us with thirty-five different verses."

"But—"

"I know what you're thinking, Mr. Monroe, and you are right. There are thirty-six righteous men. We'll come to that. For the moment, Yosef Yitzhok has thirty-five verses, staring at him from the page. He wonders what they could mean. And then he remembers the stories that children like him and like you, Tova Chaya, were raised on. Stories of the founder of Hasidism, the Baal Shem Tov; stories of Rabbi Leib Sorres."

"Men of such greatness, they were privileged to know the whereabouts of the righteous men." Will looked at Tova Chaya as she spoke: she had, he was sure, worked it all out.

"Exactly. Few men knew the mind of the Rebbe as intimately as Yosef Yitzhok, and he also knew the Rebbe's worth. He knew that he was one of the great men of Hasidic history. Some of the very greatest had been let in on this divine secret. It was not absurd to imagine the Rebbe would be one of them."

"So Yosef Yitzhok reckoned the Rebbe knew who the thirty-six were. And he goes further: he thinks these thirty-five verses he quoted are clues to their identity?"

"Exactly, Will. The trouble is, the Rebbe is no longer around to explain. He can answer no questions."

"So what does Yosef Yitzhok do?"

"He stares at the thirty-five verses for days on end. He is sure the Rebbe wanted them to be understood, that he was passing this information on for a reason. So Yosef Yitzhok is determined to break them open, so to speak, to find out what is inside. He looks at them from every angle. He translates the letters into numeric values; he adds; he multiplies. He reproduces them as anagrams. But of course there is a logical problem.

"How *could* the identities of the righteous men be contained in those verses? The identities change in every generation. Yet the verses stay stubbornly the same. Even if, say, verse twenty included the name of tzaddik number twenty for this year, where would we find the name of tzaddik number twenty for the year 2020 or 2050 or, in the past, 1950 and 1850? How could the names of men who are alive today be concealed in a text that remains static?

"And that's when Yosef Yitzhok's remarkable powers truly shone through. He remembered the answer."

"You mean the Rebbe had told him?"

"Not directly, of course. But the Rebbe had given him the answer. Yosef Yitzhok had heard it. All he needed to do was to remember it. And do you know what it was? It was the last line of the last talk at the last *farbrengen* the Rebbe ever addressed. 'Space depends on time. Time reveals space.' Those were his last words in public."

There was a pause.

"Incredible," said TC.

"You've lost me, I'm afraid," said Will, suddenly the dunce of the class.

"Don't worry. Yosef Yitzhok was baffled too. These were beautiful sentences. But they were an enigma. *Space depends on time. Time reveals space.* What does that mean? That's when Yosef Yitzhok came to me, letting me in on his theory. The Rebbe often spoke in riddles, in elliptical sentences that might take many hours—many years even—to study and interpret. Yosef Yitzhok spent a long night working away at these sentences. And then he had what you would call a brainwave, and what I would call a helping hand from HaShem.

"You may know that the Rebbe was a very close follower of science and technology. He read *Scientific American* and *Nature* and a whole variety of journals. He was always up to date on the latest developments, in neuroscience, in biochemistry. But he had a special interest in technology. He loved gadgets! He never owned them: he was the least materialistic man you could ever know. But he liked to know about them.

"Yosef Yitzhok knew that about the Rebbe. And that's what gave him his idea. Here, I'll show you."

Rabbi Freilich reached for a worn, leather-bound book and thumbed rapidly through the pages. He found the page and then the verse he was looking for.

"Now what is the year?"

Will was about to answer when TC got there first. "Five thousand seven hundred and sixty-eight."

Will frowned. "What?"

"It's the Hebrew calendar," TC explained. "It dates back to creation. Jews believe the world has been in existence for less than six thousand years."

"OK," said the rabbi. "The year is 5768. And here is a verse from chapter ten of the book of Proverbs. In fact this is a crucial verse. Verse eighteen. This is what Yosef Yitzhok tried out. We count along the line and mark the fifth letter." The rabbi's finger stopped at the selected character. "Then the seventh from there." It stopped again. "Then the sixth from there. And then the eighth. You see: 5-7-6-8. And we keep doing that till we get to the end of the line. So in this case, the fifth letter is a *yud.* The seventh letter after that is a *hay.* The sixth is a *mem.* And the eighth is also a *mem.* You keep on like that until you have a string of letters."

"Which then convert into numbers." Will was guessing.

"Precisely so. A string of numbers. Here, I'll show you one of the very earliest ones Yosef Yitzhok worked out."

The rabbi stood up, leading Will and TC over to a second whiteboard. There, neatly written in black marker pen, was a long series of digits: 699331, 5709718, 30.

"Don't tell me that's a phone number."

"No, it is not. We wondered about that, too. We even tried a few. No, this is where the Rebbe's eye for the latest advances in technology was so important."

TC was staring at the figure, as if the sheer penetration of her gaze would crack it open.

"It is"—and at this the rabbi could not deny himself a little smile of amused pride, as if he had still not got over the brilliance of it all—"a GPS number. Or rather, contained in this number are the coordinates of longitude and latitude that give you a GPS number, coordinates for the Global Positioning System."

"I don't believe it," said Will. "You mean that whole satellite navigation thing?" It sounded preposterous.

"That's it. A system that maps the entire globe, watched from space, and which gives precise coordinates for any spot on earth. The Rebbe must have read about it. Or maybe he just knew."

"You're telling me that contained in those thirty-five biblical verses are the coordinates for thirty-five righteous men?"

"We did not believe it either, Mr. Monroe. One verse gave us a number for a remote hillside in Montana: according to the map, nobody lived there. But we sent the man who runs our center in Seattle to take a closer look, and he saw a log cabin. With a man inside, living alone. Like something from our folktales, Tova Chaya: a simple man in the forest."

Pat Baxter, thought Will. The very cabin he had gazed at just a few days ago.

"Another number was an empty space in the middle of the Sudan. Again, no one was meant to live there. But then we saw from satellite pictures that a refugee camp had sprung up on that spot during the last few months, saving people who were fleeing for their lives. It was maintained by one man: the international agencies were not even sure who he was. So we began to realize that we were right. That the Rebbe was right."

"What about this number?" asked Will, pointing at the whiteboard. "What did this come out as?"

"I'll show you." The rabbi walked the few paces to where one of the young men was working away at a computer. TC and Will caught up, watching the technician over his shoulder. The rabbi pointed at the number on the whiteboard and murmured an instruction.

The young man punched in the digits, waited a few seconds, and then watched as the computer came back with an answer:

11 Downing Street, London, SW1 2AB, UK.

"So this was the verse for Gavin Curtis?"

The rabbi nodded.

Will needed to sit down and, ideally, drink something. Though nothing was around. These men would use computers and work hard, even though it was Yom Kippur, because lives were at stake. *Pikuach nefesh.* But they would break no rules they did not have to.

Now TC was speaking. "So that was what the Rebbe was trying to say. *Space depends on time. Time reveals space.* The location depends on time. If you know the time, the year—if you use the number 5678—then you will know the space. You'll work out the location." She was shaking her head in wonder at the ingenuity of it. "And I suppose if you try the same verses with different years, you get different places. Different people."

"Well, our texts are good at guarding their secrets, Tova Chaya. Yosef Yitzhok wanted to do as you say. He worked with people here to devise a computer program, to do what we just did with that one verse: stopping at every fifth or seventh character. He did it for different years. And then he ran it through the GPS system and, sure enough, he started getting place names. But what use is a place name, Kabul or Mainz, for 1735? How are we to know who lived there then? Besides, Yosef Yitzhok always wondered if that was too easy."

"If what was too easy?"

"He wasn't sure it would necessarily be the same verses for all time. Those were the verses the Rebbe had mentioned for *his* generation. But maybe the other great sages who had somehow been let in on this secret in the past—the Baal Shem Tov or Rabbi Leib Sorres—maybe they knew of the righteous men of their time in a different way. They didn't have this GPS, did they? This method wouldn't have made much sense to them, would it? They would have had their own ways—different verses, or maybe a different method entirely.

"This, I now realize, is what lay behind the Rebbe's interest in technology. I think he understood that even the most enduring, ancient truths could outwardly change very fast, that they would find new forms. Hasidim had to know about the modern world, because this too is HaShem's creation. He is found here, too."

Will and TC were silent. Awestruck, even: it was not just the lives of the thirty-six that were keeping Rabbi Freilich working around the clock, even now on the solemnest night of the Jewish year, when all work was prohibited. This man, who spoke with erudition and in calm, rational paragraphs, clearly believed he had less than twenty-four hours to save the world. Will tried to blot that out, to focus on his own, immediate need: Beth.

"OK," he said, like a police captain calling his squad to order. "So that's how the system works. The crucial question is, who else knows about this? Who else might know the identity of the righteous men?"

By now they were back at the table, where the rabbi had all but fallen into his chair. Will could see the exhaustion in his face.

"You were our best hope."

"I'm sorry?"

"When you came here on *shabbos.* On Friday night. We thought you were some kind of spy. From the people who are doing this, I mean. You were asking questions, you were an outsider. Maybe you were trying to find out about the *lamad vav.* That's why we, why I, treated you so harshly. Then we discovered you were"—Will could see the rabbi did not want to name him as the husband of their hostage—"you were something else."

Will could feel the anger rising within him again. Why did he not just shake this man and force him to reveal where Beth was? Why was he putting up with this? Because, a voice inside him began, if these people were fanatical enough to kidnap Beth for no apparent reason, they were fanatical enough to hold on to her. Rabbi Freilich might have looked weak and exhausted, but there were a dozen men in here who were stronger. If Will lunged, they would soon have him pinned down.

"All right, so it's not me. Who else knows?"

The rabbi sunk lower. "That's just it. No one knows. No one outside this community. And not even this community has any idea what's going on: there would be mass panic if they did. If they knew that the *lamadvavniks* were being murdered, every day more of them killed, there would be chaos here. They would believe the end of the world was coming."

"You believe that, don't you?" It was said in Tova Chaya's gentlest voice.

The rabbi looked up at her, his eyes wet. "I fear that what the Rebbe spoke of is coming to pass. *Di velt shokelt zich und treiselt zich*. That's what he used to say, Tova Chaya. *The world is trembling and shaking*. I fear for what judgment this day is about to bring upon us."

Will was pacing. "So no one outside this small group has any idea of this. Just you, Yosef Yitzhok, and a few of your best students."

"And now you."

"And you're sure no one breathed a word?"

"To whom? Who even knew about this whole subject? Why would anyone ask? But when Yosef Yitzhok was found dead. Well, then . . ."

"Then, what?"

"It confirmed that somebody knows what we know and wanted to know more. Until then, I thought maybe it was a strange coincidence that the tzaddikim were dying. Maybe this was the work of HaShem, for a purpose beyond our understanding. But Yosef Yitzhok being murdered, that's not a plan of HaShem's."

"You think someone was pressing him for information?"

"Just before you came tonight, I had a visit. The police. They think Yosef Yitzhok was tortured before he was killed."

Will and TC both recoiled.

"What did they want from him that they didn't know already?"

"Ah, this you tried to ask me about before. Remember, I told you about the verses the Rebbe quoted in his talks? The ones Yosef Yitzhok had memorized? Well, there was something missing."

"There were only thirty-five."

"That's right. Only thirty-five. You can use the method I just showed you, converting letters into numbers and turning those numbers into coordinates, but you would still have only thirty-five righteous men. Isn't it obvious what the men who killed Yosef Yitzhok wanted to know? They wanted the identity of number thirty-six."

CHAPTER FORTY-NINE

SUNDAY, 11:18 P.M., CROWN HEIGHTS, BROOKLYN

WILL'S FIRST IMPULSE WAS TO ASK RABBI FREILICH the name of this thirty-sixth man. It was crucial. If he and TC knew that, they could work out where the killers were heading next: whoever he was, they were bound to be on his trail.

But the rabbi would not budge. For one thing, he said, the death of Yosef Yitzhok suggested the murderers were still not in possession of this vital fact. Had YY cracked under torture? The rabbi was convinced he had not. "I know this man. His intellect, his soul. He would not betray the word of the Rebbe."

He was sure the secret was safe. If he shared it with TC and Will, it could only bring harm to them. Better that they did not know. (Will was skeptical: if the torturers came after him, they were hardly likely to inquire politely whether he had any useful information and then, once assured he did not, beat a polite retreat.)

Will tried another approach. "This thirty-sixth righteous man? Is he still alive?"

"We think so. But I really will not say any more, Mr. Monroe. I cannot say any more."

"Is he the only one alive?"

"We're not certain. Our sources of information are very patchy. We have had to scramble people to the farthest corners of the world to find these tzaddikim. Each time we have been getting there too late."

"You mean, you didn't work out these names until this week?"

"No, Yosef Yitzhok made this breakthrough a few months ago. And, as I told you, we sent people to take a look, just to see who these tzaddikim were. We planned to keep an eye on them, no more. Maybe give them food or money if they were in trouble. But, to answer your question, we did not know they were dying until this week. We're not sure, but it only seems to have started a few days ago."

"On Rosh Hashana," said TC, her mind turning over visibly. "That's when Howard Macrae was murdered."

"I'm afraid we didn't know about that until days after it happened. When the news about the others started coming through. Was it even in the papers?"

"Yes," said Will, pushing the air out of his nostrils in a sound of wry resignation. "It was in the papers." That was the trouble with page B3 of Metro; people could sail right past it.

"Anyway, it was the high holy days. We were not reading the newspapers. We were living our lives. We had no idea anything was happening. But then some of our people started hearing things. Our emissary in Seattle saw the cabin he had visited on the television news. The man who runs our center in Chennai was reading through the local paper when he saw that the tzaddik in that town—one of our youngest—had been found dead. One report after another."

"How many have gone?"

"We don't know. Remember, Yosef Yitzhok only began working

on this a few months ago. Our list was barely complete; we hadn't been able to confirm everyone. This man, for example"—the rabbi gestured back toward the whiteboard with the chancellor's number on it—"it took us a long time to find him. It turns out the GPS system is slightly different there, in England; it takes a different key. The WGS84 datum, apparently. We didn't know that then, so when Yosef Yitzhok first ran the numbers, they indicated, of all things, a prison. A Belmarsh jail. It seemed unlikely. But we didn't dismiss such a possibility. We know the tzaddikim delight in concealing their true nature.

"But when we readjusted the figures, the result was instant. Downing Street! And not the famous house, Number Ten. But the house next door. The map was very clear. At the time, this man, Curtis, was in some trouble. A scandal, I think. Another disguise."

Will was getting impatient. Enough lectures, he thought. He wanted simple, hard facts—stripped of their mystical overtones. "So, sorry, I just want to be clear on this. Do you have the full list or not?"

"We think we do."

"And of those, how many are dead?"

"We think at least thirty-three."

"Jesus!"

"You mean, they may only have to kill *three* more people? It's nearly midnight now. Yom Kippur ends in about nineteen hours!" TC, usually so calm, sounded genuinely panicked.

"Rabbi, whoever's doing this seems to be pretty clued up on Jewish religious custom, wouldn't you say?" Will began. "I mean, who else but religious Jews know all this stuff—about the righteous men, about the Days of Awe? They're following it all to the letter. And you say that no one outside this very small group even knew of Yosef Yitzhok's discovery."

"What are you saying, Mr. Monroe?"

"I'm saying, Rabbi, that you may not be behind this, despite the fact that I know you're a proven kidnapper. But somebody inside this . . . organization or community or whatever it is, almost certainly is. I reckon this is what the police would call an inside job. If I were you, I'd start looking at the people here very closely."

"Mr. Monroe, it's late, and time is running out. I don't have the time or the strength to start fighting you. What Tova Chaya said before is right: we need to work together. So I'm going to trust you, even if you cannot trust me. I'm going to let you do something that will prove we are not behind this terrible wickedness."

"Go on."

"I'm going to send you to the next victim."

CHAPTER FIFTY

MONDAY, 12:10 A.M., MANHATTAN

WILL HAD BEEN TO THE LOWER EAST SIDE a few times, to visit friends chic and savvy enough to buy up and renovate properties in the now-gentrified pockets north of East Broadway. He had seen the old-time delis, drunk coffee in the retro-chic cafés on Orchard Street. But he had not wandered beyond the safely fashionable areas. He had glided past the old tenement buildings, seeing them as cinematic backdrop. He had never looked properly.

Now he was among them, shivering from cold and exhaustion in the night air. Scrunched in his hand, safely hidden inside his pocket, was the scrap of paper with the address he was meant to find.

Rabbi Freilich had led Will and TC back to the computer whiz who had given them the earlier demonstration. He talked them through the process. First, feed the computer the Hebrew sentence: verse 16 of Isaiah 30. Then ask it to stop at the right intervals, and it will spit out a number. Feed that number through the GPS Web sites and you get coordinates for a place: a specific address on a specific street on the Lower East Side in Manhattan.

"Hang on a minute," Will had said. "Isn't this a bit unlikely? You've got thirty-six righteous men out of six billion people on the planet—and two are in New York? Howard Macrae, and now this guy? It sounds a bit convenient to me." It had not yet congealed into a full allegation, but Will's skepticism was turning into suspicion.

The rabbi explained that they too had wondered at such a coincidence. But then they had read deeper into Hasidic folklore. It turned out a truly great tzaddik radiated a "glow"—the same word Rabbi Mandelbaum had used—that might draw in others. Their calculated guess was that the Rebbe's goodness had been so powerful that a couple of tzaddikim had been pulled near. "Think of them as satellites," the rabbi had said.

But there was a problem. The address now balled up in Will's fist was an apartment building, home to dozens of people. *Which one was the tzaddik?* The Hasidim had gone down there once to check it out soon after Yosef Yitzhok had first cracked the Rebbe's code, but they had not been able to identify him. The man in this building remained one of the most hidden of the hidden righteous men.

"You will have a better chance of finding him than us," Freilich had said.

"Why?"

"Look at us, Mr. Monroe. We cannot go where you go, we cannot ask what you can ask. We are too visible. You are a reporter from the *New York Times*. You can go where you like and talk to anybody. You found Mr. Macrae, *zechuso yogen aleinu*, and Mr. Baxter, *zechuso yogen aleinu*." May his righteousness protect us. "Find this man. Go find our tzaddik."

So shortly before midnight, Will took off his skullcap and went back out into the world. As he set off, TC decided to go too.

"I'm going to call the police. I can't hide from them forever. We've done what we needed to do."

"What will you say?"

"That my phone's been dead all day, and I've only just heard what happened. Wish me luck. Or at least visit me in jail."

"This is so not a joke."

"I know. But you can see what it looks like: a dead man in my apartment, and I'm AWOL. I might be charged with murder by the morning."

"This is all my fault. I sucked you into this insane mess."

"No, you didn't. You asked for my help. I could have said no. I knew what I was getting into."

"Did you?"

"Not really, no."

And with that, Will leaned over to give TC a kiss on the cheek—only for her to pull back the moment he came close. There was a magnetic field of resistance around her face. *Of course.* She was not allowed to touch a man, let alone be kissed by one, not in the heart of Crown Heights. Will made do with a plain good-bye.

Now watching his breath form clouds before him, Will turned the corner so that he was at Montgomery and Henry. Behind him was a small triangle of park. In front, the tenement building he was looking for. He held back, wanting to gaze at it a while. He could see one, two, three, lights still on.

Now what? He had barely considered what he would do once he got here. He could not exactly start knocking on doors, claiming to be doing a vox pop for the *New York Times* after midnight. What could he do?

He would have to get into the building. That would be a start. Then he could look at the mailboxes, get some names, Google a few of them on his BlackBerry. He would think of something.

Oh, good. Someone coming out. Perfect: that would give him his chance to slip in. Except this person was moving too fast, almost running. It was hard to make him, or her, out; it was too dark, and the light above the entrance too dim. But when he stepped forward, looking nervously left and right, Will saw enough.

Most striking was the piercing brightness of his eyes, a chill, glassy blue. But it was the posture Will recognized. A physical confidence, as if this man was used to using his body. The clothes were slightly changed, but there was no mistaking him—with or without his baseball cap.

CHAPTER FIFTY-ONE

Monday, 12:13 a.m., Manhattan

Will's first instinct was to observe. He was used to watching, seeing how things unfolded. So it took a beat and then another before Will realized that he could not just watch. He would have to stalk the stalker.

He was wary. Hardly anyone was around; he would be noticed. So he kept far back, walking as quietly as he could. He cursed the black leather shoes he was wearing: they made too much noise. He tried to prevent his heels making contact with the sidewalk, to dampen the sound.

But the man in front seemed to be in a hurry as he charged down Henry Street. Not running, but a brisk walk that allowed no time for looking back. That emboldened Will; he walked faster, taking pains to keep just less than a block between them.

The stalker was carrying a black leather bag at his side, the strap worn like a sash crossing over to his opposite shoulder. He was neat and self-contained, moving nimbly. Will was no expert, but he would have been surprised if this guy did not have some connection with the military.

By now he had crossed Clinton and Jefferson. Where was he going? To meet a getaway car? If so, why had he not been picked up earlier? Maybe he was walking toward a subway station. Will cursed his limited knowledge of New York: he had no idea if there was a station near here.

Without warning, the man suddenly looked back. Will saw the movement of his head and, without even thinking, moved off the sidewalk toward the steps of the tenement block he was passing. At the same time he reached into his pocket and pulled out his keys. What the stalker would have seen was a man entering his own apartment building. He walked on; Will let out a deep sigh. He had been holding his breath.

By now the man ahead was turning a sharp right. Will tried to position himself so that he would not be caught in his field of vision.

"Yo, Ashley! You got my phone?"

Will had not seen them coming, but there they were, right in front of him. Three African-American teenage girls, filling up the sidewalk. Will tried to slide past, but they were in the mood for some fun.

"What's the hurry, handsome? You don't like how we look? You don't think we look fine?" At this the other two were screeching with laughter. He looked over their heads, to see the stalker heading down a side street toward East Broadway. He was hard to make out.

"Yo, I'm over here, honey!" It was the leader of the pack, now waving her hand in Will's face. If he had been born in New York, he was sure he would have shoved them aside with a curt "Get the fuck out of my way." But even here, on a mission to prevent a murder in the dead of night, he was still an Englishman.

"Excuse me, I have to get past. Please."

With that, he weaved around Ashley and company, hearing more whooping and calling behind him. "My friend says you can have her number!"

Will now broke into a run, desperate to catch up. He reached the junction and turned right, scanning the street up and down in search of his quarry. There was a couple making out on a stoop. But no sign of the stalker.

He could see only two nonresidential buildings; the man might have fled into either one of them. He certainly could not yet have reached East Broadway, or Will would have caught sight of him. Will slowed down, checking over his shoulder, aware that this was exactly how to walk into an ambush. After fifteen paces, Will gave up: he had clearly lost the man he had needed to follow. He must have escaped into one of these two buildings, on opposite sides of the street. Will was near enough now to see what they were. One was the Church of the Reborn Jesus, but the other was a synagogue—affiliated with the Hasidim of Crown Heights.

CHAPTER FIFTY-TWO

MONDAY, 12:28 A.M., MANHATTAN

SHOULD HE TRY TO BREAK INTO ONE OR BOTH OF THESE PLACES, to find the man he had followed? A true man of action would do just that. But as he was sizing up the first building, a police car sped past, lights flashing. He stepped back. That was all he needed: to be arrested for breaking into a synagogue in the small hours of Monday morning. And on Yom Kippur, of all days. What believable grounds for following this man did he even have? He had seen him come out of an apartment building on the Lower East Side. Oh, and he had seen him out of TC's window yesterday. He had seen him commit no crime. As Harden would say, "You've got a notebook full of nothing." Nothing except a grim suspicion that was becoming firmer every minute.

He retraced his steps toward the building on Montgomery Street. He and Rabbi Freilich had discussed what he should do in only the sketchiest terms. "Just call me," the rabbi had said. "Even if you're not sure it's him, call."

"And then what?"

"We'll come and we'll help."

Will was not quite sure what that meant.

He crossed the street and took a few furtive steps toward the entrance of the tenement. A gleam of light drew his eye to the door lock: it was not fully shut! The stalker must have left it ajar, perhaps to avoid making even that small noise. Will creaked it open and slipped inside.

Perez, La Pinez, Abdulla, Bitensky, Wilkins, Gonzales, Yoelson, Alberto. The mailboxes offered no clues.

There was a rickety elevator, but that was no use. He needed to check each floor, every apartment. He ran quietly up the stairs, stopping at each landing: but all he could see were shut doors, shabby doormats, the odd sodden umbrella left outside. Will realized the futility of this expedition. What was he looking for? A plaque announcing, "Mr. Righteous Tzaddik lives here. Available for weddings, birthdays, and bar mitzvahs"?

By the third landing, he was poised to call Freilich and press him for more information—anything else they had which might narrow it down. But the last apartment on the third floor stopped him dead.

The door was open.

Will crept toward it, lightly tapping it with his knuckles as he moved past and inside. "Hello," he called out, almost in a whisper. No lights were on, just the silver shadow of the moon, coming through the window that faced the street.

He looked to his left. A galley kitchen, small and fitted up with 1950s appliances. Not as some retro fashion statement, but the real thing: a bulky, curved fridge; a stove with oversized knobs. This was the home, Will concluded, of an old person.

Then he looked to his right. He could see a big radio on a table; a couple of wooden chairs whose seats were cushioned in thin, fake leather; one was spilling out its stuffing. Then a couch—

Will gasped, jumping back. There was a man lying on it, flat on his back. Silhouetted in the light were the bristles on his chin. He had a small, squirrel-like face framed by clunky, chunky spectacles. The rest of him looked shrunken with age, in a too-big cardigan. He seemed to be sleeping.

Will took a step forward, then another one, until he was crouched over him. He placed his hand in front of the man's mouth and waited to feel a breath.

Nothing.

Then Will touched him, placing a hand on his forehead. Cold. He put a finger on his neck, searching for a pulse. He knew there would be none.

Will moved backward, as if to take in the enormity of what he could see. As he did, he felt a crunch of glass. He looked down to see that he had just stepped on a syringe.

He was bending down to get a closer look when the room flooded with light.

"Put your hands in the air and turn around. NOW!"

Will did as he was told. He could barely see; he was dazzled by the three or four flashlights aimed directly at his eyes.

"Step away from the body. That's good. Now walk toward me. SLOWLY!"

His eyes were not yet adjusted but he could make out the small circle dancing before him, right next to the ring of flashlight. It was the barrel of a gun—and it was aimed at him.

CHAPTER FIFTY-THREE

MONDAY, 12:51 A.M., MANHATTAN

IN A WAY, IT HELPED that he was so exhausted. In normal circumstances, his heart would have been banging loud enough to wake the neighborhood. Instead, his fatigue acted as a kind of defensive shield, slowing down his reactions and even his emotions. His default mental state had become weary resignation.

He was now in handcuffs in the back of a squad car, jammed up against an officer of the New York Police Department. In front, the radio traffic was constant—and all about him. He was, it was clear, a murder suspect.

The men in the car were giving off an odor that Will recalled from his adolescence: testosterone and adrenaline, the smell of a locker room after a big win. These men were high on success, and he was the prize. They had caught him all but red-handed, looming over his victim, his fingerprints on his neck. The officers in this unit could almost touch the police medals they were bound to receive.

"I did not kill that man," Will heard himself say. The scene was so absurd, so remote from the rest of his life experience, that the voice sounded disembodied, unconnected. It was like listening to the radio, one of the BBC afternoon dramas his mother was hooked on.

"I know what it looks like, but I assure you that's not what happened." Suddenly a bolt of inspiration. "But I could lead you to the man who did do it! I followed him out of that building less than an hour ago. I know where he's hiding! I can even give you a description."

The officer in the front passenger seat turned around to give Will an ironic smile. *Sure you can, son. And I'm gonna pitch for the Yankees next Tuesday.*

At the Seventh Precinct station, Will maintained his defiance. "I just found that body!" he said as they led him upstairs. "I'd seen the man leave the building, I followed him, and then I went back. I thought he had killed someone, and I was right!"

Even as the words came out of his mouth, he knew they sounded ridiculous. The cop who had been guarding Will from the start stared at him contemptuously. "Will you shut the fuck up?"

For the first time since the police had picked him up, Will began to panic. What the hell was he doing here? He needed to get to Beth. He needed to be out on the streets, in Crown Heights or wherever else, searching for his wife—not chained up as a prisoner of the New York Police Department. He was not even thinking about the prospect of being charged with murder; merely losing vital hours battling the bureaucracy of the New York criminal justice system was nightmarish enough. Every minute spent here was another minute not finding Beth. Besides, the Hasidim had been emphatic: there was no time to lose; the fate of the world was to be decided in the coming hours and minutes. Yet here he was, doing nothing; his hands literally tied.

They took him to the sergeant's desk, where someone was waiting for him: the detective he had seen at the apartment building. He had inspected the scene while they kept Will in the car. "I got a prisoner to log in," he said, addressing the clerk and ignoring Will. Whippet-faced and in his late thirties, the rising star of the homicide department, Will guessed.

"OK, let's empty his pockets." The cop who had played bodyguard stepped forward. He had already frisked Will hard at the apartment: after the police had seen the syringe, they were taking no chances. They also took his cell phone and BlackBerry: no calling of accomplices. Now they took the rest: coins, keys, notebook.

"Let's get all this stuff vouchered," the detective said. Each item was put in a clear plastic ziplock bag and sealed. The detective made a note, witnessed by the desk sergeant.

As they opened his wallet, Will was prompted to make one of his biggest mistakes of the night. In among the plastic was his press card: *Will Monroe, New York Times.*

"OK, I'll admit it. The real reason I was in that building was that I was on assignment for the *Times.* It was undercover. I've been writing a series on crime in the city, and that's what I was doing."

The detective looked at him for the first time.

"You work for the *New York Times*?"

"Yes. Yes, I do," said Will, glad just to have got a response. The detective looked away, and the clerk went back to her work.

Will was led to another desk, where he was asked to place his right index finger on the electronic device in front of him, hold still, and then do the same with his left. Then the rest of his fingers and his thumbs. It beeped, as if he was a package at a supermarket.

Next, Will was taken toward a room marked "Interview Suite." On the way the detective handed a copy of Will's details to a colleague: "Jeannie, can you do a name search on this for me?"

Now they were inside. Just a table, with a chair on either side and a phone in the corner. Nothing on the walls but a calendar: New York, the Empire State.

"OK, my name is Larry Fitzwalter, and I'm going to be your detective for the evening. We're going to begin like this." He produced another form. "You have the right to remain silent. Do you understand?"

"I do understand, but I would really like to explain—"

"OK, you understand. Can you initial here, please?"

"Look, I was in there because I followed a man in there—"

"Can you initial here, please? That means you understand that you have the right to remain silent. OK. Anything you say can and will be used against you in a court of law. Do you understand?"

"This is a simple mistake—"

"Do you understand? That's all I'm asking right now. Do you understand the words I am saying? If you do, then initial the goddamn form."

Will said no more as Fitzwalter got to the end of the form, telling him his rights. Once it was initialed, the detective pushed it to one side.

"OK, now that you know your rights, do you wish to talk to us?"

"Don't I get to make a phone call?"

"It's the middle of the night. Who you gonna call?"

"Do I have to tell you?"

"No," said the detective, taking the phone from the back table and stretching its cord to place it on the desk between them. "Just tell me the number you want me to dial."

Will knew there was only one person he could possibly call, but the idea was appalling. How could he, with this news? He looked at his watch: 2:15 a.m. Fitzwalter was getting impatient.

Will dictated the number. The detective dialed it, then handed him the phone—staying firmly in his seat. It was clear he was going to listen in on every word. Finally, Will heard the voice he was wanting and dreading to hear.

"Hello? Dad?"

CHAPTER FIFTY-FOUR

MONDAY, 3:06 A.M., MANHATTAN

"I HAVE GOOD NEWS AND BAD NEWS FOR YOU, Mr. Monroe." It was Fitzwalter. "Which would you like first?"

Will lifted his eyes slowly. He had spent only forty minutes in this cell, but it felt like forty nights. His father had told him to invoke the first of the rights he had been read and to say nothing. Once Fitzwalter was certain Will was not going to crack, and that the interview was over, he had him locked up.

"The good news is that His Honor Judge William Monroe Sr. has telephoned to say he is on his way in from Sag Harbor."

His father's voice floated back into Will's head now, as audible as it had been when he made that call. Sleepy, then shocked, then stern, then disappointed, then purposeful. Since Will had spent his youth three thousand miles away from his father, he had never gone through that teenage rite of passage: announcing to your father that you have in some way betrayed his trust. *Dad, I trashed the car. Dad, I got caught smoking dope.* These were sentences he had never had to utter. He had never heard his father say, as all his contemporaries had, "Son, you've let me down." So to hear it now—not the words, but that tone—was an extra ordeal, to be piled on top of all the others.

"Mr. Monroe, are you listening to me?"

"Sorry?"

"You've had the good news. Don't you want to hear the bad news?"

"Not really, no."

"The bad news is, I've just come off the phone with the duty lawyer at the *Times*. He's made some calls, and guess what? They don't think you're on assignment for them at all. In fact, what they say is that you're taking a few days 'rest.' By order of the editor himself. Sounds like you got yourself in a whole pile of trouble, my friend."

Will cupped his hands over his eyes. What a basic error: to offer a lie that could so easily be disproved. His legal defense was already compromised. He had made that cardinal mistake of all guilty men: he had changed his story. As for his career, that was surely over. He would be suspended "in order to defend himself on these grave charges"—and then quietly dropped.

The door slammed shut. In some strange way, Will almost felt grateful to be in this cell. Ever since Friday morning, he had been on the move, feverishly rushing from one place to another, from one new plan to the next. He had crisscrossed the city, in and out, either to Brooklyn or Long Island or back again, trying to think, to focus, to act. Even when sitting down, he had been willing the train or cab to go faster, to get there *now*, or praying for the phone to ring or an e-mail to arrive.

Now there was nowhere he could go and nothing he could do. The scheming and thinking and frantic calculating were at an end. His jailers had not even allowed him a pencil and paper.

The pause let in the realization he had been resisting for days. Any time it had broken the surface in the last nearly seventy-two hours, Will had pushed it back down. But now he had no strength for the task.

Everything was falling apart. That was the conclusion he had refused to face, but which was now too strong to resist. His wife was missing, a captive of men whose fanaticism ran deep. He was about to be charged with murder, facing a pile of circumstantial evidence that would be hard to refute. Worse still, he had fallen for a classic setup.

After all, who had sent him to that building in the middle of the night? Was he really meant to believe it was just a coincidence that a brutal murder was in progress the minute he appeared on the scene? And how strange that the killer should almost certainly have taken refuge in, of all places, a Hasidic synagogue.

All that guff about fearing for the end of the world. They were bringing it about themselves! Will and TC had cottoned on to their plot, so Freilich had had to come up with some bullshit about "whoever is behind this," blah, blah. Will's first instinct had been right. There was no "they." The Hasidim had found the identities of these righteous men, and now, for some warped reason of their own, they wanted them dead. Will was getting in the way. What better way to take him out of circulation than to have him picked up not by them, but by the police! Will had to hand it to them: it was masterful.

He could feel a nagging intrusion—one more thought demanding to break the surface. Will had been pushing it below the waves more vigorously than the rest; he was hoping it would sink.

It forced itself up. What if the Hasidim were right? What if the moment the thirty-six men were killed, the world would no longer be upheld? Everything about this wild theory had stacked up so far. The chancellor really had performed an act of stunning goodness. So had Baxter. And they were disguised, just as Mandelbaum said they would be. Could all the details be right, but the idea itself be wrong?

Tonight he had witnessed, or just missed, the murder of a man who may well have been a tzaddik, one of thirty-six righteous ones.

If that's who this man was, then it would be one more confirmation that the Hasidim were telling the truth—or at least part of it. It would also mean the killers of the *lamad vav* were getting very close to their goal. He looked at his watch: from what TC had told him, Yom Kippur would be over in about sixteen hours. They had so little time.

He had to know: was the man in that building a tzaddik, as the Hasidim had predicted? For the first time in hours, Will had an idea.

Some time later, the cell door opened again. Will braced himself to see his father. But it was Fitzwalter.

"Come with me."

"Where am I going?"

"You'll see."

Will was led downstairs, into a room with bright fluorescent lights. There were seven or eight other men there. At least three of them looked to be stoned; he guessed several were homeless. The door was slammed shut.

"OK, gentlemen," said a voice over a loudspeaker. "If you can all take your places against the back wall." Two of the men in the group seemed to know exactly what to do, casually walking to the back, then standing and staring straight ahead. It was then Will saw the markings on the wall, indicating height. This was a lineup, an identity parade. On the other side of the one-way mirror Mrs. Tina Perez of the Greenstreet Mansions apartment building stared at the men arrayed before her.

"I know it's been a long night, Mrs. Perez." Fitzwalter was saying. "So you just take your time. When you're ready, I have two questions to ask."

"I'm ready."

"I want you to look really hard and tell me whether you've seen any of these men before and, if you have, where you've seen them. OK? Is that clear?"

"The answer's no. I haven't seen any of these men before. The man I saw had eyes you couldn't forget."

"You're absolutely certain, Mrs. Perez?"

"I'm certain. He had his hands around poor Mr. Bitensky's neck, and he looked up at me with those eyes. Those terrible eyes—"

"It's OK, Mrs. Perez. Please don't distress yourself. Jeannie, you can take Mrs. Perez home now. Thank you."

"OK, show in Mrs. Abdulla."

Will was spared the encounter with his father he had feared. Twenty minutes after the lineup, Fitzwalter had come into the cell.

"More good news and bad news. The bad news for me is that two witnesses say you were not the man they saw in Mr. Bitensky's apartment. One of them did recognize you in the lineup. She places you at the apartment building—standing outside at the time of the killing. So the good news for you is that I'm going to have to let you go. For now."

There were forms to fill in so that Will's things could be released. He pounced on his cell phone first, powering it up. Instantly it began vibrating: a voice message. TC.

"Hi, guess what. As predicted, I am in police custody. They're questioning me about the murder of Mr. Pugachov. It seems he was shot, at point-blank range. Can you believe this? In my apartment? That sweet, gentle man. And I can't bear to think it's all because . . . What? Oh, God, I'm sorry. Sorry, Will, that's Joel Brookstein. Do you remember him? He was at Columbia. Anyway, he's agreed to be my lawyer. He's telling me to shut my mouth. Let me know where you are and what's happening. Not sure if they'll let me keep this phone on." Her voice faded, as if she needed to talk over her shoulder. "All right, I'm coming. One minute! Will, I'm going to have to go. Call me as soon as you can. We don't have much time."

As he listened to her voice—which now seemed to oscillate between TC and Tova Chaya—he heard a double beep. A text message. He pressed the buttons.

Paul, sort the letters of no Christian! (1, 7, 29)

In the bombardment of the last few hours, Will had almost forgotten about the phantom texter. In his mind, he still associated these messages with Yosef Yitzhok, even though he knew, rationally, that was impossible. This latest text was definitive proof: someone else had been giving Will these coded clues all along. But who?

The meaning of this latest message seemed almost within reach. Forty-eight hours of communication with this man had given Will some sense of the workings of his mind. This must be how crossword addicts do it, Will thought: after a while, they insert themselves into the head of the crossword setter.

And this did indeed look like a crossword clue. Surely the literal meaning was irrelevant. He knew how such clues worked, with instructions in one part relating to the rest. But who was Paul? And why did the solution include a word twenty-nine letters long?

He would start with the most obvious bit, following the instruction to "sort the letters," to reorder *no Christian*. With the recklessness of a newly free man, he grabbed a pen from the desk clerk's table and scribbled on the back of the receipt she had just handed him.

On Ian Christ. That did not work. *Con this rain*. That was not much better.

And then he saw it, smiling his first smile in hours. How perfect that this message should arrive just as he was alone, without TC. The one area where he would have greater knowledge than she did.

He picked up the phone to call his father. To tell him the good news that he had been released without charge and ask him to stop on his way, maybe at a hotel, and pick up the one thing that Will realized he would need: a Bible.

CHAPTER FIFTY-FIVE

MONDAY, 4:40 A.M., MANHATTAN

FOR A MINUTE, HE THOUGHT ABOUT ASKING the desk sergeant. Then he reconsidered. It would not look great, a disheveled murder suspect alternately ranting about the identity of the true killer—"He has piercing blue eyes!"—and then demanding to read the Bible. Fine if Will was guilty and pursuing a "diminished responsibility" defense; not so great for a man who wanted to walk out of the Seventh Precinct having convinced the police he was both innocent and sane.

Instead he waited for his father pacing outside, desperate to get away. Finally William Monroe Sr., dressed in a battered sailing jacket, appeared. He looked exhausted, his eyes ringed in red. Will wondered if he had been crying.

"Thank God, William," he said, hugging his son, his hand cupping the back of his head. "I wondered what on earth you'd done."

"Thanks for that vote of confidence, Dad," said Will, pulling away. "No time to talk. Do you have the thing I asked you to bring?"

His father nodded, a gesture of sad surrender, as if he was humoring a son who was babbling about the voices in his head or demanding a hundred bucks for another fix of crack. "Here."

Will pounced on the Bible. "OK, Dad. You know those text messages I've been getting? Well, here's the latest." Will held up his cell phone.

Paul, sort the letters of no Christian! (1, 7, 29)

"What could that mean?"

Hurriedly, Will explained. "*No Christian* is an anagram for *Corinthians.* The figure 1 refers to Paul's first letter to the Corinthians—and it must be chapter 7, verse 29. Which is why I wanted a Bible. And here it is."

What I mean, brothers, is that the time is short.

"He's getting desperate."

"Will—"

"Hold on, Dad. I just want to prove something to you. Now, I know how bizarre this will sound, but at the heart of this whole fucked-up business seems to be a Jewish religious theory. It centers on men of exceptional goodness." He could see his father's face moving from pity to impatience.

"Will, what on earth are you talking about? The police brought you here on suspicion of *murder* tonight. Do you have any idea of the trouble you're in?"

"Oh, yes, Dad, believe me. I know that I am in the deepest shit imaginable. Deeper than you think. But please hear me out on this. The Hasidim who are holding Beth say that someone—it may even be one of them, for all I know—is killing good people. Extraordinarily good people. Not just here, but all over the world. What happened tonight is that I came this close to witnessing one of those killings. If the Hasidim's theory is right, the man who was murdered tonight will be a so-called righteous man. Which is why I wanted you to see this."

He took his BlackBerry out of the police ziplock bag, clicked on the Internet browser, and selected Google. Then he punched in the words *"Bitensky"* and *"Lower East Side."*

Google was searching, not fast on this handheld machine. Finally, a page of search results. A biomedical Web site, something about a classical pianist. And then a link to *Downtown Express*, "the weekly newspaper of Lower Manhattan." He clicked on it, waited an age for the page to load, and then scrolled down. It was an archive item from a couple of years ago. He prayed for it to be something of substance, something that might prove to Monroe Sr. that his son was not completely deranged.

Residents of the Greenstreet area endured a chilly start to the Passover season this week, when their apartment building was evacuated for a fire alert Tuesday.

It was after midnight when scores of residents filed together into the park, as fire crews examined the building before declaring it was safe to reenter.

While most folks were clothed only in pajamas and robes, one group were fully dressed—since they had been taking part in the traditional seder that often continues until the early hours.

They were guests of Judah Bitensky, one of the last Jewish residents of a building that was once a hub for the East Broadway Jewish community. It appears that Mr. Bitensky, janitor at one of the area's remaining synagogues, hosts an annual seder meal at his home—inviting all those who have no other home to go to.

"It's kind of a tradition," said Irving Tannenbaum, 66, a regular. "Every year Judah opens his door to people like us. Some of the crowd are elderly and live alone. Some are, you know, street people. It's quite a scene in there."

Rivvy Gold, 51 and homeless, added, "It's the best meal I get all year. This is the one night I feel like I have family."

Downtown Express *counted twenty-six people heading back into Mr. Bitensky's tiny apartment—including three in wheelchairs and two on crutches. Reluctant to give an interview to a reporter, Mr. Bitensky was asked how he was able to feed so many, despite living on a meager income himself. "Somehow I manage," he said. "I don't quite know how."*

CHAPTER FIFTY-SIX

MONDAY, 2:25 P.M., BROOKLYN

WILL MAINTAINED HIS PERCH BY THE WINDOW, regularly peeling back the curtain to look out onto the street. He knew it was foolhardy. If anyone was following him, there could hardly be a better way to attract their attention. He flapped the material back and forth so often, he looked as if he were sending a coded message.

He had said good-bye to his father only minutes after they had met up. Monroe Sr. had looked at him blankly when Will called up the Bitensky story on the BlackBerry, as if the whole business was just too deranged to take seriously. He had made a gesture with his face and hands—*let's put all this nonsense aside*—and asked Will to come back home with him. There he would have a chance to shower, sleep, and generally calm down. Linda would look after him. For his own part, he had an important case to prepare for that morning, but he would be back in the evening. Then father and son could put their heads together and work out how they were going to get Beth back. It was a tempting offer, but Will declined. He had wasted enough time already. With thanks he sent his father back to his car—and fired off a text message to TC.

To his great relief, she called back. She had been released at nine that morning. Police had just viewed the CCTV tapes from her building. The footage from Saturday night included a sequence shot by the camera above the back entrance: it showed Pugachov helping TC and an unnamed man into a large bin and wheeling them out of sight. It then showed him reentering the building a few minutes later. Not only did it confirm the admittedly strange story she had told detectives—it also showed that when TC had left Mr. Pugachov, he was alive and well.

There was something in the dead man's trousers that helped, too. In his right pocket was the spare key for TC's apartment. He would surely only have needed to use that if she was not in and the door had been locked. With that second alibi, the police released TC. They even thanked her for her time—doubtless, thought Will, with a scripted paragraph from the NYPD customer care manual.

It was Will's idea to meet at Tom's, in what was a straightforward calculation. Both his and TC's apartments had been monitored; here, they had at least a chance to meet undetected.

Besides, TC had a plan—just a hunch, she said—that required major computing brainpower. Now she was standing over Tom's shoulder as he stabbed at the keyboard.

"So you're certain of the domain name?" he was saying.

"All I can tell you is what it says on the card I took. Rabbi.Freilich@Moshiachlives.com."

"OK, OK, that's what I'll try. Spell Mosh—, you know, for me again?"

"For the third time: M-O-S-H-I-A-C-H."

Will glanced back out of the window. As much as Tom loved Beth, he could not stand TC. At Columbia Will had always put it down to jealousy, the difficulties of being a threesome. Now he reckoned it was more like organic combustion: Tom and TC were phosphorus and sulfur. They could not meet without sparking up.

In a novel form of coping strategy, Tom chose not to talk to TC at all. He talked to himself instead.

"OK, so what we need to do is run a host domain name." He punched those last three words into the "shell," a kind of empty window on the screen he had created. A few seconds later, a string of numbers appeared. 192.0.2.233.

"All right, who is 192.0.2.233?" He said the words as he typed them.

Back came an answer. Among a whole lot of blurb about "registrants" and "administrative contacts" was the address of the Hasidim's headquarters in Crown Heights. The very building Will and TC had been in last night.

"Good, now let's talk to Arin."

"Arin? Who the hell is Arin?"

"ARIN is the American Registry for Internet Numbers, the organization that allocates IP addresses—you know, the string of numbers we had before."

"But I thought you already had that for this, you know, domain."

"I had *one* of the numbers. ARIN will give us *all* the numbers allocated to this company or organization. We will have the number for every machine they have. Once we have that, we can get to work."

Soon the screen was filled with numbers, dozens of them. This, TC realized, was the entire Hasidic computer network, expressed in numerical form.

"All right, this is the range we'll scan."

"What does that mean, 'scan'?"

"I thought you didn't want me to get too technical. 'Save the geek stuff, Tom.' Remember?"

"So what do we do now?"

"We wait."

TC headed for the couch, laying herself flat out, using Tom's overcoat as a blanket, before falling into exhausted sleep. Tom was working away on a different computer, hammering at the keys. Will alternated between staring out of the window and at a photograph on the wall: a picture of himself, Tom, and Beth, wrapped up in thick winter gloves, scarves, and coats in what looked like a ski resort. In fact it was the center of Manhattan, early on a Sunday morning after a night-long blizzard. The smile on Beth's face seemed to register something more than laughter: there was, what was the word, *appreciation*, for the fact that life, despite everything, could be wonderful.

An hour and a half later, the computer beeped; not the trill of a new e-mail but a simpler sound. Will turned around to find Tom jumping back to the machine he had left running.

"We're in."

Now all three were gathered around, staring at a screen that only made sense to one of them.

"What's this, Tom?" It was Will, deciding to get the question in first—and phrase it politely—before TC had a chance to bark.

"These are the system logs for the machine we've just hacked into. This way we should be able to tell who's been in and out."

TC was biting her nails, willing everything to happen faster. Will was scanning not the screen but Tom's face, looking for any sign of progress. He did not like what he saw: Tom seemed puzzled. His lips were pursed; when he was on the brink of a breakthrough, they would part, in readiness for a smile.

"Nothing there. Damn."

"Look again," said TC. "You might have missed something. Look again."

But Tom did not need to be told. He inched closer to the screen, now slowly going through each line that appeared in front of him.

"Hold on," he said. "This might be nothing."

"What? What?"

"See, that line in the log. There. *Time service crashed.* One fifty-eight this morning. It might be nothing. Programs often crash and restart automatically. No big deal."

"But?"

"It could indicate something else."

"Yes."

Tom was not doing well under TC's interrogation. Will stepped in. "Sorry, Tom. For a know-nothing like me: what's a time service?"

"It's just a bit of the networking setup that some people forget about. They don't turn it off, so it just sits there, keeping track of the time of day."

"So?"

"The important thing is, people forget it's there. So they don't give it the tender loving care they give to the rest of the system. Old security holes that may have been closed elsewhere in the system sometimes get left in the time service bit."

"You mean, it's like a hole in the garden fence, round the back where no one notices?"

"Exactly. What I'm wondering is whether this time service crashed through, you know, natural causes—or whether somebody busted right through it. If you know what you're doing, you can send in a buffer overflow, a huge bunch of data in a specific sequence, which totally screws up the time service. If you *really* know what you're doing, you can not only make it crash but kind of bend it to your will."

"How do you mean?" asked Will.

"You can make it run your commands, which effectively gives you access to the server."

"Is that what happened here?"

"I don't know. I need to see the time service's own access log. That's what I'm waiting for now . . . whoa, hold on. This is good. See that, right there?"

He was pointing at a string of numbers by the time, 1:58 a.m. "Hello, stranger."

It was a new IP address, a string of numbers different from all the others allocated to the Hasidim and their network. This was the signature of an outsider.

"Can you see who it is?"

"That's what I'm asking right now." He typed: *whois 89.23.325.09?*

"And here is our answer."

Tom was pointing at the line on the screen. It took Will a second to focus on the words. But there they were, words that changed everything. Neither he nor TC could make a sound. The three of them stood in silence, looking at the address in front of them.

The organization that had hacked into the Hasidim's computer—reading everything they were reading, looking over their virtual shoulder to see every one of their calculations, including those that revealed the exact locations of the righteous men—was based in Richmond, Virginia, and there, on the screen, was its full name.

The Church of the Reborn Jesus.

CHAPTER FIFTY-SEVEN

MONDAY, 5:13 P.M., DARFUR, SUDAN

THE NIGHT OF THE THIRTY-FIFTH KILLING was almost silent. In this heat, and with so little food, people were too listless to make much noise. The call to prayer was the only loud sound to be heard all day; the rest was moans and whispers.

Mohammed Omar saw the heat wave shimmering on the horizon and reckoned sunset would be only a few minutes away. That was the way it was in Darfur: the sun would sneak up without warning in the morning and disappear just as quickly at night. Maybe it was like that everywhere in Sudan, everywhere in Africa. Mohammed did not know: he had never traveled beyond this rocky desert.

It was time for his evening tour of the camp. He would check in first on Hawa, the thirteen-year-old girl who had, too young, become a kind of mother to her six sisters. They had fled to the camp two weeks ago, after the Janjaweed militiamen had torched their village. The little girls were too scared to talk, but Hawa told Mohammed what had happened. In the middle of the night, terrifying men had arrived on horseback, waving flaming torches. They had set everything alight. Hawa had scooped up her sisters and started running. Only once they got away did she realize that her parents had been left behind. They had both been killed.

Now, in the corner of a hut made of straw and sticks, she held her three-year-old sister in her arms. By the doorway, on the ground, stood a battered pot. Inside, a meager ration of porridge.

Mohammed walked on, steeling himself for the next stop on the tour: the "clinic," in reality another frail hut. Kosar, the nurse, was there, and her face told him what he did not want to hear. "How many?" he asked.

"Three. And maybe one more tonight." They had been losing three children a day for weeks now. With no medicine and no food, he did not know how he could stop the dying.

He looked around. An empty corner of desert, sheltered by a few scrubby trees. He had not meant to start a refugee camp here. What did he know of such things? He was a tailor. He was not a doctor or an official, but he could see what was going on. There were columns of desperate people, often children, walking through the desert, searching for food and shelter. They spoke of village after village destroyed by the Janjaweed, the men who burned and killed and raped while government airplanes circled overhead. Somebody had to do something—and, without ever really thinking it through, that somebody had been him.

He had started with a few tents, two of them stitched together on his old Singer machine. He collected a few axes and gave them to the men to get firewood. They struggled. One, Abdul, was desperate to help, but the burns on his hands were so bad he could not hold an ax. Mohammed saw him, his hands so scorched he could not even wipe away his own tears.

Still, they chopped enough wood to start a fire, and once it burned, it worked as a beacon. More refugees came.

Now there were thousands of people here; there was no time to count them precisely. They pooled what meager resources they had. These people were farmers; what little could be conjured from the earth, they somehow teased out. But there was not enough.

Mohammed knew what he needed: outside help. In the few hours of sleep he snatched each night, he would dream of a convoy of white vehicles arriving one bright morning, each one loaded with crates of grain and boxes of medicine. Even with just five vehicles—just one—he could save so many lives.

It was then he saw the headlights, shining through the dusk. Strong and yellow, they were coming his way, their light wobbling in the heat haze. Mohammed could not help himself. He began jumping up and down, waving his arms in a wild semaphore. "Here!" he was shouting. "Here! We are here!"

The truck slowed down until Mohammed could get a better view. This was not an aid team, but just two men.

"I come in the name of our Lord, Jesus Christ," the first man began in English, rapidly translated by the second.

"Welcome, welcome," said Mohammed, grabbing his visitors with both arms in gratitude. "Welcome, welcome."

"I have some food and drugs in the back. Do you have people to unload it?"

A crowd had already assembled. After the interpreter had spoken, Mohammed nominated two of the strongest teenagers, a boy and a girl, to take the boxes off the truck. He then summoned a couple of men he could trust to stand guard: the last thing he wanted was a food riot, as hunger and desperation sparked a stampede.

"Do you think we could talk?" the visitor asked. Mohammed answered with a gesture, ushering his guest toward an empty hut. The man followed, carrying a slim, dark briefcase.

"It's taken me a long time to find you, sir. Am I right that you are in charge? This is a camp you started?"

"Yes," Mohammed said, unsure whether to look at the translator or his boss.

"And you have done this all by yourself? No one is paying you to do this? You don't work for any organization? You did this purely out of the goodness of your own heart?"

"Yes, but this is not important," Mohammed said through the interpreter. "I am not important."

At that, the visitor smiled and said, "Good."

"People are dying here," Mohammed continued. "What help can you give them? Urgently!"

The visitor smiled again. "Oh, I can promise them the greatest help of all. And it won't be long to wait. Not long at all."

He then clicked the two side locks of his briefcase and produced a syringe. "First, I want to say what an honor it is for me to meet you. It is an honor to know that the righteous truly live among us."

"Thank you, but I don't understand."

"I'm afraid I need to give you this. It's important that a man such as yourself should feel no pain or suffering. No pain or suffering at all."

Suddenly the interpreter was gripping Mohammed's arm, forcing him onto the ground. Mohammed tried to escape, but he was too weak, and this hand too strong. Now, towering over him, was the visitor, holding the syringe up to the light. He was speaking in English, lowering himself closer to Mohammed. As he did so, the interpreter was whispering directly into his ear.

"For the Lord loves the just and will not forsake his faithful ones. They will be protected forever, but the offspring of the wicked will be cut off."

Mohammed was writhing, struggling to break free. And still the voice was speaking, its breath hot.

"The wicked lie in wait for the righteous, seeking their very lives; but the Lord will not leave them in their power or let them be condemned when brought to trial. The salvation of the righteous comes from the Lord; he is their stronghold in time of trouble."

Finally he felt the needle break the skin of his arm, and as the sky darkened, he heard the words of a prayer, until the voice grew distant and all was silent.

CHAPTER FIFTY-EIGHT

MONDAY, 2:50 P.M., BROOKLYN

NOW IT WAS WILL'S TURN TO TAKE CHARGE. He all but pushed Tom out of his chair, and instantly returned to twenty-first-century journalism's base camp: Google.

"Church of the Reborn Jesus" brought up a page of entries, but they were thin. To Will's surprise, the group did not have a Web site of its own.

He clicked the first entry, a link to a paper delivered at a University of Nebraska conference.

> *Though never large in number, the Church of the Reborn Jesus achieved great influence at its height a quarter century ago, especially among young Christian intellectuals. Central to its teaching was a radical brand of replacement theology, the belief that Christians had replaced the Jews as God's chosen people . . .*

Maddeningly, the article said nothing more, rambling off into a wider discussion of campus Christianity in the 1970s. But Will was on a roll. He could tell TC was keeping up, yet both knew, intuitively, there was no time to waste on discussion. He went straight to Wikipedia, the online encyclopedia, and typed in "replacement theology."

It took a few seconds, during which Will's right foot pulsated—partly in anxiety, partly in excitement. A half-buried memory was nagging away at him. The Church of the Reborn Jesus: he had seen that name before, somewhere at the office . . .

Then a page appeared, headlined "Supersessionism." It was defined as "the traditional Christian belief that Christianity is the fulfilment of biblical Judaism, and therefore that Jews who deny that Jesus is the Jewish Messiah fall short of their calling as God's chosen people."

Will skimmed to the next paragraph. "It argues that Israel has been superseded . . . in the sense that the Church has been entrusted with the fulfilment of the promises of which Jewish Israel is the trustee."

The entry noted that while several liberal Protestant groups had renounced supersessionism, ruling that Jews and "perhaps" other non-Christians could find God through their own faith, "other conservative and fundamentalist Christian groups hold supersessionism to be valid . . . the debate continues."

And I bet I know where it continues, thought Will. He went back to Google, now narrowing his search to "Church of the Reborn Jesus and replacement theology." Three references, the first an article from the *Christian Review.*

> *. . . Replacement theology became increasingly unfashionable in this period, discredited by the politically correct crowd, said its defenders. A few years earlier, it had enjoyed a vigorous revival chiefly through a cerebral grouping known as the Church of the Reborn Jesus. According to this group, Christians had, by their recognition of Jesus as the Messiah, not*

only inherited the Jews' status as the elect, but inherited Judaism itself. The Jews had, the Reborn Jesus movement argued, ignored God's direct wishes and therefore forfeited all that they had learned from Him. They had disinherited themselves from their role as the chosen people, but—and this is what set the Church of the Reborn Jesus apart—the Jews had also abandoned their own traditions, customs, and even folklore. From now on, those were to be regarded as the possessions of committed Christians.

"Stop." It was TC, white-faced. "That's the key point, right there. *Their own traditions, customs, even folklore.* This group believes that Judaism contains the truth, not for Jews but for Christians. *Even the folklore.* Don't you see? They've taken it all. The mysticism, the kabbalah, everything."

"The story of the righteous men," said Will.

"Yes. They don't think this is some weird Hasidic tradition. They think this belongs to them. They believe it's true."

He clicked on the next Google result. It was a link to an evangelical discussion group. Somebody calling themselves NewDawn21 had written a long posting, apparently in reply to a question about the origins of the Church of the Reborn Jesus.

In its day it had quite an impact—kind of the smart end of the whole Jesus freak, sandal-wearing movement. It was centered on this very charismatic preacher who was then a chaplain at Yale, Rev. Jim Johnson.

Will looked up at TC. "I know that name," he said. "He founded some evangelical movement in the seventies. Died a few years ago." But TC was reading on.

Apparently Rev. Johnson influenced a whole generation of elite Christians. They called him the Pied Piper on campus, because he enjoyed such a dedicated following.

I can vouch for that, said the posting below:

I was at Yale in that period and Johnson was a phenomenon. He was only interested in the A-list, top-flight students—editors of Law Review, *class president, those guys. We called them the Apostles, hanging around Johnson like he was the Messiah or something. For anyone interested, I've scanned in a picture from the* Yale Daily News *which shows Johnson and his followers. Click here.*

Will clicked and waited for the picture to load. It was grainy, in drab 1970s color, and it took a while to fill the frame. Slowly it came into view. At the center, wearing a broad grin, like the captain of a college football team, was a man in his late thirties, wearing an open-necked shirt and large glasses with the curved, rectangular frames that were then regarded as supermodern. He wore no dog collar, no dark suit. He was, Will concluded, what the Victorians would have called a muscular Christian.

Surrounding him were young, serious-looking men, exuding that born-to-rule confidence that radiated out of Yale or Harvard yearbooks. The hair was long or bulky, the shirt collars and jacket lapels wide. The faces seemed to shine with possibility. These men were not only going to rule the world. It was quite clear they believed they would do it with Jesus' blessing.

"I think you need to hurry," said Tom, now taking up Will's previous position by the curtain. "There's a car outside. Two guys are getting out and coming into the building."

But Will was hardly listening. Instead he was pushed back into his seat with surprise: he had recognized one of the faces in the photograph. He was only able to because he had seen another, different picture of this same man in his youth recently. The paper had run it when he was appointed. There, at Jim Johnson's side, was none other than Townsend McDougal—the future editor of the *New York Times.*

"I don't believe it," Will said.

"It's him, isn't it?"

Will was confused. How would TC recognize McDougal?

"I didn't want to say, because I wasn't sure. But it really couldn't be anyone else."

Will looked up at her, crinkling his eyebrows to register his puzzlement. "Who are you talking about?"

"Will! They're coming up. You've got to go!"

"Look," said TC, taking her finger to the far left of the back row of the picture—an area Will had barely examined. TC stopped at a lean, handsome young man with a full head of thick hair. He was unsmiling.

"Maybe I'm wrong, Will. But I think that's your father."

CHAPTER FIFTY-NINE

MONDAY, 2:56 P.M., BROOKLYN

TOM HAD FAIRLY WRENCHED WILL FROM THE CHAIR and out the window, sending him plunging down the fire escape. He nudged TC the same way and was about to follow himself when he looked back. The computer screen was still alight with information. It would be too terrible, thought Tom, if his machine, always such a loyal ally, were to end up giving them all away.

He rushed TC out, then moved over to the desk and started frantically closing down programs. It was while he was shutting down the Internet browser that the door was flung open.

He heard it before he saw it, a splintering crash as two men shouldered their way into the apartment. Tom looked up and saw one of them: tall, thick-armed, and with the clearest, sharpest blue eyes. In an instant, Tom decided to do the one thing his every instinct rebelled against. He reached for the power cord and pulled it out of the wall, shutting down his computer and everything connected to it.

But the move was too sudden for his uninvited guests. They interpreted a man stretching downward the way they had been trained to, as someone reaching for a weapon. As he pulled on the white flex, the bullet pierced his chest. He crumpled to the ground. The screens went dark.

Will charged down the back ladder, taking two, then three rungs at a time. His head was throbbing. Who was chasing him? What had happened to TC and Tom? Where should he go?

But even as he thundered downward, story after story, his mind was racing with what he had just seen. The face was unmistakable; TC had seen it straight away. What Freudian impulse had led his eye away from it? The eyes, the jaw, the firm nose: his father.

And yet the one thing he knew for certain about William Monroe Sr. was that he was an avowed rationalist, a coolly secular man whose skepticism about religion might well have thwarted his highest ambition, to serve as a justice of the United States Supreme Court. Could he really have once been a Bible-thumper, and such a serious one?

Three more stories to go, and now he could feel the iron handrail vibrating. He looked up, to see the soles of shoes descending just as fast as his. One more level to go: Will all but jumped it.

Now he started sprinting down Smith Street, dodging people as they came out of the Salonike. He looked over his shoulder: a commotion behind him, caused by a man dashing through a crowd. "Hey, watch it asshole!"

Will body-swerved around the corner, clasping hold of a pretzel wagon to steady himself. In front of him was Fourth Avenue, with six lanes of traffic, all moving fast. At the first gap, he plunged in.

He was standing on the dotted white line separating two streams of heavy traffic. Drivers started blasting their horns; they clearly thought Will was some kind of psycho. He looked back. There, just a lane of cars away, was the stalker, the man he had nearly caught in the act of murder less than twenty-four hours ago.

As if protected by the traffic, Will stared at him. What came back was a laser-beam eye that seemed to bore right through him.

He wheeled around and spotted another gap in traffic—just a beat, and he would miss it. Will leapt across, turning around to see that his pursuer had made the same move. They were still just the width of a single car apart. He could see a bulge around the man's hip, what Will assumed to be a holster.

He looked ahead: the light was still green. But for how much longer? Soon it would be red: the traffic would slow down, and he would be able to cross to the other side, but so would the man with the gun. He would be within point-blank range. But there was no gap. The cars were moving too fast.

Will had only one option. Instead of crossing the road, he sprinted to his left, as if trying to catch up with the traffic. He ran faster, never taking his eye off the lights. He would act the second he saw a glimmer of red. *Come on, come on.* He looked around. The man was still just one lane away, but hardly moved from his previous position. Now was the moment.

As green turned to red, the traffic slowed, the cars bunching up behind each other: Will had only to dart between them, keeping himself low. Three, four, five lanes, and he was nearly there.

Once across, he had to burst through a family waiting at the crossing; he knocked the balloon out of a child's hand. Will looked back to see it soar—and to realize Laser Eyes was now just a sprint away from him.

At last, Atlantic Avenue subway station. Will hurtled down the stairs, cursing the wide woman blocking his way. Down and down, vaulting over the turnstile, hoping his ears would not fail him. Years of traveling on the Underground in London had given him a sixth sense for the mix of wind, light, and humming sounds that indicated a train was coming. Will was sure he could hear it on the opposite platform. He would have to get up the stairs and across the bridge in just a few seconds. He could hear the thudding of footsteps; the stalker was just behind him.

Only moments separated them, but as Will crossed the bridge he could see the train that had just pulled in. An instant later, he was sliding down the stairs, shoving people out of the way. There was the *beep-beep-beep* and hiss of air that announced the train was about to move off. Just one more second . . .

Will dived from the bottom stair and across the platform in what felt like a single leap. The door had almost closed behind him when it stopped—held back by four fingers of a hand. Through the glass, Will could see his face: the eyes almost translucent, fixed in a stare that turned Will's guts to ice. The door was inching back.

"What you doing? You just gonna have to wait for the next train like everyone else!" It was a woman passenger, no younger than seventy, using her walking stick to whack the knuckles protruding through the door. As the train began to move off, she rapped harder—until one by one, they disappeared. The man with the glass eyes was left on the platform, getting smaller and smaller.

"Thank you with all my heart," said Will, gasping for air as he fell into the nearest seat.

"People need to have more respect," she said.

"Yes, that's right," Will wheezed. "Respect. I couldn't agree more."

As the air came back into his lungs and the oxygen returned to his brain, he could see only one image. When he closed his eyes, it was there, imprinted under his eyelids. His father, aged twenty-one—a comrade in the army of Jesus. And not just the army, but the vanguard. A handpicked elite who believed they knew the secrets of the true faith.

What were they exactly? Christians, certainly. But with a strange edge of arrogance. It was they, not the Jews, who were the chosen people. They, not the Jews, who could regard Judaism itself as their birthright. They, not the Jews, who would quote the Old Testament and all its prophecies, they who would see the promises made to Abraham as promises made to them.

Will looked out the window. DeKalb Avenue station. He got out and jumped on another train. Keep Laser Eyes and his friends guessing.

TC had seen the significance straight away. According to this strict brand of replacement theology, if Judaism was theirs, that meant all of it. The story of Abraham's bargain with Sodom would be part of *their* inheritance—and so would the fruit of that story, the mystical Jewish belief that the world was maintained by thirty-six righteous men. For some reason, they had taken that belief as their own—and now, it seemed, they had added a new twist. They were determined to kill these good men one by one. But if it was this bizarre Christian sect who were behind the killings, why on earth had the Hasidim kidnapped Beth?

It was too much. Will needed to think, calmly. He looked at his watch: 3:45 p.m. So little time. He called TC's number, praying she had somehow got away.

"Will! You're alive!"

"Are you OK? Where are you?"

"I'm in the hospital. With Tom. He was shot."

"Oh, my God."

"I was on the roof. I heard a shot, I ran downstairs, and he was lying there, bleeding. Oh, Will—"

"Is he alive?"

"They're operating on him now. My God, who did this, Will? Why would anyone do this?"

"I don't know, but I'm going to find them, I promise. I'm going to find the people behind this whole fucking mess. And I know I'm close."

CHAPTER SIXTY

Monday, 3:47 p.m., Manhattan

"TC, I KNOW THEY'RE HERE. In New York City."

"How can you be so certain? They're killing righteous men all over the world—why would they be here?"

"For one thing, everything they know, they've got from the Hasidim. They've got all they can from hacking into their computers. Now they need to be here in person—to complete the process. That's why they killed Yosef Yitzhok. They're desperate to find number thirty-six. And they're convinced the Hasidim know who he is. And they're right. Besides, I reckon they *want* to be here."

"What do you mean?"

"Don't you see? Tonight is the climax. It's the moment it all comes together. They'll want to be in the place where all this prophecy becomes real. Because this is where it all ends, TC. The Sodom of the twenty-first century. New York City! It's here the world finally loses its bargain with God. Just thirty-six righteous men; so long as they're alive, the world goes on. Without them, it's all over. These people will want to be here to see it happen. The end of the world."

"Will, you're scaring me."

"And there's one other thing." He stopped himself. "Look, there's no time. I've got to go." He hung up and dialed a number at the *New York Times*.

"Amy Grossman."

"Amy, it's Will. I need you to do something for me."

"*Will!*" She was whispering. "I shouldn't even be talking to you. Are you getting some help?"

"Right now I need *your* help, Amy. There's a flyer on my desk, for a convention of the Church of the Reborn Jesus. Could you just read it out to me?"

Amy sighed in audible relief. "Hold on." Seconds later she was back. "OK: 'The Church of the Reborn Jesus, valuing families through family values. Spiritual Gathering, Javits Convention Center, on West 34th Street' . . . oh, hold on, it's today."

"Yes!" He sounded as if he was punching the air.

"Oh, Will, I'm so glad you're finding some comfort in your faith. I know many people facing challenges—"

"Amy, love to chat, got to go."

Thirty minutes later, he was there. The Javits Convention Center. He could see a delegates' counter, staffed by bright-eyed volunteers. That would not work. *Ah, a press desk.*

"Excuse me, I'm from the *Guardian*, a London newspaper, and I fear I'm not yet on your list. Is there any way you might be able to accommodate me?"

"Sir, I'm afraid accreditation has to be done through our Richmond office. Did you preaccredit?" *Preaccredit.* Just when Will thought he had heard every coinage corporate America could possibly come up with.

"No, I'm sorry, I just couldn't get through on the phone. But my editors would be so disappointed if I couldn't cover this wonderful celebration of family values. We have nothing like this in Britain, you see. And I know there is a real hunger back home for this kind of spiritual example. Is there any way you could let me in, just for half an hour or so, so that I could at least tell my bosses I saw it with my own eyes?"

He had pushed every button. In the years since he had arrived in America, this kind of patter had got him into Graceland for an Elvis tribute night, and into a presidential candidates' debate in Trenton, New Jersey. He hoped his eyes glowed with eagerness.

But the woman on the desk, identified by her label as Carrie-Anne, Facilitator, was not about to relent. "I'm going to need you to speak to Richmond."

Damn.

"Sure, what's the number I need to dial?"

Will wrote it down carefully—then, using his cell phone, he dialed his home number.

"Hello. This is Tom Mitchell from the *Guardian* in London. It's about today's convention. I just wondered if there's any chance . . . That's right." At the other end, he could hear his own voice, announcing that he and Beth were away from the phone right now. He tried to block out the sound and carry on talking. "So I need to look at the program. OK—" Will put his hand over the receiver and then mouthed to Carrie-Anne, "She says I need to see the press pack." Without hesitation, she passed one over.

"OK, so I should go through that now, see what interests me . . . all right, that's a very big help. Thanks so much."

As he was talking to his own answering machine, Will's eye ran down the list of sessions.

The Holden Suite: "Putting togetherness back together. Parenting after divorce with Rev. Peter Thompson."

The Macmillan Room: "How would Jesus do it? Seeking the savior's advice."

Will could not find what he wanted. He looked up; Carrie-Anne was smiling as she handed press badges to a TV reporter and her cameraman. Silently, Will wheeled around and headed for the conference rooms—his press pack held high as a surrogate credential.

He looked back at the list. Lunch breaks, crèche facilities, workshops. Then his eye stopped.

The Chapel: "Entering the messianic age. Speaker to be confirmed. CLOSED SESSION."

Will looked at his watch; it had already begun. But where in this vast complex of suites, corridors, and stairwells was the Chapel? He rifled through his press pack until he saw an internal map. *Third floor.*

There were so many doors; but finally he saw one with a sign, a diagram of a stick man kneeling, at prayer. Will pressed his ear close to the door:

". . . how many centuries have we waited? More than twenty. And sometimes our patience has worn thin. Our faith has faltered."

Will heard the *ding* of an elevator. Out came three men, around Will's age, dressed in neat dark suits—just like the one he was still wearing from his late-night trip to Crown Heights. Each held a Bible, and they were heading, purposefully, toward him.

As they got nearer, Will saw that at least one was out of breath. They were late. This was his chance.

"Don't worry," said Will as they reached him. "I think we can still sneak in at the back."

Sure enough, one opened the door, allowing the whole group to enter—the embarrassment divided by being shared. Will was simply one of the group; he even carried his own Bible.

Jammed in at the back, Will tried to survey the room. To his surprise, it was large; the size of a banqueting hall. There must have been more than two thousand people inside. It was hard to tell who they were; all heads were dipped in prayer. Will did not dare raise his eyes.

Finally an amplified voice broke the silence.

"We repent, O Lord, for our moments of doubt. We repent for

the pain and hurt we have inflicted on each other, on the planet your Father entrusted to us and on your name. We repent, O Lord, for the centuries of sin that have kept you from us."

In unison, the congregation replied, "On this Day of Atonement, we repent."

Will looked up, trying to work out who was speaking. A man was standing at the front, but he had his back to the room. It was impossible to see if he was young or old: most of his head was covered with a white skullcap.

"But now, O Lord, the Day of Reckoning is upon us. At long last Man will be held accountable. The great Book of Life is about to be slammed shut. Finally, we are to be judged."

In unison: "Amen."

The man turned around: about Will's age, studious looking. Will was surprised. He seemed too young to be a leader, and that voice too strong to have come from him.

"Your first people, Israel, strayed from your teaching, O Lord." The voice was continuing, even though the man Will had identified as the leader was not speaking. Only now did Will take in the huge screen at the front of the room. It bore just two words, black on white: *The Apostle*. At last Will realized that the voice filling this room did not belong to anyone inside it. Perhaps it was on a tape; maybe it was relayed live from the outside. It had an odd, metallic quality. Either way, the Apostle was nowhere to be seen.

"The first Israel was frightened of your word. It fell to others to honor your covenant. As it is written, 'And if you are Christ's, then you are Abraham's offspring, heirs according to the promise.' "

The congregation responded: "We are Christ's and so we are Abraham's. We are heirs according to the promise."

Will felt himself shudder. So this was the Church of the Reborn Jesus, updated for the twenty-first century. And this was the doctrine that had once captivated his father, Townsend McDougal, and who knew how many others. The men in this room—and, Will realized now, they were all men—believed it too.

They were the inheritors of the Jews' place in the divine scheme. They had taken the teachings of the Jews as their own.

"But now, Lord, we need your help. We pray for your guidance. We are so close, yet the final knowledge eludes us."

Number thirty-six, thought Will.

"Please bring us to completion, so that we may finally let God's judgment rain upon this benighted earth."

Will was surveying the room when a man in the front row swiveled around to do the same. He saw Will, did a small double take, then looked across the room, made eye contact with someone else, and gestured with his head in Will's direction.

Will did not see the hand that reached out and grabbed his neck. Nor did he spot the leg that kicked him below the knee and made him buckle. But as he fell to the ground, he caught a glimpse of the man standing over him. His eyes were so blue, they almost shone.

CHAPTER SIXTY-ONE

MONDAY, 5:46 P.M., MANHATTAN

HE HAD WOKEN UP, HE KNEW THAT, but it was still dark. He tried to touch his eyes—sending a sharp, searing pain to his shoulder. His hands were tied. His arms, his legs, his stomach, they all seemed to have had a layer of tissue removed: he pictured them as raw, red flesh.

He twitched his eyelids; he could feel something that was not skin. His eyes were covered by a blindfold. He tried to speak, but his mouth was gagged; he began to cough.

"Take it off." The voice was firm; in authority. Will started to retch; the sense-memory of the gag was still choking him. Finally he spat out a few words.

"Where am I?"

"You'll see."

"Where the hell am I?"

"Don't you dare shout at us, Mr. Monroe. I said, you'll see." Will could hear two, maybe three others close by. "Take him now."

"Where am I going?"

"You're going to get what you came here to get. All that lying seems to have paid off, Mr. Tom Mitchell of the *Guardian*: you're going to get your big interview after all."

In the darkness, he felt a thick, flat hand at his back: he was being shoved forward. He walked a few paces, then two more hands grabbed his shoulders and pivoted him to the right. Will could feel carpet under his feet. Was he still in the convention center? How long had the beating lasted? How long had he been unconscious? What if it was nighttime? It would be too late! Yom Kippur would be over. In the black of his blindfold, Will imagined the gates of heaven, slamming shut.

"Sir, he's here."

"Thank you, gentlemen. Let us remove those bonds." Even in regular speech, this man seemed to be quoting scripture. "Let's take a good look at you."

Will felt hands working at his wrists until they were free. Then, at last, the blindfold came off—flooding him with light. He stole a glance at his watch. There was still time. Thank God, thought Will.

"Gentlemen, leave us, please."

In front of Will, at a plain, hotel-room desk, sat the man he had seen earlier in the chapel. His complexion had the earnest shine of an inner-city vicar, the kind of well-meaning do-gooder Will remembered running the Christian Union at Oxford.

"Are you the Apostle?" Will winced. The effort of speaking sent a tremor of pain shooting down his spine.

"I had hoped your suffering would be easing. We took great care to bind your wounds."

Will suddenly became aware of bandages and plasters covering his arms and legs, even his chest.

"Please accept my apologies for the somewhat heavy-handed treatment you had meted out to you. 'But those who suffer He delivers in their suffering; He speaks to them in their affliction.' The Book of Job."

"You didn't answer my question. Are you the Apostle?"

A modest smile. "No, I am not the Apostle. I only serve him."

"I want to speak to him."

"And why should I let you do that?"

"Because I know what he, what all of you, are up to. And I will go to the police."

"I'm afraid that is not going to be possible. The Apostle does not meet anybody."

"Well, in that case, I'm sure the police will be very interested to hear what I know."

"And what exactly do you know, Mr. Monroe?"

The thin-lipped calm of this man infuriated Will. He strode forward, his legs aching with each movement. "I'll tell you what I know. I know that the Jews believe there are always thirty-six righteous men in the world. And that so long as those people are alive, then the world is OK. I also know that in the last few days these men have started dying very mysterious deaths. Murdered, to be precise. One in Montana, maybe two in New York. One in London, and God knows where else. And I strongly suspect that this group is behind it. That's what I know."

"I don't think 'strongly suspect' will cut much ice, Mr. Monroe. Not coming from a man who was in a prison cell himself just a few hours ago."

How the hell did he know that? Will suddenly thought back to the desk clerk at the Seventh Precinct and the crucifix around her neck. Maybe this cult had people everywhere.

Worse, the vicar was right. Will had nothing firm, just wild speculation. He had no leverage over this guy or the so-called Apostle he served. He felt his shoulders slump.

"But let's say this theory of yours is right. Purely hypothetically, of course." The man was twirling a pencil between his fingers, letting it fall from one hand to the other. Will wondered if he was nervous. "Let us say there was such an effort to identify the thirty-six and to . . . bring them to their final rest. And let us say that a holy group was involved in this. I strongly suspect, to use your own phrase, that you would have a divine obligation to get out of their way, wouldn't you? I think you would understand the wounds to your flesh as some kind of sign. A warning, if you like."

"Are you threatening to kill me?"

"No, of course not. Nothing so crude. I am threatening you with something much worse."

Will felt an ice in this man that terrified him. "Worse?"

"I am threatening you with the reality of the holiest teachings ever given to mankind. The hour of redemption is upon us, Mr. Monroe. Salvation will come to those who have brought the hour closer. But those who sought to delay it, to thwart the divine promise, those souls will be tormented for all eternity. A thousand years will be like the passing of just one day, and there will be a thousand more and a thousand more after that. So think carefully, Mr. Monroe. Do not stand in the path of the Lord. Do not stand in the way of our Father. Do not aid those who seek to frustrate Him. Try instead to light the way."

Will was attempting to absorb all this man was telling him when he realized the meeting was over. From behind, he felt hands once again grabbing his arms and replacing his blindfold. He was led out of the room and into what sounded like a service elevator. It shook when it had plumbed what Will calculated was five floors. The doors moved apart, and he was shoved out. By the time he had removed the blindfold, to see he was in an underground car park, he was alone.

Upstairs, the man who had spoken to Will a few minutes earlier checked to make sure it had all come through loud and clear on the speaker phone. "I think we have given him enough," he said to the older man at the end of the line.

"Yes, you have done well. Now all we can do is wait." If Will had heard the voice, he would have recognized it. For it was the voice of the Apostle.

CHAPTER SIXTY-TWO

MONDAY, 7:12 P.M., CROWN HEIGHTS, BROOKLYN

IT HAD BEEN BLACK; TONIGHT IT WAS WHITE. The synagogue seemed to glow with whiteness, moonlight reflected on snow. There were as many men in here as Will had seen on Friday night, except now they were dressed not in black suits but clothed almost entirely in white.

They wore what seemed to be thin white bathrobes over their dark suits, covering them from their ankles to their shoulders. Instead of the regulation black leather shoes, their feet were now in white sneakers. Many of the prayer shawls were all white, as were the skullcaps of those not wearing hats. And they were packed together, a swaying mass of white, a swaying mass of prayer.

This, TC had told him in the briefest of calls from the hospital, was *ne'eilah*, the concluding segment of what would have been a marathon, day-long service. Tradition demanded that the congregation—denied food or water for the previous twenty-four hours—stand for the duration, in recognition of the gravity of the moment. For this was the final hour of Yom Kippur, the Day of Atonement, the day of reckoning. In this hour, the gates of heaven were closing. Repentance was urgent. As TC described it, Will imagined it: the last-minute penitent slipping through the crack in the door, just as it thundered shut. Those who had not atoned, or left it too late, were left outside.

All day, this vast hangar of a space had echoed with ancient incantations, as several thousand voices sang together:

B'Rosh Hashana yichatayvun . . .

On the first day of the year it is inscribed and on the Day of Atonement it is sealed. How many shall die and how many shall be born; who shall live and who shall die, who at the measure of man's days and who before it . . .

The heaviness of the hour descended on Will as soon as he walked in. Faces were funeral-serious; acknowledging each other, but unsmiling. Most men had eyes only for the prayer books they held as they bobbed back and forth in supplication.

Sha'arei shamayim petach . . .

Open the gates of heaven . . . Save us, O God

"Excuse me," said Will, trying to squeeze his way through this football crowd of a throng. It was too packed; his progress was too slow. He needed to get to Rabbi Freilich as quickly as possible if he was going to have any chance of striking a bargain. He would reveal the real pursuers of the righteous men, and, in return, they would release Beth. He looked at his watch. He had perhaps thirty minutes to act. Will had calculated that he had to move now, while the threat remained at its highest. If he waited till after Yom Kippur, and if the thirty-sixth man remained safely hidden, the Hasidim might conclude that the danger had receded. Will's leverage would vanish.

He began to ask. "Excuse me, do you know where Rabbi Freilich is? Rabbi Freilich?" Most ignored him. Occasionally a hand would wave him left or right while the eyes stayed fixed on the page ahead or, just as often, firmly shut.

It was like wading through water. All these unfamiliar faces. He looked at his watch: twenty-three minutes.

Then a hand on his shoulder, sending a bolt of pain through his back. He turned around, his hand balled into a fist in readiness.

"Will?"

"Sandy! You frightened me. Jesus. Sorry."

"What are you doing here?"

"No time to explain. Listen, I need to speak to Rabbi Freilich. Now."

Sandy did not reply, but grasped Will's wrist and dragged him first right, then back, and finally around the tables where Will had seen the men studying so hard three days earlier. There, rocking backward and forward, his eyes closed and facing toward the heavens, was Rabbi Freilich.

"Rabbi? It's Will Monroe."

The rabbi lowered his head and then opened his eyes, as if from sleep. His face betrayed great weariness. Then, seeing the bruises on Will's face, it registered shock.

"Rabbi, I know who's killing the righteous men. And I know why they're doing it."

The rabbi's eyes widened.

"I will tell you and I will tell you right away, while you still have time to stop them. But first you have to do something for me. You must take me to my wife. This instant."

Freilich's brow tensed. He took off his glasses and rubbed the bridge of his nose. He looked at his watch: twenty minutes to go. Will could see he was weighing up the right course of action.

"All right," the rabbi said finally, though he still looked anguished. "Come with me."

It was easier to walk out of the shul than it had been to walk through it; the crowd parted in deference to Rabbi Freilich, even if a few curious glances were directed at the rabbi's battered companion.

They emerged into the dusk, the sound of the prayer within filling the air. The rabbi walked fast, turning left at the first corner. Will looked at his watch: fourteen minutes left. Each step hurt his calves and thighs, but he was almost running. He glanced over each shoulder, to see if he was being followed. No sign.

Suddenly Rabbi Freilich stopped, turned, and faced a small brownstone house.

"Are we here?"

"We are here."

Will could hardly believe it. It was just around the block from the synagogue; he must have passed this house several times. He had been so close to Beth without even knowing it.

His heart began to pound. So much had happened, it felt as if so much time had passed, since he had seen his wife. The need to hold her tight was so intense, he could barely contain it.

The rabbi knocked on the door. A woman's voice called out, in a language Will did not understand. The rabbi replied with what Will guessed was a password, in Yiddish.

Finally, the door opened to reveal a woman in her mid-thirties, wearing one of those twin sets his mother might have worn twenty years ago. Her hair was styled the way all the women of Crown Heights had their hair—which meant its was not hers at all, but a wig. Will let out a sigh; he realized he had expected to see Beth straight away.

"Dos is ihr man. Bring zie ahehr, biteh." This is her husband. Bring her here, please.

The woman disappeared upstairs. Will could hear doors opening, then footsteps, then the sound of two people coming down.

He looked around, to see a long dark skirt descending the stairs. More disappointment. But as the woman walked lower, he recognized her hips and her posture. And then he saw her face.

He had no control over his eyes. They filled the instant he saw her. Only at that moment did he realize just how deeply he had missed her, how his whole body had ached for her. He jumped the two remaining stairs and clasped her right there, on the staircase. His vision was too blurred to see her face clearly, but as he held her tight he could feel her shake, and he knew she was trembling with tears. Neither could say anything. He was squeezing her so hard, but it was not tight enough. He wanted there to be no space between them.

At last he peeled himself away, to look at her properly for the first time. Her eyes met his, with a kind of bashfulness he had not seen before. It was not modesty but something else: it was awe, awe for the enormity of the love they felt for each other.

Finally she spoke, through her tears. "You see, I told you. I told you I believed in you. Remember the song, Will? I knew you would come and find me. I knew it. And look. Here you are."

He brought her head to his chest, the two of them clinging fast, unaware of the woman who had opened the door, unaware of Rabbi Freilich standing at the foot of the stairs, unaware that each one of them had shed their own tears at the sight of this couple back, at last, in each other's arms.

"Mr. Monroe, I am sorry," the rabbi began, as if clearing his throat. "Mr. Monroe."

"Yes," said Will, using the back of his shirt cuff to wipe the tears from his cheeks. "Yes, of course." He turned to Beth. "Have they told you about all this—"

"She knows nothing," the rabbi interrupted. "And there isn't time. Now please."

Will hardly knew where to start. A tiny Christian sect that believed it had inherited Jewish teaching, all of it, even the doctrine of the *lamad vav.* How they had picked up on the messianic fervor of Crown Heights and had started hacking into its computer network, eventually discovering the identities of the righteous men. How they had used their people all over the world to kill them, one by one—timing the murders for the Days of Awe, the Ten Days of Penitence. "Which," Will added, "will be over in twelve minutes."

"But why?"

"I can't be certain. At the service, this voice, the Apostle, was explaining it, but that's when they started beating me. He and the other man, the younger one, talked about redemption and judgment and salvation, but I couldn't make any real sense of it. I'm sorry." Will glanced at Beth and took her hand: she looked completely baffled.

"Can someone tell me what on earth is going on here?" No one said anything. Will gave a small shake of the head. *No time. Later.*

By now Rabbi Freilich was sitting, stroking his beard, deep in thought. "And you have seen this group with your own eyes?"

"I was with them an hour ago. They're here in New York. I'm convinced it's them. And I'm convinced they're here to finish the job. The Apostle said that 'the final knowledge eludes us.' I think they still don't know the name of the thirty-sixth righteous man. But they are determined to find him—and to kill him. You have to protect him. Where is he? Is he safe?"

"He is in the safest place in the world."

"You must tell me. Otherwise, we can't be sure they won't find him."

Rabbi Freilich looked at his watch again and allowed himself a small smile. "He is right here."

CHAPTER SIXTY-THREE

MONDAY, 7:28 P.M., CROWN HEIGHTS, BROOKLYN

THE SOUNDS OF *NE'EILAH* WERE DRIFTING THROUGH, not just from the synagogue but from houses along the street—intense prayer at this, the most climactic hour of the holiest day of the year.

"Here?" Will said. "You mean . . ." He stared at Rabbi Freilich himself.

"No, Will, it's not me."

Will looked around. There were no other men in the room; no other men in the house. His stomach began to turn over. Was it even possible? "No, it can't be. You can't mean—"

"No, Will," said the rabbi, his smile stretching wider. "It's not you." And then, with only the slightest tilt of his head, he nodded toward Beth.

"Beth? But I thought the thirty-six were all men. You told me they were all *men*!"

"They are. And your wife is carrying inside her the thirty-sixth righteous man. She is pregnant, Will, with a boy."

"You've made a mistake. We've been trying—" Will stopped himself when he saw Beth's face. She was smiling and crying at the same time.

"It's true, Will. I finally got to use that tester I've carried around in my bag for so long. It's true. We're going to have a baby."

"You see," said Rabbi Freilich. "Your wife didn't know she was pregnant. But the Torah knew. The Torah told us. It was the Rebbe's last message, given to Yosef Yitzhok in his dying hours. Nobody realized it at the time, but his last words led us to the thirty-sixth verse—from the book of Genesis, the book of new beginnings. This one verse—the tenth verse of the eighteenth chapter—was kept separate from all the others; not written down in any of the Rebbe's papers or speeches. No one could have picked it up from our computers. But we counted off the letters in the usual way, and it brought us a location: your home. At first we assumed that meant the *tzaddik* was you. But then Yosef Yitzhok looked closer at the words themselves. That verse describes the moment when God speaks to Abraham and tells him his wife, Sarah, is to have a son. She had been childless so long, yet she was to have a child. Yosef Yitzhok understood what the Rebbe was telling us. We weren't to look at you, but your wife. We found the hidden of the hidden, Will. And he is your son."

Will pulled Beth toward him. But as they hugged, he felt something dig into his chest through the bandages. He heard the words of the vicar, repeated in his ears. *We've bound your wounds. I hope your pain is easing.*

Will ripped open his shirt and tore off the bandages underneath. He cursed himself. How could he have been so stupid! He had followed the script exactly as the vicar had laid it out for him. *Try instead to light the way*—and that was exactly what he had done. Sure enough, there it was, concealed between the bandages: a simple wire, tipped at one end by a microphone and at the other by a tiny transmitter.

A second, maybe two, passed before they knocked down the door. As it smashed against the wall, Will saw a blur with only two distinct features: a pair of laser-blue eyes and the barrel of a revolver, sheathed in a silencer. Instinct rather than judgment made Will shield Beth. He stole a glance at his watch. Nine minutes to go.

Rabbi Freilich and the woman of the house froze, petrified. Laser Eyes barely looked at them.

"Thank you, William. You did what we asked."

The voice was not the gunman's, but belonged to the figure behind him, now stepping into the room. The sound of it made Will's brain flood. He realized he was looking at the head of the Church of the Reborn Jesus, the man behind the murder of thirty-five of the most virtuous people on earth, the man who wanted to bring about nothing less than the end of the world. And yet the face he was staring at was one he had known forever.

CHAPTER SIXTY-FOUR

MONDAY, 7:33 P.M., CROWN HEIGHTS, BROOKLYN

"HELLO, WILLIAM."

Will could feel his head pounding. The room seemed to spin. Beth, cowering behind him, grabbed his wrist and gasped. Rabbi Freilich, the woman—everyone was frozen.

"What? What are you . . . I don't understand."

"I don't blame you, Will. How could you possibly understand? I never explained any of this to you. Nor to your mother either. Not in any way she could understand."

"But, I don't, I don't . . ." Will was stammering. Nonsensically he said, "But you're my father."

"I am, Will. But I am also the leader of this movement. I am the Apostle. And you have just rendered us the greatest possible service, as I knew you would. You have brought us to the last of the just. For that alone, you have earned your place in the world to come."

Will was blinking, like a fugitive dazzled by headlights. He could not compute what he was seeing or hearing.

His father. How could his father, a man of the law and justice, be the architect of so many cruel, needless deaths? Did his father, a stern rationalist, really believe all that replacement theology, all that stuff about becoming God's chosen people, about the end of the world? Of course he must believe it: but how had he hidden it all these years, convincing the world that he was a man whose only god was the legal code and the United States Constitution? Had his father really drawn up a plan to strangle and shoot three dozen good men, the last best hope of humanity?

For less than a second, an image popped into his head. It was the face of someone he had not seen in years. It was his grandmother, serving tea in her garden back in England. The sun was shining, but all he could focus on was her mouth, as she uttered the words that had intrigued him at the time and ever since: *Your father's other great passion.* So this was it. The force that came between his parents, both so young. It was not another woman nor even his father's dedication to the law. It was his faith. His fanaticism.

Will had so many questions, but he asked only one.

"So you knew all along, all this time, about Beth?" As he said it, his arms went backward, shielding his wife from both sides.

"Oh, I had nothing to do with that, William. That was your Jewish friends' initiative, theirs alone." Monroe Sr. gestured toward Rabbi Freilich. "But once you told me Beth was kidnapped, I had my suspicions. Once you had tracked her captors down to Crown Heights, I knew for certain. It took me a while to work it out. At first, I wondered if it was somehow meant to stop you working on the story. You were doing so well—first Howard Macrae, then Pat Baxter—it seemed you were about to discover everything. But then I realized that the Hasidim had not taken Beth to stop you. That would make no sense. They had taken her to stop *me.* And there could only be one explanation. They needed to give her shelter because she *was* shelter—the shelter of the thirty-sixth righteous man."

"You knew what was going on, but you didn't help me, you didn't—"

"No, William. I wanted you to help *me.* I knew you would not rest until you had found Beth, and in so doing, you would bring us to her. And I was right."

Will was struggling to stay standing. The room was beginning to turn. His lungs seemed to be emptying of air. He could only manage a few words. "This is madness."

"You think this is madness? Do you have even the first idea of what's going on here?"

"I think you're murdering the righteous of the earth."

"Well, I wouldn't use those words, William. I surely would not. But I want you to look more widely, to see the whole picture." It was a tone Will had never heard before, or not until an hour ago at any rate. It was the voice of a strict teacher who expected to be obeyed. Whatever electronic voice distortion had been used in the Chapel at the convention center, it had not concealed this tone: the authority of the Apostle.

"You see, Christianity understands what Judaism never could: what the Jews stubbornly refused to understand. They did not see what was staring them in the face! They believed that, so long as there were thirty-six just souls in the world, all would be well. They took comfort from the idea. They did not realize its true power."

"And what is its true power?" It was Rabbi Freilich.

"That if these thirty-six men uphold the world, then the opposite must be true! The instant the thirty-six are gone, the world is no more." Monroe Sr. turned back to face his son. "You see, that didn't interest the Jews. They thought if the world ended, then that would be that. It would all be over: death, destruction, the end of the story. But Christianity teaches us something else, doesn't it, William? Something glorious and infinite! For we Christians are blessed with a sacred knowledge: we know that the end of the world spells the final reckoning. And now we discover that all we have to do to make that happen—to make absolutely sure that happens—is to end the lives of thirty-six people.

"If we can do that before the Ten Days of Penitence are complete, the true Judgment Day will be upon us. It's as simple and beautiful as that."

Will could not quite believe these words were coming from his father's mouth. It was a mismatch, as if he had become a ventriloquist dummy for a madman. With dread, Will realized that maybe this was the real William Monroe. Perhaps the father he had known was the fake. He forced himself to speak. "And why would you want to bring about 'the true Judgment Day'? Why would you want this final reckoning?"

"Oh, come on, William. Don't play the fool. Every Sunday-school child in Christendom knows the answer to that. It's all there in the Book of Revelation. The end of the world will bring about the return of Christ the Redeemer."

Will rocked on his heels, as if the words themselves were a physical force. "So you're trying to bring Christ back into the world by killing thirty-six innocent people?" Will was conscious of the gun pointed directly at him. "And these men are not just innocent. They are men of remarkable goodness. I know that for a fact."

"Don't look at me as if I'm some common murderer, William. You must see the genius of this plan. Only thirty-six. Just thirty-six men need die. You should read the scriptures, my son. It was assumed that millions would have to lose their lives in the battle of Armageddon, the final conflagration hastening the Second Coming. The dead piled on the dead, oceans of blood. 'Every island fled away and the mountains could not be found.'

"But this avoids all that. This finds a new way to paradise, via a path neither strewn with bones, nor drenched in tears." Will's father was closing his eyes. "This is a just, peaceful way to bring about heaven on earth. Think of it, William: no more suffering, no more bloodshed. The messianic days, brought about by the sacrifice of only thirty-six souls. That's fewer than die every minute on the roads; fewer than die needlessly in house fires or train wrecks. And those deaths are for nothing. But these—these lives are given so that others, the rest of humanity, may live forever. In paradise. Isn't that what these righteous men would have wanted?

"And these were not brutal murders, William. Each one was carried out with love and respect for the blessed soul within. We gave them anesthetic so they would feel no pain. Of course, sometimes we had to disguise what we were doing. Sometimes that meant a more violent end than we would have liked." Will thought of Howard Macrae, stabbed and stabbed again, so that his death might look like a gang killing.

"But we tried to give them a measure of dignity." Will remembered the blanket laid over Macrae's corpse. The woman he had interviewed a thousand years ago in Brownsville—Rosa—had insisted that the only person who could have done that was the killer himself, and it turned out Rosa was right.

His father was still talking, his voice softer now. "Imagine it, William. Let yourself imagine it. A world without war. A world of peace and tranquility, not just for now or next week, but for ever and ever. And you could make all that a reality, not by the sacrifice of millions but by sacrificing three dozen righteous souls. If you could do that, William, wouldn't you do it? Wouldn't you *have* to do it?"

The Apostle stopped preaching, letting his words hang for a while. Will could feel his head aching. All this talk of the end of days, of the Second Coming, of redemption and Armageddon, was too vast. It seemed to engulf him. Out of nowhere, an image of his past floated before his eyes. He was six years old, jumping the waves on a beach in the Hamptons, clinging to his father's hand. But now there was no hand to hold.

Everything rational told Will his father had lapsed into a kind of insanity. How long he had been like this, Will had no idea. Perhaps ever since he started following Jim Johnson at Yale. But insanity was what it was. An international killing spree to bring back Jesus? It was certifiable.

But another voiced tugged at Will. It certainly sounded crazy, but the evidence was hard to deny. The Hassidim of Crown Heights yearned for Messiah; so did Christians the world over. Could all those hundreds of millions of people be wrong? A world without violence or disease, a world of peace and eternal life. His father was a clever, serious man—his intellect was as formidable as any Will had ever known. If he believed the truth of this prophecy, that this might really bring about heaven on earth, was it not gross arrogance for Will to insist he knew better?

Besides, it was too late to save the righteous men themselves. Thirty-five of them were dead; that damage had already been done. And the decoding of ancient texts—finding these men by converting letters into numbers and then numbers into coordinates on the map—all that sounded loopy, but it had been vindicated. Those men were indeed righteous. Will had seen that for himself. Could he be so sure that he was right and his father wrong?

Suddenly Laser Eyes was gesturing at his watch, pressing Monroe Sr. to hurry. "Yes, yes. My friend is right. We have so little time. But Will, it's important you know something. How I worked it out, how I understood that Beth is the mother of a tzaddik." Will flinched. The word sounded strange, unnatural, in the mouth of his father.

"Because I saw the beauty of it. *The pattern.* Don't you see it, Will? None of it is a coincidence, none of it. Not the stories you wrote for the newspaper, not this." He gestured toward Beth. "Not you, not me. It's not a coincidence at all. The rabbi here can tell us all about that. You'd call it *beshert*, wouldn't you, Rabbi? 'What is meant to be.' Destiny.

"Time is running out, William. And it's time for you to face your destiny. You've been chosen for this holiest of roles. Don't you see how perfect it is? How God wants to end everything the way it all began? It started with Abraham and the request God made of him. You know what God wanted Abraham to do, don't you, William?"

Will swallowed hard. Cold realization seeped through his veins.

His tongue felt glued to the roof of his mouth. "To sacrifice his son."

"Exactly. To sacrifice the son he and his wife had wanted for so long." Monroe Sr. turned to the blue-eyed man, who suddenly produced a long, gleaming knife. Will's father handled it gingerly. With respect.

"That's why it has to be you, William. Abraham was willing to slay his beloved Isaac merely to prove his faith. But I'm asking you to do this for the sake of every human being that ever lived, including all those now long dead. Let them rise again, William! Let the kingdom of heaven reign on earth!"

Will's nervous system seemed to flood with rage. "And would you do it, Dad? Would you murder your own son? Would you murder me to bring about the end of the world?"

"Yes, I would, William. I would do it in a heartbeat."

Will needed to sit down, to close his eyes. He felt dizzy.

Suddenly, just on the edge of his field of vision, he could see a haze of movement. It was the woman, charging toward Laser Eyes with some kind of stick: Will realized it was a loose wooden upright, pulled from the banister. With barely a turn, the man aimed his gun directly into the woman's face. He shot twice, sending a cascade of blood and bone across the room. The body slumped to the ground. There was a second or two of silence. And then Will could hear and feel Beth behind him, moaning. His own hands were trembling.

"We need to act fast, William. We cannot tolerate any more delays. The Almighty has designated a time and even a person to take this step. The time is now, and the person is you."

Will guessed there could only be a couple of minutes to go. Outside he could hear a chorus of voices, now swelling.

Avinu Malkeinu Chatmeinu b'sefer chaim . . .

Our father, Our King, seal us in the book of life . . .

Even muffled by the walls, the intensity of their plea was unmistakable. He did not understand the words, but he knew their meaning. They were praying, in the fifty-ninth minute of the eleventh hour, for salvation.

The blade was glinting now, as bright and fierce as the flame in his father's eye. He spoke calmly, but his eyes were on fire. "Take this knife, Will, and do what is right. Do what God has commanded you. Now is the time."

Will glanced at the rabbi, who finally spoke, his voice querulous. Will saw that his face was splattered with the blood of the woman who had been murdered in front of them. He seemed to be panting. "Your father is right, Will. This is the moment for you to act. That is what God himself, in his wisdom, has given to us all: free will. He gives us choice. And now this choice is yours. You must decide what to do."

Will gave one last look at his watch. If he could just spin this out a few moments longer . . .

But the next second took the decision away. With a cry of "Enough talk!" Laser Eyes aimed his gun toward Will, his eye squinting as he took aim. Will could see that the gunman's real target was not him at all: he was shooting at Beth and the baby she was carrying.

Uselessly he held up his hands to cry, "No!" But the word barely came out. Instead, Will felt himself shoved from the side. As he toppled over, he heard first one gunshot, then another—and saw the falling, almost flying, figure of Rabbi Freilich. The rabbi had leapt up and pushed Will out of the way, smothering Beth with his own body. The rabbi had made his own decision: to take the bullets aimed at Will's unborn son.

Will seized the moment, charging at Laser Eyes, rushing at his gun hand. The man squeezed the trigger, but he had been knocked off balance: the shot went through the glass of the street-facing window. Will had to get the gun from him. But now he could see his father, the blade bright in his hand, moving toward the corpse of Rabbi Freilich—looking for Beth.

Finding a strength he had never known, Will was now gripping the assassin's gun arm, trying to pull it behind his back: the nelson armlock he had learned at school. The man began to squeal, his hold on the weapon weakening. Will got a finger on the handle, but it was not enough. With one eye, he could see that his father had nearly pulled Freilich free: in a matter of seconds, he would be able to plunge the knife into Beth.

Will wanted to pull away from Laser Eyes and stop his father, but he knew it would be no good: he would be shot before he had crossed the room. He had to get the gun. He gave one more pull on the man's arm in a desperate attempt to wrench the pistol away, but it did not work. The gun did not fall from his hand. Instead the assassin instinctively tightened his grip, inadvertently squeezing the trigger.

Will heard the noise and looked down at his hands, expecting to see them blown away. He was covered in blood, but, he realized a second later, it was not his own. Laser Eyes had shot himself in the back.

Now there was a clear line of sight to his father, who had briefly turned away from his task at the sound of the gunshot. For a moment, Will caught his eye. He turned back, his face flushed, as he finally shoved Freilich's lifeless body to one side. He raised his knife high, ready for the plunge into Beth's stomach.

Will flew at him, the same rugby tackle his father had taught him perhaps twenty years earlier. It knocked the older man down, away from Beth but still with the knife in his hand. Now Will was on top of him, staring straight into his face.

"Get off me, Will," he rasped, his neck muscles engorged. "We have so little time." His father's strength shocked him. It took a supreme effort to keep his arms pinned to the floor; his own wrists were straining. Monroe Sr.'s neck was swelling with the effort to throw Will off. And still he kept the knife in his hands.

Suddenly, Will felt a new pressure. His father was using his knees to spring Will off him, and it was working; Will was being pushed back. With one more kick, he threw Will off and jumped to his feet. Still with knife in hand, he took three purposeful strides toward Beth, who was now backed against the side wall.

Will could see his father draw back his hand, ready at last to stab Beth's womb. But Beth grabbed Monroe Sr.'s wrist with both hands, using all her strength to push it back. The knife hovered for a second—held in suspension by the equal strength of a true believer's desire to bring about heaven on earth and a mother's determination to protect her unborn child. The two forces were a match for each other. Will realized he had seen this fire in his wife's eyes once before: it was the same feral determination he had glimpsed in his dream. Then too Beth had been defending a child from terrible harm.

Now the man's greater muscle began to show. His hand was advancing, the knife cutting wild arcs in the air, just in front of Beth's belly. The blade made contact, scoring a deep gash in the cloth of her skirt.

Will was filled with a sudden hot burst of adrenaline, the adrenaline of the truly desperate. Staggering toward the slumped body of Laser Eyes, he uncurled the assassin's fingers, still rigidly gripping the weapon, and wrenched the gun away. Standing parallel with Beth, he aimed precisely at his father's head.

He had already begun to squeeze the trigger when he heard his father gasp, his throat jerking back, suddenly exposed. The older man was tottering backward, clutching at his chest. A dry rasp was issuing from his mouth; his shirt was now a spreading stain of crimson. It took Will a long second to see that his father had been stabbed in the chest. Standing before him, her face frozen, was Beth. She was holding a knife slick with blood.

EPILOGUE

Six months later

Will always liked the office ritual of a cake. A group e-mail would go around the office, or at least one part of it, announcing that someone was marking a birthday, celebrating a landmark anniversary, or, most often, leaving.

These little ceremonies—a speech from the department head, a response from the honoree—always gave Will a warm pleasure. Mainly it was because he was still new enough to the *Times* to enjoy the sense of membership of a grand old institution—and these occasions ladled out that sentiment by the bucketload.

"Farewell to Terry Walton. 4:45 at the Metro Desk." It hardly mattered that Will was no fan of Walton's; it would still be fun. Not that he had seen him much in the six months since everything happened; Walton had scarcely been around. Maybe he was winding down for his retirement or the job running a local paper in Florida or whatever else it was he was going to do next.

Six months. It felt longer. Everything about that week felt long ago, even far away—as if it had happened on a distant planet or in a different age.

He had had so many hard conversations, the hardest with Tom, at his bedside, explaining why exactly he had taken a bullet. There was no good reason, Tom had concluded, cooly logical even in the intensive care ward. Just as there was no good reason why the bullet had missed his heart by a few inches, lodging in his shoulder bone instead. "If I'd been shorter, I'd be dead," Tom had said, woozily. "Or do I mean taller? You see what I mean? There is no logical reason for any of it. We live in the absence of reason." After that, he had fallen back to sleep.

TC and Will visited him often in those first few days, but neither of them was guest of honor. That place was reserved for Beth. When she walked in, Tom managed a wide beam, rather than a watery smile. She bent over for a mini-hug and told him he had helped save her life and the life of her child. He said, "Any time."

Will had had to recount the events of that night and that week over and over again. First to detectives and lawyers, explaining that his wife had killed his father in defense of herself and her unborn son—an account that was soon born out by forensic examination of the house in Crown Heights and subsequent inquiries into the Church of the Reborn Jesus. The police could also see the terrible fate that had befallen Rabbi Freilich and Rachel Jacobson. Both Will and Beth spent hours reliving that dreadful night, giving statement after statement, until they were exhausted.

When they were on their own, Beth described how she had been well treated, how Mrs. Jacobson had mothered her in that house—constantly apologizing for her captivity, promising that soon all would be explained. Beth had been first scared, then furious, and finally desperate to get word to Will that she was safe. But, she said, she never once doubted that she would survive. The

Hasidim swore they would not harm her, and, for a reason she had never quite understood, she believed them.

So they went together, Will and Beth, to the funerals of Rabbi Freilich and Mrs. Jacobson, which, following Jewish custom, were held quickly, as soon as the coroner released their bodies. There were huge crowds, perhaps three thousand for Rabbi Freilich, a mighty show of collective grief. Only then did Will appreciate Freilich's position among the Hasidim: he had been their surrogate father, guiding them ever since they had lost their Rebbe.

A handful of people at the funeral approached Beth, making a small bow of their head as they came close. Will understood they were showing respect not to her or him, but to their unborn child, destined to be one of the *lamad vav.*

Will saw a familiar face, and he headed over immediately. "Rabbi Mandelbaum, I need to ask you something."

"I think I know what you want to ask, William. Perhaps you'll allow me to give you some advice. Don't think too deeply about what we discussed that night. It would not be good for you. Or your child."

"But—"

"It does seem as if the Rebbe understood that your son will have a special responsibility, that he is to be one of the righteous men. That is a great honor. But the other matter we discussed, I think this is best left alone."

"I'm not sure I understand."

"I told you that our tradition suggests one of the *lamad vav* is the candidate to be the Messiah. If the time is right, if mankind is worthy, then that person will be the Messiah. If the time is not right, they will live and die like anyone else."

"But in the last hours of the Day of Atonement, the child my wife is carrying was the only one left. All the other righteous men had been killed—"

"But now that moment has passed—and the world is still standing. Which means there are thirty-six in the world once more.

A new group of tzaddikim. Any one of them could be the candidate." Rabbi Mandelbaum gazed deeply into Will's eyes. "Any one of them."

"You see," said Beth, drawing her husband away, "we don't have to dwell on all that. There are other things to think about." She had been urging Will not to focus on the distant future but on the immediate past—specifically his father. For she knew that Will would be experiencing a triple trauma. First, he had to cope with the shock of what she, his wife, had done. No matter that it was a desperate act of self-defense, Beth warned her husband that both of them would need years to absorb what they had been through. Second, she said, he was experiencing a son's grief. No matter how insane the circumstances, Will had lost a parent, and he needed to acknowledge that. But third, and perhaps hardest, he had to mourn the father he thought he had known. That man would have been lost even if William Monroe Sr. had lived.

For that man had been a fiction. To the world he had presented a front—the secular judge, the ultimate man of reason—so that no one would ever suspect him of his true beliefs or real intentions. It was a sustained lie, one that was doubtless plotted years in advance. It had cost him dearly, almost certainly denying him the seat on the Supreme Court he coveted so badly. Or, Will thought now, maybe that ambition too was a fraud. Probably such earthly goals meant nothing to his father. He dreamed, it seemed, only of heaven.

In the days that followed that night in Crown Heights, there was a series of arrests across the globe; missionaries and church activists charged from Darfur to Bangkok—all with connections back to the Church of the Reborn Jesus. The suspect in the Howard Macrae case turned out to be a local pastor who had known the victim for years. In Darwin, Australia, the female chaplain of a hospice was charged with murdering an aboriginal care assistant. In South Africa, police arrested a former fashion model who had joined the sect once she left the industry: she had killed an AIDS researcher she picked up on the beach.

It turned out that only a relatively small group around the man the newspapers now referred to as the Apostle knew of his plot against the righteous men. The movement's new leadership announced that the doctrine of replacement theology would be "under review," and that they hoped all their members would soon come into line with the "majority of the modern Christian family who have only respect and reverence for the validity of Judaism as a path to God."

Townsend McDougal issued a statement, declaring that he had cut his links with the Church of the Reborn Jesus nearly a quarter of a century earlier—and that he had no idea that Monroe Sr. had maintained his secret involvement. He sent Will a note, with condolences, an apology for the suspension—"a hasty decision"—and a promise that his desk was waiting for him whenever he was ready.

Will looked at the piles of paper in front of him, still unsorted. The light was flashing on his phone: two messages.

"Hi, Will, it's Tova. Looking forward to tonight. Tell me if there's anything you want me to bring."

He had forgotten; TC was coming over for dinner. Beth had it all mapped out: she had invited some gorgeous single doctor from the hospital and two other decoy singles. Will had opposed the move: far too blatant, he had said.

He wondered how TC would handle such a setup. Her life had changed as much as his that week. She had been the first person, after the police, to come to the house in the minutes after Yom Kippur was over. She had been calling and texting Will frantically, and when she got no response, she headed straight for Crown Heights. She followed the flashing lights. Later she told Will, "I know you were determined to get your wife to meet me, but there must have been an easier way than that."

Will had told her to go home and get some rest, but she said no. "There are some things I need to do here," she said, as they hugged good-bye on the street corner. "Some people I need to see." Surrounded by police and flashing red lights, Will wished her luck.

"Oh, and Will?"

"Yes?"

"Can I ask you to do something for me? I've been thinking. I'm not really Tova Chaya anymore. And TC doesn't really sound like me either. Too much like a disguise. So. Will you call me Tova?"

Six months ago.

"OK, people, listen up." It was Harden, snapping the newsroom to attention and Will out of his daydream. "It's time to boot out of the door one of our number, so please gather round in loving memory of Terence Walton!"

Soon thirty or so people were huddled around the Metro desk as Harden offered a galloped tour of Walton's career on the *Times.*

"Well, you gotta hand it to this guy for sheer versatility. He's done just about every job on this paper: police reporter, city hall reporter, business desk, National editor, Delhi correspondent—you name it, Walton's done it. Would you believe that for two years, this guy edited the puzzle section at the back of the magazine? Even wrote the goddamned crossword clues. Well, now he has decided that he has had enough of our fair city and is going to share his talents with the good people of India. He's off to train journalists there so that they can pick up all his bad habits. But we're grateful to him, and so, let's all raise a paper plate laden with cheap cake and say, 'To Terry!' "

"To Terry!" they chorused, followed rapidly by the demand for a speech. Walton obliged with a roll call of former colleagues, many long since gone and unknown to Will, and a few barbed jokes at the management's expense. Finally, he began to wrap it up.

"Well, if my Yale education taught me anything, it's better a short address than a long lecture. And, as the good book says, 'Brothers, time is short.' I fly to Delhi this very night. So I'll conclude. It's been a pleasure and a privilege . . ."

The room broke into warm applause; even Amy Grossman allowed herself a little cheer—though maybe that was just relief to see Walton gone. Will tucked into his cake, shook hands, and wished his desk-neighbor all the best.

Maybe it was the reference to Yale that did it, but five minutes later Will was seized by a thought. He sat back at the computer, still nibbling at the icing on the carrot cake. He typed in "Church of the Reborn Jesus," scrolled, and clicked until he found the picture showing the Rev. Jim Johnson and his acolytes.

Now Will's eye went straight to his father. So serious, even then. Will's eye shot across to Townsend McDougal and then, methodically, started at the right of the back row. Face, face, face . . .

He increased the magnification on the image. There he was, in the middle row, four away from McDougal. With long, hippie hair he was almost unrecognizable: Will had certainly glided right past him the first time he had looked. But the supercilious smile was unchanged: Terence Walton.

Suddenly a shiver ran across Will's shoulders. He could hear Walton's voice from just a few moments ago: *As the good book says, "Brothers, time is short."* He knew it was familiar: it was the message the texter had sent when Will was in jail, from Paul's letter to the Corinthians.

Will sat back in his seat, a wry smile breaking on his lips. What had Harden said? Walton had done every job on the paper, including a stint editing the puzzle section: he even wrote crossword clues.

"I'll be damned," said Will out loud. "It was him."

A founder member of the Church of the Reborn Jesus with a knack for riddles: suddenly Will had no doubt. *Don't stop*; the ten proverbs; *Just men we are, our number few.* Walton knew it all and wanted to pass it on. He must have been scared. Too scared to tip anybody off directly. If the Apostle or his heavies had discovered his betrayal, they would not have hesitated to kill him. No wonder he had had to resort to code.

But why Will? Why had he picked him to receive all those clues? He must have seen Will's stories in the paper and realized he was on to the killing of the righteous men. *Don't stop.* It did not refer to finding Beth; it referred to the story of the *lamad vav.* Don't stop at Macrae and Baxter: *more's to come.* No wonder he had stolen Will's notebook: he wanted to know what Will knew. He might even have been keeping it safe.

Then a doubt surfaced. If Walton was the informant, a mole inside his father's circle, why had he taunted Will after the Macrae story? Surely he should have encouraged him?

And then Will remembered their conversation after his story had hit the front page. He had bullied him about beginner's luck: *Very hard to pull off that trick twice*, he had said. And yet that was exactly what Will had done, by recounting the life and death of Pat Baxter. Walton had all but drawn a map—and Will had followed it.

Once he saw the Baxter piece, Walton must have realized Will was the man to expose the Church of the Reborn Jesus. To expose his own father. Or had Walton's plan been hatched even earlier; had he even engineered the Baxter story? What had Harden said when he dispatched Will out west? *I scraped the bottom of the barrel and offered them Walton, who was all set to go, but now, at the eleventh hour, he's cried off with some lame-assed excuse.* Was it even possible? Had Walton ducked the assignment, knowing that Will would go instead—and walk right into the Baxter story? And that flyer for the Church of the Reborn Jesus, mysteriously lying on Will's desk. Had Walton put it there?

Will would ask him direct, right now. He swiveled around to see the next desk even barer than usual. Will called to Amy. "Hey, where's Terry?"

"He's already gone. Straight to the airport, apparently."

It was too late. Will slumped back into his seat, deflated. He would have liked to thank Walton and to ask him a hundred questions. Now he would never have the chance.

"Shame, I wanted to say good-bye properly."

"Didn't he leave you a gift? He gave me a book," she said, holding it up. "*The Juggler: How to Balance Work and Family.* Thanks a lot, Terry."

Will had not spotted it until then: a neatly wrapped box, balanced on the partition between their desks.

He brought it down and tore off the paper to reveal a brown

carton, no more than six inches square. He opened the lid: bubble wrap. Underneath, Will pulled out what seemed to be a desk toy, perhaps a gyroscope. It was only once he got it fully out of the box that Will understood what Walton had given him.

It was a model of Atlas, the statue outside Rockefeller Center. A man carrying the universe on his shoulders, holding up the world. There was a note:

> *An ancient Jewish teaching holds that to save a life is to save the whole world. I know you did one; you may even have done both. Good luck, T.*

Will put it down on his desk, next to the Saddam Hussein snow dome he had stolen from Walton and never returned. It was not yet on the Grossman scale, but Will was developing his own, personalized corner of office real estate. Pride of place went to a framed photograph of Beth, now showing the full curve of pregnancy. Next to it was a picture of Will and his mother. And next to that was an empty space, ready for a picture of the boy he already loved.

AUTHOR'S NOTE

The Righteous Men is a work of fiction—but it is rooted in several key facts. First, the legend of the *lamad vav*, of thirty-six exceptional individuals whose virtue upholds the world, is a thread that runs through Jewish tradition. The books and essays Rabbi Mandelbaum cites in his conversation with Will are real—and, for those whose interest has been piqued, worth consulting. The obvious starting point is Gershom Scholem's *Messianic Idea in Judaism* (New York: Schocken, 1971), especially the chapter entitled "The Tradition of the Thirty-Six Hidden Just Men."

Scholem tells the story recounted by Mandelbaum, one that appears in the Palestinian Talmud and dates back to the third century. It speaks of the rabbi who notices that, when a certain man is in the congregation, the community's prayers for rain get answered. That man is known as Pentakaka, a Greek-derived name whose literal meaning is "five sins": he rents out whores, even dancing and drumming in front of them. And yet when a woman offers to become a whore to raise bail for her jailed husband, Pentakaka prefers to sell his own bed and blanket rather than see her suffer that indignity. In other words, Howard Macrae is not entirely an invention: his act of righteousness is documented—and at least 1,700 years old.

Jean-Claude Paul's good deed in Haiti—creating a secret chamber that preserves the anonymity of both the givers and receivers of charity—has even deeper roots. The "chamber of secrets," as it was known, existed in the Temple of Solomon, which stood as Judaism's holiest site in Jerusalem from 953 B.C. until its destruction in 586 B.C. It was the physical embodiment of a core principle: that the act of giving should entail neither glory nor humiliation for those involved, but should instead be a simple act of justice.

It is also a matter of fact that there is a large Hasidic community in Crown Heights, one that still mourns for the Rebbe it lost a few years ago and which continues its outreach efforts across the globe. The Rebbe of the Lubavitch or Chabad movement was a remarkable figure, whom some of his followers hailed as the Messiah. Some still do.

Finally, replacement theology and supersessionism are no inventions. Many Christians do indeed hold that the Jews have forfeited their role as the chosen people, a status that has been passed on to those who follow Jesus Christ. The Wikipedia entry Will reads on the topic is not made up but quoted directly.

That much is fact. As for the rest, who can know for sure?

ACKNOWLEDGMENTS

Any book, I have discovered, is a collaborative effort, and this one is no exception. I owe thanks to a variety of people who guided me through what was a new and complex process.

First thanks must go to the Hasidic community of Crown Heights, Brooklyn. The late Gershon Jacobson and his wife Sylvia welcomed me into their home during a reporting assignment in 1991—and made me welcome again nearly fifteen years later. Their guidance, along with the warmth and wisdom of their sons Rabbi Simon and Rabbi Yosef Yitzhok, was vital. Along with Rabbi Gershon Overlander of London, they ushered me into what was an entirely new world—one I continue to admire greatly. I am also indebted to Dr. Tali Loewenthal, who acted as tutor on some of the finer points of Jewish and Hasidic doctrine. It goes without saying that any errors on this score are mine alone.

I owe a debt, too, to the staff of the *New York Times,* who showed me some of the workings of that great newspaper. Warren Hoge was especially generous, enlisting the essential help of Bill Keller and Craig Whitney as well as the editors of the Metro and

Foreign sections. Lest there be any confusion, the *New York Times* of the Righteous Men is a work of the imagination.

Specific guidance came from Alex Bellos and Hilary Cottam on life in a Latin American slum, Peter Wilson on Australia, and Stephen Bates on the Church. The Yiddish appears courtesy of the redoubtable Anna Tzelniker. Lee de-Beer literally walked the streets of New York on my behalf, tracing some of the more awkward steps of Will Monroe and his pursuers. Eleanor Yadin and her team at the New York Public Library could not have been more helpful. Sharyn Stein proved a crucial source on both the law and police procedure of New York.

Tom Cordiner and Steven Thurgood allowed me to dip into their enormous expertise on computing and technology. Monique El-Faizy deserves special thanks for advising on matters New York, spotting details both large and small. Kate Cooper at Curtis Brown proved a zealous advocate of the book—and a perceptive reader. Chris Maslanka showed why he is the king of the puzzlemasters, coming up with one ingenious riddle after another to confound Will and TC. I am in awe of his skill.

My parents read early drafts and gave sage advice as well as moral support: their influence can be spotted in several places in this book. My in-laws, Jo and Michael, once again allowed me to turn their Suffolk home into a writer's retreat, while Michael proved an eagle-eyed reader. A special mention should go to my late great-aunt, Yehudit Dove, whose very real righteousness inspired this story.

At HarperCollins, Jane Johnson proved herself to be a model editor, worthy of her towering reputation. Not only did she root for this book but, backed by the hugely able Sarah Hodgson, improved it at every stage. In the United States, Claire Wachtel was acute, perceptive, and sharp: now I know why she's the best in the business.

Three people should be singled out. Jonathan Cummings did more than just research; he devoted boundless brainpower and energy to this project. He is a genuine comrade. I owe Jonny Geller a great deal. He is not just a world-class agent but a true friend, a man who believed a late-night conversation could become a novel—and whose belief, support, and insight never flags. It is no exaggeration to say this book would not have happened without him.

Finally my wife, Sarah, shared in the excitement of this project from the very beginning. She managed not only to be a wonderful mother to our children, Jacob and Sam, but to provide shrewd advice, a fine eye, and constant love. Marriage is one of the themes of this book—and I am loving every day of ours.